Rafe

the Walkers of Coyote Ridge

PIER 70
Reckless
Fearless
Speechless
Harmless
Clueless

PRIMAL INSTINCTS
Chase (Volume 1-3)
Capture (Volume 4-6)
Claim (Volume 7-9)

SNIPER 1 SECURITY
Wait for Morning
Never Say Never
Tomorrow's Too Late

SOUTHERN BOY MAFIA/DEVIL'S PLAYGROUND
Beautifully Brutal
Without Regret
Beautifully Loyal
Without Restraint

STANDALONE NOVELS
Unhinged Trilogy
A Million Tiny Pieces
Inked on Paper
Bad Reputation
Bad Business
Filthy Hot Billionaire
RULE

NAUGHTY HOLIDAY EDITIONS
2015
2016
2021

Rafe

THE WALKERS OF COYOTE RIDGE, 11

NICOLE EDWARDS

NICOLE EDWARDS LIMITED

A dba of SL Independent Publishing, LLC
PO Box 1086
Pflugerville, Texas 78691

RAFE

The Walkers of Coyote Ridge, 11

COVER DETAILS:

Image: © Wander Aguiar (Model: Manuel)| WanderBookClub.com
Design: © Nicole Edwards Limited

INTERIOR DETAILS:

Formatting: Nicole Edwards Limited

AUDIO DETAILS:

Image: © Wander Aguiar (Model: Manuel)| WanderBookClub
Narrators: TBD

ISBN-13: (ebook) 9781644180839 | (paperback) 9781644180846 | (audio) 9781644180853

BISAC: FICTION / Romance FICTION / LGBTQ+ Bisexual

Dedication

To the fans of the Walker universe.
Something is coming, and this is the beginning.

Chapter one

Wednesday, July 13, 2022

RAFE SHARPE SAT QUIETLY AT THE BAR, tucked in the corner, watching the room as he sized up the few people who'd graced this establishment with their presence. You didn't need to be a mathematician to count the eleven people, including the bartender and the waitress.

Aside from those who worked here, there was a group of guys at the pool table bumping fists to celebrate the round they won against the guy they didn't yet realize was a hustler. When they figured it out, those fist bumps would have a bit more power behind them and be aimed at a nose, not knuckles.

A couple of old-timers were at the opposite end of the bar, drinking beer like it was fine wine, sipping from time to time while fully engaged in a fascinating conversation involving a rusty well pipe and a couple of frolicking fillies. Horses, not women.

And, of course, the three stay-at-home moms who came in every Wednesday like clockwork to celebrate a few hours without heathens—the term they used to refer to their kids. Lovingly, of course. They were chatting it up over some not-so-fine wine but, based on the giggles erupting from their corner, enjoying themselves regardless of the vintage.

And then there was her.

Bailey Weber, Moonshiners' most tenured waitress and easily the most beautiful woman Rafe had ever laid eyes on. He'd been captivated from the moment he looked into those big hazel eyes and received a smile in return.

Being that it was Wednesday, there wasn't a lot going on, but it was still active enough that Mack was willing to keep the place open. Rafe got the feeling the man purposely worked on nights like this to avoid the rowdy crowd that ventured in on the weekend. Rafe had been taking those shifts regularly for the past few months, offering because it gave him something to do and kept him out of trouble.

Trouble. He liked that word. Especially when it was used as an adjective to describe him. And while plenty of folks in this small town remembered him as such, it'd been a damn long time since he'd gotten in any. Did that mean he was getting old? Twenty-nine wasn't old, was it? Or had he been running in the wrong direction all those years, and his wild youth had caught up to him?

If he had to guess, he would say it was the latter because his wild and rowdy days seemed to be behind him. He'd been back in Coyote Ridge for three years—two years and ten months, to be exact. A helluva lot longer than he'd intended to stay when he showed up on his brother's doorstep that warm September day to find Rex remodeling the old farmhouse where they grew up, transforming it into a bed-and-breakfast, which was just a fancy name for a small backwoods hotel from what he could tell.

Since then, Rafe had somehow put down roots, although he damn sure hadn't planned on it. Maybe not the roots you'd find from a walnut or a hickory tree. Nothing too strong or sturdy. More like pine or maple. Yet, they were roots all the same.

Hell, he'd even gotten a job. Right here. At Moonshiners.

Rafe

It was the only bar in the small town, and as of three weeks ago, only one of two places you could get your grub on. Since Mack finally conceded to Rafe's request to serve appetizers, they'd been seeing a different clientele moving through. Of course, the regulars weren't gonna stray far. If you didn't get your liquor here and weren't looking for a forty-ounce at the Gas 'n Go or the box wine the general store recently started selling, you had to head down the road a good twenty minutes to get to a store that sold it. So here it was. And now they could get French fries and chicken wings to go with the cheap booze, bottled beer, or the few tap brews they served.

Rafe took a long pull on his beer, the one he'd been nursing for the better part of an hour now, while he waited for Bailey to finish her shift. She didn't necessarily need him to stick around, but he did it simply so he could see if she needed a ride home. It was pathetic, he knew. One of two days he had off this week, and here he was, inhabiting the place he spent most nights working behind this very same bar he was bellied up to now.

Rafe looked over at the gray-haired man with the bushy beard behind the bar. Michael "Mack" Schwartz dried a glass and tucked it away before moving on to wipe down the lacquered bar top, careful not to disturb the old-timers. Rafe considered calling him over, pitching his idea to Mack for the eleven thousandth time. The one that would take Moonshiners from just a bar to something the entire town could enjoy.

Not that it was his place to suggest converting the small bar into something resembling a roadhouse, but during the year and a half he'd been working here, Rafe had gotten comfortable around Mack. The man had continued to give Rafe more and more responsibilities, now trusting him to open and close on his own while manning the bar several nights a week. Truth was, Rafe would be content to do just that for the rest of his days. It wasn't a fancy joint, and Rafe appreciated it for that fact. However, he did see some potential. Maybe slap a coat of paint on the place and give the rest a little refresh, add a few things to the menu, and they'd be in real business.

Too bad Mack hadn't committed yet. According to him, it was one thing to serve up fries and wings, something else entirely to give this place a makeover. It was long overdue, considering some of the decor was as vintage as the bartender. Like the ugly ass flamingo painting that was straight out of the 50s.

"You want good luck, might wanna hit on *that*," one of the gloating assholes at the pool table said as he lined up for a shot and missed.

Rafe's attention shifted to the guy chalking his cue stick and openly ogling Bailey's ass. Rafe had been keeping an eye on them since they strolled in two hours ago. Looked like the hustler had amped up his game, throwing the other two off theirs in the process.

"Hey, honey," one of the assholes called out as Bailey sauntered back with empty glasses from the chatty ladies who were gearing up to make an exit.

As usual, Bailey beamed them a radiant smile as she carried the glasses behind the bar and tucked them into the dirty bin.

"I'm about done here, Mack," she told her boss. "You need me to do anything else?"

"We're good. Gonna close it down in a bit."

She smiled and grabbed the cleaning rag before heading back to the table to wipe it down as the ladies made their way to the door.

And then there were eight.

"Hey, girl, you wanna help a man out?" the asshole called out on Bailey's return trip to the bar.

Bailey stopped, giving them her full attention, including a smile—the one she used in hopes of earning more tips.

"I think my buddy here needs some luck, sweet cheeks," the drunk one said. "Maybe you'd like to help him out with a kiss."

Rafe sat up straight, glared in their direction.

"She can hold her own," Mack grumbled in that not-so-polite way of his. "She don't need you fightin' her battles."

Rafe briefly cut his gaze to the bartender, then back to Bailey and the assholes.

Rafe

Mack had a point, but that didn't mean Rafe wasn't ready and willing to do just that. And while he had no intention of starting any shit, that didn't mean it wouldn't happen anyway. Rafe was a magnet for shit. Had been his whole life. Didn't matter if he was here at Moonshiners, at the diner, or hell, at the bakery, for that matter. Wherever he went, it seemed someone wanted to rag on him for something. The douchebags in this town thought he was an easy target. They generally learned their lesson with a bloodied nose, hand-delivered—pun intended—by him.

Over the past ten years, Rafe had learned there were only two ways to silence the chaos in his head. Fighting or sex. Never together, of course. The fighting was saved for the assholes who deserved it, and the sex was reserved for the women who could handle him. For the record, there weren't all that many of the latter. Not these days, anyway.

Although he was abstaining from his promiscuous lifestyle, the anger was still a living, breathing thing inside him, churning hot, bright, and powerful. It had been that way for the past seventeen years. Ever since the night his crazy fuck up of a father forced Rafe to kill him. Even with the old man rotting in hell, Rafe still hated him with a passion.

Every time he thought about that night, he remembered how Rex had been chained to the bed, crying, terrified as Jolene Snyder, his father's warped and twisted girlfriend, had dared to put her hands on him. Rafe remembered his brother's sobs. Hell, he still heard them in his nightmares. They were what had woken Rafe from his hiding place in the closet that night. Without hesitation, he'd grabbed their grandpa's shotgun, pushed to his feet, and squared his bony twelve-year-old shoulders. There hadn't been any rage at that point, only single-minded purpose and a desperate need to save his brother from the hands of the devil.

"What, honey? Your bodyguard won't let you have no fun?" one of the assholes crooned at Bailey.

Rafe didn't move, but his gaze was honed on the fucker.

"Leave well enough alone, son," Mack told him. "There's no sense lettin' 'em rile you up. They're just tryin' to get you to cause trouble."

There was that word again. And today, it could very well be his middle name. That was what these pricks expected of him, wasn't it? They expected Rafe to detonate with the slightest provocation because he was the outcast, the deviant who'd gone and killed his father. Didn't matter that he'd claimed self-defense—which had been the truth—and the jury had agreed. It also didn't matter that Rafe hadn't spent any time in prison for ridding the world of the insane bastard.

Nope. They simply knew him from the bullshit story that had drifted through the grapevine: the spoiled brat who'd pulled the trigger because he didn't like his father's new girlfriend.

At least part of that was true. Rafe had hated Jolene Snyder with a fucking passion. If he'd been a homicidal maniac, he would've killed her that night, too. In fact, he should've killed her the first night she put her fucking hands on him. Rafe still had fucking nightmares about it. Had he taken her out then, she never would've had the chance to put her hands on Rex. That was his only regret. That he hadn't done something sooner. And he'd lived with it for nearly two decades, unable to face his brother because if he'd been stronger, his big brother would never've been put in that situation.

Rafe hadn't shed a single tear when Jolene overdosed just a month after Rafe had filled his father full of lead. The bitch could rot in hell right alongside Rafe's old man for all he cared.

"You got a problem, boy?" the redneck at the pool table asked, glaring daggers at him from across the room.

Rafe didn't say a word. He tipped his beer bottle to his lips and held that bleary-eyed stare.

Daryl Hogan was a piece of shit who deserved to get his ass kicked, but Rafe had been making strides lately. He'd kept himself out of trouble, focusing on working and nurturing the few relationships he'd established since he got back. Rumor was Rafe had turned over a new leaf. He wouldn't go that far, but he'd admit he wasn't trying to buck the system as much these days.

Granted, he wouldn't turn away from a fight if it came knocking on his door. The mere thought of it had his hands flexing, his muscles coiling as the adrenaline slithered through his bloodstream.

"Rafe?"

Rafe

The sweet, almost musical lilt of her voice had Rafe turning to look at Bailey as she approached. With a smile, she slipped off her apron and tucked it behind the bar before coming to stand beside him.

"I'm ready to go. Can you give me a ride home?"

Rafe wasn't sure how he'd gotten so damn lucky to have Bailey as a friend, but at some point, that was exactly what had happened. And he liked her. A hell of a lot more than he should, considering.

Granted, it hadn't been her sweet nature or kind eyes that had originally turned his head. No, he attributed that to her ass. Yeah, Bailey had an ass that deserved a fucking shrine. The way she filled out a pair of jeans should've been illegal. But the moment she'd turned those pretty hazel eyes on him, Rafe had been a fucking goner.

Although he certainly enjoyed spending time with her, Rafe hadn't come back to land a relationship. He wasn't looking for love, romance, or even a hookup. Hell, he hadn't even been looking for a friend, but then there she was.

And damn near every day since, Bailey had been right by his side, making him laugh with her stories, giving him insights into all the goings-on in this small town.

Rafe valued her friendship because those were damn hard to come by for him. She had grown up here, heard all the stories from whoever shared the tale of woe that pertained to the Sharpe brothers, yet she still insisted on hanging out with him. Rafe couldn't figure out why she wanted to be around the likes of him, but he was long past questioning her motives. The woman was the only light in an entirely too dark world.

"Come on," she said with a nudge of Rafe's arm. "Let's go."

"You slummin' it tonight, Bailey?" Daryl asked with a yellow-toothed grin. "'Cause, honey, you just hafta ask. I'd be more'n happy to oblige. I could take you home, spend some time foggin' up the windows in my truck."

Bailey cast him her signature sweet smile, but her voice held a slight edge. "Oh, Daryl, I'm not sure what your wife would think about that."

When she turned back to Rafe, she rolled her eyes and feigned gagging.

Setting his beer on the bar, Rafe stood. He pulled out a twenty, tossed it beside the bottle.

"Your money ain't no good here, boy," Mack grumbled.

"Put it in the tip jar, then."

Mack merely shook his head and grinned.

"I'm drivin'," Bailey announced.

"No, ma'am. *I'm* drivin'," Rafe told Bailey as they started for the door.

"Uh-uh. You've been drinkin'. That means your butt's in the passenger seat."

It was Rafe's turn to roll his eyes. "One beer, Bailey. I only had one beer." And he hadn't even finished it.

Chatter erupted behind him, but Rafe ignored it. Or tried to, anyway. It helped that Bailey put her smooth hand on his arm and steered him in the right direction.

"But I like drivin' your truck," she drawled, probably more of a distraction than anything. "Plus, you look cute sittin' in the passenger seat."

That had only happened once, and that night, Rafe had been too drunk to walk, much less focus on the road.

"Look at the pussy runnin' out the door," Daryl called from behind him, laughing like a hyena. "Still can't fight like a man. Someone oughta check, make sure he ain't got a gun."

Daryl's drunker sidekick laughed along with him while the hustler looked on with interest.

"Ignore them," Bailey whispered, her tone no longer cordial.

"Girl, if you had a lick of sense, you'd steer clear of that one," the sidekick hollered. "You ain't safe with him. One wrong move, and he'll likely shoot you, too."

Rafe stopped when Bailey's feet abruptly came to a halt. She spun on her little white tennis shoes, a finger coming up as she pointed in the direction of the words. Her dark blond ponytail swung around, hanging over her shoulder.

"You keep your mouth shut, Flynn. I don't quite like your tone."

Rafe grinned at the cute little woman now fuming mad beside him. That was one of the things he loved about Bailey. She took no shit from anyone. At five-foot-three, a strong breeze could knock her over, but she would stand up to the orneriest of men.

Rafe

"We're just watchin' out for you, sweetness," Daryl said as he moved closer.

Rafe did turn then, positioning himself between Daryl and Bailey when Flynn and the hustler moved in to offer their support.

"You don't wanna do this," Rafe warned softly.

"And what if I do, boy? Whatcha gonna do about it?"

Rafe didn't speak, didn't move. He inhaled slowly, exhaled. His mind was clear as he tracked every person in the room, every move. Without a doubt, Rafe could take Daryl in a fair fight, but he knew this wouldn't be fair. Daryl wasn't about to get his ass kicked in front of his friends. Those fuckers would be on Rafe like stink on shit as soon as Daryl took the first fist to the face.

Bailey moved to stand in front of Rafe. "You start somethin', Daryl, and I'm gonna go tell Lulu how you were suckin' face with that floozie last Friday night. That what you want?"

Daryl's dark eyes shot to Bailey's face.

"That's what I thought," she said firmly, then waved toward the bartender. "Mack, you'll keep him in here till we leave?"

"You know I will," the man said, used to keeping these rednecks in line.

"Come on." Bailey turned and placed her hands on Rafe's chest, forcing him backward.

It wasn't until his back came in contact with the door that Rafe turned, pushed it open, and motioned Bailey outside. They stepped out into the hot, muggy July night, and Rafe felt like he could breathe again.

"I'm so glad you're here tonight," she said as she marched around to the driver's side. "But I don't like the way those buttholes talk to you."

"Buttholes?" Rafe laughed. "Are you twenty-four? Or fourteen?"

"Oh, you hush up."

Rafe followed her to the driver's side, opening the truck door for her. When Bailey climbed in, he did the same, right behind her.

"Hey! I said *I* was drivin'."

"Scoot on over, darlin'," he insisted, not giving her a chance to argue.

Bailey huffed. "Rafe Sharpe, I do *not* like your high-handedness."

Rafe chuckled. "Get used to it, woman."

"I don't have to get used to nothin'." She sighed but crawled over the console to the passenger seat.

He held out his hand for the keys, which she'd snagged from his pocket, and waited patiently until she dropped them into his palm. With a twist of his wrist, Rafe started the truck, backed it out of the space, and headed toward Bailey's house.

Even after all this time, Rafe still couldn't believe he was back here, back in the town where he grew up. Couldn't believe his brother was still here, living in that old house that he'd turned into a fancy bed-and-breakfast where strangers traipsed through every day and night.

The day Rafe turned eighteen, he'd left Coyote Ridge and everyone he knew, swearing he would never come back. He walked away from Uncle Owen, his aunt, his cousins, even his brother, the only person he gave a shit about in the world. And he didn't look back. Not necessarily because he didn't want to, but because he couldn't. Rafe had killed his bastard of a father, and the stigma associated with it and the events leading up to it had brought a dark cloud over his family. To alleviate some of their stress, Rafe had moved on.

But not without consequences.

Back then, Rex had been expecting Rafe to move into the farmhouse, to go to college, to let Rex take care of him. Rafe hadn't been able to do it, hadn't wanted to drag his brother down like that. So, he'd bought a bus ticket and headed for the coast. Ended up working in the refineries in Corpus Christi for a while. Not glamorous, but he made ends meet that way. For a few years, he managed to stay off the grid. How Rex eventually found him, Rafe didn't know. For the years that followed, he'd kept in touch with his brother, replying to a text every so often so Rex knew he was alive. And that had been his plan. Carry on elsewhere and not be a burden on the family he had left in Coyote Ridge.

Until three years ago.

Something had compelled him to come back here. Perhaps it was that he missed his brother, or maybe he'd simply been running from something else, and this was the only direction to go. Whatever it was, he had woken up one morning, hopped in his truck, and started driving.

His destination had turned out to be his brother's front porch.

"Did Rex mention I've got an interview with him tomorrow?" Bailey asked when they'd driven in silence for a few minutes. "He called me this mornin'. Outta the blue."

Rafe cut his gaze to her. "Interview for what?"

"To work at the B and B."

He knew Bailey had never intended to waitress forever. She claimed she enjoyed it, but she was constantly on the hunt for something more fulfilling. Why she didn't want to work at her family's bakery, he didn't know, but he didn't question it either.

"Well, I figured that. Doin' what?"

"Whatever he wants me to do. I know he's lookin' to hire someone to manage the place, but I don't have that kind of experience."

Having spent the better part of the last two years confined to the B and B since they were doing a good amount of business, Rex had become serious about hiring a manager for the Double R Retreat—a ridiculous name for a bed-and-breakfast if Rafe had ever heard one. Being that Rex was married to Jack, the two of them had been forced to see less of each other because of Jack's job. Evidently, being a world-famous graphic novelist required you to trek across the country—and sometimes the globe—to make appearances at various comic conventions dedicated to whatever it was he wrote about. Because Rex was hoping to cash in on some of those travel opportunities, he was looking for someone to take over full-time.

"You've got a degree, don'tcha?"

Bailey sighed again. "Yeah. From an *online* college."

She said it like it was a four-letter word.

"And what's wrong with that?"

"Nothin', I guess. But that doesn't always make up for experience."

"What kind of experience do you need?" Rafe glanced her way.

Bailey chuckled. "It's not nearly as easy as it looks. You've gotta manage reservations, take care of the guests, ensure the house is in workin' order, cook meals, coordinate events."

"You could do that easy," he told her, his attention on the road.

"One day, maybe." Bailey sighed and leaned back into the seat. "I'm just lookin' forward to workin' somewhere I don't have to worry about wanderin' hands."

Rafe glanced over and frowned. "Whose hands are wanderin'?"

She waved him off with a grin. "It's nothin'. I'm just excited about doin' somethin' different, that's all."

Rafe let the subject drop but vowed to find out who was putting their hands on this woman without permission. She might not belong to him, but Rafe felt protective of her. Not that Bailey couldn't take care of herself. She was sweet as molasses, but the woman had a fire in her. It took something big to draw it out, but it was there.

"What about the bakery?" he asked.

Bailey shrugged. "Mama said she could handle it just fine. Shelly's takin' more hours, helpin' every day now that her kiddos are gettin' older. Mama told me it'd be smart to branch out into somethin' more."

Rafe didn't care to talk about Bailey's mother. He'd met Ramona Weber because she owned and worked at the bakery, but he didn't know her thoughts on him and his brother. Everyone else in town seemed to have an opinion, and he figured she did too. But Ramona kept it professional when their paths crossed, and Bailey was far too nice to let him think differently.

"You sure you wanna work for my brother?"

"Well, technically, I'd be workin' for both of you," she said quickly. "Rex said you're as much an owner as he is."

"Whatever." Rafe hadn't lifted a finger to help his brother with the B and B, hadn't even stepped foot inside that house since the night the police took him away all those years ago. He damn sure didn't deserve to be part owner of the place, no matter what Rex said. Which was why he'd refused every check his brother had tried to pay him since the Double R opened its doors.

Rafe

"I've got my fingers crossed. I think it'll be fun," she told him as her eyes shifted out the window.

Fun.

Seventeen years ago, fun ceased to exist for him, and Rafe wasn't even sure what it meant anymore.

Chapter Two

THE BEST PART OF BAILEY'S DAY—OR night, as was usually the case—just so happened to be when Rafe drove her home.

Kind of oxymoronic, considering the worst part of her day was the *being* at home part. Was that an oxymoron? Or perhaps ironic? English never was her best subject.

Whatever it was, when Rafe drove her home, Bailey had the chance to enjoy the few minutes it took to get from Moonshiners, where she worked, to her boyfriend's house, where she was currently living. Like now, it was often quiet unless she instigated the conversation. Rafe wasn't much of a talker. He was a brilliant listener, but she suspected that was a side effect of him not wanting to talk about himself. When it came to getting Rafe to open up, Congress made more headway during a legislative session.

Not that government was a subject she'd excelled at, either.

The point was she enjoyed the time she spent with Rafe even if she preferred he take her anywhere else but home. Out on the town would've been nice. Even a quiet dinner for two.

Of course, those things would never happen for a couple of reasons.

One: instead of being social, Rafe preferred to hole up in the tiny one-bedroom, one-bath apartment above the bookstore where he'd been living since he returned to Coyote Ridge. Granted, Bailey'd never seen the apartment, so maybe there was some major appeal to it that she wasn't privy to. It could be like a carnival on a fall night; she didn't know.

Rafe

And two: Bailey harbored a major crush on Rafe, and since she was in a relationship with someone else, her interest in Rafe could only be as friends. It wasn't necessarily a bad thing. Rafe was a great friend.

So here she was, settling for the quiet drive to her house in the middle of the night.

If it were up to her, she would be staying at the Double R Retreat, and she wouldn't need a ride home because she could walk. Or better yet, it would *be* her home. Not in the sense she would own it or anything, but the idea of managing the place filled her with so much excitement Bailey could hardly contain it.

God, she loved that place. It was a well of inspiration. Twice now, she'd managed to take her camera and snap pictures of various things. It was a hobby of hers, one she hoped might lead to some extra money one day. She'd been searching around the Internet and stumbled across a stock photo site. It had given her the idea of selling some of her photographs. Maybe she wouldn't make a lot, but surely, she could make something. From what she'd read, there was decent money in it. Which was why she'd focused so much on the farmhouse. Based on her research, those seemed to sell the best.

She sighed, thinking about the place. Full of so much light and character. It was the little things like how the evening sun hit the shiplap wall in the living room, lighting it up and casting shadows on the stone fireplace. She loved that picture. So much she hoped one day to have it framed in her own house.

One day. But not yet. Not until she took the reins of her life back. Until then … well, until then, she was stuck in the rut that she'd inadvertently dug in her most recent attempt to find a happily ever after. And while she didn't want to go home, didn't want to see her boyfriend, it was her only option because it was the right thing to do. Plus, she had an important interview tomorrow, so sleep was in her future.

When Rafe pulled down the long, gravel-pitted road in front of the tiny two-bedroom house she currently lived in, Bailey drew a deep breath and let it out slowly.

"Somethin' wrong?" Rafe asked, his dark eyes darting over to her briefly.

He had the most mesmerizing eyes. She could get lost in his bottomless brown gaze.

"Nope." She made sure to inject sunshine into her tone. That was what everyone expected of her.

"You're a shitty liar, Weber," he said with a chuckle.

God, she loved when he laughed. It was a rusty sound that she didn't hear nearly enough, but when she did, it made her insides light up.

Rafe pulled the truck to a stop in front of the house, directly behind Seth's Ford Explorer.

"Your boyfriend home?" Rafe asked, nodding toward the porch with his chin.

"Yup," she said, glaring at the SUV in the driveway.

Bailey had asked Seth if she could borrow the Explorer to go to work, but he always told her no. Said he wasn't going to be stuck at home while she was running amok in town. While she didn't consider working to be the same as running amok, it never benefited her to argue with him.

"He asleep?"

Bailey shrugged. She doubted it. Since it was Wednesday, Seth didn't have to work tomorrow, so he was probably getting drunk on the couch, waiting for her to come home and cook him dinner. Didn't matter that it was almost midnight. He was still expecting her to do her girlfriend duties which included cooking and cleaning for him. He claimed it was her contribution to the household since he didn't expect her to pay half of the utilities, only half of the rent.

"Why are you still with him?" Rafe asked after several heartrending seconds of silence.

Bailey shifted to look at the handsome cowboy. He was wearing his favorite Astros baseball cap tonight. Backward. As usual. For some reason, it gave him a playful, bad-boy vibe. Not to mention, it made the dark stubble on his jaw stand out. The man was insanely attractive. In ways Bailey sometimes felt overwhelmed by.

"Truth?"

"Always."

Bailey was ashamed to admit it but let the words come out anyway. "Because I have nowhere else to go."

"*That's* why you're with him?" Rafe did not sound pleased by that. "Well, shit, Bailey, that's a stupid fuckin' reason."

"That's a crappy thing to say, Rafe Sharpe," she countered hotly, fidgeting her fingers in her lap. Defending her relationship with Seth had become a natural part of her life, even if she didn't believe half the crap that came out of her mouth. It was easy enough to tell people they'd hit a rough patch; however, with Rafe, she couldn't bring herself to lie to him. "It wasn't the reason in the beginning."

At first, she'd thought she was in love with Seth. Turned out, it was a passing fancy. Slight infatuation would better describe it. Now that the honeymoon period of their relationship was over, Bailey realized she didn't love him. Sometimes she didn't even like him. But she'd made her bed which meant...

When she first met Seth, he made her feel things. Good things. Like making her heart go pitter-patter and her palms sweat whenever he was near. Those were the same things she felt whenever she was around Rafe, so she knew what they meant. And since Rafe hadn't been receptive to any of her flirting, she embraced the emotional security she had received from Seth and pegged him as a safe bet.

Ha! *Safe, my ass.*

Unfortunately, she'd learned the hard way that not all men were what they pretended to be. Looking back, she realized she should've spent more time with Seth before deciding to take their relationship to the next level. Since she didn't, she was stuck. At least until she could end things with him the right way. Even though he didn't deserve it, she was loyal and faithful. Physically, at least. As for emotionally ... well, that was another story. Did she consider her deep-seated infatuation with Rafe cheating? Maybe. But there was nothing she could do about it. During the three years since she'd befriended Rafe, she had fallen in love with him a little at a time.

Not that he knew how she felt. Oh, no. She'd never told him. In fact, she'd pretended otherwise and set out to fall in love with someone who wanted her back. Enter Seth.

Even if Seth hadn't been an asshole of the highest order, Bailey knew there was no future for them. Back when they'd first started dating nine months ago, back when he swept her off her feet with sweet gestures and even sweeter words, Seth had said he wanted to one day get married, settle down, have children, and live happily ever after. Those were all things Bailey wanted. But evidently, Seth had only been pretending.

Turned out Seth was a liar. That's what he was. He had snowed her, made her believe he was something he wasn't, and now she was stuck with him because she had nowhere else to go.

That would change one day, though. And getting the job at the Double R would be a step in the right direction.

"Does he hit you?"

Bailey frowned and cast a sideways glance at Rafe. "Why would you ask me that?"

He adjusted his hat on his head and his eyes narrowed. "Does he?"

"No," she said adamantly. "And if he did, he'd only do it once; I promise you that."

Rafe's gaze shifted out the window. He seemed somewhat interested in the little house she lived in. Bailey doubted he was curious about the crooked shutter or the hole in the rotten floorboards of the porch. More than likely, he was wondering what Seth was doing on the other side of that door.

Bailey didn't care what Seth was doing. If she had her way, she would be living there alone. Except the house belonged to Seth's godfather—or maybe he was an uncle, she couldn't remember—so there was no option of flipping a coin to see who got to stay. Bailey had moved in with Seth roughly three weeks after they'd started dating. As she was prone to do, she'd jumped in with both feet without gauging the temperature of the water. And here she was, just eight months later, wishing Rafe had been man enough to call her to the carpet before she leaped.

Not that she would admit she'd been holding out for Rafe's attention, but it was true. She'd initially gone out with Seth in the hopes of pushing Rafe to make a move. She should've known it wouldn't work. The man had no problem being her friend, but he clearly wasn't interested in anything more. So, she'd let Seth woo her into believing he was her happily ever after.

If she hadn't jumped at the opportunity of moving out of her mother's house, she figured there was a slight chance her life would've been different at this point. She blamed her impulsive nature. And the fact that, before moving in with Seth, she'd always lived with her mother, and being that she was twenty-four years old, Bailey knew it was time to fly the coop. If only she could go back in time, ignore that rash desire, and accept that living with her mother was the right thing to do for a little longer.

Yeah.

If only.

"Can't you move back in with your mom?" Rafe prompted.

Bailey shook her head. "She rented out my old room."

He frowned. "Seriously?"

"She needed the money, and having a roommate makes it easier on her."

He seemed to consider that for a minute. "Why don't you move into the farmhouse?"

"I can't afford to pay that kind of rent."

"I'm sure Rex'll give you a discount."

"I'm not lookin' for handouts, Rafe."

He shook his head. "There's plenty of room. If Rex gives you the job, it'd make sense."

"Yeah, if he gives me the job. But like I said, no experience." She sighed and smiled, forcing sweetness in her tone. "Plus, if I lived there, I'd just be buggin' you all the time."

"I won't go in that house, Bailey. Not now, not ever."

Yeah. She knew that. Rafe refused to step foot into the house because of the hell he'd lived through. She couldn't blame him. From the stories she'd heard, he and Rex had suffered at the hands of their abusive father and the tramp his father had been shacking up with after the death of their mother. No one seemed to know exactly what had transpired, but the folks in town who'd known them back then were convinced his father's death was justified.

"It doesn't look the same at all," she told him. "Rex changed everything."

Not that she knew what the house had looked like when Rafe had been a kid, but shortly after the B and B opened, Bailey had gone by with her mother just to check it out. Jack had given them the dime tour, bragging about all the changes Rex had made. According to Jack, Rex had put tremendous amounts of sweat equity into it, repairing whatever he could and replacing the rest.

"Doesn't matter," Rafe muttered. "I can't. I just…"

He didn't finish the sentence, and he didn't have to. She wanted to say she understood, but the truth was Bailey had no idea. She'd never endured a hell so awful you were forced to kill the man who'd sired you. Although she grew up without a father, she had a mother who loved her to the moon and back.

Bailey hoped that one day Rafe would come around, maybe share with her so he could get it off his chest. However, she wasn't going to push him. What had happened to him and Rex when they were kids was tragic. Bailey was a few years younger than Rafe, so she didn't remember any of it, but she'd lived in Coyote Ridge her entire life, and people talked. Plus, her uncle had been a friend of their mother's, so he had some firsthand knowledge. The stories still circulated, mostly gossip at this point. Some she wished were gossip but rang with far too much truth, no matter how heinous they were.

They sat in silence for another minute. Bailey was considering getting out when Rafe finally spoke.

"You'd tell me if he hurt you, right?"

"Of course," she lied.

Seth had never laid a hand on her, although there were a few times she thought he might. Still, if he had, Bailey wouldn't tell Rafe. She knew he would go after Seth, and the last thing she wanted was for Rafe to get in trouble. Then again, she wouldn't be living with Seth if he had physically hurt her. As for emotional abuse … yeah, that was beginning to be an issue.

"Like I said, horrible liar, Weber."

Bailey chuckled. "Whatever. Thanks for the ride. Maybe I'll see you tomorrow?"

"No maybe about it. I wanna know how the interview goes."

Bailey reached for the door handle. "Thanks again."

Before she could get it open, Rafe's hand was on her arm. She turned slowly, met his hooded gaze. Her breath lodged in her throat, the heat of his skin seeping into hers.

"Stay with Rex, Bailey. At the farmhouse. Please."

Oh, how she wanted to tell him yes. Even if it meant staying in the farmhouse, which he would never visit, it would still mean she was closer to him. And her heart wanted that more than anything.

Only she had obligations, and until she could end things with Seth the right way, she couldn't do that to herself or Rafe.

"Let me think about it," she whispered, hoping that would appease him.

His thumb brushed over her wrist. Once, twice, but then his touch and his warmth disappeared.

"I'll see you tomorrow," he said as she climbed out of the truck.

"I'm lookin' forward to it."

More than he knew.

AFTER RELUCTANTLY LEAVING BAILEY, RAFE CAME HOME to an empty apartment, which was located in the small retail space that lined Main Street.

Not for the first time, Rafe realized how lonely this place was. As was the case on any given night, all the businesses were closed up tight, the streets empty. According to Bailey, that was how country towns were meant to be. She said Coyote Ridge was exactly the sort of small town they wrote romance novels about.

Rafe didn't know about that. But it was small, and despite the larger cities encroaching, the town held true to its roots. There were community events on any given weekend and damn near every holiday. The businesses were independently owned and run by people whose families had lived there for generations.

Aside from the light shining from Rafe's apartment, the rest of the shopping center was dark. There wouldn't be life outside these walls for a few more hours when Bailey's mom arrived at the bakery across the street to start baking for the day.

As for his apartment … well, it was exactly what you expected for a converted retail spot in a small town. It wasn't much to look at, but it was nice enough. There were no holes in the plaster walls, no electrical sockets hanging loose. The lights worked, as did the A/C in the summer and the heater in the winter. And during the day, it was insulated enough he wasn't bothered by the traffic outside his window. Plus, Violet Anderson, the owner of the bookstore, had given him a good deal on the rent because she liked that someone was there to keep an eye on her stuff when she wasn't.

Small though it was, it worked for him. Rafe didn't need much room, only a bed to sleep in, a recliner to sit on, and a refrigerator and microwave to get him by. And that was pretty much all there was. One bedroom, one bathroom, nothing fancy. He had a living room and a kitchenette. His brother had insisted he get a television, and when Rafe didn't buy one, Rex did. Unless it was football or hockey, Rafe rarely ever turned it on. He spent his spare time reading, one of the perks of living above a bookstore.

Despite the fact he had minimal furnishings, this place felt more like home to Rafe than any place he'd lived his entire life. Even the farmhouse, back when his mama had been alive. Back when life had been full of warmth and light and something to look forward to. While he hoped never to part with the memories of his mother, Rafe had long ago accepted that the farmhouse was not where he wanted to be. Too much had happened in that place, and he was content never to step foot back inside.

Rafe marched across the living room and headed for the refrigerator. He grabbed a beer, popped the top, leaned against the rickety little island, and stared at the brown suede recliner. It was a housewarming gift from Rex, one of many his brother had tried to slip by him when he got back.

His gaze shifted to the window. In the distance, he could see the farmhouse, one of the only remaining residences downtown. The houses that were still standing had been converted into retail space.

Rafe

It stunned him how different this place was when so much was still the same. Especially the main square of downtown. Sure, the names of the businesses were different than he remembered, but the layout was the same. Strips of retail space formed a U around the park, with the B and B and acres of land on the other side.

As was the case in many small towns, there was a bookstore, a drugstore, and a barber shop, complete with the old-fashioned pole with the spinning helix of red, white, and blue stripes. A florist, a vintage record shop, and of course, the bakery. Those were all in the main square. Downtown was also home to the hardware store, a plant nursery, the diner, and of course, Moonshiners.

But the B and B stood proudly there, beautified over the years to reflect his brother's dream. Part of him was curious as to what the house looked like now. He remembered every square inch of that place. The secondhand furniture his mother had worked so hard to keep nice, the knickknacks she dusted every week, the yellow tile countertops she had insisted were charming but were simply ugly. Rafe knew the third step on the back staircase squeaked when you stepped on it, and the newel post on the front staircase wasn't attached because Rafe had broken it off when he was four.

But the room he remembered most was Rex's old bedroom. The blood that had splattered on the white wall behind where his father had been standing when—

The memory hit him with the impact of a freight train.

"Don't … please don't … God, don't…"

Rafe came awake with a start, his ears perked to his brother's coughing and sputtering, his inconsolable cries.

"Don't!" Rex yelled. "Don't fucking touch me!"

A horrible hacking laugh followed, drowned out by metal clanking on metal.

Rafe knew what was happening, knew he had to do something to stop it. Jolene had sounded the same way when she'd trapped Rafe in his bedroom that first time. If he was right, she was even using those same cuffs she'd strapped him to his own bed with.

Grabbing the shotgun Rex had hidden in the closet, Rafe stumbled to his feet. He knew it was loaded because Rex had shown him how to do it, and Rafe didn't go to sleep without checking it every single night.

His breaths raced in his lungs, his heart pounding painfully in his ears.

"Be still, you—"

Oh, God, no. Billy Don was here. It was bad enough that Jolene was doing what she was doing, but if Billy Don watched Rex the way—

Shuddering at the memory, Rafe twisted the knob and shoved the door open. As it slammed into the wall, he lifted the shotgun to his shoulder.

"Stop it right now!" he screamed.

Rex's tormented face turned his way as Rafe racked their grandpa's shotgun, aiming the barrel at the bitch standing over his brother.

"Let him go right now, I said!" Rafe yelled. "Let him go, or I'll shoot you. I will. Let my brother go!"

"Get yer boy, Billy Don!" Jolene screamed, her hand wrapped around Rex's—oh, God. She was touching him. That nasty bitch was touching his brother! "Take that gun away from him and get him outta here. I got a job to do, and I ain't leavin' till it's done."

Rafe looked at his brother, saw the tears and the shame glittering in his eyes. Rafe should've stopped her before. He should have. Then Rex never would've had to know what it was like to have her touching him. Rex always told him it was the big brother's responsibility to protect, but Rafe didn't believe that for a second. Rafe wanted to protect Rex, too. He should've done better.

Billy Don moved, and Rafe took one step back, but he didn't lower the gun; he merely swung it so the barrel pointed at their father.

"Come closer and I'll shoot you, old man. I'll do it," Rafe snarled, teeth bared. "Don't fucking test me."

Not listening, the old man closed the distance between them, stumbling once but righting himself.

"Don't you come closer, you asshole," Rafe warned, his voice calm as determination set in.

Billy Don took another step, and Rafe's finger shifted on the trigger.

"Rafe, no!" Rex shouted, but his voice was drowned out by the unmistakable sound of a shotgun blast, followed by Jolene's scream.

Rafe

Rafe stumbled away from the counter, shoving the memory down deep as he went to his bedroom. He refused to think about that night, refused to relive that hell. He forced his thoughts to shift to Bailey.

For some damn reason, if he thought of her, everything seemed right in the world. Didn't matter that she had a damn boyfriend—a fucking loser who didn't deserve her—either. Rafe still thought about her. Day and night, from the first moment he laid eyes on her three years ago when he had pulled into the little Gas 'n Go to fill up his truck.

Bailey had been inside at the counter, paying for a soda and a bag of chips, talking to the clerk in that animated fashion of hers. Evidently, that was her idea of dinner before her shift at the bar, and she'd been defending the benefits of carbs. While he'd ogled her ass, he had overheard her telling the clerk that she would be waitressing at Moonshiners that night, and Rafe had found himself going over there just to get another glimpse of her. When she had checked on him after he'd downed his first and only beer, her smile had been so damn bright it nearly blinded him.

For whatever reason, Rafe had stuck around until she left, watching as she climbed inside a silver Toyota Corolla, then as it disappeared down the road. He did that many times, having learned her mother was the one who picked her up.

It didn't take long for them to become friends. Rafe had welcomed her into his life with open arms, desperate for a distraction, something to keep his mind off his reason for running the last time. He'd never told her that coming back to Coyote Ridge hadn't been in his plans, but he'd told her more than once that she was the reason he stayed. It was true. Their friendship had grown from there. He couldn't count how many hours they'd spent together over the years. Going to the movies, the lake, the park. Whatever Bailey wanted to do, Rafe had gladly signed up to take her because being with her was the one good thing he had in his life.

But all that changed eight months ago when Bailey up and moved in with Seth.

By then, Rafe was already working at the bar, and he usually finagled his schedule to align with hers. He told himself it was so he could keep an eye on her, make sure she wasn't hassled. Maybe that had been the case at first, but the night he followed her outside, waiting while she pulled on her jacket and started walking toward the street, he'd finally asked her where she was going.

"Walkin' home," she said with a blinding smile, as though she didn't care that it was December and the nights were cold.

"Where's your mom?"

She shook her head, continuing to take steps backward. "I moved in with Seth."

Rafe hadn't known that but hearing her admit it had been like a sucker punch to the gut. To cover, he'd asked her how far she had to go. When she said three miles, he nearly lost his shit.

She had a fucking boyfriend who made her walk three miles home. Who fucking did that?

So, he drove her home that night, and the next day, he ran into Josh Weber, Bailey's uncle, at the auto parts store. Josh had thanked him for taking his niece home, and they'd chatted for a while. Turned out Josh wasn't exactly fond of Seth, either, but Bailey was adamant he was the one. Josh told him that when a woman was as insistent as Bailey, you wouldn't change their mind.

Rafe believed him.

Since then, Rafe had found every reason he could come up with to be around Bailey. He drove her home after her shift every night, refusing to let her walk the dark roads alone. It wasn't a hardship because she was the only person he cared to be around. And since he was her co-worker, it was the perfect excuse to give her a lift after they closed for the night.

"Sweet dreams, Bailey," he mumbled as he pulled his shirt over his head and tossed it on the chair.

He would leave his jeans and boots on for now. He'd never gotten accustomed to sleeping without clothes. Considering the hellhole he'd grown up in—first with his psycho father, then the brief but horrific stint at the boy's home—Rafe had learned not to let himself become too vulnerable. Even when he'd moved in with his Uncle Owen, Rafe could never relax.

Rafe

Lying back on the plush bed with its thick comforter and down pillows—more gifts from Rex—Rafe rested the beer bottle on his chest as he stared at the ceiling. He could see Bailey's beautiful face in his mind's eye. He could still smell her sweet, lavender scent, feel her baby-soft skin against his fingertips.

What he wouldn't give to have her in bed with him, curled up against his side, keeping the damn nightmares at bay.

But those damn nightmares were why he could never sleep with a woman beside him. No way was he subjecting anyone to that. Hence the reason he'd gone through dozens of women after he'd left Coyote Ridge. He couldn't remember most of their names, some he never even bothered to ask. Since he'd been back, Rafe hadn't been with anyone. Not because the opportunity hadn't arisen. It had. Often. But there was only one woman Rafe wanted, and she just so happened to be far too good for the likes of him.

Bailey wasn't one of those women a man would bed for the night, ride like a wild stallion and then disappear on come morning. She was the sweet type, the woman a man wanted to keep close, to protect, to … love. There was no doubt Rafe loved her, although he would never admit it to anyone. His love wasn't worth shit. Hell, just look at Rex. Rafe had proven that his love didn't have an ounce of value. Rather than stick around to be with his brother, Rafe had bailed. And still, Rex had worked his ass off to build a place for the two of them because that was the sort of man Rex was.

Rafe's phone buzzed in his pocket.

He set the beer on the nightstand, dug the phone out, and stared at the screen. A smile tilted his lips at the simple words from Bailey: *Good night, Rafe. Sweet dreams, cowboy.*

Damn that woman.

She was going to be the death of him, making him want things he knew he didn't deserve.

Never had he wanted a woman the way he wanted her. It was easier not to want anything at all. At least that way, you weren't disappointed. And until he met Bailey, until she'd managed to burrow under his skin, Rafe had stuck to that.

But even as each day passed, he felt himself changing, wanting something he'd never had before. He wanted to love and to be loved. And he knew Bailey Weber would be the woman who could give him that. If he even entertained the notion, he knew he would eventually give in because she was a temptation too great to ignore for long. In his fantasies, he would convince her to leave that jackass, and he would promise to be her man for eternity.

But those were fantasies because Rafe was the last thing a woman like Bailey needed in her life. He would only bring her down, cause her pain. He had secrets that no one knew. Some were even unforgivable. She would forever be weighed down by the sins that haunted him.

If only his mother hadn't died.

If only Billy Don hadn't brought Jolene around.

If only Rafe hadn't pulled the trigger that night.

He was doing the right thing by keeping Bailey at arm's length. Yeah, pretending he merely wanted to be her friend was hell. It hadn't been so bad in the beginning, but as the days ticked by, as they spent more and more time together, he couldn't stop thinking about her. The mere idea of her crawling into bed with another man had his stomach twisting in knots.

But it was the best thing for her. She needed a man who was whole, not a broken wanna-be cowboy who'd shot and killed his old man.

Nobody needed that.

Nobody.

Chapter Three

Bailey woke up the next morning to an empty house.

She made toast, took a shower, and even dried her hair. All while on edge that Seth would return any minute and ruin what she hoped was going to be a great day.

By the time she was dressed, she no longer cared where Seth was. She was grateful he was gone because it gave her time to primp in the mirror. Whenever he was around, he always poked fun at her. Usually, it was about her hair or makeup, often about her clothes. She got the feeling he found it amusing, but she rarely found anything funny about his snide comments. They were downright juvenile, and most of the time, they were mean.

She knew he would have plenty to say about the black silk pantsuit she was wearing. She'd paired it with a silky white shirt, a pair of ruby red flats, and the ruby earrings her mother had gotten her for her birthday last year. She thought she looked cute, plus the suit gave her a businesslike air, which was what she was going for since her interview with Rex was in an hour and a half. She'd ensured she had enough time to call for an Uber so she wouldn't have to trek into town on foot. She'd asked Seth last night if she could borrow his car to run some errands today, but he'd turned her down flat. In fact, he'd told her she could do well with some exercise.

Usually, Bailey wouldn't mind the walk. She'd gotten used to it, even enjoyed listening to an audiobook while breathing in the fresh air. Today was the exception because she did not want to show up at the bed-and-breakfast sweating or stinking. She didn't imagine either of those things would draw favor with Rex, and right now, she wanted him to hire her. She didn't even care if it was to clean toilets. As long as the pay was better than what she was earning now, she would gladly do it.

Well, maybe *gladly* was a bit too optimistic, but there was still a good chance she would jump at the opportunity.

"You've got this," she told her reflection, smiling. "You're smart and friendly, and you've got plenty of experience with customers."

Bailey had started her career in hospitality when she was ten, helping in her mother's bakery. Although she didn't earn a paycheck—then or now—she still helped as often as her mother needed. When she was fourteen, she babysat for several people from her church. Then when she turned sixteen, she got a job at a small grocery store in the neighboring town. That lasted only a couple of months before she had to quit because her schedule didn't align with her mother's, and leaving her mom without a car wasn't an option. When she turned eighteen, she started working at the diner since it was within walking distance of her mother's house. She worked there until she learned Mack was hiring a waitress at Moonshiners, also within walking distance. She'd been working there since she was twenty-one, serving drinks to her friends and neighbors.

She loved working in the small town she grew up in. When she thought about working in the big city, it made her nervous, which was likely why she'd put off applying for those jobs. Or part of it. Since transportation was limited, she didn't have many options.

But the moment she'd learned of Rex's need for someone to manage the Double R Retreat, she'd immediately sent him her resume. She would've been elated if she hadn't been one of about three dozen, according to the conversation she'd overheard between Jack and Rex. Instead, she was merely determined.

She took another moment to smooth down her hair. She contemplated pulling it up in a ponytail when her cell phone buzzed.

Rafe

Snagging it from the bathroom counter, she smiled when she saw it was a text message from Rafe.

> ⋯ **What time's your shift tonight?**

Bailey responded with:

> ⋯ Mack gave me the night off so I could either celebrate or sulk, depending on how it goes with my interview.

As she always did, Bailey stared at her phone as though that would make Rafe respond faster.

Deep down, she knew it was wrong to harbor these feelings for a man who wasn't Seth. She tried to tell herself it was okay because they were only friends, that as long as she didn't admit it aloud, no one would be the wiser. With that said, if Rafe would simply ask for something more, she'd jump at the chance.

She didn't want to think too long or hard about what that said about her. She should've ended things with Seth long ago, but she'd gotten comfortable with her life. She wouldn't go so far as to say she was happy, but she was familiar with it. She knew what to expect from him, even if it wasn't wine or roses or even a sweet gesture from time to time.

It was the same with her jobs. She didn't hate them, but she wouldn't go so far as to say she liked them, either. On the plus side, they were in Coyote Ridge, but aside from being able to work with her mom at the bakery and Mack and Rafe at Moonshiners, Bailey didn't look forward to going. She did it because she'd made the commitment, and if her mother had taught her anything at all, it was that she was to follow through on them.

Hence the reason she was twenty-four years old, living with a man she wasn't sure she even liked anymore and working at a job that paid her bills but did little else for her.

At the same time, she knew neither the bakery nor Moonshiners would be the stopping point on her career highway. She couldn't say the B and B would either, but she figured she wouldn't know unless she tried.

Bailey gave up waiting for Rafe to respond. She finished getting ready, adding another coat of mascara and a quick swipe of gloss on her lips before grabbing her phone to pull up her Uber app. As she was doing that, another text message came through from Rafe.

> I'll give you a ride to the B and B when you're ready.

She smiled at the phone, feeling a warmth in her chest that no one else could put there. It felt good to know Rafe cared enough to do something like that. And while she appreciated the gesture, Bailey knew it was wrong to lean on him like that. The last thing she wanted to do was get comfortable with Rafe and screw up what had turned out to be a great friendship.

> You're very sweet to offer, but it's okay.

> I'm already here. Quit making excuses.

That warmth in her chest turned into a glow, one she thought would have sunlight coming out of her eyes.

"Rafe Sharpe, don't you know I'm already in love with you?" she whispered. "Things like this aren't helpin' me with it."

Rafe

Bailey went to the window, peeked through the sheer curtain to see that, sure enough, his truck was parked out front. The giddy feeling that charged her insides was something she'd gotten used to. Although she'd thought Seth was capable of making her feel that way, she'd realized too late that Rafe was the only one who could.

Because there was no way she could say no, she messaged him back.

💬 Be out in 5.

She took that allotted time to look at herself once more in the mirror. Satisfied, she grabbed the small crossbody purse she carried everywhere and tossed her phone and lip gloss inside. It took effort, but she managed to stop the riot of nerves long enough to march out the door, down the creaky porch steps, and out to Rafe's truck.

Before she could get to it, Rafe was out and walking around to open the passenger door, something he always did for her. It melted her heart that he was such a gentleman. Just one more thing she loved about him.

"Hey," she greeted with a smile. "You didn't have to do this but thank you."

"Anytime, darlin'." He smiled, a flash of white teeth on his beautiful face.

Her heart melted just a little more.

"You look ... all professional-like," Rafe told Bailey after he climbed into the driver's side.

What he wanted to tell her was that she looked good enough to eat, but that wasn't appropriate, considering.

"Thank you," she said sweetly, swiping her hand down the front of her suit jacket.

He couldn't recall the last time he'd seen a woman wear a suit, but he knew for a fact no one wore it like Bailey. Hers was black and fit perfectly to her petite form. The jacket was short enough to show off her cute little ass, and not for the first time, he wondered what she looked like naked.

Granted, he shoved that thought away because it was inappropriate, and while he would like nothing more than to flirt ruthlessly with this woman, to lure her away from the douchbag boyfriend of hers, Rafe had made a promise to himself that he would never do that to her. Bailey deserved better than that. Hell, Bailey deserved the world, and since he was no more equipped to give it to her than the shithead she lived with, Rafe had to settle for being her friend.

"You don't think it's too much?" she asked, peering over at him as he backed out of the driveway.

"I think it's perfect," he mumbled, not meeting her gaze.

"I just hope Rex can see past the bar waitress he knows."

"I doubt you have anything to worry about," he assured her, not bothering to tell her that he'd already attempted to interrogate his brother on his intentions. Rex hadn't been forthcoming with details, but he'd ended the text conversation with a thumbs-up emoji, and Rafe decided to take that as a good sign.

"What're your plans for after?" he asked, attempting to make small talk as he weaved through the older neighborhood and onto the road leading into town.

"Thought I'd hang out," she said casually. "I told Violet I'd swing by the bookstore and hang out for a bit."

"Once you're done, maybe we can grab some lunch."

Bailey's smile was brilliant, something he found he looked forward to seeing daily. "I wouldn't say no to that."

"Good."

A few minutes later, he was pulling into the B and B, parking in one of the empty spaces in the lot out front. From here, he could see that Rex had already started taking down the Fourth of July decorations. Pretty soon, he'd start up with his fall decor, and the wraparound porch would look like one of those craft stores, overflowing with pumpkins, hay bales, and signs announcing, "It's fall, y'all."

Rafe

Rafe rested his wrist on the steering wheel and shifted his body toward Bailey. "Text me when you're done. I'll pick you up."

Bailey's beautiful hazel eyes skimmed his face. "I can walk across the park, you know."

"But you don't have to," he clarified, gesturing toward the big farmhouse. "Now go on. Get."

She giggled, just as he'd hoped she would. "Wish me luck."

"Darlin', you don't need luck."

"Everyone needs luck, Rafe." She took a deep breath, exhaled heavily, then opened the truck door.

He watched her cute little ass sway until she disappeared inside the house.

There was no doubt about it. He was a glutton for punishment. That was the only way to explain his insane need to be around Bailey, day in and day out, knowing he couldn't have her.

Then again, he figured if she was single and for the taking, Rafe would've already fucked it up by now.

Chapter Four

WALKING INTO THE BED-AND-BREAKFAST FELT almost like stepping into another dimension.

From its spot in downtown Coyote Ridge, the place didn't look like it could be a soothing home away from home, but the inside was a different story. Although it was apparent it wasn't someone's cozy living space, thanks to the check-in desk at the bottom of the stairs, it still made one feel welcome.

Rex had somehow managed to modernize the space by opening it up but still maintained the house's original charm. Bailey loved how bright and open it was. The way the sunlight highlighted the details and the dark beams on the ceiling—an addition Jack had talked Rex into—drew the eye up, which meant you couldn't help but notice the fireplace.

Glancing around and realizing she was alone, Bailey stepped behind the desk and smiled toward the door, imagining a sweet couple coming in to claim their reservation and enjoy a wonderful weekend of small-town, country living.

"Welcome to the Double R Retreat. Do you have a reservation?"

"Technically, no," a voice sounded from behind her.

Bailey spun around to see Rex walking toward her, an amused grin on his face. Unlike his brother, Rex did a lot of smiling, especially these days. Ever since he'd fallen in love and married Jack Cunningham, he had done a one-eighty. No longer was there a dark cloud hanging over his head the way it still did with Rafe.

"Sorry," she said sheepishly. "I couldn't resist."

A bark sounded, and a second later, Duke, Rex's six-year-old, floppy-eared retriever, came bolting in her direction, stopping shy of taking her down. He yipped happily up at her until she gave his head a rub. "Hey, Duke," she greeted. "Good to see you, too.

"Well, if you'd like to give your pretend guest their keys, we keep 'em locked up in that cabinet right there." He pointed to a large lockbox mounted to the wall.

Bailey stared at him for a moment, wondering if he was teasing. She decided it didn't matter because she wasn't about to pass up the opportunity he was handing her.

"Great idea, Mr. Sharpe," she said with a smile as she turned toward the box. It was locked, but she gestured for him to open it for her.

Clearly amused, his eyebrows rose, but Rex strolled over, used his thumbprint to unlock the biometric lock.

She stared at the rows of keys with numbers.

Figuring it was better to be safe than sorry, she leaned toward him and kept her voice low. "Are all of the rooms vacant?"

"As long as there are two keys, it is."

One, four, and seven only had one key. She skipped over them.

Squaring her shoulders, she grabbed the set with the number 3 inscribed on the plastic tag.

"Right this way." She motioned toward the stairs. "I'll show you to your room."

Playing along, Rex and Duke followed behind her as she slowly ascended the stairs.

"I hope your trip was good," she said conversationally. "I noticed on the reservation you had a plus one. Will your significant other be joining you?"

"He's tied up right now," Rex teased. "But he'll break free eventually."

Bailey laughed, hoping it covered her blush. She had no idea if he was serious and a graphic novelist was currently handcuffed to his bed, nor did she really want to know.

"Here we go," she said when they approached room number three.

She used the key to unlock it, then opened the door inward, stepping inside and just out of the way so Rex could follow. Duke opted not to come in, turning around and flopping down in the hallway as though standing guard.

"As you can see, you've got a small kitchenette, and over there's the bathroom." She gestured toward the far corner of the room. "Your room overlooks our beautiful grounds, and you've got a balcony where you can enjoy your morning coffee." She turned and beamed a smile at Rex. "Breakfast is served daily between six and eight. Come down and join us if you'd like, or you can place that"—she pointed toward a small piece of paper on the desk—"on your doorknob the night before, and we'll deliver your selection to your room."

Rex was staring at her, his eyes twinkling with amusement. "That's not a service we offer, but I like how your mind works, Ms. Weber."

"Please, call me Bailey," she noted. "I was improvisin'."

"But you knew about the kitchenette and the balcony?"

She felt her cheeks heat. "I might've stalked your website to learn the details of your options. I also know the dates for all the upcoming festivals and activities taking place in town. I figure that's good information to have so the guests can see the sights while they're here. I thought maybe we could do some marketing around those events. Maybe some promotional deals."

"I'm impressed." He tilted his head toward the hallway. "Why don't we head back down?"

Bailey took the liberty of locking the door back before passing the key to Rex as they headed back down to the main floor.

"I know you've been here, but I'm not sure if you've had the grand tour yet. Do you have any questions about the amenities?"

She figured she should probably have some questions, but she couldn't think of any. "I've seen most of it, so I'm comfortable with the layout. I'd like to understand the process, but I figure that's an on-the-job sort of thing. Something I can do as I work my way up the ladder."

"There's not much to it, although it'll keep you busy day and night."

"I'm sure."

"As far as the ladder goes, there's only one rung, and you're on it. This is a full-time gig. We're lookin' to hire a manager to live on-site."

"I understand. And I know I don't have the qualifications, but I'm a hard worker. I don't mind cleanin' rooms and learnin' the ropes. Once——"

"You misunderstand," Rex said, interrupting. "There's only one position. Someone who can live here full-time. And that's non-negotiable. I don't think it's a secret we've been buildin' a house at the back of the property. We've just started movin' stuff over now that it's finished. I don't think apartment living is workin' all that well for us."

"Apartment?"

Rex pointed toward the ceiling. "Third floor. Two bedrooms, one bath, small eat-in kitchen, nice-sized den. There's a lot of light from the windows and a balcony, as well as a private entrance at the back."

Bailey felt her heart thump hard in her chest. She'd thought they'd offer a manager the use of one of the guest rooms, and she'd been thrilled with that. But the idea of having a real place of her own … it would solve so many of her problems. She hoped one day, she could work her way up to that position.

"It's part of the compensation package," Rex informed her. "There's also a salary, time off. All the stuff Jack informed me was a requirement for getting a strong candidate in here."

Bailey laughed.

"There might be a small transition period," Rex continued, "while Jack and I move out, but there's a private room on the main floor in the interim. We use it for those in need of handicap-accessible accommodations. You're welcome to stay there if that helps."

Bailey's eyes widened. Was he saying…?

"That is, if you want the job, Bailey."

Her smile widened until her face hurt. "Really? Me?"

"Yeah, really. Shit. We'd be lucky to have you."

"But I thought y'all got a lot of applications?"

"We did, but we got yours first. As soon as it came in, I told Jack you were the one."

"But aren't there people with more qualifications? I've never managed anything on my own."

Rex's eyebrow quirked. "Are you trying to talk me *out of* hirin' you?"

"No," she blurted. "Definitely not."

"You're it, Bailey. You're the one we want."

She smiled as wide as she could, trying to hide the tears that threatened.

"I'll still be around most of the time, but I'll lean on you to manage the place. I'll handle the maintenance and repair, shit like that. You'll oversee the guests, plus cookin' and ensurin' the rooms are cleaned. I suggest you hire someone to help with that. If you think you can do it yourself, you'll quickly learn you're wrong. We've been usin' a service, but I'd prefer to keep it local. Unfortunately, keepin' up with demand's been difficult. We've been booked solid every weekend for the past fourteen months, and the weekdays aren't doin' too bad, either."

She was still hung up on the part where he'd offered her the job.

"Why don't I show you the compensation package," he said, turning and retrieving a file folder that was lying on the counter.

He handed it over, and Bailey opened it. Her eyes widened when she saw the yearly salary. It was twice as much as she made at Moonshiners, not counting tips. She skimmed the page, saw that room and board were included, as well as two weeks of vacation each year to start.

"I can't do much on givin' you all holidays off," Rex noted, "but we can work together to come up with a fair schedule."

When she looked up, Rex was staring at her expectantly. She honestly didn't even know what to say.

"Sorry, kiddo, but I've shown you all my cards. I don't have any more to play."

Bailey frowned. "What?"

"You want the job?"

She shook herself out of her stupor and smiled giddily. "Yes. Absolutely, yes. I promise you won't regret hirin' me."

"Like I said, from the day we got your resume, the job's been yours," he said kindly. "We've just been waitin' for you to show up."

"That's ... wow! Thank you, Rex." She felt tears filling her eyes as a new hope emerged.

"But there's still one more question before we can finalize everything."

Squaring her shoulders and attempting to resume an air of professionalism, she stared up at him.

"When can you start?"

She smiled, then ran over and hugged him before she could think better of it.

Thankfully, Rex laughed.

RAFE WAS STANDING OUTSIDE HIS TRUCK, LEANING against the passenger door, when Bailey emerged from the B and B, grinning ear to ear.

Jesus, she could knock him down with just her smile. He was easily as fascinated with the way she tried so hard not to skip when it was obvious her excitement was attempting to break free from her body.

"Well?" he asked when she approached.

Her smile somehow managed to grow wider seconds before she launched herself at him, throwing her arms around his neck. "I got it! I got the job."

Every bit of air was expelled from his lungs the moment he had her in his arms. He held on tight, soaking up her lavender scent and the sweet sound of her joy. It took tremendous effort to release her and pretend he hadn't just witnessed the equivalent of the Second Coming just from having her in his arms.

"I can't believe it," she said, her tone urgent. "Two weeks. Rex said they'll be moved out in the next two weeks, and I can move in."

Disappointment landed like a boulder in his gut. "You and Seth are movin' in here?"

She flinched back, frowned. "Absolutely not. Just me."

Relief gripped him by the throat, but he choked it down. "Are you ... uh...?"

"Breakin' up with him?" Bailey nodded. "As soon as I have a place to go." Her eyes widened. "I mean … I know that sounds bad, but I'm not usin' him. I swear it. I just … he's not the guy I thought he was, but I—"

Rafe placed his finger over her mouth, effectively silencing her. "You don't have to explain it to me."

A soft gasp whispered between them as her breath caught, her soft, glossy lips parting as he forced his finger away from her mouth. She had the nicest fucking lips. He couldn't count how many times he's fantasized about all the places those lips would go on his body when they were naked together.

Jesus.

His traitorous cock fought to break the damn zipper on his jeans.

"Come on," he said, opening the truck door and gesturing for her to get inside. "I'll drop you at the bookstore."

When she got in, he shut the door, adjusted himself in his fucking jeans, and marched around to the driver's side. He climbed in, refusing to look her way as he started the truck and put it in gear.

"Rafe?"

"Hmm?" He busied himself by reversing so he could avoid drawing attention to his extreme discomfort.

"Could we go somewhere else? I mean, before the bookstore?"

"I'd be happy to drop you anywhere," he said, shifting into drive, then heading toward the parking lot exit.

"Not me," she clarified. "*We.*"

He had no choice but to look at her as he waited for an oncoming car to pass. His mouth opened with an instant rejection perched on the tip of his tongue. But as soon as his gaze locked with hers, he knew he couldn't reject her. He would do anything for this woman.

"Where?" he asked softly, admiring her beautiful face.

"The lake?"

Rafe knew going to the lake was a mistake just waiting to happen. He wanted this woman with a passion he couldn't ignore, but he'd never crossed the line with a woman in a relationship, and he didn't intend to start now. It didn't matter that she claimed she was breaking up with her boyfriend. Rafe wouldn't do that to anyone. There was a damn good chance her idiot-ass boyfriend would get with the program once he realized he was about to lose the best damn thing that had likely ever happened to him.

"It's okay if you don't—"

"It's fine." He nodded, then pulled out of the lot and headed in that direction.

Evidently, he wasn't listening to his better angels today.

"What's at the lake?" he prompted, desperate to break the stifling silence.

"No one."

He smiled. "I didn't say *who*?"

"I know. No one is the *what*."

Rafe cast a sideways glance her way, grinning. "Are you fuckin' with me?"

She laughed. "No. What I mean is the lake is quiet, and there's no one there askin' you to get them somethin' or do anything for them. It's just ... quiet. And right now, quiet sounds perfect. I need a few minutes to process."

"Quiet, huh?" He propped his forearm on the steering wheel and leaned forward. "I can do quiet."

Half an hour later, he'd found a patch of dirt tucked in amongst the trees not too far from the pier that launched out over the water. It wasn't used much, although he suspected someone thought putting a gazebo out over the water, several yards from shore, was a good idea.

Despite being in a familiar summer drought, the leaves were firmly planted on the trees, still vibrant and green as tended to happen here. It would be like that for most of the year since they didn't get the various colors of fall like the decor his brother used to celebrate the season. It was green or nothing around these parts.

Rafe backed his truck close to the water, then shut off the engine. He ordered Bailey to stay where she was so he could open her door. When he walked around, he had his mask firmly in place, his dick wrangled into submission, and his priorities in order. He could spend some time alone with her. No problem. He had mastered the art of resisting this woman. Hell, he'd been doing it for three years. What was another hour?

Once she had slipped off her suit jacket, he helped her out of the truck. To avoid ogling her ass, he led the way to the rear of the truck, intending to lower the tailgate.

"Could we walk out on the pier?" Bailey asked.

Probably a good idea. The tailgate was likely hot enough to singe with the sun beating down, scorching the earth with its intensity.

"Yeah, sure."

Rafe tucked his hands in his pockets and began walking alongside her as they weaved their way around the outer banks of the lake. Although the kids in town referred to this spot as the beach, it didn't resemble one with its rocky, unsteady terrain. They were near the pier when Bailey stumbled. Rafe managed to catch her before she fell, his arms curling under hers to keep her upright.

"Thanks," she rasped, clutching his arms as she attempted to get her footing.

Rafe grunted, holding onto her despite his better judgment. Her breath hitched, but so did his. It took every ounce of self-control he possessed to release her and take a step back, urging her toward the wooden step to the pier.

"Sorry."

"For?"

"Makin' you uncomfortable."

He should've told her he was the farthest from uncomfortable as a man could be, but what good would that do? Rafe knew hope when he saw it, and Bailey's glittered brightly in her beautiful eyes. It was best to let her think he wasn't interested.

"It's fine," he grumbled, gesturing toward the wooden pier. "Ladies first."

Bailey led the way to the gazebo. Her gaze swung to the ceiling when she stepped inside, shifting quickly.

"What're you lookin' for?" he prompted.

"Wasps."

He grinned, then did a sweep of the space. There weren't any, which meant this place was used more than he thought.

Bailey took a seat on one of the wooden benches facing the water. Rather than sit beside her—his damn dick wasn't keen on being compressed in his jeans—Rafe leaned his hip against the railing as he stared at the glassy water. Bailey was right. It was quiet. The only sounds were the rustle of the leaves in the light breeze and the birds chirping.

His thoughts drifted back to another time when his view had been as serene as this one. Only that body of water had been the Gulf of Mexico, and the sounds had come from the waves crashing against the shore. Nearly three years had passed since the incident that triggered his fight or flight instinct. He'd opted for flight that time, refusing to look back, desperate to forget the incredible night that had changed what he knew about himself.

"You know, Seth's not who I thought he was."

Bailey's soft apologetic tone pulled him out of his reverie, bringing him back to this moment and the other person who'd altered his life in ways he hadn't anticipated.

"That's why I'm breakin' up with him," she explained. "Not because I've got a place to go."

Rafe didn't want to talk about Seth, but he indulged her. "Who did you think he was?"

The silence lingered for so long he thought she was avoiding his question. He was about to comment when she finally spoke.

"When I met Seth, he was kind and attentive. He would take me on dates and plan special nights. Then I moved in with him, and that stopped. He rarely even buys me dinner these days. If I want groceries, I have to buy them. And if I want them cooked, that's my job, too."

"Maybe that's part of settlin' down with someone."

"What? That they morph into a completely different person? *Pfft.* Definitely not."

Rafe honestly had no idea what it meant to be in a relationship. He'd never been in one, and he'd never casually dated anyone, either. The most he'd done was screwed the same woman more than once, but only a couple of times, and only when he knew the woman wasn't interested in anything more than that.

"I thought he was different."

"Most people aren't who you expect them to be," he muttered.

"You are," she said firmly.

Rafe shifted so he could look at her. "No, Bailey, I'm not."

She smiled, but it was sad. "I knew you were gonna say that because I know you better than you think I do."

He shook his head again, looking back at the water. If she really knew him, Bailey would've questioned what she was doing here with him. What he wanted and what she had to offer weren't exactly aligned. There were certain desires, even if she tried, she could never fulfill.

"I know you're smart and funny and kind."

Rafe closed his eyes and took a deep breath. "Bailey…"

"You care about your brother and your friends. You'd give the shirt off your back if one of them needed it."

He ground his molars together, trying to hold back the biting retort that was desperate to escape. She gave him far too much credit. Rafe did what he needed to do to survive each day. The ghosts that haunted him came from a darkness he couldn't forget, no matter how hard he tried.

"I know—"

"Stop," he demanded, crossing his arms over his chest. Rafe refused to look at her. "I know you *think* you know me, but you don't. Like everyone else, I let you see who I want you to see."

He hadn't meant for his tone to be so sharp, but this was why he avoided being alone with this woman. He knew that Bailey was looking for the white picket fence and all that shit. He'd heard her talk about it with her friends. Rafe couldn't give her any of that. Hell, he was a bartender making barely above minimum wage with no prospects of a future. The only thing he had to his name was a ten-year-old truck. He lived paycheck to paycheck without a penny in savings. And that didn't even begin to touch his emotional demons, which kept him up at night. She deserved a man who could give her a better life. That wasn't him, which was why he'd kept her at a distance. Even when he'd hated the idea of her dating Seth, he'd managed to stay far enough away so she could find a real chance at happiness.

"I don't believe you, Rafe."

His tone cooled, but he didn't look at her. "It's true."

"Then who are you, huh?"

Feeling the familiar rage running through his veins, he faced her. He fell back on the tried-and-true excuse that usually worked to push people away. "I'm the guy who murdered my father, Bailey."

"You were a kid," she countered. "That's—"

"I'd do it again the same way today," he bit out. "I'd gladly take his ass out for—" He cut himself off before he revealed a secret he'd held onto for nearly twenty years.

"For what?"

"Nothin'," he snapped. "Drop it, Bailey." He jerked his chin toward the truck. "We should get back to town. I forgot I've got some shit to take care of."

Bailey nodded, and he pretended not to see her disappointment.

He allowed her to walk down the pier before he followed a few feet behind. When she slipped on the rocks, his muscles tensed, but he resisted the urge to help her. Touching her was a bad idea.

When they reached the truck, he walked her around to the passenger side, opened the door, and stepped out of the way so she could get in.

He was seconds away from safety when Bailey grabbed his arm and tugged, forcing him to look down at her.

"I didn't mean to upset you."

Rafe looked away, grinding his teeth, trying to think of anything except for her soft fingers on his skin.

"Rafe. Look at me."

When he didn't, she slid her hand up his forearm.

"Bailey," he warned. "You need to stop touchin' me. My impulse control is shit on a good day, and you…"

"Finish that sentence, Rafe," she said firmly.

Because he knew she wouldn't let it go, Rafe looked down at her. "You tempt me, goddammit. Is that what you wanna hear?"

Her eyes widened, shock etched on her smooth skin.

"It's true, okay? You fuckin' tempt me, but you're too fuckin' good for me."

"You tempt me, too," she said. "You've always tempted me, Rafe. That's—"

"I'm not gonna be your fallback guy, Bailey," he ground out. "It's not my fault your relationship didn't work."

She looked as though he'd slapped her, and it pained him to know he'd hurt her, but this was nothing compared to the damage he'd do if he allowed her to believe her feelings were reciprocated. He had to put an end to this now.

"That's not what I meant. I just—"

"Drop it, Bailey," he barked, forcing himself back a step as he focused his gaze over her head. "I knew this was a mistake. Get in."

No matter how much he wanted her, Rafe vowed he would not fuck up her life because he was selfish. As far as he was concerned, Bailey Weber was and always would be off-limits to him. No exceptions.

Chapter Five

AFTER THEY LEFT THE LAKE, BAILEY HAD Rafe drop her at her house instead of the bookstore. As much as she wanted to hang out with Violet and celebrate her new job, her argument with Rafe had put a damper on her mood. She spent the better part of the afternoon trying to process what he'd said, but more specifically, the anger she'd detected in his tone. It wasn't the first time she'd seen Rafe angry, but it was the first time he'd directed it at her.

She didn't like the way they'd left things between them. She hadn't meant to give him the impression she wanted things to change. She didn't. Breaking up with Seth had nothing to do with how she felt about him. It was something she needed to do for herself. Unfortunately, she could see how he might think otherwise. After all, now that there was a light at the end of the tunnel, she was going to end things with Seth. To others, that probably looked like a selfish move.

If nothing else, Rafe was her friend, and she didn't want to do anything that would upset that balance. Clearly, she'd overstepped, and she wanted to make it right. She'd called him once and texted him several times since, but he hadn't messaged her back. She had apologized twice, thinking that would earn her some sort of response but still nothing.

In an effort not to dwell on the crickets she was getting back from him, Bailey began organizing her things so she could start packing. When she realized she didn't have enough to matter, she ended up cleaning the house from top to bottom. She did the laundry—hers and Seth's—vacuumed and mopped, emptied the dishwasher, and dusted all the furniture. She would admit that part of it was out of guilt. She was going to move out, and she didn't intend to have a lengthy conversation with Seth about it. She didn't think he would care, but that didn't mean she wanted to hurt him. He was an ass, but Bailey wasn't wired for retaliation or revenge.

It had taken her until late into the evening to get all her chores accomplished. Long enough, she'd forgotten all about dinner. When she realized the time, she texted Seth to find out when he'd be home. Unlike Rafe, Seth quickly responded, letting her know he was hanging with a friend so not to wait up.

If only she'd taken his advice. Instead, Bailey had vegged on the couch with a bag of Doritos, watching *Suits* because it wasn't something Seth let her watch when he was home. At eleven thirty, she gave up and decided to go to bed so she could read for a while. As she was washing her face, she heard Seth come in. As was his routine, he didn't come to the bedroom, and she was grateful. They didn't sleep in the same bed much anymore. On the nights he went out, he chose to pass out on the couch, and on the off chance he was in bed when she came home from work, she would sleep there so she wouldn't wake him. Or so she told herself. Bailey sensed that Seth didn't want her there any more than she wanted to be there.

Two weeks and counting, she reminded herself. She merely had to hold out for two more weeks, and then she wouldn't have to endure this anymore. In the meantime, she would at least have the bed to herself.

After freeing her hair from the ponytail, Bailey went to the dresser to get her pajamas, checking her phone again, hoping to find a text from Rafe. She frowned at the screen when she saw there wasn't one. With a huff, she set it on the dresser.

"What are you doin'?"

Bailey shrieked, spinning around to find Seth standing in the bedroom doorway, his face contorted with what looked eerily like excitement. Like he'd caught her doing something she shouldn't, and he now had the upper hand.

Or maybe that was her guilt creating an illusion.

"Getting ready for bed. Why?"

Seth placed a hand on the doorjamb to keep himself upright, his chin jerking in the direction of her phone. "What's that?"

He'd been drinking. She knew because his face was blotchy, his eyes glassy. Those were both signs he'd overindulged, which was usually when she saw this side of him.

"My phone." *Duh.*

"Who're you calling?"

"No one." It was the truth. Technically, she hadn't been calling anyone.

Seth moved toward her, and Bailey picked up her phone, clutching it tightly and hiding it behind her back. The move made her look guilty, she knew, but she honestly didn't care.

"What's goin' on, Bailey? Who're you on the phone with in the middle of the damn night?"

Figuring Seth wouldn't be happy unless she told him, she opted for the truth. "I texted Rafe. Wanted to make sure he got home all right."

"Got home?" He glared at her. "From where?"

"He drove me home from my job interview," she said, unable to come up with a better answer. She didn't know *what* she'd say if Seth remembered that it was earlier in the day.

"Interview? Did you get fired?"

Well, at least she didn't have to worry about coming up with another lie. He didn't remember. He never did.

"No, I didn't get fired." Did the man *ever* listen to her? "I applied for a job at the B and B."

He rolled his eyes. "Tired of bussing tables? Thought you'd clean rooms instead. Jesus, Bailey. Can't you stick to one job?"

She'd only had one job for the past three years, but she didn't remind him of that. There were times Bailey wondered if the guy knew anything about her at all.

"Wait." Seth's forehead scrunched, and his head turned so he could regard her with a sideways glare. "The B and B? With Rafe's *brother?*"

"Yes."

"Is this you tryin' to get closer to Rafe fucking Sharpe?" His words were drawled slowly, and she wondered if he was having difficulty keeping up with the conversation.

"I work with him *now*, Seth. I'm not sure I could get much closer."

"I knew it! I knew you were tryin' to hook up with that bastard."

Oh, geez.

"I am not."

"Then why're we talkin' about him?"

"You're the one who brought him up!" Bailey snapped.

"Rafe fucking Sharpe," Seth said as though he was trying to wash the taste out of his mouth.

"Yes. For the last time, yes!"

For a moment, Bailey expected steam to come out of Seth's ears. He didn't like it when she showed she had a backbone. His face turned redder, his glassy eyes got bigger as they bounced from her face to the phone, then back again.

Realizing they were getting nowhere fast, Bailey slowly turned away and opened the drawer to get her pajamas. She held them to her chest as she moved around Seth to the bathroom.

"Rafe fucking Sharpe, Bailey?"

Bailey sighed as she stepped into the bathroom. Before she could close the door, Seth slammed his hand against the wood, causing it to hit her shoulder. She stumbled backward but remained upright.

"Are you fuckin' him, Bailey?" he shouted, the stench of beer wafting on his breath.

"God, no," she declared, her anger building. "You know I'm not."

"I don't know anything about you anymore. You're always gone, out till all hours of the damn night."

Was he serious?

"I work at night," she hissed. "Every night."

"That's what you say. Now I'm not so sure that's the case."

The more he spoke, the more he slurred, which meant Seth was way past drunk.

Hoping to diffuse the situation, Bailey softened her tone. "You know I work with Rafe. And he drives me home, Seth. Since you refuse to let me take your car."

"You have no right gettin' in a car with him."

She did not want to argue with him. Not tonight. She'd had enough arguments for one day.

Bailey rolled her eyes. "And how do you expect me to get home, huh?"

"You're a smart girl. You can figure it out. You got two legs. Use 'em."

Of course he would say that. Seth didn't care that she had to walk three miles to get home from the bar, usually at two o'clock in the morning.

"Or maybe that's what you're doin'," he snarled. "Are you spreadin' your legs for Rafe Sharpe, Bailey? Lettin' that bastard fuck you in his truck every night?"

Her anger ignited, but she swallowed it back. She'd never cheated on Seth, and he knew it. He merely wanted a fight.

Seth watched her for long seconds before finally saying, "I don't want you anywhere near that damn murdering son of a bitch. You hear me? I catch you with him again…" He turned to go.

His words pissed her off, and though she knew she should let him walk away, let him sleep off the alcohol, she couldn't.

"Maybe if you gave a shit, Seth, I wouldn't have to get a ride with other people. You'd think you could stay sober long enough to pick me up."

Seth spun around, stabbed a finger in her direction. "You're a grown woman, Bailey. I didn't sign on to be your goddamn chauffeur. Get your own fucking car. Drive your own ass to and from."

"You're right. You didn't sign on to be my chauffeur," she yelled. "You signed on to be my boyfriend!"

He barked a laugh. "And you think a boyfriend drops everything to cart his whiny ass girlfriend all over the place? Hell no, Bailey. I've got better things to do than sit around and wait for you."

"Well," she said with a huff. "I've got better things to do, too."

"Good. I suggest you do them."

Bailey stared at him for a moment, ignoring the way her chest squeezed. "Why'd you ask me to move in with you, Seth?"

His eyebrows angled down.

"I thought you loved me."

He snorted. "You want the truth?"

Mentally, she shook her head, but outwardly, Bailey nodded.

"For one, I didn't think you'd agree. And two, it was the only way I could get you to let me fuck you."

Bailey gasped in shock.

Seth laughed. "Yeah. That's right. I wanted to be the one to prove Bailey Weber's not the good girl everyone thinks she is. It worked. But somewhere along the way, you got it in your head that I was gonna be your Prince Charming."

"You're certainly no Prince Charming," she huffed.

His smile was vicious. "You're right. And your pussy's not made of gold like you think."

She knew they were headed for the conversational gutter. Whenever they argued, Seth always degraded her.

With her phone in her hand, Bailey headed into the closet. "I'll make it easier for you." She yanked down an overnight bag and grabbed a few things, stuffing them inside.

"Where do you think you're goin'?" Seth hollered. "Runnin' to your mama's house?"

Not caring that it would piss him off, Bailey pulled up her contacts on her phone, then tapped the screen. As had been the case earlier, the call to Rafe went straight to voicemail. She stared Seth right in the face when she said, "Hey, Rafe. I'd like to stay at the Double R tonight. Can you come get me?"

"You cheatin' bitch," Seth hissed. "You fucking whore. I should've known."

"Thanks, Rafe," she replied to no one. "I'll see you in a few minutes."

She tapped the screen to end the call and glared at Seth as she moved toward him. "For one, I've never cheated on you. And two, I'm not sleeping with anyone. I'm gonna stay at the B and B, where I'll be movin' in two weeks anyway."

"Moving?" He rolled his eyes. "If only I could get so damn lucky."

Although she didn't expect anything less from Seth, Bailey couldn't deny his comment stung. She'd moved in with him because she thought they had something. And she'd stuck it out because she thought they could make it work. She'd been so wrong.

"It's true," she said, keeping her tone from reflecting the pain lancing her insides. "Rex offered me the job. I start in two weeks. I'm movin' into the manager's apartment."

"Thank Christ," he chortled. "I didn't want to kick your ass to the curb, but you don't seem to take a hint. I don't know how much more I could've taken."

He could've slapped her and it wouldn't have hurt as much. While she needed some space from him tonight, a little time to get her thoughts together, Bailey hadn't expected Seth to dismiss her so easily.

She watched as he stormed out of the room. Honestly, she hadn't expected their little argument to end so quickly. Once riled, Seth's rampage generally lasted a good hour.

Since the walk into town was going to be brutal enough, she traded the overnight bag for a rolling suitcase, filling it with as much as she could, then stuffing a few more things in a bag she could sit on top of it. When she dragged her stuff into the living room, she found Seth sitting on the couch, his phone to his ear.

"Yeah, baby. I told you she'd be gone soon. Mm-hmm. She moved out tonight." Seth's eyes lifted to hers. "It's been goin' to the shitter for a while now. But the good thing is, we no longer have to keep our relationship a secret."

Bailey's ears heated, fury raging in her chest as she held Seth's gaze. He was talking to a woman. He'd been cheating on her. The bastard!

"You're a fucking asshole," she snarled. "I can't believe I wasted any of my time with you."

"The feelings mutual, sweetheart," he grumbled. "No, not you, babe. Yeah. She's leavin'. Give me a few minutes, and I'll come pick you up."

What a jerk.

"Make sure you tell her she'll probably have to walk home!" she yelled, hopefully loud enough the woman on the other end could hear.

"Ignore her," Seth crooned. "She's a mooch, and she whines about every damn thing."

Seething but determined, Bailey spun away from him and headed for the door, dragging her bags with her.

Fuck him. She didn't want to be with him anyway. It didn't matter that he was fucking someone else. It wasn't like she'd been sleeping with him. Maybe once a month, at most. Thank God for alternating schedules and condoms because God only knows what diseases he might've passed to her.

The bastard.

Once she'd crossed the threshold with all her shit, Bailey jerked the door shut as hard as she could. It hit her foot and bounced back, ruining her dramatic exit. She heard a cackle from Seth and decided he could get his happy ass up and shut the door his damn self.

She grunted and groaned as she jerked her suitcase down the stairs. It twisted and tumbled, dumping her bag when it fell. With tears in her eyes, she crouched down to clean it up.

"You're gonna be fine," she mumbled to herself.

Of course, that was a platitude she told herself because she honestly didn't know where she was going to go. Her mother's? It was always an option, she knew, but the thought of putting her mother out like that didn't sit well. Plus, she didn't want her mom to think she'd gone and screwed everything up with Seth. After all, Bailey was the one who'd defended him to her family when they'd attempted to make her see reason.

Stupid Seth.

Standing tall, Bailey repositioned the bag so it wouldn't fall, then grabbed the suitcase handle and started down the driveway. Her suitcase bounced and wobbled until she reached the asphalt road. When it leveled out, she set her feet in motion and started the trek into town.

Maybe she should go to Moonshiners. There was a small room in the back with a single cot. It would do in a pinch. Then in the morning, she could call Rex and take him up on the offer to stay in the guest room until she could move her things into the apartment. She had enough money in the bank to cover the cost of renting the room for a little while. Maybe he'd give her a discount until she officially started working there.

But first, she had to get to town.

She'd gotten good at getting the three-mile walk down to an hour and fifteen minutes. It wasn't as easy with the suitcase bogging her down, but it was doable. She managed a decent pace, so it only took an hour for her to near the outer edge of downtown where the sidewalks began. At least here, she wasn't dodging cars. Not that there'd been many. Not this time of night.

Lucky for her, Moonshiners closed at midnight on most weeknights if the crowd was thin, so she wouldn't risk anyone seeing her pathetic entrance.

What wasn't so lucky was that, based on the empty parking lot, it appeared Rafe had shut things down already. Which meant she couldn't get in the building because only Rafe and Mack had keys.

Her gaze swung toward the B and B, then across the park to the bookstore. More specifically, the apartment above it.

Truth was, she hated to impose on either of the Sharpe brothers. She knew Rex would let her in, but it would require her to wake him up, and setting that sort of precedent with her boss felt wrong. The idea of asking Rafe for a place to stay didn't feel any better. He was clearly pissed off at her, and until she could figure out why, she wasn't eager to rehash that argument.

"Well, Mom, I sure hope you've got that extra blanket in the back," she muttered as she tugged her suitcase toward the bakery. She *did* have keys to that.

Rafe closed the bar shortly after midnight when the last customers left. It had taken tremendous effort not to toss them out on their ass, but he figured they'd call Mack, and since his boss didn't give a shit that his cell phone was dead and there wasn't a spare charger sitting around, Rafe had reined in his patience and waited them out.

Now he was waiting for the damn phone to get enough juice to turn on.

Pulling his shirt off and tossing it onto the chair, he strolled to the refrigerator and grabbed a bottle of water. He would've preferred a beer, but that would require a trip to the grocery store in the next town. Something he would not be doing in the middle of the damn night.

Granted, a trip out would be far less pathetic than pacing the floor, waiting for the air conditioner to cool the room down from sauna to tolerable and for his cell phone to turn on. Waiting to find out if he'd missed any calls or texts from Bailey. He hated how he left things with her this morning. It had been a complete dick move on his part but keeping her at a distance was the best thing for her.

He glanced at his phone, willing the damn screen to flash on. *How fucking long does it—*

The screen flashed with the glowing red battery symbol, showing it was charging.

"Finally. Shit." Rafe capped the water bottle and set it down before snagging his phone.

He tapped the screen. Nothing happened. He could see the little lightning bolt showing it was charging, but apparently, there wasn't enough juice to pull up the unlock screen.

He took a deep breath and dug for more of the patience he'd relied on earlier. It wasn't nearly as easy as it looked. He wasn't a patient man. Never had been. And this was beyond ridiculous. Rafe couldn't remember the last time his cell phone had died. Of all days for it to happen…

His phone beeped.

"Fuckin' finally," he grumbled, picking up the phone and tapping to pull up the notifications.

A relieved sigh escaped when he noticed four text messages and two missed calls from Bailey, one call from a number he didn't recognize, and a voicemail.

Rafe

He tapped to open the messaging app, then clicked on the image of her.

> Hey. I wanted to tell you I'm sorry about this morning. I don't know exactly what happened, but I didn't mean to upset you. Text me back when you get a minute.

How the woman could think it was her fault was beyond him.

> I'm hoping you're busy and haven't had time to text me back. That's better than you ignoring me.

The next one came two hours later.

> I guess I upset you. Again, I'm sorry. You think maybe we could just start over? To, like, yesterday.

Of all the days for his battery to die.

> I'm not sure what more I can say. Especially if you refuse to talk to me. I won't bother you anymore.

"I could never refuse you, Bailey," Rafe mumbled. "And you damn sure aren't a bother."

And that was the problem.

With a sigh, he glanced at the clock. It was almost two in the morning. No way he could call her now, and since this conversation was far too important to hash out over text, he would have to wait until daylight.

He pulled up his voicemail screen and tapped to listen to the first one from Bailey. While she rambled, pretty much repeating everything she'd said in her texts, Rafe moved to the window and glanced out over the park.

When her first message ended, he pressed play on the second.

Hey, Rafe. I'd like to stay at the Double R tonight. Can you come get me?

Rafe glanced at the phone to see when the call came in. Almost an hour and a half ago.

"Shit."

He heard a man's voice coming from the phone's speaker, so he put it to his ear.

You cheatin' bitch. You fucking whore. I should've known.

Then Bailey's voice sounded again: *Thanks, Rafe. I'll see you in a few minutes.*

Rafe was about to disconnect the call but realized the voicemail was still going. Bailey hadn't disconnected but her voice now came from a distance, as though she'd meant to.

For one, I've never cheated on you. And two, I'm not sleeping with anyone. I'm gonna stay at the B and B, where I'll be movin' in two weeks anyway.

Moving? If only I could get so damn lucky.

Rafe hated that little fucker even more than he had.

It's true—

Rafe lowered the phone and stepped closer to the window, convinced he was seeing things. No way was Bailey dragging a suitcase down the sidewalk at two in the damn morning.

"What the fuck?"

Rather than wait for him, she'd walked.

Goddammit.

Rafe

Setting his phone down so it could continue to charge, Rafe grabbed the water bottle and headed out the door. He followed the second-floor landing to the side of the building, then took the stairs down. He stepped out onto the main porch that ran in front of all the businesses at the base of the U and peered to his left.

"Bailey?"

As soon as he said her name, she stopped walking, spinning around with her hand over her chest.

"You scared me to death," she announced. "Shouldn't you be asleep?"

Rafe strolled toward her, closing the distance as he studied her from head to toe. She was wearing blue jean shorts and a black T-shirt which clung to her lovely curves. Unfortunately, it clung to her because she was drenched in sweat.

He frowned. "What're you doin'?"

"I'm walkin'. What does it look like I'm doin'?"

Remembering his manners, he held out the bottle, offering it to her.

She shook her head. "Thanks. I'm good."

"Tell me you didn't walk from your house."

"Why do you care?" She spun away from him and began dragging her suitcase toward the bakery.

"Where are you goin'?"

"To work."

"At two in the mornin'."

"It's a bakery, Rafe. We start early."

But not this early, he knew.

"Dammit, Bailey. Talk to me."

This time when she spun around, her suitcase fell over, and the bag she had on top tumbled to the ground. She ignored it, planting her hands on her hips and glaring at him.

"I tried talkin' to you. All damn day. You obviously don't want to talk to me."

"That's not true," he told her, refusing to step any closer. "My fuckin' phone died earlier today. I didn't have a charger." He tilted his chin in the direction of his apartment. "It's up there right now. Plugged up. I just saw your messages a few minutes ago."

Her chin tipped up slightly. "For real?"

Rafe grinned. She always said that when she believed him but wasn't sure she should.

"For real," he assured her.

"So, you're not mad at me?"

"Of course not."

Bailey took a deep breath and exhaled slowly.

"But I will be if you don't tell me why you're luggin' your suitcase through downtown."

"I moved out of Seth's house," she explained. "I'm gonna stay at the bakery tonight, then talk to Rex in the mornin'."

Rafe knew the gentlemanly thing to do would be to invite her to stay at his apartment for the night. He wanted to. But if he did that, every ounce of gentleman would slip away with the gesture, and he damn sure didn't want to risk ruining their friendship because he couldn't control his desire for her.

The other option would be to let her stay at his apartment, and he could sleep in his truck. Then again, she would likely take that as a snub, thinking he didn't want to be that close to her.

A no-win situation here.

"Anyway," Bailey said with a sigh before grabbing for the handle of her suitcase to set it upright. "I'm gonna go before Sheriff Endsley gets a call about looters."

Rafe nodded.

He knew he should help her, but he couldn't do that either. Right now, the only thing he wanted was to crush her to him and hold on until the sun crept up over the horizon. It was the only thing he ever wanted to do, but if he did, Bailey would expect more from him. Unfortunately, Rafe couldn't pull *more* out of a hat, which meant he didn't have it to give.

"Okay, then," she said. "I guess I'll see you tomorrow." Her eyebrows rose. "Or today. Whatever."

"Goodnight."

She flashed a half-hearted smile. "Goodnight."

Rafe waited until she was safely inside the bakery before he returned to his apartment, cursing himself the entire way.

Chapter Six

FOUR A.M. CAME FASTER THAN BAILEY ANTICIPATED, but she managed to take a quick nap and stow her suitcase under the cloth-covered table in the prep area in the back room so her mother wouldn't see it. To keep up the ruse of coming in early to get started, she started prepping the equipment so it would be ready when her mother arrived to start baking.

She was setting out the last baking sheet when she heard the bell over the front door. A moment later, her mother appeared in the kitchen.

"What in the world are you doing here so early?"

Bailey smiled. "Couldn't sleep. Thought I'd help out."

As usual, her mother regarded her carefully, likely trying to detect the lie in her statement.

It wasn't that Bailey was prone to lying to her mother. Not about the important things, but she was good at keeping her feelings under wraps. For that reason, Ramona Weber was skeptical.

With a twitch of her nose, her mother said, "I'm glad to have you. I've got to work on that cupcake order for the Walkers."

"Which Walkers?" There were quite a few, so it was always good to clarify.

"The ones with the most grandbabies. They're having a big party for the July birthdays this weekend."

Bailey grinned. Curtis and Lorrie had recently started a new birthday celebration trend due to the fact their family had gotten so big. Although they still had a special meal on the special day for the kids, they'd started coordinating birthdays by month, and July was a big one for them.

"How many did they order?"

"Three dozen."

"That's not too bad."

"And a quarter sheet cake for Lorrie."

"Is that *all*?" Bailey laughed. "Well, I can do whatever you need me to do."

"You can start by prepping the coffee pots."

"Already done."

Ramona looked impressed. "All right. Then why don't you stock the front cooler while I start mixing batter and making dough? When you're done, you can start today's muffins. Then Shelly should be in to help."

With that, Bailey got to work, thankful her mother didn't look too hard. Had she, she would've surely noticed that Bailey was on the verge of a nervous breakdown.

By the time the morning rush cleared and only a couple of people were hanging around to enjoy the free Wi-Fi, Bailey was exhausted. To the point her arms and legs felt like noodles.

The only time she took a break was to send Rex a text and ask if they could talk today. His reply was almost instant, with an agreement to meet up around noon. Bailey didn't think she could wait that long since she hoped to be horizontal with her eyes closed at that point. If she wasn't, there was a good chance she would be too loopy to hold a conversation. Since she had to work tonight, looking like a zombie wasn't ideal, either.

The bell over the door jingled, alerting that someone was coming in or going out. Bailey stepped out of the kitchen to see Rafe walking through the door.

He looked good, but that wasn't anything new. The man always looked good. Today he was wearing a black short-sleeve Henley and his Wranglers and boots. His ball cap was on his head, shielding his eyes but not the scruff growing darker on his jawline.

Rafe

"What can I get you?" she offered, stepping behind the pastry case.

As he moved closer, he tilted his head so she could see his eyes. "Coffee."

She didn't ask if he needed room for cream or if he wanted sugar to go with it. She knew he drank his coffee black, so Bailey flashed a smile and turned to the coffee machine, grabbing the fresh pot and pouring a large foam cup full before placing a lid on it.

He was waiting at the register counter when she finished.

"Anything else?"

"You doin' okay?"

His question surprised her, but she managed a nod. She was exhausted, but she wasn't really in a chatty mood. For whatever reason, things felt off between her and Rafe. She wasn't sure if it was the argument they'd had yesterday morning or the fact that she'd been disappointed when he didn't invite her to stay at his apartment last night when she didn't have a place to go.

Not that she had any right to insinuate herself into his personal space, but his lack of offer had felt intentional. As though he didn't want her to be that close.

She entered the cost of the coffee into the register and waited for him to swipe his credit card. Refusing to look at his face, she stared at his hands as his words from yesterday reverberated in her head.

I'm not gonna be your fallback guy, Bailey. It's not my fault your relationship didn't work.

As had been the case when he said them, Bailey felt the echo of pain in her chest. Somewhere in the vicinity of her heart.

"Thanks for stoppin' in," she told him, forcing her customer service smile. "Have a great day."

Rafe's gaze swung over her face, lingering long enough to make her want to fidget, but she managed to refrain. Instead, she directed her attention to organizing the napkin holder on the counter before turning toward the back. Part of her expected him to call out her name, but the only sound she heard was the jingle of the bells over the door as he left.

Her chin wobbled, but she fought back the tears. Good thing, too, since her mother was waiting for her when she made it to the kitchen.

Ramona's eyebrows were lifted, and she was pointing at Bailey's suitcase, which was no longer hidden beneath the table but at her mother's feet.

"Care to explain?"

Not really, no. But she did anyway. "I moved out of Seth's house."

"What? Why?"

Bailey shook her head. "We've been havin' problems for a while. It was time."

"When was this?"

"Last night." She wrung her hands together. "Or this mornin'. I walked here from his house."

"Bailey Anne Weber…" Her mother clenched her teeth together to hold back the tirade that she was eager to let loose.

"I'm fine, Mom. I promise."

Her mother put her hands on her hips and took a deep breath. "Although I can't say I'm disappointed you dumped him, I hope you don't think you can camp out here, honey."

She shook her head quickly. "No. Definitely not." She managed a smile. "I got the manager job at the B and B. It comes with room and board. I'll be living there."

"Oh, honey!" Her mother moved toward her. "That's fantastic news. I know how much you wanted that job."

Bailey accepted her mother's hug and forced her thoughts on her new job and the promising future ahead. If she didn't, there was a good chance she would break down and cry on her mother's shoulder.

"Speaking of the B and B…" Bailey pulled back. "I need to head over there and talk to Rex." She pointed at her suitcase. "Would you mind if I keep that here for now? I promise I won't sleep here again."

Her mother's light brown eyes swept over her face, again scrutinizing, looking for untruths.

"I won't be gone long, I promise."

Ramona finally nodded.

Bailey didn't waste any time before pulling off her apron and grabbing her purse. She was out the door and making haste across the park, wanting to talk to Rex before she lost her nerve. She was so engrossed in working through what she wanted to say she didn't notice the truck in the lot. Nor did she realize Rex was sitting on the front porch, his brother leaning against the railing while they chatted.

Unfortunately, Rex saw her before she could turn and head in the opposite direction.

"Hey, girl. What's up?" Rex called out.

Rafe glanced back over his shoulder, his expression shifting as his familiar mask fell into place, concealing whatever he'd been feeling before she arrived.

"I know you said we'd talk at noon…"

"Now's good, too." Rex got to his feet. "Rafe was just tellin' me you spent the night at the bakery last night."

Bailey's gaze darted to Rafe. He wasn't looking at her, but the incredulous look on his face was directed at his brother. Obviously, Rafe had told Rex that in confidence.

Rex smirked. "Like I told you yesterday, you're welcome to stay here until we're completely moved out."

"I'd like to take you up on that. Thank you."

"No problem. And if you don't mind helpin' with a few things in the evening, perhaps I can move the date up by a couple of days."

Bailey's chest squeezed with both relief and gratitude. "Gladly. I can work up until my shift at the bar."

The screen door opened, and Jack appeared, glancing at Bailey, then Rex, then Rafe.

"Looks like y'all are having a party out here." Jack smiled. "Hey, Rafe. Bailey."

"Hi, Jack," she replied when Rafe merely grunted.

Rex tipped his chin at his husband. "Why don't you show Bailey her temporary accommodations, and I'll get her employment paperwork. We can knock it all out in just a few minutes."

Leaving Rafe and Rex to talk, Bailey followed Jack inside. If he noticed the tension between her and Rafe, he was kind enough not to mention it.

"HOLY SHIT. YOU FEEL THAT?" REX SAID when Bailey disappeared inside with Jack.

"Feel what?"

"The cold chill. If I didn't know better, I'd think winter came early."

Rafe should've known his brother would give him shit.

"Fuck off."

Rex laughed. "Lover's quarrel?"

"It's not like that, and you know it."

"So you say."

As usual, Rex was pushing his buttons, angling for a story, but Rafe had no intention of giving him one. He'd told Rex more times than he could count that he and Bailey were merely friends. Nothing more. Not that Rex believed him. And no amount of denying the accusations would convince him, either. So the best thing to do was for Rafe to brush it off and move on.

"I should head out. I've got some errands to run. Then I need to get some sleep before my shift tonight."

"You work too much, little brother."

Rafe snorted, gesturing toward the house. "You're one to talk."

"Touché." Rex turned toward the door. "Maybe we can grab dinner one day next week. Catch up."

Rafe started down the steps. "I'd like that."

"Oh, hey!" Rex called, letting the screen door slap shut.

Stopping, Rafe turned to look up at his brother.

"You know a guy named … Shit. What was his name?" Rex moved closer. "Colt. No wait. That's not it."

Rafe stared at Rex, waiting patiently.

Rex snapped his fingers. "Holt. Holt Callahan, I think."

Rafe did his best to hide his reaction, but the mere mention of his name had his blood pumping faster and hotter. "Yeah. I know him. Why?"

"He's booked to stay here in a coupla weeks. He mentioned your name to Jack when he made the reservation. Apparently, he's lookin' for you."

"That right?" Rafe shrugged as though it was of no importance to him. It wasn't. Like his feelings for Bailey, Rafe had gotten good at pretending certain things didn't exist. Holt Callahan was one of those things.

Rex scratched his chin. "Should I be worried?"

"Naw. Just a guy I used to know."

"Friend or foe?"

Rafe snorted a laugh. "Who asks shit like that?"

"An older, protective brother," he said with a grin. "Which is it?"

"Friend."

At least, Rafe hoped so. He hadn't talked to Holt in a long damn time. And the last time Rafe saw him, Holt was passed out cold, and Rafe had taken the opportunity to run for the hills. In all fairness, Holt had been the closest thing he'd had to a friend and one of the only people in the world Rafe had ever opened up to about what happened with his old man. Not all the gory details, but some.

"Well, now you know he's comin'."

Rafe nodded. "Yeah. Thanks."

The question was, why now? After all this time?

As Rafe was parking his truck along the curb behind his apartment, his cell phone rang. He glanced at the screen and frowned. It was the same number that had called him last night. He hit decline. Whoever it was hadn't left a message last time, which meant it clearly wasn't all that important.

Was it Holt? Was he calling to let Rafe know he was coming here?

He got out of his truck and took the stairs up to his apartment, ignoring the itch on the back of his neck that told him he needed to react to this. The same itch had caused him to get in his truck and head home after the night he'd spent with Holt Callahan.

Rafe managed to make it into his apartment before the memory assaulted him. He wasn't sure why, but it always came with vivid clarity, bringing emotions that were better left in the past.

"I think I'm gonna head up to the house. Grab something to eat. Want to join me?"

Rafe peered at the friends sitting around the small camper they'd brought to crash in on the weekend. It had become a ritual of theirs. Every weekend for the past two months, ever since summer kicked off, they'd driven down here to shrug off the dregs of the real world for a little while. It had started with only three of them, but more people had latched on as the weeks passed. Now there were seven, and as was usually the case, they'd paired up, with Rafe being the odd man out.

Which was how he'd found himself forming a friendship with the writer who was staying in the house just over the dunes. He'd met the guy the first weekend they'd come down, and Rafe was pretty sure he used Rafe's presence as a distraction from what he should've been doing.

Not that Rafe minded. Holt Callahan was a good guy. More than once, he'd splurged for pizza for everyone, and he didn't have a problem restocking the beer when the supply got low. For those reasons alone, he'd become a favorite of the group.

Problem was Rafe couldn't help but feel like there was something between them. Something that Rafe wasn't sure he could acknowledge.

"You don't have to," Holt added. "I can make some sandwiches. Bring them down."

Rafe glanced up at the three-story house on the other side of the dune. If he went up there with Holt, there was a good chance Rafe would have no choice but to acknowledge the foreign sizzle that he'd sensed on more than one occasion when Holt was around. Maybe that was what he needed. That final shove to help him figure out why he hadn't stopped thinking about the man since they met two months ago.

"Yeah, I'll go up. Food sounds perfect," he told Holt, pushing to his feet and brushing the sand off his legs.

"Ignore the mess," Holt told him a few minutes later when he slid the glass door open. "I've spent the entire week rebelling against my protagonist."

"As in a fictional person in your book?"

Holt laughed. "You make it sound like he doesn't exist."

"Does he?"

"In my head, yeah."

77

Rafe

Rafe peered around, and sure enough, it looked like Holt had gone on strike from anything chore related. There were clothes tossed everywhere, a few even hanging out of the laundry basket sitting on the dining table. You couldn't see the countertops in the kitchen for all the dishes—both clean and dirty—that were lying around.

"I tend to rummage through shit when I'm trying to figure something out."

"Sounds … messy."

"Don't worry. I haven't yet destroyed the third floor. We'll make some sandwiches and eat 'em on the balcony up there. Turkey and cheese good for you?"

"Yeah." Rafe wasn't picky.

While Holt went to work making sandwiches, Rafe looked around, curious about all things Holt. He had to admit he never would've pegged him for a slob. He was always so put together when they hung out at the beach. Every Friday night for the past seven weeks, Holt had come down shortly after they got the camper set up. Rafe knew the moment he arrived because he could smell him. It was his cologne. It was intoxicating, addictive almost. Rafe had found himself smelling it a few times when Holt wasn't around.

"Just out of curiosity…" Holt prompted as he passed Rafe a plate with a sandwich and chips. "I've noticed your crew keeps growing."

"Boyfriends and girlfriends," Rafe explained, following Holt up the narrow, curved staircase to the third floor.

"And why haven't you brought one?"

Holt led the way through a bedroom to another sliding glass door. He opened it and walked out.

Rafe followed. "I don't date."

Holt laughed, pointing toward the beach. "I'm not sure that necessarily qualifies as dating."

Rafe followed his pointing finger to see Mario leaning against the camper while Angie was kneeling in the sand in front of him. It was clear what she was doing even from this distance.

"I think they're too eager to worry about an audience," Holt said, shoving one of the plastic Adirondack chairs toward Rafe.

Clearly.

Wanting to avoid talking about his friends' sex lives, Rafe decided to broach a safe topic. "What seems to be the problem with your character?"

Holt took a bite of his sandwich and looked at Rafe, evidently surprised by the question.

He chewed and swallowed. "He's confused."

"About?"

"Who he is."

Rafe raised his eyebrows. "I don't even know what that means."

Holt sighed, setting his sandwich on the plate and balancing it on his knee. "When I'm writing, I find it necessary to understand my character's motivation. Whether it's the hero or the villain, I need to know what drives him to understand why he would do certain things. Do you read?"

Not expecting to have to answer, Rafe had his mouth full, but he managed a nod.

"Fiction?"

Another nod.

"Romance?"

He shook his head as he swallowed. "More of a crime thriller kinda guy."

"Ah. Perfect. That's what I write. Anyway. The series I've been writing has been optioned for television."

Since that sounded like a good thing, Rafe said, "Congrats."

"Thanks. It'll be interesting, I think. Problem is my protagonist isn't exactly mainstream material. He doesn't believe in monogamy, and he's bisexual. My editor wants me to dial it back some. She says it'll reach a larger audience that way."

"And that's the goal, I assume?" Rafe set his empty plate on the ground.

"For some, probably. I've never wanted to work within the confines of a box."

"Then don't."

Holt grinned. "I wish it were that easy."

"Why isn't it?"

When Holt didn't respond, Rafe glanced over to see he was studying him closely.

"What?"

"Have you ever been with a man?"

Rafe's entire body went still. "No."

"Have you ever wanted to?"

That question wasn't nearly as easy to answer. It would've been back before Rafe met Holt. Before then, Rafe had been certain of his sexual orientation. He'd never been stirred by a man before.

"Rafe?"

Jerking his attention back to the beach, Rafe stood up. "I think I should get back."

Holt was on his feet instantly, getting between Rafe and the door. "Don't go."

Rafe met his gaze.

"I didn't mean to make you uncomfortable."

"You didn't," Rafe lied.

Holt took a step forward. Rafe stood his ground, refusing to let Holt know he'd lied.

"Tell me you don't feel it," Holt whispered.

The gap between them had been eliminated. They were toe to toe, close enough Rafe couldn't look him in the eye anymore.

"From the day I met you, I've felt something," Holt continued, his voice a soothing rasp between them. "I've never felt this before. Not for anyone."

"Let me guess," Rafe retorted. "Your character's not bisexual. You are."

Holt leaned in until his lips nearly touched Rafe's. "I've never wanted anyone this fucking much."

His body was betraying him. Rafe didn't want to react to his nearness or the promise in those words, but he couldn't help it. There was something there, something more potent than anything Rafe had ever felt before. It was the reason he kept coming back to the beach. The reason he continuously looked for Holt when he wasn't around.

"Tell me to stop, and I won't ever bring it up again," Holt said, his breath fanning Rafe's lips.

He knew he should. It wasn't like Rafe was interested in anything more than sex, and since he'd never found a man attractive enough to make him swing that way, he figured this was an anomaly. If he allowed this to happen, it would forever change him. If he enjoyed it, he would crave more. Why would he do that to himself when this was temporary? Holt was temporary.

But wasn't that a reason to do it? Rafe wouldn't be required to commit to anything more. This could be an end-of-summer fling; afterward, they could go on with their lives like nothing happened.

"One night," Holt said, his lips now only a breath away.

He didn't mean to, but Rafe tilted his head, allowing their lips to touch.

"One night," Rafe agreed, taking the lead by grabbing Holt's head and crushing their mouths together.

"Fuck," Rafe hissed, dragging himself out of the memory.

He had his cock in his fist, and he was jerking himself roughly, his back still pressed to the front door.

Every fucking time he thought about Holt, about that night, he couldn't help himself. But it had grown exponentially worse when he'd first fantasized about what that night would've been like if Bailey had been there. His favorite fantasy was the one where Rafe was buried balls deep inside Bailey while Holt fucked him from behind. The three of them locked in the throes together, grunting, groaning ... *oh, fuck ... coming!*

"Son of a bitch!" Rafe's body tightened as his cock jerked in his fist.

He came with a muted cry, his eyes closed as he imagined coming deep inside Bailey while Holt came inside him. He gasped for breath as the revulsion hit him in waves.

"You're an idiot," he growled at himself as he forced his legs to carry him to the bathroom.

He met his gaze in the mirror and glared at that man.

"You've got nothing to offer one person, let alone two, you dumbass." He leaned in. "It's best you remember that."

Chapter Seven

Three weeks later…
Friday, August 5, 2022

"GOOD AFTERNOON. WELCOME TO THE DOUBLE R Retreat," Bailey greeted as she looked up from the reservation book.

Thankfully, she'd spent a reasonable amount of time around customers in her lifetime because she'd learned how to school her expression. The moment her brain registered the sexy man standing in front of her, she relied on that honed skill to keep her jaw from falling open and her eyes from bugging out of her head.

A couple of inches over six feet with sandy brown hair and navy-blue eyes, he was the sort of man you might expect to grace the cover of a magazine. Not necessarily the ones with the suit-clad guy strutting because this guy was dressed casually in a navy-blue T-shirt that was cut to fit his muscular torso perfectly and a pair of lightly distressed jeans that somehow looked both comfortable and stylish. The work boots on his feet spoke to a life of leisure rather than traipsing through a dusty construction site, but Bailey wouldn't hold it against him.

In a word, he was gorgeous. And based on that wicked grin, he knew it, too.

His gaze seemed to linger on her even as he closed the front door behind him. "Afternoon, ma'am."

Bailey cleared her throat, hoping her voice still worked. "Are you checking in?"

"I am. Holt Callahan."

Even his name was sexy.

"Welcome, Mr. Callahan."

"Please call me Holt."

It was safe to say she was going to enjoy this job.

Bailey had already memorized the guests arriving today, so she said, "So glad you're here. I've got you for three days, two nights."

As soon as the words were out of her mouth, she realized how they sounded.

"I mean … you … uh … you're here. At the Double R." She swallowed past the ball of mortification clogging her throat. "You're set to stay here for three days and two nights."

He chuckled and grinned, causing a dimple to form on his left cheek. "And here I was thinkin' this vacation was lookin' brighter already."

Oh, that drawl. It was even more prominent than most. It wasn't a Texas twang. No, instead of talking fast and dropping the g's at the end of words, his vowels were drawn out, and there was a softer lilt to his tone. It was nice.

Bailey could feel the blush infusing her cheeks. "Don't mind me. I'm still getting my bearings."

"I've been told I have that effect on people."

She choked on a laugh. "No. I mean, that's not the reason. Well, it's not *not* the reason. I'm not tryin' to insult you. I'm just sayin'…" *What the hell* was *she saying?* "I've only been workin' here for a little while. Only full-time this week, so I'm just feelin' my way through."

Holt winked. "You're welcome to feel your way with me anytime."

Oh, heavens.

"And you're right," he said, stepping closer. "I'm here for three days and two nights, but when I called, I spoke to someone about the option to extend my stay for a few weeks."

Bailey peered down at the reservation book. She didn't remember seeing any notes about it.

"If it's a problem…"

"Of course not." She peered up at him. "We're not completely full through the summer, so I'm sure I can make it work."

"I appreciate it."

She got lost in his tumultuous blue eyes for a moment too long before remembering what she was doing. Bailey turned to the lockbox and used her fingerprint to unlock it, then retrieved a single key for room five. She passed it to Holt as she jotted down the time he arrived.

She stepped out from behind the reservation desk and motioned toward the stairs. "Your room's at the top of the stairs to the right. Number five." She gestured to the main floor. "Feel free to use any of these rooms if you'd like to interact with other guests. We serve wine in the livin' room at seven every evenin'."

She led him past the stairs to the open living area so he could check it out.

"There's an air-conditioned sunroom at the back if you'd like a pool view. The laundry area is also back there, so it might sometimes be a little noisy." She turned back to the room opposite the reservation desk. "This was originally a parlor, but Rex converted it into a business center in case you need it. And this over here is the dinin' room. Breakfast is served between six and eight every mornin'." She pivoted to point that room out. "It's buffet style, but if there's anything specific you'd like to request, I can see what I can do."

"I'm not picky about breakfast. Unless my choice is to share it with a pretty lady."

Bailey fought the urge to giggle at his charm. His lines were cheesy, but his delivery was sinful. She doubted he had any problems getting women to agree to join him for breakfast.

"The kitchen is open day and night if you're hungry. We keep everything for sandwiches on hand, plus several single-serve snacks. But if you're lookin' for dinner, might I suggest the diner." She kept walking until they reached the windows overlooking the pool. "We close the pool and hot tub at ten each night, but they're available throughout the day. And every Friday night in August, there's a band in Walker Park." She pointed toward the front door. "It's right across the street."

He shifted his bag on his shoulder. "Sounds like a good time all around."

"It is, yes." Feeling her cheeks warm again, she met his stare and aimed for professionalism. "Anyway. My name's Bailey if you need anything. Oh, and if you need somethin' and can't find me, feel free to text the number on the back of your keychain. Someone will be here to assist."

"Good to know." He winked again, then turned toward the back stairs.

"As a head's up, there's a door at the top of these stairs. It opens into the game room, so don't be alarmed when you get up there. It kinda surprised me the first time I went up there. I worried I was gonna walk into someone's room."

Holt laughed. "I guess that could've been awkward. Maybe I should use the main stairs the first time."

Bailey walked him to the front of the house, then shifted her attention to the reservation desk in an effort not to stare at his ass as he walked up the stairs. For the record, she failed.

She was pretty sure Holt noticed because his muffled laughter followed him to the second floor.

Shaking her head, Bailey found herself smiling as she headed for the kitchen to put together some afternoon snacks. She'd ordered two dozen chocolate chip cookies from the bakery that her mother had hand-delivered a short time ago. Bailey knew it was merely a way for her mom to check on her and to get a glimpse of her at work. Bailey'd been so busy these past few weeks that she hadn't been able to spend much time with her mom. After giving Mack her two-week notice, she worked her shifts at Moonshiners while Mack interviewed candidates to fill her position. Thankfully, he found a suitable replacement just two days before her last day, so she had a little time to help the woman adjust.

Not that Bailey had done much. From the moment Ivy Tilman stepped onto the polished wood floor, she'd dominated the room. As far as waitressing went, she was a natural. Quite possibly perfect. Unlike Bailey, who'd dropped more dishes than she delivered her first night on the floor.

But waitressing didn't seem to be Ivy's only specialty. She had an absurd ability to juggle multiple tasks at once. Not only could she balance six beers and two glasses of wine on a tray, she was also quite skilled at flirting with the bartender when Rafe was the one behind the bar.

Rafe

To say Bailey had hated her instantly would've been an understatement.

But Ivy wasn't her problem anymore. Bailey had put the busty blonde out of her mind as soon as her last shift ended. Or at least she'd tried to. Unfortunately, her last image of the woman was when she was leaning over the bar, grinning at Rafe while he smiled back at her. Bailey had wanted to drive a corkscrew through her eye.

That had been a week ago. Bailey hadn't seen Ivy or Rafe since then and didn't want to. Even the thought of seeing them together or hearing someone mention he was now dating her made her stomach churn. It would happen. The rumors. Even if they weren't together, the rumor would be that they were. And then what? Maybe it *would* come true?

Not that she cared.

She couldn't.

She wouldn't.

Nope.

Rafe Sharpe was free to do whatever and whoever he wanted. His lack of communication these past few weeks made it painfully clear that their friendship was pretty much a thing of the past. When she'd been working at the bar, he'd been cordial. But she hadn't heard a single thing from him since her employment ended. Now that she wasn't seeing him at Moonshiners, her imagination was running away with wild and crazy ideas. And since that wasn't the best use of her time, she was putting every ounce of brainpower into her new job.

Several hours later, after the cookies were snagged by guests wandering through and after all the expected arrivals had been checked in, Bailey was finishing the last of the dinner dishes when Rex strolled in through the back door. He sniffed the air and groaned.

"No one told me you were makin' meatloaf."

"We had some late arrivals, so I thought I would make it easy on them."

"You're gonna spoil these people."

That was her plan. If it meant they would tell their friends, Bailey was more than happy to serve home-cooked meals on Fridays.

She grinned over her shoulder. "I saved you and Jack some. It's in the Tupperware in the fridge."

"Have I mentioned I love you?"

Grinning, she turned off the sink and grabbed a towel to dry her hands.

"All the guests have arrived. The Coopermans are out visiting the family they have in the area. Mr. Ingram and his lady friend went into Austin for the evenin'. Ms. Bellamy turned in early after askin' for information on Austin's nightlife. I think she'll venture out tomorrow night," she informed him. "Rooms four and six are ready for tomorrow's arrivals."

"And Holt?" Rex prompted.

"Um." Bailey swallowed. "I ... uh..." Once again, her cheeks flamed from embarrassment. "He asked me to join him for music in the park. I told him I was workin'."

Rex's gaze bounced over her face. Bailey wasn't sure what he was looking for, but his response surprised her.

"You should go."

"What?"

Okay, maybe that came out slightly more abrupt than she'd meant for it to.

"Go. It's Friday night; as you said, all the guests are checked in. Sounds to me like you can spare an hour or two to enjoy yourself."

"I need to finish gettin' my things unpacked in my apartment."

Rex rolled his eyes. "If I know you, that was done a couple of hours after me and Jack delivered the last of your bags from Seth's."

Fine. He had her there. Rex had been kind enough to go to Seth's and get her things so she didn't risk another encounter with him. To her surprise, Rex said Seth had been completely cordial, helping Rex and Jack to pack it all up. She had no idea what Seth's angle was, but she'd come to learn the man didn't usually do nice things for the hell of it. She figured, if nothing else, he did it to keep her on edge because she would be until she figured out what he was up to.

"It'll be good for you," Rex said. "Relax and enjoy yourself."
Bailey considered it for a moment. "Fine."

As soon as she committed to going, excitement fizzled in her veins. She wouldn't mind spending a little time outdoors with some good music and the company of a handsome man.

What could possibly go wrong?

"What in the world are you up to, husband o' mine?"

Rex peered over his shoulder when Jack came through the back door. "What ever do you mean?"

"I never thought you to be the meddling kind."

Grinning, he turned toward Jack. "Meddlin'?"

Jack shrugged. "Yes, meddling. Sticking your nose where it doesn't belong."

"How exactly did I do that?"

"You just sent that sweet girl out with ... with..." Jack sighed dramatically. "Well, I don't *know* what Holt Callahan is, but surely he's got an agenda."

"Because he's an author?" Rex nodded. "They *are* a mischievous lot."

"We are not," Jack said defensively.

Rex knew his husband was the suspicious sort, as was Rex most of the time. However, he decided to play along. "Then why would you possibly think he has an agenda?"

"For starters, he asked about your brother when he called to make the reservation."

Yes, Rex was rather curious how they knew each other. A guy Rafe used to know shows up almost three years exactly from when Rafe returned. And though Rex hadn't seen Rafe in years before that, he'd suspected something was different about him. Now he had to wonder whether Holt Callahan played a part in that, and if so, how?

But he wasn't ready to relay that to his husband quite yet. Rex figured it needed to play out a little more before he connected the dots completely.

"So? They know each other. People know people, Jack. That doesn't make them bad."

"I never said he was *bad*," Jack defended.

"I guess he couldn't be, huh?" Rex picked up the plastic food containers and turned to pass them to his husband. "He's an author, after all."

"Exactly." Jack's eyes widened. "Wait. How did you know he was an author?"

"Because you told me."

Jack shook his head. "No, I didn't. You brought it up first."

"Fine." Rex grinned and stepped closer. "I know because *my* author likes to doodle on notepads when he's ponderin' somethin'."

"Fuck." Jack rolled his eyes. "You weren't supposed to see that."

"What? That you've got a crush on a hot thriller writer, and you were scribblin' his name all over your notebook?" Rex teased.

"I do not," Jack insisted, his expression turning deadly serious. "I swear it, babe. No. I—"

Rex silenced him with a quick kiss. "Trust me. I'm not worried. If I were, you'd be spread eagle on the bed right now, tryin' to figure out how to get yourself free."

Jack's eyebrows jumped. "Would I be naked?"

"Most definitely."

"I guess he is kinda—"

"Don't you dare finish that sentence."

Jack laughed as he stepped back. "Fine. I won't. But are you sure sending Bailey on a date with him is a good idea?"

"I'm not sendin' anyone anywhere. He asked her, and I could tell she wanted to go. Where's the harm in encouragin' her to enjoy herself?"

"But she just got out of a relationship."

"Seth was merely a placeholder," Rex told him as he opened the back screen door and urged Jack outside. Rex was starving, but he had no desire to eat dinner at the B and B. He happened to enjoy having some privacy, and now that they'd moved into their new house, more rooms were waiting to be christened.

But first, nourishment.

"Who's gonna watch the house while Bailey's out?"

"We've got cameras. Plus, if someone needs somethin', they'll text as they were instructed to do."

"That was a good idea Bailey had."

Rex nodded as he urged Jack toward their house.

Jack huffed but continued walking. "I don't know why, but I thought for sure Rafe was going to make his move the moment she was single again. That man's been pining for her for so long."

That was the damn truth. And perhaps that was part of why Rex had *encouraged* Bailey, as Jack had so kindly accused. Deep down, he suspected Rafe and Bailey would end up together. If history were anything to go by, it would take Rafe some time or possibly the right situation to realize what a dumbass he was being. But Rex held out hope that his brother would come around eventually.

And maybe seeing her out with a handsome, charming man would light a fire under his ass.

As far as Rex was concerned, it was the least he could do to help his brother along.

"I CAN'T BELIEVE YOU AGREED TO COME with me."

Technically, Rafe hadn't agreed to anything.

Mack was the one who'd done the encouraging, practically shoving Rafe out the door, urging him to show the new girl what their quaint little town had to offer.

Mack's words, actually.

"This is incredible," Ivy exclaimed, a giddy excitement in her tone. "I've never been to a small-town festival. I'm so glad you offered."

Again, he didn't. But it was pointless to tell her he really hadn't had a choice. Mack was his boss, not to mention he was rather devious when someone defied him. The last thing Rafe wanted was to find out Mack had replaced the vodka with water again. That had happened shortly after Rafe informed Mack that he wasn't going to be the one to clean vomit off the wall in the women's restroom. They'd argued, but Rafe had won the round. Or so he thought. He learned the error of his ways a couple of nights later. *After* he poured six shots for a group of college kids passing through town. Shots of water, it turned out. He'd gotten an earful from the ornery little shits. It had cost him a round on the house. Mack thought it was hilarious.

So tonight, when Mack mentioned it, Rafe had told the old man to go, and he would stay behind at the bar. Unfortunately, his boss was having none of it, so here he was with Ivy clutching his arm as though he'd asked her to marry him, and they were on their way to a church, not the center of town, to watch some up-and-coming band the chamber of commerce managed to get on the docket tonight.

"Oh. Wow. Is that a shaved ice truck?" Ivy squeezed his arm.

Although the first adjective Rafe would use to describe Ivy was *annoying*, he liked her. At twenty-two, she was still trying to figure out what she wanted to do with her life and determined to enjoy every second in the meantime. For the past week, he'd gotten the low down on all things Ivy Tilman straight from the horse's mouth. It seemed there was nothing she wouldn't talk about, so he'd learned that her family had money—lots and lots, apparently—which meant they had high expectations for her. Her dad wanted her to be a lawyer like him. Her mother wanted her to be a doctor. Preferably a surgeon. And Ivy ... well, she wasn't even sure she wanted to go to college. Her primary goal appeared to be to see the world, preferably with a woman on her arm.

Yes, Ivy was a proud lesbian, although she seemed to enjoy flirting with Rafe because she said it was funny to watch the other waitresses give her the stink eye.

Did he mention she was kind of bratty?

Of course, he wasn't sure how Ivy would see anything now that she'd hunkered down in this small, backwoods town, but he didn't think it was his place to mention it. Although he liked her as a person, Rafe had no intention of being the ear she could bend when she had a hard day and certainly not the shoulder she could cry on. But Rafe didn't want to hurt her feelings, so he was giving her some time, hoping she would make friends with other people before he started enforcing the distance he wanted to keep from her.

"Let's get some," Ivy suggested. "My treat."

Rafe allowed her to lead him by the arm toward the food truck convoy at the far end of the park. The sun was starting to set, and before long, it would be dark, but that seemed to encourage more and more people to show up. A group was setting up the stage for the band, and several more were putting up tables and lights so they could hawk their wares during the festivities. Rafe had realized that was part of the appeal of these Friday night venues at the park. Kind of like mini flea markets with entertainment during the summer months.

To be fair, he didn't mind it. He liked the scenery and the small-town camaraderie, even if he wouldn't admit that to anyone.

"What flavor would you like?" she asked as they approached the line. "I'm gonna go with half cherry, half blue raspberry. You seem like a grape kinda guy."

"No. I'm good. But thanks for the offer."

He could feel her eyes as she peered up at him, a wide grin on her face. "You're a cheap date, Rafe Sharpe."

Not wanting to give her the impression he considered this a date, Rafe kept his gaze straight ahead, watching as the two people at the front of the line received their overpriced chips of frozen water and paid. There were several people between him and the truck, but at the pace they were setting, it shouldn't be a long wait.

Rafe was still watching the couple at the front when the man turned around. A man Rafe hadn't seen in nearly three years.

"Fuck," he muttered.

Ivy gripped his arm tightly. "What's wrong?"

At that point, nothing was. At least not until Holt put his hand on his companion's back and steered her away from the line. Only then did Rafe realize who he was there with.

Rafe narrowed his gaze on Holt and waited to see if he would look his way. When he did, he saw the instant recognition on the man's face. Along with that wicked smirk he was famous for.

"Well, I'll be damned," Holt said in that rich bass of his. "I thought it'd be harder to track you down. After all, you won't take my calls."

"Because you didn't call me," Rafe countered before he could stop himself.

Holt's response was a slight lift of his left eyebrow.

Forcing his gaze away, Rafe looked at Bailey, waiting until she acknowledged him. When her eyes met his, he tried to mask his emotions but wasn't sure he did so in time. Instantly she glanced at the woman still clinging to Rafe's arm before her lips pursed tightly, and she looked at him again. He noticed the way her chin tipped up just slightly, as though she was refusing to accept that it bothered her that he was with another woman.

Not that he was with another woman. It merely looked that way.

Of course, he couldn't very well tell her that. Not without drawing attention to the fact that Rafe had feelings for Bailey. The last thing he wanted was for Ivy to get it in her little head that she should play matchmaker while she was hunting for her own love interest. He wouldn't put it past her.

"You know each other?" Bailey asked, glancing up at Holt.

"Friends from way back," Holt answered, then shifted his cup of colored ice to the other hand and thrust his right hand in Rafe's direction. "Good to see you."

Because it would've been rude to refuse, Rafe returned the handshake and steeled himself for Holt's touch. As had been the case the last time he'd seen the man, heat blasted through him as soon as their palms touched. His brain flashed memories of a long, hot night by the beach. Based on the gleam in Holt's blue eyes, he was reliving that very same night.

Rafe forgot all about Ivy standing at his side until she squeezed his arm and cleared her throat.

Right. Manners.

Pulling his hand from Holt's clutches, Rafe nodded his chin toward the man. "Ivy, meet Holt Callahan. Holt, this is Ivy. She's a waitress at Moonshiners."

Rafe

Holt shook her free hand, but Ivy refused to let go of Rafe's arm.

"Your name's familiar," Ivy noted. "Have we met before?"

"Not that I know of," he said easily, as though it wasn't every day that women were trying to figure out how they knew him.

It was, Rafe knew. Men and women alike heard his name and realized they'd heard it before. And if they weren't avid readers, addicted to Holt's bestselling novels, they'd likely seen him doing interviews for the television series that spawned from those books. Over the past three years, life had been good to Holt Callahan.

Not that Rafe was tracking his career.

Definitely not.

"I'm from Dallas," Ivy explained. "Maybe you and I crossed paths up there?"

As soon as she was distracted by Holt, Rafe attempted to pull away, but Ivy clung more tightly, a move that had Bailey frowning.

It's not what it looks like.

When Bailey's eyes met his, he saw the hurt in them even though she quickly hid it.

"So, what brings you kids out tonight?" Holt asked them.

Realizing Holt had steered the conversation back from himself, Rafe looked at his former friend.

Ivy answered for him. "Rafe was kind enough to show me around town. Not a bad venue for a first date, I must say."

Not a date.

"I think the band's settin' up," Bailey told Holt. "Maybe we could head that way?"

"What the lady wants, the lady gets."

Bailey glanced Rafe's way again. "It was good to see you. Have a good night."

"You, too," Ivy chimed, assuming Bailey was talking to her.

Holt put his arm around Bailey's shoulders, and Rafe was tempted to punch him in the fucking face. In fact, it took every ounce of willpower he possessed to refrain.

"We'll catch up later," Holt said.

Not if Rafe could help it, they wouldn't.

"Did you two have a thing?" Ivy asked when they were alone again.

Rafe's head snapped around, his eyes slamming into her face. "What?"

"You and Bailey. Did you break her heart or something?"

His racing heart slowed when he realized what she meant. Or rather, that she hadn't been referring to him and Holt. Because they didn't. Have a thing. What they'd done that night ... what Rafe had done ... it wasn't a thing. It was an experiment, that was all. Nothing more. And it would never, ever, *ever* happen again.

"We're friends," he said, hoping that would satisfy Ivy's curiosity.

"I think she was hoping for more than that."

"I don't have more than that to give anyone."

Ivy's green eyes held a hint of skepticism as they moved over his face. A second later, a smile formed. "I'm making it my mission to change your mind."

Oh, hell.

Someone tapped him on the shoulder, causing him to look back and see a kid pointing toward the shaved ice truck. Evidently, it was their turn. And not a moment too soon.

Chapter Eight

BAILEY LOST HER APPETITE THE MOMENT SHE saw Rafe with Ivy. She'd spent the better part of the past ten minutes attempting to look like she wanted the shaved ice, but she didn't. She now wished she hadn't agreed to come to the park at all. If only she'd stayed at the B and B...

"Here," Holt said, holding out his hand. "Why don't I take that for you?"

Bailey glanced from him to the paper bowl of ice and back before passing it over with a sheepish smile. "Sorry."

"No worries." He tossed both hers and his into the nearest trash receptacle before returning to her side. "Was it something I said?"

"Of course not."

"Then, by deduction, I'd say it had something to do with either Rafe or Ivy."

Bailey chuckled. "You could say that."

"Question is, which one?"

"Both."

"Ah. You swing both ways, huh?"

Bailey choked on her surprise as she turned to stare up at him. "No. That's not..."

His eyebrows rose. "Trust me. I don't judge."

"No. I don't. I mean ... I don't have anything against people who ... you know. But I don't. I like..." She groaned and dropped her head. "This is goin' badly."

A large finger tapped under her chin lightly, urging her to look up. When she didn't, Holt helped her along, curling his finger sideways and nudging until she was staring up at him.

He was smiling, and damn it if the man didn't have an amazing smile. Most notably, his perfect lips. She briefly wondered what they would feel like pressed against her own.

His eyes locked with hers, shifting slightly as though he was attempting to peer deep into her soul. She didn't want to acknowledge that there was some sort of unfamiliar connection forming. An arc of electricity that shimmered and sparkled as it moved between them. Like those electrostatic plasma balls. The kind you touch and the colored lights follow your fingertip. She imagined those colorful lights stretched between, glowing brighter the longer they remained like that.

Of course, she'd thought the same thing about Rafe not too long ago. Up until he made it very clear that what she felt was one-sided. It was safe to say she wasn't a good judge of chemistry.

Taking a deep breath, she looked away from Holt. "I'm sorry. I'm just havin' an off night. You were kind enough to invite me."

Holt's voice dropped an octave or two. "Would it help to know kindness hadn't played a part?"

Her skin tingled from the seduction in his words. Something about this man had appealed to her from the moment she saw him, and she couldn't shake it. In fact, with every second she spent with him, she found her attraction to him intensifying. Since she didn't know much about him, it was merely physical, but it was quickly consuming her.

"We should probably move closer to the stage," she whispered, trying to break the spell he had on her.

It took effort, but she managed a smile and broke eye contact.

Before she could walk away, Holt touched her cheek. The barest sweep of his fingertip across her skin, urging her to look at him again. This time when she did, he leaned down and pressed his lips to hers. The sweet melding of his lips to hers stole her breath and made her vividly aware of those sparks again. Something compelled her to lean into him, to press her palm to his chest, to feel the rock-hard muscle that shifted as he stepped closer, deepening the kiss as he licked his way into her mouth. She slid her hand to his neck, the soft hair at his nape tickling her fingertips. The gap between them disappeared, the hard press of his body warming her through her clothes.

She got lost in him. That was the only way to describe it. She felt his kiss deep in her core.

In those few precious moments, she was bared to him. As vulnerable as she'd ever been. Never had she put much stock in love at first sight, but she was beginning to think there might be something to it. That connection. It felt deeper now. As though he'd succeeded in baring her soul and finding the deepest, darkest parts of her.

Bailey knew she should step back. Knew they were in public and everyone could see them. For some reason, she didn't care. She was so tired of doing the right thing, the honorable, respectful thing. Being the good girl had gotten her nothing but disappointment. She wanted to be free for a little while, to let loose and let the foreign sensations within her carry her away. She'd done the right thing with Rafe, waiting for something that would complete her, and look where that had gotten her. Maybe if she'd done something back in the beginning, she wouldn't have gotten her heart broken.

Thankfully, at least one of them had some sense left because Holt pulled his mouth from hers, but he didn't move away. With his hands on her face, he met her gaze, and she saw the same flames burning in his eyes that she felt in her bloodstream.

"I take that to mean Rafe's the one who has you up in arms."

He couldn't have doused the moment any faster if he'd poured a bucket of ice water over her head.

Bailey tried to pull away, but he grabbed her hand.

"Don't you run, little rabbit."

Frowning, she glared at him.

"I didn't mean it like that." Holt shook his head and closed his eyes. "And I damn sure didn't mean to ruin that incredible moment."

"Well, you did," she said firmly.

"By bringing up Rafe."

"Could you please quit sayin' his name," she bit out.

"Tell me one thing first."

She swallowed hard. "What?"

"Is there something between you and him? Something I might be stepping in the middle of?"

"No." She shook her head for emphasis. "There's never been anything between me and Rafe."

"Good. Then I'm gonna do this."

Before she knew what was happening, Holt was kissing her again. This time her common sense left for a shorter period, and though she kissed him back, she managed to stop it first.

Someone hit the drum snare and snapped Bailey out of her hormone-induced mental coma, bringing her front and center.

"Don't worry, little rabbit," Holt whispered, his eyes still locked with hers. "I know how to be a gentleman."

That was good because she certainly wasn't behaving like a lady. And if he were to leave it up to her, there was a good chance her lust for him would obliterate her decorum.

True to his word, Holt played the role of the perfect gentleman during the concert.

It wasn't an easy feat, that was for damn sure.

Well, he figured it was, and it wasn't.

He wasn't a bad guy. He didn't take things that weren't offered, but from the moment Bailey kissed him back, he'd felt something. Something he'd never felt before. And yeah, that was a fucking cliché if he'd ever heard one, but that didn't make it any less true. He wouldn't pretend to be a saint, but he had never felt what he felt when he kissed Bailey.

Okay, fine. That wasn't exactly true. He'd never felt it for a *woman* before, and he'd kissed plenty. Only one other person had caused that molten eruption in the center of his being, but that had been so long ago that Holt had started thinking it was merely a figment of his imagination. That was why he was here in this small town Rafe Sharpe called home. Holt had come here for a repeat, if for no other reason than to determine whether it was real.

A repeat he seriously doubted would happen based on Rafe's reaction to his presence earlier. No, Holt hadn't anticipated a warm welcome from Rafe since the man had up and left the morning after. And not merely Holt's bed, either. He'd left town. Disappeared. That was nearly three years ago. Holt had intended to track him down long before now, but life had gotten in the way, and he'd vowed he wouldn't make a move until the timing was right for him to do so.

The timing was finally right, although it could be too late to matter.

The lack of reception from Rafe was expected. But meeting Bailey Weber certainly was not. From the moment Holt walked into the Double R Retreat, he hadn't stopped thinking about the woman with big hazel eyes and silky hair the color of rich caramel. He'd never seen a woman who looked more pure and wholesome as she did. But that kiss made him think there was a fire banked deep inside her, and the moment she shed that virtuous outer layer, she was going to do some serious damage to some poor man's heart. Holt only prayed it wasn't his.

"You want to grab a drink?" he offered when the park began clearing out after the last song.

Bailey brushed her hair back from her face, still avoiding eye contact with him. "I should probably get back."

"I'll walk you."

"You don't have to." This time she did look at him. "It's right there."

Holt tucked his hands in his pockets to keep from reaching for her. "Then it won't take us long."

They'd only taken a few steps when Bailey spoke up.

"How do you know Rafe?"

"We met several years ago down in Corpus. I booked a condo on the beach so I could finish up a project. I couldn't focus for shit, so I found a place that wouldn't allow for any distractions. I learned there was one fatal flaw in my plan when a group of people came down to camp out the first weekend I was there. Turned out they did it every weekend in the summer to blow off steam, so I started hanging out with them. Rafe and I became … friends." He nudged her with his arm. "How do *you* know Rafe?"

"I grew up here. He's from here. We worked at the same bar for a while."

"But you never dated him?"

Bailey shook her head, her eyes focused on the ground in front of her. "Not for lack of tryin' on my part."

That was interesting.

"Rafe can be a stubborn one," Holt told her.

Bailey chuckled. "Understatement of the century."

Holt smiled as they strolled up the walkway to the B and B. When they reached the stairs, Bailey went up one before he reached for her hand, urging her to turn around.

"I had a great time tonight." He stepped closer. "I hope I was gentlemanly enough that you'll consider doing it again sometime."

Her smile was sweet. "You get an A for effort."

Holt held her gaze. "That doesn't mean I don't want to kiss you again."

Her eyes shifted to his mouth, but Holt refrained from moving in. As much as he wanted to seal his lips to hers, it was obvious she was skittish. And until he figured out the reason, he would let her lead.

He waited until those pretty hazel eyes met his again. "All you have to do is ask."

Bailey's eyebrows lifted. "Ask?" She smiled shyly. "For you to kiss me?"

"Or you could kiss me. I certainly won't mind."

He could tell she was contemplating the idea, but she didn't lean in.

"Whenever you're ready, little rabbit. I'm not going anywhere."

"I thought you were only stayin' for a couple of days."

Holt shrugged. "That was before I met you."

Bailey's expression sobered. "You're a charmer, aren't you? The guy who beds every woman he meets?"

"At one time in my life, I might've been," he said honestly. "That's not the case anymore, I assure you."

"Well, Holt Callahan, I can tell you, I've never been into casual sex. So, if that's what you're expectin'…"

Fuck, she was sweet, and he decided he really liked it. Far more than he should.

"If it's any consolation, I'm not looking for casual either."

He could tell she didn't believe him.

She finally smiled and brushed her hair behind one ear. "Well, I guess I'll see you in the mornin'."

"I sure hope so."

Holt remained where he was until Bailey disappeared inside the B and B before he turned toward the park. He'd driven through town earlier today, so he knew where the bar was. It was true he'd taken a little detour with his date with Bailey, but Holt had every intention of confronting Rafe as soon as possible. The last thing he wanted was to find out he'd come all this way, only for the man to disappear again. Once was more than enough for him. Especially after the incredible night they'd shared.

Even now, he couldn't help thinking about it.

"One night," Holt said, holding back from kissing the man by sheer force of will.

Rafe tilted his head and their lips brushed. Holt inhaled sharply, surprised by the electrical current that simple touch had caused. Holt had never met a man who turned him on the way this man did.

"One night," Rafe agreed.

The next thing Holt knew, Rafe had taken over, grabbing his head and crushing their mouths together. Holt banded one arm around Rafe's back and jerked him closer, needing to feel that hard body pressed to his. He'd spent the entire summer fantasizing about this moment, and nothing short of a tsunami would ruin this night for them.

Thankfully, they were only steps from a soft, horizontal surface. Holt steered them into the house and across the few feet to the bed. Before he could push Rafe down so he could ravish every inch of him, the man stopped him.

"I'm in charge," Rafe growled softly.

Holt had never given up control in the bedroom, but based on the sparkle in Rafe's eyes, this was non-negotiable.

Luckily, Holt was adaptable.

"You're in charge," he echoed, stepping in to resume the kiss.

It sparked the same as before, and this time, Rafe had him flat on his back in seconds. Holt refrained from grabbing Rafe and holding onto him. Something told him Rafe's need for control wasn't merely to maximize pleasure.

But Holt had no problem stripping Rafe bare from where he was. He tugged on Rafe's shirt until he was forced to lift his upper body, allowing Holt to pull it over his head. He tossed it aside, then did the same with his own.

Rafe's eyes slid over Holt's chest as he leaned forward again. The heated appreciation Holt saw there filled him with warmth and told him he couldn't let a minute pass them by.

Lifting his head, Holt sucked Rafe's nipple, teasing the tiny disc until it hardened against his tongue. Rafe pushed his chest forward, making it easier for Holt to tease him and allowing him to slide his hand into Rafe's shorts, cupping the hard-rounded globe of his ass.

"Fuck, yes," Rafe hissed, spreading his knees wider. "Touch me."

Taking that as permission, Holt teased Rafe's hole with his finger as he sucked on his nipples. Rafe controlled the force with which he sucked by pressing his chest down. Holt had never had a problem being on the bottom because he found you could control as much from that position if you wanted it badly enough. And Holt fucking wanted this man.

He scooted down on the bed, holding Rafe in place so that he could reach his cock with his mouth. Since they were both still wearing shorts, Holt couldn't get to him the way he wanted, but he managed to lick the swollen head of Rafe's dick by pulling the waistband of his shorts down. He tugged and jerked, forcing Rafe to lift his knees in order to get the cotton down his legs. Once he was naked, Holt returned to his task, sucking him into his mouth.

"Greedy, aren't you?" Rafe groaned, shifting forward and pressing his knees under Holt's arms, eliminating his ability to touch. "Open wide. Let me feed it to you."

With his arms stretched over his head, Holt opened his mouth and allowed Rafe to push his cock in slowly, inch by inch. Grabbing the headboard for support, Rafe stared down, clearly mesmerized by what he was doing. Holt let him use his mouth, sucking and licking, then opening his throat to give Rafe room to push in deeper.

Rafe

"Oh, fuck, that's good." Rafe grabbed his hair, holding his head so he could ram in deeper.

Holt choked on the thick cock filling his throat, but he didn't pull away. If Rafe felt the need to punish him, Holt was more than willing to pay the penance merely for this opportunity.

"Ah, hell," Rafe gasped, jerking back, his cock dislodging. "I'm not ready to come yet."

"No?"

Rafe shook his head, then moved down Holt's body until he was straddling his knees. He pulled Holt's shorts down to his thighs, leaned forward, and took him to the root with one downward slide of his wicked mouth.

For a guy who claimed he'd never been with a man before, Rafe sure as fuck didn't need lessons. Holt pumped his hips up as he groaned, the warmth enveloping him. He watched as Rafe bobbed up and down, lubing him with his saliva while tormenting him in the best way possible.

"You sure you've never done this before?" Holt grunted. "'Cause damn, you're good at that."

Rafe chuckled, and the vibration sent flares firing down Holt's spine.

He held on for as long as he could, ensnared by the way Rafe sucked him like a starving man. He slowed his pace as though knowing Holt was close before lifting his head and meeting Holt's gaze. He smiled, then crawled forward, straddling his hips and kissing him again.

"I want you inside me," Rafe rasped against his mouth.

Holt was surprised by the request. He thought for sure Rafe was going to be the top.

"I'll make it good for you, I swear."

Rafe stared down at him, and for a moment, Holt was pretty sure the man was emotionally bare. "I don't know why, but I trust you."

Holt felt a strange heat move through him. It coalesced in the center of his chest, and he knew in that moment this was a night he would never forget for as long as he lived.

"So, I was thinking maybe you'd want to come back to my place after work."

Rafe grabbed two more beers for customers and pretended he didn't hear Ivy's proposition.

"We can hang out. Share some popcorn. Watch a movie. Talk."

It wasn't the first time she'd made a similar comment since they'd returned from the park. Based on her determination, he doubted it would be the last.

"You can't ignore me forever, Rafe Sharpe," Ivy sing-songed. "I'll eventually wear you down."

He was about to tell her that was impossible when the door opened, and several people chimed, "Welcome," to the newcomer.

Rafe was grabbing a glass from the wine rack when he saw the man stroll inside.

As had been the case the last night he'd been with Holt, his heart thumped painfully hard against his chest wall, and a strange churn stirred lower. Only one other person's presence had the power to send his cardiovascular system into chaos, but Bailey Weber wasn't with him. Which meant the response was solely for Holt Callahan.

The bastard.

Was it a good sign that Bailey wasn't with him? Had that all been an act earlier? Had they not been at the park *together*, rather just a coincidence?

And honestly, why the fuck did he care?

He didn't. He *couldn't*.

He wouldn't pretend he didn't care about Bailey. He did. She was his friend, and he wanted the best for her. A fly-by-night writer wasn't something she needed. The man had all but told Rafe he didn't put down roots because his craft allowed him to go wherever he wanted, whenever he wanted. Rafe hadn't needed an engraved invitation to see himself out.

So why the fuck was Holt here?

Rafe tried not to stare, but it wasn't easy. When Holt walked in, people noticed. Some because he wasn't a familiar face around these parts. Others because he had one of those faces that required you to do a double take. To say the man was handsome was an understatement. He had a movie star vibe about him that drew people in, and when he spoke, people listened. At one time, Rafe had been one of those people.

Not tonight.

"Is anyone sitting here?" Holt asked one of the old timers bellied up to the bar.

The man glanced over, his expression reflecting his irritation until he saw Holt. How the man could shift a mood with merely a smile, Rafe would never know.

"Nah. All yours."

"Thanks." Holt took a seat on the stool. "Any chance you've got a single malt back there?"

Rafe retrieved the bottle of Johnnie Walker Blue Label from the top shelf and held it up for Holt to see. It wasn't single malt, but it was the best they had.

"Make it a double." He tapped the bar near the old timer's beer. "And put this guy's beer on my tab."

Retrieving a tumbler, Rafe added a large ice cube and poured, giving his full attention to making the drink, although he could do it in his sleep. It was better than looking at the man who'd sent Rafe's world into a death spiral at a point when he thought his life was finally moving in the right direction.

When he set the glass in front of Holt, the man passed over his credit card with a mumbled, "Thanks."

They were busier than usual, nearly at capacity, thanks to all the stragglers who'd relocated here from the park. It ensured Rafe didn't have time to chat with Holt or any of the other patrons who'd managed to sidle up to the bar. For a solid hour, he worked to make drinks—evidently, music in the park meant specialty cocktails all around—and keep the waitress' trays full while Mack manned the fryer in the back, cooking up French fries and onion rings, now that they were out of chicken wings.

But as they said, all good things must come to an end because, at 1:45 A.M., Mack yelled, "Last call."

The few minutes that followed weren't nearly enough, and before he knew it, Rafe was closing things up while Holt remained sitting at the bar. At that point, ignoring him was futile, but Rafe wasn't one to back down from a challenge.

"All right," Mack said when he emerged from the kitchen. "All cleaned up in—"

When he stopped mid-sentence, Rafe peered over at him.

Mack turned his attention to Holt. "Sorry, man. We're shuttin' it down for the night."

"He's with me," Rafe said grudgingly.

Holt took that as a reason to introduce himself to Mack. They shook hands, and before their palms separated, Mack realized who he was.

"My husband's gonna shit bricks when he realizes you're in town."

Holt grinned. "Doesn't sound comfortable."

Mack barked a laugh. "Probably not. But you're in his top three favorite authors of all time list."

"Top three, huh? Who do I share the honor with?"

"James Patterson and Michael Connelly. He switches the order based on how he feels about the latest release."

Holt chuckled. "Good to know."

Mack spared Rafe a glance, likely wondering what their relationship was.

It *wasn't*. That was what it was.

Seeming to see through Rafe's hard exterior, Mack smirked and looked back at Holt. "How long you stayin'?"

"Haven't decided," Holt told him, his gaze briefly swinging to Rafe. "I'll be at the B and B for a few weeks. Figured this was a good place to start working on my next book."

"A few *weeks*?" Rafe bit out, hating himself as soon as the words were out of his mouth.

Holt's eyes moved over him, and Rafe saw his amusement. He pretended not to notice, returning his attention to closing out the register for the night.

"Maybe I'll get to meet your husband while I'm here," Holt told Mack.

"He's the sheriff, so there's a good chance you'll see him around."

"The sheriff? That's good to know. I always like to get the low-down of an area when I start to write. Maybe if I name-drop, he'll give me a tour."

Mack grinned, and Rafe shook his head. He rarely saw his boss excited about something, but apparently, meeting one of his husband's favorite authors did it for him.

"I can take it from here," Rafe told Mack. "You can go on home and tell Jeff the excitin' news." He emphasized the last two words with a dramatic eye roll.

"Don't think I won't. See you tomorrow."

"Later."

"Good night," Holt told Mack as the man headed out the front door. "I think I'm gonna like it here."

"No, you won't," Rafe countered, wiping down the bar once more. "Before you know it, you'll be movin' on to bigger and better things."

"Like you did?"

There was obviously a glitch in his wiring because that was the only way to explain why those words gave him pause. Rafe pulled himself together quickly. "Not the same thing, and you know it."

"Oh, I know something, all right," Holt said, leaning toward him.

Rafe stood tall and tossed the rag onto the shelf below the bar. "Why are you here? Did you come all this way to give me shit? Because I don't wanna hear it."

"Well, that's too damn bad because I've got some things to say."

"The statute of limitations on your chance is long over," Rafe snapped. "You shoulda said what you had to say before now."

"Tough shit. You're the one who walked away. Not me. You owe it to me to listen."

"The hell I do."

Rafe stormed toward the hallway that led to the storage room. He swung the door open and grabbed the broom. When he turned around, Holt was standing less than a foot away.

"You need to go back where you came from," Rafe hissed, hating that his entire body was humming.

It did that. Whenever Holt got close to him, his body was no longer his own. There was something about the man that he connected with, although he didn't fucking understand it. He might've been attracted to a couple of men over the years, but he'd never given in to those feelings. They'd never enticed him enough. Rafe had never believed you were either gay or straight. He'd always wondered why anyone thought there needed to be a delineation. Attraction was attraction. And it could happen to anyone at any time, regardless of gender.

But that was the thing. Attraction was *attraction*. It wasn't love, and at some point during the night at the beach, Rafe had crossed the line into thinking it might be.

So, no, he wasn't in fucking denial. This was him protecting the people he cared about. Since he'd failed at it so spectacularly as a kid, it was his turn to do what was right. And protecting people like Bailey and Holt from the likes of him was the right thing to do.

And if keeping his distance from anyone who enticed him hurt, then it was a punishment he rightly deserved.

"You still feel it," Holt said, stepping closer.

"I don't feel shit," he countered, attempting to step around Holt.

The man blocked his path.

"Don't do this," Rafe warned. "I'm not in the mood."

"No?" Holt stepped closer.

This time Rafe didn't move. He couldn't. His breath was lodged in his throat. He was overwhelmed by the rich spice of Holt's cologne, a scent that still lingered in his memory from time to time. More than once, he thought he'd smelled the man and found himself looking around for him, only to realize his senses were playing tricks on him.

"I don't believe you."

They were close to the same height, with Rafe being a couple of inches taller. But that minimal difference had never been noticeable because Holt Callahan had seemed larger than life from the day Rafe met him.

"Last warning," Rafe whispered when Holt leaned closer.

"I've never stopped wanting you," Holt said, his breath fanning Rafe's lips. "I've never stopped thinking about you. About that night. About what we could've been."

Rafe could feel the tension in his muscles, his brain directing him to shove Holt away, but he didn't. Long seconds passed as Holt's lips hovered only a whisper away. Rafe wanted his kiss. He wanted to feel what he'd felt all those years ago. Wanted to steal a taste so he could savor it again, even if it could never last. But he knew one kiss would lead to endless months of agony, and he refused to go through that again. It was the very reason he hadn't kissed Bailey, why he'd kept her at arm's length. He was only so strong. Eventually, he would cave, and he would ruin the life of whoever was in his path. He couldn't do that.

Planting one hand firmly in the center of Holt's chest, he pushed him back. "I'm not goin' back there. Not now. Not ever."

Holt's blue eyes glittered with need and anticipation, and it mirrored the emotions that churned within him. That was one thing about Holt. He never hid his desires. He went after them without apology. Rafe envied him for that, but he wasn't Holt. He couldn't be that man. Not with the sins he'd committed weighing heavily on him.

Shouldering his way past Holt, Rafe emerged from the hallway and got to work sweeping the floor.

"I'm gonna assume you won't have a problem with me going out with Bailey."

Rafe nearly tripped over the broom but caught himself.

Did he care? Hell no. It wasn't like Bailey would want anything to do with Rafe or Holt once she learned they'd been together. And there was no doubt in his mind that Holt intended to tell her. For the shock value, if nothing else.

But Bailey was pure and sweet, the kind of woman looking for a man who could and would put her on a pedestal and worship at her feet. She deserved that. A man who could give her one hundred percent of himself. Since Holt had never been the sort to lean one way for too long, Rafe figured it was only a matter of time before she told him to take a hike.

"You need to stay away from Bailey."

Holt didn't respond, and he still didn't respond, so Rafe made the mistake of turning to look at him.

"You're in love with her."

It sounded like an accusation, so Rafe let it stand. He didn't need to confirm or deny his feelings for anyone.

"Shit." Holt shook his head. "And she has no fucking idea."

"It's not like that," Rafe bit out.

"So she's fair game?"

Knowing Holt would keep pushing until he got the answer he wanted, Rafe delivered the only one he was willing to give. "I don't give a shit what you do."

Holt chuckled softly. "You never were a very good liar. You know that?"

He was wrong about that. Rafe was a brilliant liar. When it counted.

How else did you explain why Bailey had no idea that Rafe was head over fucking heels in love with her?

Chapter Nine

BAILEY WOKE UP ON SATURDAY MORNING WITH a smile on her face.

She wanted to attribute her newfound happiness to the new bed she was in or the apartment that belonged solely to her. She wasn't so sure that was the only reason for the grin. She couldn't stop thinking about Holt or the impromptu date they'd gone on last night. More specifically, she couldn't stop thinking about that kiss.

Never had she kissed a man who had the ability to obliterate her brain cells. With one sweep of his tongue against hers, Holt Callahan had turned her brain to mush and sent her hormones into chaos.

It had been glorious. So much so that she'd relived it in her dreams.

As some of the sleep fog faded, she recalled the dream more clearly. Her breath caught, and the smile faded.

"Oh, my God." She stared up at the ceiling. "What is *wrong* with me?"

In her dream, Holt had certainly kissed her, but he hadn't been the only one. Rafe had been there, too. All three of them had been at the park waiting for the concert. She'd been holding their hands, waiting for the music to start, when Holt slid his fingers down her cheek, urging her to look up at him. She had, and he had kissed her.

Bailey drew in a deep breath as she remembered what happened next.

Rafe had been standing behind her, pressing his big, hard body against her back while Holt was against her front. She'd been sandwiched between them with Holt's mouth on hers and Rafe's lips caressing her neck. She recalled worrying that people would see them, but Rafe assured her everything was fine. She was right where she belonged. Between them.

"Holy shit." Now her body felt tight and achy—in the best possible way. But how could that be? How could she possibly have a dream about two men?

Hopping up, Bailey padded to the bathroom to brush her teeth, wash her face, and pull her hair into a ponytail. While she flossed, she avoided meeting her own eyes in the mirror. She brushed her teeth with her head hanging down. And when she washed her face, she opted for cold water, hoping it would cool the heat from her cheeks. Why she was blushing from a dream, she didn't know, but it wasn't going to look good when she went downstairs to feed the guests.

"Pull it together, girl," she muttered, turning off the water and patting her face dry. "It was just a dream. A crazy fantasy. Nothing more."

Taking a deep breath, she exited the bathroom and went back to her room. For the past few days, this had become her routine. It was pointless to put effort into her appearance when she would be bustling around the kitchen, so she didn't bother with makeup. Instead, she pulled on a T-shirt, shorts, and a pair of sandals and went downstairs to start coffee for any early risers.

Once that was underway, she washed her hands again, then started on the biscuits. Southern-style buttermilk biscuits were her specialty, and her mother had taught her to make them from scratch when she was little. She pulled out all the utensils she would need—measuring cups and spoons, glass bowls to mix in, a pastry mat and pastry mixer, a baking pan, and a biscuit cutter.

From there, she pulled out the ingredients—flour, butter, baking soda, baking powder, buttermilk, and salt.

It took her roughly fifteen minutes to prepare the biscuits, and while those were cooking, she started making the gravy and sausage. She made separate batches of gravy, one with sausage crumbled in it, the other plain. She was in the process of plating everything when she heard footsteps coming down the stairs. A moment later, Holt appeared in the doorway, wearing jeans, a T-shirt, and a sexy grin.

"I take it you like to cook," he said as he moved toward the coffee maker.

"I like to bake mostly, but I'm comfortable in the kitchen," she said. "I get it from my mother."

"She owns Batter and Bliss?"

Surprised that he knew that, Bailey glanced over her shoulder. "Yes."

He gifted her with another smile. "I've done my homework on this small town."

"Have you?"

"Of course. When it's the basis for a book, I want to know what I'm dealing with."

Bailey turned around fully, frowning. "Book? You're a…"

"Writer? Author?"

She was trying to process that.

Holt continued, "Wordsmith? Man of letters? Novelist?"

"Yes. That."

"Full-time," he confirmed.

That was … Bailey wasn't sure what that was. She'd never met an author before. Well, besides Jack but he was a graphic novelist. It wasn't the same thing. Right?

"And you're basing a book on Coyote Ridge?"

"A series, actually."

"What's it about?"

"I've started an outline, although I use that word loosely. It's more like notes on a page, but I'll tell you when I figure it out."

Smiling, Bailey returned to her task of taking the food into the dining room and setting it up on the warming stands. Holt followed.

"Wait."

Holt abruptly stopped.

Bailey chuckled. "Sorry. I didn't actually mean for you to…" She gestured toward his legs. "I meant … anyway. You're an author."

He nodded, then glanced at the kitchen. "I think we had this conversation a few minutes ago."

She laughed, then shook her head. "What I mean to say is … do you think that's why Ivy recognized your name? Because you're an author."

"More than likely."

Well, that made more sense. Bailey had gone to bed last night wondering if Holt knew Ivy. If maybe they'd once been…

She shook off the thought. Nope. She wasn't going there.

"Can I get you anything?" Bailey offered when Holt took a seat at the large dining room table with only his coffee mug.

"Thank you, but no." He held up his coffee mug. "This is the extent of breakfast for me. At least this early in the morning."

"Well, if you change your mind…"

Bailey started for the kitchen but stopped when Holt reached for her arm, his long fingers gently circling her wrist. She glanced at the point where he was touching her, then up to his face, praying he didn't see what that slight touch did to her. Fireworks were igniting in her womb, and she was sure parts of her body—like her toes and fingers—had gone numb to accommodate the rush of sensation to other parts.

"Last night was memorable," he said softly, his blue eyes glittering with sincerity.

Her mind flashed an image of Holt and Rafe pinning her between them. She erased it, but not before her cheeks heated with embarrassment.

"I hope we can do it again sometime."

She met his stare. "They have music in the park every Friday in—"

"I wasn't talking about the concert, Bailey."

"Oh."

His grin widened.

"I'd like that too," she admitted before she even realized she was going to.

A creak sounded above them, and Bailey pulled away. More guests were coming down, and she certainly didn't want to give the impression she was neglecting her duties.

As she slipped into the kitchen, she felt Holt's eyes on her, a fact Bailey liked far more than she was willing to admit.

HOLT COULDN'T REMEMBER THE LAST TIME HE shared breakfast with anyone. And while he didn't eat, he remained in the dining room and drank coffee while more guests came down to devour what was touted as the best biscuits ever by more than one person. If Bailey thought she was hiding how much that pleased her, she'd failed. But it was a good look for her. The way her eyes turned shiny and her cheeks pink.

She was absolutely adorable, and he found himself looking forward to having breakfast here for the foreseeable future.

Admittedly, Holt led a relatively solitary life. He spent a good majority of it writing. And when he wasn't, he was generally researching—a lot of it online. He ventured out when he was in search of a muse or when he needed to delve deeper into a character's motivation and sometimes when a scene merely wouldn't form. But rarely did he encounter people in this capacity.

It was refreshing. And it gave him a new perspective since the guests at the Double R Retreat were not residents. They were looking at this town from the outside. It allowed him to see it through their fresh eyes, which would help when he got the perspective of those who'd lived here their entire lives.

Because he was in no rush to leave Bailey, he stuck around until the space cleared out. When Bailey holed up in the kitchen to take care of her chores, he took that as his cue to give her some space, so he ventured over to Batter & Bliss to meet the woman Bailey called Mom.

"You're a new face," Ramona Weber said by way of greeting from her post behind the pastry display case.

"Yes, ma'am. I'm staying at the B and B for a little while."

"Oh?" She seemed quite pleased by this news. "My daughter manages the place. Bailey?"

"We've met," he said casually, skimming the variety of baked goods inside the case. "She escorted me to the concert in the park last night."

"I guess if you've had a date with my daughter, it's only fair that I get your name."

"Holt." He stood tall. "Holt Callahan."

"It's a pleasure to meet you, Holt Callahan. I'm Ramona."

"Pleasure's all mine," he said with a grin, then gestured toward the case.

"What can I get for you?"

He scanned the rows of muffins, scones, and croissants. "I'm not sure I can choose."

"Just say the word, I'll pick somethin' for you."

Holt smiled at her. "I have a feeling I'll be stopping in daily, so perhaps you can surprise me with something each day."

"I can certainly do that. Any allergies or aversions?"

"No, ma'am. However, I do have a sweet tooth, but it tends to lie dormant first thing in the morning."

"Noted. Why don't you start with a croissant? Those sell fast around these parts."

Ramona picked out a giant, fluffy croissant, and Holt added a coffee to go with it. He paid for both, then moved to one of the empty tables. He made note of an available plug and saw a sign for free Wi-Fi, and decided this might be a perfect place to work when he needed a change of scenery.

Speaking of scenery...

His grew infinitely more appealing when he noticed Rafe coming out of Shelf Help, the bookstore across the way. He was carrying a large wooden box mounted on a post with a crossbeam base. Holt watched as Rafe set it on the porch in front of the store, then went back inside. A minute later, a woman came out carrying a stack of books. She opened a plexiglass door on the front of the box and began tucking the books inside. Rafe returned with more books, passing them to the woman before they exchanged a few words and some smiles, then Rafe went back inside.

Interesting.

Rafe

Holt finished his mid-morning meal, cleaned up his mess, then said goodbye to Ramona, promising he would be back tomorrow. Once outside, he felt the summer heat beating down on him. It was only ten, and the temperatures were already in the mid-80s. With the humidity, it felt even warmer. Not uncommon in Texas, but that didn't mean he had to like it. Granted, he grew up in Mississippi, so he knew all about balmy heat.

Figuring there was no better time than the present to seek Rafe out for another attempt at a conversation, Holt headed for the bookstore.

When he walked inside, the bells over the door jingled, and Holt briefly wondered if they got all those damn bells wholesale. Every place he'd been so far had them. Except for Moonshiners. Evidently, you didn't need jangling to announce your presence when everyone inside did it for you.

He was instantly greeted with the scent of a familiar laundry detergent and the hint of vanilla. Not exactly the scent he expected in a bookstore, but to each his own.

Or *her*, as was the case here. Based on his research, Holt knew Shelf Help was owned and operated by Violet Anderson, daughter of Daphne Walker, a member of the town's founding family.

"Good morning," Violet greeted with a charming smile as she stepped out from behind the small wood counter that served as a centerpiece of the store. "I figured you'd be stopping in soon enough."

There was something about the woman that put him at ease. Perhaps it was her low-key demeanor or the fact that he felt like she *saw* him when she looked his way. Violet wasn't making idle chit-chat while she tried not to focus on something else. She was completely present and accounted for.

"Yeah?" Holt smiled and moved toward her. "Because I'm new in town or because you've got my books in your window?"

Violet's smile grew even more radiant. "Both." She held out her hand. "I'm Violet. Welcome to my store."

He shook her hand. "I'll admit, it's not what I expected."

In fact, he wasn't sure he'd ever seen anything like it.

She peered around. "What did you expect?"

"These days, the bookstores I'm in are more of a coffee bar with a few books lingering on shelves."

"Yeah, well. If you want coffee, you can go to the bakery two doors down."

"I just came from there," he admitted, admiring how the entire back wall was designed to look like someone's personal library—three separate and distinct ones.

Since there were no windows, Violet had created them by having life-like, three-dimensional murals that resembled enormous windows overlooking various scenes. One was a fairy tale illustration, complete with a dragon flying high over sparkling water. The shelves around it were designed as a tree, the branches filled with books that reached the ceiling.

The middle window had gauzy curtains bracketing it, and the drawing was of mountains. Off in the distance, a princess was talking to a prince. The shelves surrounding it weren't as elaborate, but they were designed around various ornamental decorations that seemed to go with the fairy tale theme.

And the third and final window design was...

"Okay, so I get the fantasy," he told Violet, motioning toward the window with the dragon and then over to the middle drawing. "And I get the fairy tale. But I'm not sure I'm comprehending the third one."

Violet turned toward the window that was a scene right out of a fall decorating catalog. "The moms in town enjoy having a bit of peace from time to time. And fall is festive and something to look forward to, so I went with that."

That made strange sense.

It also explained why there were two comfortable chaise lounge chairs near that window and the other areas had various wooden chairs and a couple of beanbags on the floor. On the bookshelves in that section, there were flameless candles that created a serene ambiance.

"It's not only about the words on the page, Mr. Callahan," Violet said, turning back to him.

"And at the same time, it is," he countered with a smile.

"You win. The words build the world, so I'll give you that."

He turned and scanned the rest of the store. As with a typical bookstore, there were rows of shelves and a variety of tables that held books in every genre. At the front, near the windows that overlooked Main Street, the books were set out to accentuate the best sellers and recent releases for both traditionally and independently published authors.

As he turned around, Holt's gaze snagged on the wooden box Rafe had carried out front.

"And that?" he pointed to where it stood.

"That's the Little Free Library."

"Ah." Holt nodded. "I've heard of those. The take-a-book, share-a-book concept?"

"Exactly. I finally got around to building it. I'm hoping it'll spur people to find something they might not know was out there."

"Don't you think it's a direct conflict with your business?"

"Reading's reading, Mr. Callahan. As long as people are doing it, that's all that matters."

Holt appreciated her do-gooder attitude, but he wondered whether that had a place in a small business. Since it wasn't his place to criticize, he decided to shift topics.

"I noticed Rafe was here helping. Is he around?"

Violet's gaze narrowed, and the talkative woman from a moment ago closed up tight.

"I mean no harm," he explained. "We're friends. You can ask him yourself."

"He's not here."

Holt glanced toward the back, wondering if he'd slipped out when Holt came in. He wouldn't put it past the man.

"Do you know when he'll be back?"

"I'm not Rafe's keeper, Mr. Callahan."

"Okay, then." Clearly, he wasn't going to get anything more from her on the subject, so he switched again. "Your shop is lovely. If you're ever looking for authors to do signings, I know quite a few. Several who write children's books if that's the audience you target. Just let me know."

"I assume that means you're here permanently?"

"The foreseeable future," he corrected. "The more I learn about this town, the more appeal it seems to have."

"Well, thank you for the generous offer. And if I see Rafe, I'll let him know you're looking for him."

Taking that as a dismissal, Holt skimmed the room again before heading for the door.

As he walked outside, his brain was working overtime trying to figure out why Violet Anderson seemed so protective of Rafe. Were they in a relationship? Or was it something else entirely?

Chapter Ten

RAFE WALKED INTO THE DINER A LITTLE before six. He stopped in every night he worked to grab a meal hearty enough to tide him over until closing time. When he'd first arrived in town a few years ago, they hadn't welcomed him the way they did now. The fact his family tree branched out from the Walkers—Lorrie Walker was his aunt—went a long way in getting people to stop giving him the side eye when he walked by. At least those who respected the Walkers.

Plenty didn't, and unfortunately, those people had to eat too.

"I wonder if they checked him for weapons at the door," someone muttered from a nearby table.

It amazed him that they couldn't come up with something more clever.

Rafe ignored them. He didn't give a shit what people said about him as long as it didn't hurt anyone he cared about. When they dragged innocent people in, he tended to take offense. When it didn't … well, he'd learned how to be the verbal punching bag for every asshole in this town.

"Yeah, thanks," a deep voice said from a booth to his right.

Rafe glanced over to see the back of Holt's head. He was facing away from Rafe, likely the only reason he hadn't engaged him in conversation. He knew Holt hadn't given up after his failed attempt last night because Violet had informed him that he'd come by the bookstore inquiring about Rafe's whereabouts. Thankfully, she hadn't told Holt where Rafe lived, so he figured he still had at least one place to go to avoid the man.

When Holt stood and tossed his napkin on the table, Rafe tipped his head, letting his cap shield his face.

"You can't hide from me forever," Holt said as he passed. "We're gonna talk."

"Nothin' left to say." Rafe realized his mistake as soon as the words were out of his mouth. Holt would've continued toward the door if he hadn't engaged the man.

"You might not," Holt stated, turning to face him. "But I've got a few things to get off my chest."

Rafe was tempted to tell him to lay it all out now because he wouldn't get another chance, but knowing Holt, he would. And Rafe got enough shit from the residents of this small town. No reason to add more ridicule.

"Hey, Mister. You might wanna be careful with him. He'll shoot you where you stand."

Ah, hell.

Rafe met Holt's gaze. He shook his head, urging Holt not to respond, but he knew it was pointless.

Holt slowly turned, then walked toward the table of teenagers. His tone was cool and calm when he said, "Anyone ever hear of a spoiler alert?"

The kids glanced at one another. "What?"

"Spoiler alert," Holt repeated. "It's what you say when you're about to give away something crucial to the plot, and you're not sure whether your audience has read the book or watched the movie."

"What are you talkin' about, dude? This ain't a movie."

"It's old news," one kid said.

Holt engaged the kid. "Older than you, I'm pretty sure."

"Yeah. Duh."

Holt put a hand in his pocket. "Which one of you gave away the ending?"

The kids all looked at each other.

"It's cool. I'd just like to know the whole story. Who knows it?"
The kids shrugged.

"No one?"

They traded looks between them.

"Did you know it was self-defense?" Holt asked, his tone still casual. Completely unaffected by the topic of conversation.

"It doesn't matter," the girl closest to Holt said. "He shot his *dad*. You don't have to like your parents, but you can't kill them."

Evidently, she didn't know the definition of self-defense.

"True," Holt told her. "I take it your parents are cool?"

"They're all right," she grumbled. "I wouldn't shoot 'em."

"You shouldn't."

"So why's it okay that he killed his dad? It makes him a killer."

"Technically," Holt agreed.

"So why's he not in prison?" one of the other kids asked.

"If he were a danger to anyone, don't you think they would've arrested him?" Holt countered.

"They did," one kid insisted, then waffled as he looked around. "Didn't they?"

Rafe tuned out the conversation because he didn't want to hear Holt share a story he'd told him in confidence. Granted, he'd told him not even as much as what had come out in court, but he figured Holt had gotten more details by reading about it online or in the archived newspapers. Rafe certainly hadn't told him the events that led *up* to that night. Hell, he'd never even talked to Rex about it. It wasn't something he wanted to share, which was why they'd relied on Rex's testimony to find Rafe not guilty. As for the events Rafe had endured that led up to that night … no one knew. No one but him and Jolene. And since Jolene was dead, the horrors of what had transpired in that house after his mother died would never see the light of day.

"Ignore those kids," Rachel said as she brought Rafe's food.

He took the plastic sack, which contained the Styrofoam container.

"We were all ignorant at that age."

Rafe couldn't help but smile. She was probably right.

"But tell your friend I like how his mind works." She winked and then strolled back to the kitchen.

Not wanting to hear the end of Holt's history lesson, Rafe headed for the door. He was almost to his truck when Holt called after him.

He made a mental note to start walking faster so he didn't risk follow-up conversations with people he wanted to avoid.

"You working tonight?" Holt prompted when he approached.

"Yes." Rafe opened the passenger side door and set his food on the seat. "If you plan on followin' me, I won't have time to talk."

He closed the door and turned to look at Holt.

"I'll make you a deal."

Rafe narrowed his eyes. "A deal? For what?"

"I won't come harass you at work tonight, but you need to pick a day when we can meet up this week. I don't care where or when, but we need to talk."

"And then you'll leave?"

"Coyote Ridge?" Holt grinned. "Ah. Probably not."

"Why the fuck not?" he asked as he walked around to the driver's door.

Holt followed. "Because I happen to like the people here. One in particular. And until I see where that might lead…"

Rafe spun around. "What do you mean 'where that might lead'?"

"It's simple. I like her. She likes me. I'd like to see where it goes."

Rafe's hands balled into fists. "Don't fuck with her."

"Awfully defensive for a guy who doesn't give a shit."

"She's my friend."

"Coulda fooled me. She seemed bothered by the fact that you flaunted Ivy in her face last night."

"The hell I did."

Holt's eyebrows rose, which gave Rafe a moment to recall that encounter. Specifically, the way Ivy had clung to his arm like he was her life jacket and she didn't want to drown.

Fine. He could see how that might've given Bailey the wrong impression.

"It's not like that with Ivy."

"I know."

"How the fuck do you know?"

Holt stepped forward. "Because I know the look you get when you like someone. I've seen it before."

Rafe swallowed, hating himself for making it so easy for Holt.

"And I've seen the way you look at Bailey." His voice lowered. "What I don't understand is why didn't you take the chance?"

"That's none of your goddamn business."

Holt's expression sobered. "Just know something, Rafe. I have no intention of hurting Bailey."

"Go fuck yourself," he hissed. Holt was baiting him. He was pushing him to see if he'd break. Rafe hated him for that. More importantly, he hated himself for wanting to go to Bailey and … and… Rafe wasn't even sure what he wanted because the thought of losing Bailey to Holt was as unbearable as the thought of losing Holt to Bailey.

And wasn't that just righteously fucked up?

"Nor do I intend to be hurt by her. You had your chance."

"Then I wouldn't tell her about…"

"About us?" Holt asked, a gleam in his eyes.

"There never was an *us*," Rafe snapped.

Holt moved so fast, Rafe didn't have time to react before he was pressed up against the door of his truck, Holt's big, powerful body pinning him there.

"You make a habit of lying to yourself?" Holt's voice pitched low. "Because that's not the impression I got when I was balls deep inside you."

"Fuck you," Rafe hissed, thrashing in an attempt to get Holt off him.

It didn't work. Holt was strong.

"An invitation?"

"Get off me." Rafe shoved him, but Holt held firm, leaning in until their mouths nearly touched.

Rafe hated himself for wanting to cave. He hadn't felt this alive in … well, it'd been years. The closest he'd come were those precious few times he'd found himself alone with Bailey. She breathed life into him with a simple smile.

But what he could have with Bailey was the opposite of what he'd had with Holt.

With Bailey, he wanted to love and cherish, to hold her, protect her. He wanted to make love to her, to feel every breath, every sigh. With Holt, he wanted hard, dirty, and fast. He'd never felt that before until that night. Until he'd manhandled Holt and then gave himself over to him.

Even if he was willing to be honest about his feelings, his desires for each of them ran in opposite directions, making it impossible to know which way was up.

"Tell me you don't want me," Holt growled softly, his hips pressing forward, the hard ridge of his cock sliding along Rafe's.

Rafe moaned, surprised by how fucking good that touch felt. It'd been so damn long. Although the town thought he bedded every woman who looked his way, Rafe hadn't been with anyone in nearly three years. No one since the night he'd spent with Holt in a condo on the beach. These days, his hand was the only comfort he had.

"Goddammit, Rafe," Holt groaned, grabbing Rafe's jaw and tilting his head. "I've missed you. Don't you get that?"

It was now or never, Rafe knew. If he gave in, he could enjoy himself for a few nights, succumb to the pleasure and quench that thirst that had been building for years. If he did, they could fuck until they got it out of their system, and then Holt could move on. He could leave Coyote Ridge. Leave Bailey. And Rafe's life could go back to the way it had been before Holt strolled into town.

Rafe swallowed a whimper that damn near escaped when Holt ground his hips against him, rubbing against his cock. He was driving him insane, and they were both fully clothed.

You don't deserve either of them. You've got nothing to offer.

With that little voice screaming in his head, Rafe brought himself back from the brink.

He cleared his throat. "For a man who just told me he wouldn't hurt Bailey, you sure aren't thinkin' with the right brain."

That seemed to click with Holt because he released him, standing tall. Their eyes remained locked together. It was all Rafe could do not to kiss him. He merely wanted to remember what it had been like. Just a few minutes to spur that memory so he could make it another three years.

"Don't fuckin' hurt her," he told Holt, reaching for the handle and flinging his door open.

He climbed inside and slammed the door, then waited for Holt to walk away. Only when he was alone did Rafe drop his head to the steering wheel and wish his life had been different.

WHEN HOLT RETURNED TO THE B AND B, he intended to march up to his room, pull out his laptop, and put some of these heightened emotions to good use. He tended to write better when he was worked up, and he couldn't remember a time when he'd been this confused.

Unfortunately—or perhaps fortunately, depending on how you looked at it—fate had other plans for him because when he walked in, he found Bailey sitting in the living room by herself, a book in her hand. The room was dark except for the glow from the lamps at each end of the couch.

"Whatcha readin'?" he drawled.

She lifted the book and showed him the cover.

Holt grinned. "Good choice. First in the series."

"I know." She shifted, putting her back into the corner of the sofa so that she was facing him. "Violet suggested it. Said it was your best series."

"And here I thought she didn't like me."

"She's good at pretending." Bailey set the book in her lap, keeping it open so she didn't lose her place. "Did you enjoy your day?"

"I did. Worked my way through town, checking out what Coyote Ridge has to offer."

"Sounds like fun. And what's your first impression?"

Holt considered giving her some sort of glossy answer he would've told a stranger, but he didn't want to treat Bailey like a stranger. He wanted to know her. Everything about her.

So he opted for the truth. "I think this town has a lot to offer someone like me."

She tilted her head and regarded him with a smile. "How so?"

He moved closer, taking a seat on the sofa near her but not too close to crowd.

"For starters, it's got the best bakery I've ever been to."

She laughed softly. "My mom called. Told me she met the handsome writer who's staying here. She asked my opinion on which breakfast pastries to treat you to while you're here."

"If you want a hint, it's blueberry. I love blueberry."

Bailey laughed again, and he realized how much he loved the sound. "I'll make a note of it. What else did you learn?"

"That the bookstore very well could be a doomed enterprise." Holt leaned back and propped his ankle on his knee. "Did you know Violet puts free books on the front porch? Who does that?"

Another laugh. "I heard she wanted to do the Little Free Library. I'm glad she's doin' it. Keep in mind, we're a small town. It started as a farming and ranching community. Then the Walkers parsed out the land and *gave* it to the town. Although some folks are doing rather well, most of the residents don't have a lot of money."

"Fair point."

"What came after the bookstore?"

"I stopped by the sheriff's department."

"You mean the jail?"

Holt nodded. "Yeah. Yeah, that's what it is. I don't know what I expected, but it wasn't a few cells and a couple of desks."

"We don't have much crime here." She reached over and rapped her knuckles on the end table. "Knock on wood."

Holt grinned. Fuck, she was adorable.

"Mostly drunk and disorderlies, sometimes public intoxication. Rarely, we'll have a B and E."

He had no interest in those accused of breaking and entering, but he considered bringing up the three events he'd uncovered when researching the town.

The first one had surprised him, but evidently, there were suspicious circumstances surrounding Rafe's mother's death, although no one had ever delved too deep. According to a few articles he'd come across, some thought it had been a cover-up by the sheriff at the time.

The next was Rafe's father's death. He knew the how of it, but he was still fuzzy on the why. He didn't doubt for a second that it had been self-defense, but Holt was curious as to what had led up to that night. Since there were very few details, he figured only Rafe and Rex could answer those questions.

And the other was the death of Kylie Walker and the events that led up to it. From what he could tell, the beginning of the end started with a house explosion—a gas leak, supposedly, at a house owned by Jessica James, who happened to work for the Off the Books Task Force, the team who'd been pursuing the woman responsible for Kylie's death. According to the articles Holt read, Travis Walker had been there at the house at the time of the explosion. Coincidence? He seriously doubted it.

But Holt liked seeing that smile on Bailey's face, so he decided to steer clear of the morbid topic for now. He damn sure didn't want to do anything to make it disappear. There would be plenty of time for him to find out more on his own.

"What else did you do today?"

"I took some time out of my day to play," he admitted.

"Play? Really? And what did you play with?" Her forehead wrinkled. "Or should I say *who*?"

Holt met her stare and gave her a sensual look. At least, he hoped that was how it came across. Then he said, "The toy store."

Bailey huffed a laugh. "You know that place is catered to little kids."

"I know," he said for dramatic effect. "I had a great time playing with the Lincoln Logs. I didn't even know they still sold those."

"They don't." She laughed again. "Well, not like they made 'em back then, anyway. But if there are any around, that's where you'll find them. They've probably been there since the beginning of time."

"I think you might be right. And just when I thought I'd created the ultimate Lincoln Log masterpiece, I got schooled by these two little boys. Matthew and Brody. Evidently, there's a height limit to be a master. Three feet, according to Matthew."

"Sawyer and Kennedy's boys. They were there?"

"They were. Brody's birthday's coming up. At least, I think that's what he was trying to tell me. He talked fast, so I didn't catch all of it."

"He does talk fast," Bailey agreed. "Plus, he's got a potty mouth."

"I didn't even know fuckapotomous was a word until he said."

Bailey giggled.

"Damn, they were cute."

"What else did you do?"

Holt exhaled slowly and leaned back, relaxing into the cushion and resting his head. "I honestly don't remember. I spent so much of my day thinking."

"About?"

"A woman."

"Really? Someone I know?"

He rolled his head, looking at Bailey. "You probably know her better than anyone."

Holt saw the color rise in her cheeks, and he found her blush endearing. Hell, he found everything about this woman endearing.

But then her expression sobered. "There's something you should know about Coyote Ridge."

"What's that?"

"The rumor mill is a real thing."

"Yeah?"

Bailey nodded. "And what happens here spreads fast if there's someone around to see it. And there's *always* someone around to see it."

Holt got the feeling she was referring to something specific, and he had a good idea what it was. Still, he decided to see how much she'd heard.

"Someone saw you and Rafe havin' an argument in the diner's parkin' lot."

"We might've exchanged a few words."

Her eyes skimmed his face. "Is there somethin' between you two that I should know about?"

Holt figured he should come clean about his reason for coming here, but he thought about Rafe's warning. If she learned he had an intimate history with Rafe, would that be the end of whatever this was? Since he didn't know her well enough, he was hesitant to be that open, but he decided she did deserve some honesty.

"Rafe and I have history."

"Romantic history?"

"What would give you that idea?"

Bailey shrugged and looked away. "It's not anything I *saw.*"

"Bailey?"

She looked at him. "The other night, when we saw Rafe and Ivy at the park, I felt something between you. And it felt like something more than friends."

He reached over and took her hand, lifting it. He brought it closer and outlined her fingers with his fingertips. Her skin was so soft. Simply touching her made every fiber of his being tighten.

"Can I ask you for a favor?"

"Sure."

"Could we possibly put Rafe on the back burner for a while? Not because I don't want to tell you everything there is to know about me, but because I'd like to get to know you better, and I'm not sure Rafe has a place in that. Unless I'm wrong."

"You're not," she said a little too quickly. "I mean, that's weird, right? You, me, and Rafe?"

Her eyes widened, and her mouth opened as though she couldn't believe she said that.

"You know what I mean. It's … yes. You're right. We *should* put Rafe on the back burner."

He noticed she said they *should*, not that they *would*.

"Good. Because I can't stop thinking about you," he admitted, turning his attention to her small, dainty fingers. "I don't know what it is about you."

When she didn't respond, Holt peered over. Bailey was watching as he glided his fingertip over her palm, following the lines.

"Tell me I'm not the only one."

Her eyes shifted to his face. "You're not."

"And you're okay with that?"

The subtle flex of her jaw and the way she swallowed told him there was something she wasn't telling him.

"Talk to me, Bailey."

———

FROM THE MOMENT HOLT TOUCHED HER, SHE'D been mesmerized by the feel of his fingers moving on her skin. Her entire body felt that simple caress, as though they were completely naked and he was moving over her, skin to skin.

And though nothing was stopping her from pursuing whatever this was between them, Bailey wasn't sure she was ready for something new. Not yet.

"I might've heard a rumor, too," Holt said softly.

Her gaze shifted to his face. "I'm sure you heard plenty but let me guess. You heard I recently got out of a relationship."

His eyebrows slowly rose, and he nodded.

If only that were the issue. For Bailey, she'd left Seth behind that night and hadn't looked back. For whatever reason, her heart wasn't holding onto her past with him. Probably because she'd moved on from him long before it was over.

No, her hesitance had nothing to do with Seth and everything to do with Rafe. Unlike him, she couldn't merely turn off her feelings. It didn't matter that he'd brushed her off like a speck of lint, Bailey had developed feelings for him long ago, and they'd grown stronger as their friendship had.

But the strange thing was, she genuinely liked Holt. And she wanted to get to know him. Holding out for something that would never come seemed foolish, so why shouldn't she do what Rafe did and move on?

"Bailey?"

If there was even a remote chance things might go somewhere with Holt, she knew he had to know the truth.

"It's Rafe," she admitted, her gaze shifting to where he still held her hand.

"He's the relationship you recently got out of?"

"No." She shook her head to emphasize. "But I've..." Bailey exhaled heavily. "It's complicated."

"You love him."

It wasn't a question, but she figured he deserved some sort of clarification.

"I think I do, yes." She forced herself to meet his gaze. "It's not reciprocated, and I know there's no future there, but it doesn't change the fact it hurts to see him with other women."

Bailey thought about Rafe and Ivy and the way she'd been hanging on him. She'd done everything in her power not to think about what they'd done after that. She'd imagined him taking her back to his apartment...

Rafe

Her chest squeezed, and her sinuses burned. It was stupid to get so worked up over something that had never been, but what she felt for Rafe wasn't a passing fancy. It had solidified over the years, and though she knew he wasn't interested in anything with her, she couldn't make the feelings disappear.

Holt shifted closer, his hip bumping her knee. Bailey didn't move. Not even when his big, warm hand rested on her thigh.

"What if I could help you think about him less?" Holt offered. "Just for a little while."

"I told you I'm not a casual girl, Holt. That hasn't changed."

"I know. And I'm not talking about sex."

Bailey felt her cheeks warm. She'd never met a man who told it like it was before. She liked that about him. She liked knowing where he stood on things. Especially since she'd spent so long trying to decipher Rafe's secret code.

"But I'd like to see where this goes," he said softly, twisting his upper body so he was facing her.

When he slid his hand under her hair, cupping the back of her neck, Bailey didn't resist him. She let him urge her closer, and the next thing she knew, she was leaning into him, their lips lightly brushing.

"I'd like that," she admitted. Bailey couldn't promise she would stop loving Rafe, but she wasn't opposed to seeing where things went with Holt. Maybe he was just what she needed to get over the man who'd stolen her heart the first day he rolled into town.

His lips moved over hers. Lightly. Briefly.

"There's something you should know, Bailey."

"Hmm?"

He paused, and the sound of his breaths hypnotized her, the feel of them against her lips. Her body temperature rose one degree at a time until she thought she would combust.

"I can't promise I won't fall in love with you."

Her heart swelled, and she thought for a minute it would beat right out of her chest. Those were words her romantic heart had always wanted to hear. Bailey had longed for the day she would find a man who would promise her things that would make her fall in love with him.

"Me either," she admitted, then kissed him, needing that connection.

Holt groaned softly, his hand tightening on her neck as his tongue slid past her lips. Bailey kissed him back, savoring his taste and the warmth of his body. Every cell came to life; every electrical impulse fired hotly as she succumbed to his mouth. A throbbing started between her legs, intensifying as the kiss did. Before she knew it, Bailey was fisting the front of his shirt, desperate to keep him there.

No one had ever kissed her the way he did. With wild abandon. As though nothing in the world mattered except her. And just like last night at the park, everything else disappeared except for his warmth, his touch. He consumed her in ways no one ever had. And for one brief, fleeting moment, Bailey didn't think about Rafe.

But then he pulled back and reality returned.

When she tried to sit up, Holt's hand tightened on the back of her neck, keeping her there. He pressed his forehead to hers as they both breathed heavily.

"Let's see where it goes," Holt said softly. "For as long as I'm here, let's enjoy it."

Bailey didn't like that there was a looming expiration date for this, but she couldn't find a reason to say no. Holt was just what she needed. A man who could show her there were men out there who knew how to treat a woman and one capable of helping her get over a broken heart. If she were lucky, when he did leave, she would be whole again.

Or he'll be the one to shatter you completely.

She ignored the pessimism and nodded. "Yes. Let's see where it goes."

After all, if a heart was already broken, would it really hurt more if it cracked again?

Chapter Eleven

Thursday, August 11, 2022

"I'D LIKE TO TAKE YOU TO DINNER tonight."

Bailey looked up from the reservation book, then peered around the empty downstairs. The B and B was surprisingly slow for the first time this week. Aside from Holt, the last of their guests had checked out that morning, and they weren't expecting any new arrivals until tomorrow afternoon. Technically, this meant she could have the night off and wouldn't have to disrupt Rex's schedule.

"What did you have in mind?" she prompted, smiling up at the handsome man.

Based on his smile, he seemed relieved that she was agreeing. "I figured I would leave that up to you."

"Would you mind if we went to the diner?" she suggested. "It's been far too long since I've eaten there, and I love their Thursday night special."

Holt's eyebrow quirked. "Which is?"

"Fried chicken livers."

His forehead creased, and she was pretty sure he turned a light shade of green.

"They make other things," she assured him.

His smile returned. "Then it's a date. What time should I pick you up?"

Bailey glanced at her watch. It was quickly closing in on dinner time, and since she'd skipped lunch… "Now would be good."

As though he'd known she would say that Holt retrieved his keys from his pocket and dangled them in front of her.

"Let me text Rex first and tell him I'll be out for a bit."

"He already knows," said a voice from behind her.

Bailey turned to see Rex coming out of the kitchen, his dog trotting at his side. He tipped his chin in Holt's direction, giving him that silent gesture for *What's up?*

"I figured I'd do my due diligence," Holt explained. "I asked him if he could spare you for a couple of hours."

"Go on," Rex said, jerking his chin toward the door. "I'll lock up down here."

"Thanks." Bailey turned to Holt. "You *will* have to give me a few minutes to freshen up, though. I've been cleaning all afternoon. You can come up if you'd like."

"Good night," Rex called after them as they headed up the stairs.

By the time they reached the third floor, Bailey was out of breath. Could've been from the trek up the stairs or because she was so close to Holt. Perhaps both. Ever since they agreed to see where things went, his presence induced quite the reaction.

Probably didn't hurt that he'd been treating her to small things, letting her know that he was thinking about her even though they hadn't been able to spend much time together.

On Sunday, he brought her a cowboy cookie—a fancy name for oats, chocolate chips, coconut, and pecans—from the bakery. Her favorite.

On Monday, he brought her a copy of the second book in the series she was reading. She didn't start reading it until last night, but when she opened the cover, she saw that he'd signed it and left a sweet note inside.

On Tuesday, he brought her a pint of mango sherbet from the corner store. Evidently, he'd asked her mother what her favorite ice cream flavor was. Bailey had shared it with him that night by the pool.

And last night, their roles had reversed because he had locked himself away in his room to write. She interrupted briefly to bring him mini blueberry whoopee pies, which were essentially soft, cake-like cookies made with blueberries in the mix, pressed together with cream cheese icing. She made them herself, then paired them with an Irish coffee topped with just a little whipped cream to help him work.

To say she was enjoying this new relationship was an understatement. Bailey liked having Holt around. When she wasn't helping guests, tidying up the place, or cooking for the masses, she would get to talk to him. She was slowly learning some of the more secretive things about him. Like he'd grown up in Mississippi, and his parents had divorced when he was seven, but they'd remained friends after that and had mastered the art of co-parenting. According to him, they still lived in Biloxi, and both had established careers in the casinos.

Despite all their conversations, she was no closer to understanding his history with Rafe, but to be fair, she hadn't broached the subject again. He'd asked that they put Rafe on the back burner, and she was doing her best to oblige. Not that it had helped her dreams because the more she tried to pretend Rafe didn't exist, the more he haunted her when she was asleep. To make matters worse, Holt was always there, too, and somehow Bailey had found herself caught in the middle of two sexy men. Only they didn't know about it. And she didn't plan to tell them, either.

"There's not much to my place," Bailey explained when she opened the door to her apartment. "I just moved in, and this is the first place I've lived on my own. Rex was kind enough to let me steal a few pieces of furniture they weren't using anymore. I'm waiting to save a few paychecks before I buy anything to start decorating."

"I wasn't looking at the furnishings."

Bailey turned to see he was actually looking at her butt.

"Perv," she teased as she moved around him. "This is the living room. Kitchen's right there. There are two bedrooms, but one's empty. I'm not sure what I want to do with it yet."

"Maybe a reading room," Holt suggested.

Bailey considered it. "That's not a bad idea. It has great light and a nice view of the back of the property. I'll just be a few minutes."

"Take your time."

She hurried down the hall to the bathroom. It didn't take long for her to wash her face, apply a little bit of mascara and eye shadow and brush her hair. She spritzed body spray on her arms, chest, and belly, then headed for her bedroom. She changed into a white skirt and a light blue sleeveless summer top, then slid her feet into sandals. Thanks to the ridiculous heat, she'd kept up with her pedicures since she could wear sandals to work.

When she came out, she found Holt standing in the living room, peering out the window toward the park across the street.

He turned when he heard her, and Bailey's breath caught when he slid an approving gaze over her.

"You look beautiful."

She grinned. "You're not so bad yourself."

He flattened his hand on his chest and smoothed out his maroon T-shirt. "This ol' thing?"

When Holt led the way toward the door, it was her turn to ogle *his* butt.

"I can feel you looking, little rabbit."

Her cheeks warmed, and she choked on a laugh.

Fifteen minutes later, they were seated at a booth along the front wall of the restaurant. It overlooked the parking lot, and with the sun beginning to set, the view wasn't half bad.

Of course, the view across the table was far more impressive.

"So chicken livers, huh?" Holt asked as he skimmed the menu, his nostrils flaring in disgust.

"Have you ever had them?"

"No." His eyes lifted. "And I can't say I'm eager to."

"They've got great chicken fried chicken."

The waitress arrived to take their order. Bailey went with the livers, Holt the chicken fried chicken with mashed potatoes. Once the waitress jotted it all down, she promised to bring sweet tea and rolls as soon as possible.

"You know, I've had dinner here almost every night since I got to town."

Bailey's eyebrows rose. "I'm so sorry. I didn't—"

"I'm not complaining. Not at all. I'm quite impressed with their selection. I haven't had the same thing twice." He grinned. "Well, except for the chicken fried chicken. Tonight'll be the second time."

Her smile formed slowly. "So you didn't need my suggestion."

"Suggest away. I don't mind at all."

Bailey blushed and glanced down at her hands.

"How's the writing going?" she asked, ignoring how hot her ears had gotten.

That seemed to relax him because Holt leaned forward, resting his forearms on the table and giving her his full attention.

"I've got the first chapter written. But now that I can envision the story better, I'm not sure it's the first chapter."

"So, what is it?"

"I think it might be the prologue."

"How do you know which it'll be?"

"In this instance, it feels more like backstory, providing a glimpse at what set him on his path."

Kinda like your history with Rafe. Thankfully, she kept that to herself, but she knew there was a reason Holt was here in Coyote Ridge, and it had everything to do with Rafe. Sure, he might be staying because of her, but Bailey couldn't help but wonder what could've happened between them that would have Holt coming here in the first place after several years had passed.

Wanting to keep the subject of Rafe in the dust-riddled corner, she tried to come up with a question related to his fictional character's motivation, but before she could, she saw a familiar face.

"Crap. He's comin' over here."

Holt frowned and glanced over his shoulder. "Who?"

"My ex-boyfriend." She met Holt's gaze. "I apologize in advance for anything he says."

Holt reached across the table and took her hand. Her gaze snagged on the move, watching as he rubbed his thumb over her fingers. He had really nice hands. Big and strong and—

"Hey, Bailey."

She forced herself to look at him. "Hi, Seth."

A deafening silence descended as Seth stood there, glancing between her and Holt. Bailey figured he was waiting for her to introduce him to her date. If that were the case, he would be waiting a long damn time.

Finally, he turned to Holt. "I'm Seth."

Holt acknowledged him with a nod of his head.

"You're Holt Callahan, aren't you?"

Holt briefly looked up. "Tonight, I'm Bailey's date. And I don't mean to be rude, but you're interrupting."

It took everything in her not to laugh. The expression on Seth's face was priceless. Almost like he'd never been dismissed before. And clearly, he wasn't impressed.

"How long's this been going on?" Seth asked her when he pulled himself together.

Holt was the one to respond. "Since the moment I laid eyes on her because only an idiot would meet a woman like Bailey and not want to spend time with her."

Bailey chewed on her lips to keep from grinning.

"Are you callin' me an idiot? Because I *spent* time with Bailey."

"You didn't let me finish." Holt canted his head and stared at Seth. "Only a *dumbass* would ever let her go."

That wasn't what Bailey expected as a response, and she could tell Seth hadn't expected it, either. Especially the emphasis on dumbass.

"Not tonight, junior," Holt said before Seth could launch into a tirade. "You're interrupting *us*. Not the other way around. I'd appreciate it if you'd move along."

She had to give Seth props for attempting to be somewhat civil. The last time she saw him he'd been on the phone with what she assumed was his side piece, so Bailey didn't care to have this conversation at all.

Luckily, the waitress returned with their drinks and gave them a brief reprieve. But then the awkwardness intensified when the bells over the door jingled, and Rafe walked in.

Bailey didn't mean to do it, but she pulled her hand from Holt's as she met Rafe's stare. She knew she looked guilty, although she had nothing to feel guilty about. She wasn't dating Rafe. She never had. But for some reason, she didn't want Rafe to see her holding hands with another man.

The move had Holt glancing over his shoulder, and his demeanor changed. It was slight, but she noticed how his shoulders squared, and the muscles in his neck tightened.

Her breath halted in her lungs when Rafe moved toward them, not sparing her a glance as he narrowed his gaze on Seth.

"You need to move along," Rafe told Seth, his tone cold and hard.

"Fuck you. You're not the boss of me."

This time Bailey did laugh because that was the most juvenile response she'd heard in a long time.

"Move. Along."

Seth glared at him, then turned to her. "When you get a chance, I'd like to talk to you."

"We don't have anything to talk about."

"I need to apologize, Bailey. I was a real ass."

"More accurately, a *dumb*ass," Holt added.

"Yes, you were." She shifted her attention to her tea glass. "But it's in the past. We've got nothing more to say to each other."

Rafe cleared his throat.

Holt scratched his chin.

Bailey felt incredibly awkward.

And Seth being Seth, said the cruelest thing he could probably think of.

"So that's how it is? You're letting them both bang you at the same time. I knew you were a—"

The last word died on his lips when Rafe grabbed him by the shirt and jerked him right off his feet. Seth fell on his ass, then scurried to get up.

"Out!" Rafe growled, shoving Seth toward the door.

The sound in the room had died, all eyes directed at the commotion.

Mortified, Bailey looked at Holt and whispered, "I'm so, so sorry," before jumping to her feet.

She didn't make it one step before Holt grabbed her wrist and pulled her into the booth with him. He put his arm over her shoulder and pressed his mouth close to her ear.

"You don't get to apologize for other people. And you damn sure don't get to run, little rabbit."

"It's embarrassing," she said softly, wishing everyone would stop looking their way.

She knew that by tomorrow there would be rumors running through town that Bailey was messing around with three men. She could practically hear the stories now. How the men she was seeing found out about each other. She wouldn't be surprised if there were an article in the Coyote Ridge Gazette.

WITH BARELY RESTRAINED FURY, RAFE SHOVED SETH toward the door, then out into the steamy August night.

"Fuck with her again, and I won't be fuckin' nice about it."

"Screw you, Rafe," Seth hissed, spinning around as though he was going to come at Rafe. He changed his mind at the last second when Rafe stepped forward. "You're the one who needs to stay away from her."

That was exactly what he'd been doing. And look where it got him. She was here on a date with Holt. Yes, Holt had warned him it would happen, but Rafe had been able to pretend otherwise until now.

"You had your chance with her, Seth. You fucked that up. Now leave her alone."

"I love her!" Seth shouted as Rafe returned to the restaurant door. "I was just too blind to see it."

Rafe knew exactly how that felt. Only his feelings for Bailey were real, and Seth was merely a fuck-up who didn't like to lose. If he had loved Bailey, he damn sure wouldn't have treated her the way he did. Any man who would make his woman walk three miles to and from work didn't deserve to experience life with anyone. He deserved to be relegated to jacking off every fucking night. Alone.

"That guy in there's right. I was a dumbass."

With no interest in listening to Seth's bleeding-heart blues, Rafe turned to go back inside.

"But I'm not the only one, huh? You didn't even *try!*" Seth shouted. "And now she's with some asshole."

"He's less of an asshole than you. But that's not sayin' much," Rafe muttered as he opened the door and stepped inside.

He spared a glance at Holt and Bailey, noticing she was sitting beside Holt this time, his arm over her shoulders.

As though he knew he was there, Holt looked back, their eyes meeting across the distance.

And just like that, he was transported back to a time when Holt had given him a similar look.

"Shower with me."

Rafe sat up straight, staring down at Holt. "What?"

The man smirked. "You heard me. Shower with me."

"I just asked you to fuck me, and now you wanna shower?"

"I get one night with you. I'll be damned if I'm not gonna get the deluxe package."

"Deluxe package?" Rafe grinned. "Is that what I am?"

Holt chuckled, then bucked his hips, causing Rafe to fall to the side. Holt was on his feet and heading for the bathroom, stripping his shorts off as he went.

"What the hell are you doin'?" Rafe muttered to himself. He had two choices at this point. He could pull on his clothes and walk out the door before he went through with this. Or he could join Holt in the bathroom and explore more of what Holt had introduced him to a few minutes ago.

It wasn't an easy choice; he had to admit. It also wasn't difficult, but he wasn't sure why that was. Rafe wanted Holt like he'd never wanted anyone before. He couldn't explain the chemistry or the connection, but he felt it. And though he didn't intend to let this turn into more than one night of passion, Rafe couldn't imagine tomorrow without experiencing tonight.

Holt peeked his head out of the bathroom. "Get in here. My mouth needs to be on every inch of you."

The heated gleam in Holt's eyes was all the invitation Rafe needed.

The moment he stepped into the glass enclosure, Holt was on him. Hard hands moved over every inch, soaping his slick skin and making his dick ache and throb. Their lips and teeth clashed as their tongues trashed and dueled. If he'd thought Holt was looking for a moment to regroup, he'd been wrong. This was foreplay that involved water and soap.

Rafe gasped for air, pulling his mouth from Holt's when the man wrapped his fists around his cock and stroked. The soap lubricated his efforts and intensified the sensation.

"Keep that up, I'm gonna come," Rafe warned.

"Isn't that what you want?"

Rafe shook his head. "Not yet. Not until you're inside me."

Holt grunted, releasing his grip and stepping back. While Rafe caught his breath, Holt ran his soapy hands over his rock-hard abs, his well-defined chest. Rafe wasn't sure why, but he'd never expected a writer to be quite so ripped.

When Holt began stroking his cock, Rafe watched, mesmerized by the sight. He wanted that cock inside him. He wanted Holt to fuck him so hard that he forgot his damn name. For so long, Rafe had been using sex to obliterate the horrific memories that plagued him, but it never failed that they would return. Hell, even the new memories sometimes took on the shape of those horrors. With Holt, Rafe knew that wouldn't happen because this wasn't something he'd ever had before. Rafe had never shared intimacy with a man, and these memories would be his alone.

Standing tall, Rafe moved toward Holt, pushing him back against the wall and letting the water pour down over them, rinsing away the soap.

"I want you to fuck me," Rafe told Holt. "And then I want you fuck me again and again until the only thing I remember is you."

Holt pulled back, his inquisitive gaze seeking as it bounced over his face.

"Can you do that?" Rafe asked when Holt didn't respond.

Holt nodded. "All fucking night."

Rafe had no business remembering his time with Holt, but the past three days had been filled with memories of their time together. Not only that one incredible night but all the nights that had led up to it. But whenever he thought about Holt, he thought about Bailey. Truth was, he had changed in so many ways since that night with Holt. Even if he were capable of committing to anyone, he knew he couldn't be with either of them because it would mean being without the other. At this point, Rafe was emotionally invested in both of them. It wouldn't be fair to his heart to have to pick only one.

Because Bailey hadn't yet confronted him, Rafe had to assume Holt hadn't told her about their history together. She would've wanted to know more. Of that, Rafe was certain.

They were friends, and while he hadn't opened up about everything, Rafe had shared some things with her. And vice versa. He missed that. He missed the long conversations they'd had over the years. But after everything that had happened, Rafe didn't know how to resume his friendship with Bailey. He wanted to. God, he fucking wanted to. And for once in his life, the risk would be worth the reward, but Rafe wasn't sure he could keep his distance if they got close again.

But until Bailey made the first move to talk to him, Rafe was going to steer clear.

For her benefit.

"CAN WE GET OUR FOOD TO GO?"

Holt peered down at Bailey and frowned. "We could. But why would you want to?"

She shrugged. "Everyone's lookin' at us."

He chuckled. They weren't, but she wouldn't know that because she still had her chin tucked against her chest, as though the silky fall of her hair would make her invisible.

"They're looking at *me*," he said, keeping his voice low. "They're wondering how the fuck I got so lucky to be out on a date with you."

Bailey lifted her head and met his gaze.

Gone was her exuberant smile. It had disappeared the moment Rafe walked through the door. At the same time that she'd pulled her hand away from him. He'd instantly seen the guilt on her face. It was then that he realized there was more between Rafe and Bailey than either of them was letting on. Sure, he'd known Rafe had a thing for her. A man didn't look at a woman the way Rafe did if he didn't have feelings for her.

Holt hadn't realized their feelings were so recent. He'd sensed something at the park the night of the concert when they'd seen Rafe with Ivy, but Bailey had played it off well. Enough that Holt had thought perhaps what they had was in the past.

That definitely wasn't the case. At least not far enough behind them to move forward without feeling guilty.

"I'm sorry about my reaction," Bailey said, her eyes sheened with unshed tears. "You know, when Rafe walked in."

Holt let his gaze skim her face momentarily before he leaned in and pressed his lips to hers. Just a light brushing against them to let her know he had no interest in backing off.

A better man would've told her he didn't want to come between her and happiness if she thought she might find that with Rafe, but Holt wasn't a better man. If he were, he wouldn't be harboring feelings for Rafe. And he wouldn't be quickly falling in love with a woman Rafe clearly had feelings for.

What they had here was a convoluted love triangle.

"It doesn't bother me," Holt told Bailey, and he realized how true that statement was.

She studied his face, her eyes reflecting her skepticism. "You don't care that I have feelings for another man?"

"I didn't say *that*." Another man he would have a problem with. But it was only fair that she had feelings for Rafe since he did too.

A small smile curved Bailey's lips. "Then what *are* you sayin'? Because it's startin' to sound like a riddle."

At the very least, he got her to focus less on their surroundings and more on him.

"What do you say we table this discussion until *after* dinner?" he said softly as the waitress approached.

Bailey pulled back as though surprised, then shifted in her seat, putting a little space between them. Before she could get out to switch to the other side of the table, he put his hand on her leg.

"Stay. I like having you close."

She relaxed, and if he wasn't mistaken, that was a sigh that escaped as she moved her leg and his hand caressed smooth, bare skin.

Perhaps they should've gotten the meal to go. At this rate, his perfect gentleman routine was going to fizzle out before they made it to dessert. He wanted this woman with a passion he hadn't felt in a damn long time.

Chapter Twelve

Monday, August 15, 2022

THE WEEKEND PASSED IN A BLUR OF excitement and energy. Every ounce of it contained within the walls of the B and B.

Bailey barely had a minute to take a breath, much less to spend with Holt, although, after their date on Thursday, she was eager to spend some time with him. Even though their dinner hadn't been exactly smooth, the night ended with Holt kissing her until she was sure fireworks were launching behind her eyelids. To her dismay, he'd left her in a state of arousal that rivaled anything she'd ever felt before.

That arousal had translated into her dreams, filling them with erotic encounters that would start between her and Holt but end with Rafe there with them. One of those subconscious fantasies had even involved Rafe and Holt exchanging a heated kiss. Needless to say, when Bailey woke up, she was both ashamed and incredibly turned on. Somewhere along the way, her subconscious mind had started writing the story of the past. She had no idea whether their history involved the two of them together, but evidently, her hormones thought, *why the hell not?*

Yes, she was both embarrassed and horny thanks to those ridiculous dreams, but there wasn't much she could do about it because here she was, cleaning up the Monday morning dishes after a full house had consumed every bit of food she'd prepared. Every single room they had was booked for the entire week, and for the first time, there were two families of four checked in, so there were even little mouths to feed.

Rex had warned her that they usually had an influx of guests right before the new school year started. Bailey figured the families were out and about trying to get in some last-minute summer fun before they had to buckle down for nine months of learning. Also, the fact that the town was setting up a mini carnival in the park didn't hurt business.

Bailey dried the last dish and tucked it into the cabinet before pulling off her apron and setting it on the counter. She took her first breath of the morning and peered over at the coffee pot. Enough for one last cup and she was going to take it for herself.

As she was pouring the last drop from the carafe, she heard footsteps behind her. She glanced back in time to see Holt coming her way.

"Good morning," he greeted in that throaty growl that she found obscenely sexy.

"Mornin'." She held up the cup. "I'll split it with you."

He chuckled. "It's all yours. I'm gonna stop at the bakery before heading to the sheriff's office."

Bailey turned around and leaned against the counter. "Is somethin' wrong?"

His blue eyes raked over her from head to toe and then back up. "Definitely not."

"I meant because you're goin' to talk to the sheriff."

He met her gaze. "I'm doing some research. Thought if anyone could give me facts, it would be law enforcement."

"Of?"

"Kylie Walker's death."

A lump formed in Bailey's throat, and she suddenly didn't want her coffee. She turned and set the cup on the counter. When she turned back, Holt was watching her.

Hoping to have this conversation without tears, she swallowed past the knot in her throat. "Why are you researchin' that?"

"I came across an article when I was digging into the town's roots."

"Oh."

Kylie's death wasn't something people around here liked to talk about. It'd been a year and a half since it happened, but it felt like just yesterday. Bailey hadn't known her well, but they'd interacted enough that the woman's death had impacted her.

Holt moved closer. "What are *you* up to today?"

Bailey appreciated that he changed the subject. And that he moved closer. "I've got to do laundry and clean rooms. We're booked, so it'll take all day."

"You don't have help?"

"Rex said he'd pitch in, but I'm interviewin' someone this afternoon. He tried tellin' me I would need help maintainin' the place, but I didn't listen. He said I could hire a full-time housecleaner."

"Mmm." Holt stepped directly in front of her and put his hands on her hips. "Will that mean you'll have more free time?"

"If I'm lucky."

"Good. Because I'd like to spend more time with you. I haven't seen you nearly enough since our date."

"I was thinkin' the same thing." She leaned closer and lowered her voice. "I was hopin' to get you all to myself. Somewhere private."

The soft rumble in his chest made her nipples tighten.

It didn't surprise her that his hands remained on her hips, not roaming to other parts of her body where she would've preferred them. Holt had this gentleman routine down pat. It had been nice at first, but now Bailey was looking to take things to the next level.

She tried to help him by leaning forward and pressing against him. "Unless that's not what you want."

His fingertips pressed more firmly on her hips. "Oh, I want it all right."

"Then why aren't you takin' it?"

"I'm trying to be good, little rabbit."

"No one can be good all the time." She flashed him a smile.

"Not even you?" he taunted.

"Not even me," she confirmed as she slid her hand behind his neck and urged him down to kiss her.

Bailey was tired of being good. Good had never gotten her what she wanted. It had never made her so hot she thought she would catch fire. And it certainly hadn't given her a chance to enact the fantasies that were plaguing her dreams. If being bad meant having incredible, mind-numbing orgasms, she wanted to be bad. And she was almost positive Holt was a master at delivering mind-numbing orgasms.

Plus, he made her feel safe enough to explore more of her wild side, so she figured she might as well.

"Careful," he whispered against her mouth when she nipped his lower lip.

She heard the sexy warning in his tone, felt the flex and release of his fingers on her hips. "Or what?"

"A man's restraint can only be stretched so far. And you, Bailey Weber, are a temptation far greater than any man can resist."

When he said things like that, she wanted to climb him like a tree.

"What if I don't want you to resist anymore?"

He pulled back and met her gaze. "Just say the word."

Bailey swallowed. She was tempted. So very tempted, but at the same time, she was hesitant. It had nothing to do with Holt and everything to do with her residual feelings for Rafe. Try as she might, she couldn't stop thinking about him. And since Holt told her he didn't have a problem with her having feelings for Rafe, her crazy fantasies were becoming more intense. Sometimes to the point she wondered whether they could one day be real.

Which was obviously bananas. Bailey was not the sort of woman who could be with two men. People would think she'd lost her mind if anyone even learned she'd fantasized about it.

"Just know one thing." Holt gripped her hips firmly and lifted her onto the countertop. He stepped between her legs and cupped her face. "When I have you, I don't want you to have any reservations."

When not *if*. He knew it was a foregone conclusion because it was. Bailey wanted to give herself to this man.

She slid her hands over his chest. "I don't have any reservations. I know exactly what I want."

"Right this moment, maybe."

Not understanding, she tilted her head and tried to read between the lines.

"Rafe," Holt said, as though she needed help filling in the blanks.

"What about him?"

"What happens when he learns about us? And he will. You told me yourself it's a small town."

She sat up straight and tried to inch back from him. "I don't know what you mean."

"The other night at the diner … you pulled away when he walked in. You didn't want him to see me touching you."

Then why, in my dreams, is it all that seems to happen?

She kept her dreams out of it and said, "I didn't mean to."

"I believe you. That doesn't change the fact you have feelings for him."

"But … that's…" She wasn't even sure how to explain it.

"That's what, Bailey?"

"Rafe doesn't want me," she blurted, feeling guilty all over again.

"I'm pretty sure you're wrong."

She wasn't, but how would Holt know that? He hadn't been here that long and as far as she knew, he hadn't spent much time with Rafe. If they were old friends, she would've expected them to catch up, but from what she could tell, Rafe was keeping his distance. Because of her? Because of their history? She didn't know.

And since Holt had avoided talking about it when she'd asked, she knew it wasn't any of her business.

"I don't want to talk about Rafe," she said, the heat between them slowly diminishing.

"Then I won't bring him up again."

"Me either." She seriously doubted either of them could hold to that promise, but for now, it was settled.

"Provided you do one thing for me."

Her head tilted again. "And what would that be?"

"Kiss me."

She leaned in and pressed her lips to his, smiling despite the awkwardness of the situation.

Holt's voice lowered again. "Like you mean it, little rabbit."

She really loved that gravel thing he did with his voice. He sounded so assertive, so … dominant. It turned her on, made her want to do whatever he told her to do.

Bailey held his gaze, then gave herself free rein to prove to him that she could be bad when she wanted to be. She slid her fingers along his corded neck and urged him down until their mouths touched. She licked his lower lip, then slipped her tongue inside when his lips parted.

"Your lips are sweet," Holt rasped against her mouth. "I want to run my tongue over every inch of you to see if you're as sweet all over."

She shivered, her brain practically building out the fantasy of him stripping her right there in the kitchen and ravishing her on the countertop. She wanted his mouth on her. On her lips, her breasts, between her legs.

She groaned, unable to hold the sensations inside.

"You want that, too. Don't you?"

Bailey nodded, never letting her lips move from his.

Holt took over. He pulled her in close, banding his arms around her, his tongue thrusting against hers. It was zero to sixty in a single second, and Bailey lost herself to the passion that engulfed them. Her body heated and throbbed with a desperate need that he created with his presence. She was intimately aware of every inch of him, his hands moving along her sides, his thumbs almost grazing her breasts. *Almost* but not quite.

"Touch me," she whimpered, trying to shift to get his hands where she needed them. She was desperate for him. Hell, she wanted him to make love to her right here in the kitchen. She was that far gone.

Actually, no. She didn't want him to make love to her. She wanted him to *fuck* her. Bailey had never wanted a man to fuck her before. She'd always considered the terminology crass and unnecessary, but Holt inspired dirty, raunchy thoughts, and she figured that was deserving of a good fuck.

"Slow down, little rabbit."

"I don't want to," she said defiantly, shifting closer so her thighs bracketed his hips and the hard ridge of his cock was pressed intimately between her legs.

Her entire body shuddered at the sensation that ripped through her from the friction alone.

Holt grunted, his palm flattening on her lower back as he pressed his hips forward, adding enough friction to make her cry out. Unable to hold back, Bailey grabbed his hand and forced it between her legs.

"What do you need?"

"You." She kissed him hard, holding his head to keep him from moving back.

"You need me here?" His hand moved down to her thigh, his thumb sliding along the crease of her leg, teasing the edge of her panties.

"Yes." She didn't care how it made her look; Bailey spread her legs wider, inched her butt forward, eager for him to satisfy this overwhelming ache.

"Holt..." She kissed him harder. "Please..."

The need was so intense she wasn't sure she would survive it.

His lips trailed down to her neck, and Bailey placed one palm on the counter, leaning back, giving him room. His thumb caressed her through her panties, gently rubbing circles on her clit, but it still wasn't enough.

She was coming undone, utterly oblivious to where they were, when she tugged her panties aside, letting Holt know exactly what she needed.

"Fuck, you've got a pretty pussy."

Bailey was vibrating, his words making her pussy clench and release. She was dangerously close to implosion. It would only take one touch.

"More," she whispered, seconds from begging.

"If I touch you, I won't stop until you come."

Bailey trembled violently, his words nearly setting her off. "Yes."

"Yes, what?"

Her cheeks heated, but she forced herself to say the words. "Make me come."

They both watched as Holt's thumb moved to her clit, pressing firmly at first before he teased the nub with a vigorous circling motion.

Bailey's hips bucked. She couldn't look away, mesmerized by the sight of him touching her so intimately.

She could hear him breathing near her ear as he rubbed circles on her clit until she couldn't take anymore.

"Come for me, little rabbit."

Unable to stop the tsunami-forced orgasm from cresting, Bailey pressed her nose into his neck and came with a muffled cry.

His words came in a gruff whisper. "Fuck, you're so damn sweet."

As the ecstasy faded, Holt held onto her, his mouth grazing her neck. Bailey didn't want to let go. She'd never had an orgasm like that before, and she wanted to experience it again in case it was a temporary thing.

But then her sanity returned as her heart rate slowed, and she realized they were in the middle of the kitchen. Anyone could've walked in. Hell, maybe someone had, and she hadn't seen them.

A creak near the back door had her head snapping over.

There was Rafe. Standing on the back porch, his eyes peeled wide.

When she blinked, he was gone.

RAFE STOOD ON THE BACK PORCH, HIS lungs burning as he held his breath, his heart wedged somewhere in his throat.

He'd come to the B and B to talk to Rex, but when no one answered the front door, he moved around to the back. He heard voices coming from the kitchen, so he went to the back door. Finding it open, he expected to see his brother talking to Bailey.

Instead, he found Holt and Bailey.

At first, they'd been talking. When he heard his name, he'd been curious why he was a topic of their conversation. He hadn't meant to eavesdrop, and he damn sure hadn't meant to stand there and watch what happened when they stopped talking, but his feet wouldn't move.

What happened next wasn't what he expected. His reaction to it was even worse.

Rafe

Sure, he was jealous. To the point his insides felt shredded. How dare Holt touch her when Rafe never had? All he'd wanted was to kiss Bailey, but his stubbornness had gotten in the way. Now there was a good chance he would never get the chance.

But jealousy wasn't what kept him there, had him watching as Bailey wantonly gave herself to Holt, begging him to make her come. He'd never seen anything as sexy as her telling Holt to make her come.

All the fantasies he'd had of her had involved sweet, gentle lovemaking. Never had he considered she might need something more than gentle caresses. The version he'd seen a moment ago had brought something inside him to life. He imagined himself walking into the house, joining them. He envisioned making Bailey come with his mouth while Holt watched, then trading places so he could have the pleasure of tasting her sweet pussy.

Realizing he was still staring through the screen door, Rafe jerked out of his reverie, intending to leave. He hadn't managed a single step when Holt pulled back, and Bailey's gaze shifted to Rafe. Their eyes locked for a single heartbeat before Rafe put his feet in motion and marched off the porch.

How the fuck had he let this happen?

If Holt had his way, he would've spent the rest of the day with Bailey. It didn't even matter where. Preferably naked with his cock lodged deep inside her, but he could do casual, too. He simply wanted to be around her.

Instead, he managed to walk out of the house so she could deal with the chores she needed to tackle and so he could wrangle his fucking dick into submission.

Not so surprising, the distance didn't help at all. He was absolutely useless. He only managed to walk to the bakery because it required no brainpower whatsoever. His mind was occupied with their encounter in the kitchen, the sound of Bailey's muffled cry resounding on an endless loop. Touching her ... feeling the heat of her ... Holt had never known anything as precious as Bailey's surrender.

How the hell was he supposed to get anything done now?

He made it to the bakery without incident. He ordered a black coffee, and Ramona chose a cranberry-orange scone for his daily pastry surprise. He ensured he gave her his high praise before he left to focus on the task he'd set out to accomplish today. The walk back to his truck gave him time to shift his mindset and plan out the questions he wanted to ask Sheriff Endsley when they met in a little while. But first, he wanted to make a trip to the cemetery to see Kylie Walker's gravestone for himself.

By the time he arrived at Coyote Ridge Cemetery, his thoughts were clear. Mostly. He'd managed to tuck thoughts of Bailey away for a little while. He would certainly be pulling them out later to relive that moment again and again, but for now, there was something he was curious about.

Holt parked his truck on the side of the narrow road and got out, strolling through the perfectly manicured grass to what he believed were the plots dedicated to Curtis Walker and his family. Turned out he didn't have to search. He merely headed for the fresh flower arrangements that seemed to be centered over one particular grave.

The gravestone gleamed as though someone polished it daily. Someone had placed a dozen roses in the small cylinder meant to hold flowers, and someone else had placed a magnolia flower on the edge. There were also daisies and sunflowers, and Holt suspected someone kept up with the decor on a daily basis.

As he stared, he had to wonder what it would mean to have a love like that. To know that when you left this world, there were people who would mourn you for not weeks, not months, but years. Not until recently had Holt even considered settling down and having a family, but something changed about six months ago. Something that made him realize life was fleeting, and he needed to find somewhere to go unless he wanted to be moving from one city to the next without roots to keep him in place. Funny, but his first thought had been of Rafe.

Holt had come to Coyote Ridge to validate those feelings, to confirm that what he'd felt that night had been real, and if it had, he'd intended to change Rafe's mind. One night was all it had taken for Holt to fall in love, and the man he happened to fall in love with did not think he deserved love from anyone. Never in his wildest dreams would he have expected to encounter a woman who might've stolen his heart within the first minutes of meeting her.

Talk about complicated.

"I won't lie, Kylie," Holt said, talking to her headstone. "I want what you had. In more ways than I expected."

He wondered whether Sheriff Endsley would have the same reaction that Bailey had when he brought up Kylie's name. If so, how should he approach the subject? It was clearly not an easy thing to talk about for the folks in this small town. People were still grieving a year and a half after it happened.

Holt understood loss. He'd never experienced it to this magnitude, no, but his grandparents on both of his parents' sides had passed away when he was young. He'd been close to all of them, so he'd been heartbroken. The difference was they'd died when they were older and not at the hands of violence. The same couldn't be said for Kylie Walker.

Problem was, during his research, Holt had encountered a few things that didn't add up. Not with Kylie, per se. She'd married Travis Walker when she was nineteen, and they'd gone their separate ways shortly after Travis joined the army. Later, they'd found each other again, and from what he could tell, that was partially thanks to the interference of Gage Matthews, also known as Chance Reed, a former undercover cop responsible for taking down some pretty severe government corruption.

Since this was right in Holt's wheelhouse, he'd started digging deeper to understand. Curious, he'd started to pull on the thread, trying to unravel the story behind Chance Reed. Somewhere along the way, that thread led him to Meredith Prescott, Kylie's mother, but he wasn't entirely sure how. It would take some backtracking to figure it out, but he was curious whether he could get the lowdown from those who'd known Kylie. And the thriller writer in him wanted to understand exactly what led to her death because something about the whole thing didn't sit well with him.

Figuring there was no time like the present to find out, Holt said goodbye to Kylie and headed back into town.

Chapter Thirteen

RAFE WOKE TO THE SOUND OF HIS cell phone. He rolled over and squinted at the screen.

"Fuck," he muttered, grabbing the phone and answering. "Sorry. I must've overslept."

"You're not late," Mack grumbled in his ear. "But I'd like to talk if you can get here before your shift starts."

"Sure. Somethin' wrong?"

"Nope. Just get yer ass here."

Not one to mince words, Mack disconnected, and Rafe was left holding the phone to his ear, his eyes closed. He forced them open to see what time it was and realized he still had two hours before he was supposed to be in.

In all the time he'd worked for Mack, never had the man called him to come in to chat. Hell, Rafe wasn't sure they'd ever really carried on a conversation that wasn't had with a few drunk cowboys bellied up to the bar.

He forced himself out of bed, then stumbled to the shower. The water was lukewarm by the time he'd finished shaving, so he tolerated the slight chill because he didn't want to waste time. All the while, he tried to figure out what he'd fucked up. Surely that was why Mack was calling. Had he left the bar unlocked, and someone came in and stole all the liquor? He'd had a dream that he'd done that once, shortly after Mack gave him a set of keys. Rafe had been so worried he'd gotten out of bed and hurried back only to find it locked up tight.

Or maybe this was about Ivy. She wasn't getting along so well with two of the waitresses, and Rafe had gotten an earful this past week about it. Ivy was stealing tables, or so she was accused. Rafe hadn't had a chance to talk to Mack about it, and he'd purposely avoided talking to Ivy because every time he did, she suggested he come over. Rafe didn't want to hurt her feelings, but he wasn't interested in making new friends. There was only one he cared about—Bailey—and finding a way to fix things between them was all he had time for right now. He figured if he were going to burden anyone with his baggage, he would go for the one he was in love with.

Once dressed, he grabbed his cell phone, keys, and wallet and was out the door.

Twenty-three minutes had passed between when Mack called and when Rafe walked into Moonshiners.

It wasn't empty. A couple was sitting at a table on the far side of the room, and Sheriff Jeff Endsley was seated on a stool at the bar. Since he was out of uniform, Rafe figured Mack's husband had the night off.

"Take a seat," Mack commanded, pointing to the bar stool on Jeff's left.

Yeah, he was pretty sure he'd fucked something up.

Rafe straddled the stool and rested his arms on the bar top. "Afternoon, Sheriff."

"Are you ever gonna call me Jeff?"

"Not as long as you're the sheriff."

Jeff chuckled.

Rafe appreciated that the man was in good spirits, but it didn't help the knots twisting in his belly.

Mack stood directly across from Rafe, his expression solemn. "It's been a long time comin', kid. I didn't wanna do it like this, but—"

"Are you really gonna screw with him like that?" Jeff asked his husband.

Mack's gaze slid to Jeff, but his countenance remained the same. "It has to be done."

"Well, I know that. And *you* know that, but your delivery needs some work. I mean, it's not like he killed somebody."

Rafe turned to look at the sheriff, his jaw unhinged in disbelief.

Jeff glanced over and grinned. "Too soon?"

He couldn't help it; he barked a laugh. Not in all his life had anyone made a joke about what happened, and though there wasn't anything funny about the situation, the fact that the sheriff, of all people, could say that…

"I knew I could rely on you to lighten the mood," Mack told Jeff.

"Of course you could. I'm the fun one."

Rafe noticed a smile under Mack's bushy mustache and beard, but it disappeared as quickly as it had arrived, and he was back to looking grim.

"I've been doin' some thinkin'." Mack tapped the bar with his index finger. "About all those changes you keep askin' me to make."

Oh, shit.

"I know you think it's a good idea and all, but I just can't commit to takin' on a task like that. I'm too damn old."

"You're sixty," Jeff snapped. "The same age as me. If you're old, that makes me old, and *I'm* not old."

"Fine," Mack huffed and rolled his eyes. "I'm not old. But I've got too much shit I wanna do outside these walls."

Rafe nodded. "I understand. I—"

"I wasn't finished."

Rafe closed his mouth.

Jeff chuckled and shook his head. "Why anyone would want to work for you is beyond me."

"Well, the good news is, no one has to," Mack countered.

Rafe waited for someone to tell him what was going on. Was Mack firing him? Seriously?

Mack took his sweet fucking time before finally looking at Rafe again. "I've decided to sell the bar."

The air released from his lungs in a rush, but it wasn't relief. Mack wasn't firing him, but Rafe figured the new owner certainly would. Rafe was a good bartender, but he lacked the experience most people would want. He made a mean martini and could sling beers with the best of them, but he didn't spend much time learning all those fancy drinks because no one around here bothered to order them.

"You ain't got nothin' to say to that?" Mack prompted.

Rafe glanced between the two men. "I didn't realize I was supposed to say somethin'."

"I figured you'd wanna buy it," Jeff noted.

Rafe shook his head. "I don't have that kinda money."

"He's right," Mack told Jeff, looking forlorn. "He doesn't."

The knots in Rafe's guts twisted even tighter. What the hell was he supposed to do now? If the new owner fired him, he'd end up out on his ass without a fucking thing to his name. It was bad enough he didn't have anything to offer a woman he loved, but now he would have to lean on his brother for help. That would make him doubly pathetic. At that point, *no one* would want him.

"But I thought you said…" Jeff's face scrunched as he studied Mack.

"What?" Mack's bushy eyebrows rose. "What did I say?"

"Somethin' about twenty bucks." Jeff shook his head. "Maybe I was wrong."

Mack's eyes widened. "Oh, right. The twenty bucks Rafe gave me for that beer he had … what was it? A month or so ago?"

Jeff nodded. "I think it's been that long, yeah."

Mack chewed his lip and looked at Rafe. "I told him his money was no good here."

"You lied," Jeff said.

Rafe wasn't sure what the fuck they were talking about or why they were talking *about* him but not *to* him. His head was spinning. Maybe he needed some air.

"I did," Mack said. "I lied." He cocked an eyebrow. "Because those twenty bucks bought you a bar."

Rafe choked.

He took a breath, and he fucking choked on air. He coughed and sputtered, pushing away from the bar to try and clear his throat and get oxygen into his lungs.

"I didn't think you could do it," Jeff said. "I didn't think you had it in you."

Rafe managed a breath and turned to look at the two men. "Are y'all fuckin' with me?"

"No," Mack said seriously. "You got yourself a bar. But Jeff did tell me I couldn't make you think you were gettin' fired when you haven't done a damn thing wrong. You make it too easy, kid."

"You think this is funny?" Rafe accused.

"It *is* funny." Mack stood tall and grinned. "*I'm* funny."

"Since when?"

Mack winked at Jeff. "Since I married this guy."

"What can I say?" Jeff chuckled. "I rubbed off on him."

"Hey. What happens in the bedroom stays in the bedroom," Mack said, deadpan.

Jeff snorted and nearly spat out his beer.

"Fuck off," Rafe rasped. "Both of you."

Jeff slapped Rafe on the back. "Congrats, man. I think you're gonna do this place justice. Just do me a favor, will ya?"

"Hmm?"

"Burn that damn flamingo picture."

BAILEY FINALLY FOUND A MOMENT OF PEACE around seven o'clock that night.

When Rex offered to keep an eye on things so she could take a break, she jumped at the opportunity and extended an invitation for Holt to come to her apartment for dinner. He had accepted without batting an eye.

Now, here she was, pacing the kitchen, second-guessing everything. The food, the sundress she was wearing, the earrings. Even the wine she'd chosen.

Was she expecting too much? She hadn't had a minute alone with Holt since that morning in the kitchen, and she was pretty sure that was partially his doing. Was he purposely keeping his distance? Did he accept her invitation so as not to be rude? Was he no longer interested? Had she moved too fast and turned him off?

To be fair, he had said he was writing. And it wasn't like she'd had a minute to spare with the B and B filled nearly to capacity. But wouldn't they make an effort if they cared about each other? Maybe exchange a text during the day? Say hello in passing?

She figured, technically, that was what tonight was about. Maybe she was overthinking this.

The knock on her front door surprised her. She shrieked, then broke into a fit of laughter at her stupidity.

"Comin'!" she called out as she grabbed her glass of chardonnay and carried it with her. Surviving tonight would only happen under one condition: there would have to be alcohol involved. Lots and lots of it. Good thing this was her first glass. From the second bottle.

Bailey composed herself and stood tall before opening the door.

Holt was standing in the hallway with a beautiful bouquet in his hand. Orange orchids and yellow sunflowers formed a lovely arrangement that, oddly enough, matched the colors in her dress.

He held them out.

"They're beautiful," she said with awe, taking them and stepping back out of the way. "Thank you."

"Something smells amazing."

Nerves rioted in her belly, but Bailey managed to reply with, "I cooked. It's homemade chicken pot pie."

She flashed him a smile as she carried the flowers into the kitchen. She retrieved a vase out of the bottom cabinet. It was one she'd "borrowed" from the extras pile that Rex and Jack had in the furniture building. She hadn't been sure she would ever need it, but her romantic heart had hoped this would happen someday, and she wanted to be prepared. Good thing she was.

"Would you like some wine?" she offered as she filled the vase with water.

"Love some."

While she arranged the flowers in the vase, Holt poured wine into the extra glass she'd left on the counter. When he was done, he added more to hers.

"How long until dinner?"

Bailey glanced at the clock on the wall. "Twenty-two minutes."

"Good."

"You're not hungry?"

"Oh, I'm hungry," he said, moving closer. "But twenty-two minutes gives me plenty of time to do this."

Bailey found herself in his arms, his lips moving over hers. Her body acted on instinct, her arms wreathing his neck as she held on, reliving the exquisite sensations as his tongue moved against hers. She'd missed this. The strength in his hands, the warmth of his body, and that unique spicy scent. It was a heady masculine mixture of vanilla, amber, and woody floral notes that went right to her head.

"You don't know how badly I've wanted to do that," Holt murmured against her mouth.

"Then why didn't you?"

"You've been so busy; I didn't want to be selfish."

Bailey grinned. "I won't mind if you're selfish sometimes."

Holt kissed her again, and she was pretty sure the kitchen heated a few more degrees from the intensity. This time her hands roamed, sliding beneath his T-shirt to find smooth, warm skin. He groaned, and she felt the reverberation move through her, lighting every nerve ending, and they all seemed to have a direct correlation to her pussy because she was throbbing with anticipation.

He eliminated the space between them, their bodies pressed together. She felt the muscles in his back flex and shift beneath her fingertips, and she had the sudden urge to slide her tongue over them so she could memorize every plane and angle of his body. She'd never been the kind to get swept away like this. Sex was something she enjoyed but not something she'd ever craved. She'd never been with a man who could light her up from the inside, but Holt didn't seem to have a problem. Almost like he knew exactly where the buttons were that would turn her to maximum voltage.

When his lips trailed down her jaw, Bailey fought the urge to climb him. As she clutched him tighter, she opened her eyes and saw the door that led to the back stairs. For a moment, she imagined Rafe standing there watching them the way he had when they'd been doing something very similar downstairs. A shiver snaked down her spine at the same time her clit pulsed.

"What's wrong?" Holt asked, pulling back and meeting her gaze.

Bailey frowned. "Nothing. Why?"

"I can feel the tension in you. And I'm not sure it's the good kind."

Oh, it was good, all right. As for whether it was normal or appropriate… that was something else entirely.

"Sorry." She forced a smile and managed to release him so she could back up a step. "I just… how'd it go with the sheriff today?"

Holt continued to watch her, but he took the redirect easily. "It didn't. He canceled. Said he had something else to deal with."

"Did you reschedule?"

"I told him I'd get back to him in a week, see if he has some time then."

Bailey heard the words, but her gaze shifted to the back door again. She imagined Rafe standing there, watching them. In her mind, Holt was stripping off her dress while Rafe's heated gaze caressed her from a distance.

"Bailey?"

Jerking her attention to Holt, she realized that wasn't the first time he had said her name.

"What's wrong?"

She shook her head. "Nothing."

"You're distracted. Talk to me."

Bailey shook her head and reached for her wine glass. She drank it like water, downing half the glass in one gulp.

"Bailey?"

"Rafe saw us," she blurted.

Holt's body went rigid as he turned toward the door.

"Not now," she said with a huff, moving around the small island. "This mornin'. In the kitchen."

She felt her face flame from embarrassment. Bailey didn't know why she was even telling him this. Rafe had no business in her thoughts, much less coming between her and a man she was already developing feelings for. A man she wanted to get to know on the most intimate level.

"He *saw* us?"

She nodded. "I don't know how long he was there, but after … you know … I saw him. He was on the back porch."

The small smile that pulled at Holt's mouth was not the response she expected.

"Why are you smiling?"

"It explains why I couldn't find him today. I think he's avoiding me." Holt picked up his wine and carried it into the living room.

Why wasn't he bothered by the idea? More importantly, why wasn't *she*? From a privacy perspective, of course. For reasons she would never understand, Bailey had thought about that incident so many times throughout the day, but never once had she been bothered by the idea of Rafe watching her and Holt in an intimate moment. The only concern she had was that Rafe was upset with her. He might not want the same things she did, but that didn't mean Bailey wanted to hurt him. She valued their friendship more than she could ever express.

No, when Bailey relived the encounter, she was turned on by the idea of Rafe watching. And that ... well, she figured that was unacceptable behavior. It wasn't fair to Holt.

"Your cheeks are pink," Holt noted. "Is that from the kiss? Or because you're thinking about Rafe watching us?"

Bailey nearly dropped her wine glass. It took everything in her not to spill it as she hurried to set it on the counter. "That's—I...uh...why—*what* would make you say that?"

"Does it turn you on?"

She stared at him in disbelief. "Of course not."

"Little liar."

There was no heat in his tone, and Bailey didn't understand it. "It's okay if it does."

Really? *Really?* How could he possibly be so cavalier about this?

"Tell me the truth, Bailey."

"Fine," she snapped. "Maybe it does. I'm a bad person, okay?" She hung her head in shame. "I'll understand if you don't want to see me anymore."

Holt laughed as he came toward her. She held her breath as he set his wineglass on the counter beside hers. Her chest tightened with fear. He was going to walk out that door, and she would never have another moment with him. She didn't blame him, of course, but she wasn't ready for him to go. She wanted more time with him. Lots of time. She—

His fingertips brushed along her cheek, sliding down her jaw. He urged her to look up at him, so she did.

"What if I told you it turns me on, too?"

Her pussy clenched at the thought. It was wrong, but that was her body's first response. How? How could she possibly be turned on by this?

"Then again, little rabbit, everything about you turns me on."

His other hand glided down to her ass, cupping it gently as he urged her closer. Bailey leaned in, unable to resist the magnetic pull.

"I've wanted you from the moment I laid eyes on you," he said, his voice deep and smooth. "Even more with every second I've spent with you."

"The feeling's mutual," she whispered.

His thumb brushed over her bottom lip. "I knew the first time I kissed you that there was a fire burning inside you. One that's been smoldering for a long time."

She wasn't sure that was true, but at the moment, it felt like it.

"Tell me you want me, Bailey."

"I want you," she said without hesitation.

"Tell me you want to feel me inside you."

She trembled and whimpered, her knees weak. "Yes."

"Tell me."

"I want..." She gripped his arms to keep herself from melting into a mushy puddle. "I want to feel you ... inside me."

His knees bent as he pressed his hips to hers, grinding his erection between her thighs. She curled her leg around his, urging him closer, needing to feel the friction. She wanted him naked. She wanted to feel the hard steel of his cock moving inside her. She wanted him to ease this insane ache that had taken up residence inside her since the day she met him.

Holt groaned low in his throat, and his beautiful blue eyes smoldered like the fire he said was inside her. Whatever he thought of her feelings for Rafe, she could tell it hadn't diminished his desire for her.

"This is wrong," she said, holding his stare. "You shouldn't be okay with this."

"With what? Knowing you have feelings for Rafe?"

Bailey nodded. "I do. I can't help it."

"I know."

Did he? Because Bailey didn't. She didn't know why she couldn't get over a man she'd never had a chance with. Rafe had never made her any promises, never insinuated he would reciprocate her feelings. That hadn't stopped her from falling for him, and now that he wasn't in her life, she missed him. So terribly much.

But not to the point it had stopped her from falling for Holt Callahan. She wasn't sure when or how it had happened, but sometime over the past week and a half, her wires had gotten crossed, and she found herself longing for him in ways she hadn't intended.

Her breaths were racing in her lungs. "But it's worse than that."

Holt kneaded her ass, pulling her closer, the hard ridge in his jeans rubbing against her clit, making her tremble.

"Tell me."

"I liked it," she admitted, digging her fingernails into his arms. "I liked that he watched."

Holt growled, jerking her against him. His hands were urgent but gentle, gliding over her as the friction between her legs intensified. Bailey was close. So close. He was going to make her come like this.

"It doesn't feel wrong to me, Bailey."

No, it didn't. But it should. Bailey didn't understand what was happening.

"I want to feel you wrapped around me, little rabbit."

She shuddered, but before she could tell him she wanted that too, the timer went off.

Holt chuckled, releasing his firm grip on her but not letting her go. "We really should try this when we're not in the kitchen."

Bailey laughed, some of the tension draining away. "We really should."

HOLT HAD BEEN SECONDS AWAY FROM FUCKING Bailey in her kitchen.

Milliseconds, maybe.

He honestly couldn't remember ever wanting a woman as much as he wanted her. He couldn't remember being so turned on that he thought he might shatter. She did that to him. He merely had to *think* about her and his cock thickened, making it impossible to concentrate on anything except memories of the precious time they'd spent together.

But he wanted more, which was why he didn't want to rush this. Holt wanted her to understand that he wasn't here for physical gratification. Well, in a sense, he was, but there was far more to this than sex. Being that she was a small-town girl and he was technically only a guest for a short while longer, Holt didn't want her to get the impression he was here for one thing. Or worse, he didn't want Bailey to see this as temporary because he couldn't see himself leaving. Not this small town, not Rafe, and certainly not her.

He composed himself as best he could while Bailey pulled the pot pie from the oven. He poured more wine into their glasses and watched as she worked. She was at ease in this space and beautiful as she went through the motions. So graceful, so self-assured. As though this was where she'd always wanted to be. Baking was obviously something she loved.

She gifted him with a smile as she dished up the food, arranging it on white plates with care and attention to detail. He couldn't stop watching, mesmerized by the little things like her small fingers curled around the spoon, the way she delicately scooped the food as though it would taste better if she were gentle.

Yeah, he was falling for her. Never in his life had he admired the little things. Hell, he rarely slowed down long enough to notice them. But with Bailey, he noticed everything.

When she was satisfied with her work, she picked up both plates and turned toward the two-seater table in the nook. "You hungry?"

Holt managed a nod. He was starving. For both food and for her, but he couldn't find his voice. It was lodged somewhere in his sternum because, at the moment, he was overwhelmed by it all.

Bailey set the plates on the table. "Let me get some napkins."

Holt pulled out his chair but didn't sit, waiting for her to do so first. When she finally eased into the chair opposite him, he managed to plant his ass in the chair, adjusting to accommodate the hard-on he was still sporting.

She was apparently waiting for him, so he picked up his fork and took a bite. Her eyes glazed over as she followed his movements, watching as he chewed.

"Bailey?"

She took a sip of wine, her eyes lifting to his. "Hmm?"

"I won't be able to do this with you looking at me like that."

She set the glass down, and he expected her to pick up her fork, but instead, she got to her feet.

"I can't do this either," she said, stepping closer.

He turned in his chair as she approached. "If this is about Rafe—"

She put her finger over his lips and grabbed his wrist. When she tugged, he stood up.

"I think dinner's gonna have to wait," she whispered.

He didn't think this was her way of kicking him out, but Holt needed her to spell it out for him. He needed her to be the one to instigate this so she would remember that he'd held firm to his gentlemanly routine, although it had been ridiculously hard.

"What did you have in mind?"

Her hazel eyes moved over his face before locking on his gaze. "Holt."

"Yes?"

Bailey's lips parted, and he waited with bated breath.

"Fuck me."

"Christ Almighty," he growled, lunging for her.

Curling his hands behind her thighs, Holt lifted her off the floor. Her arms circled his neck as she crushed her mouth to his. He stumbled his way through the apartment, refusing to look where he was going because there were more important things to focus on, like rubbing the damp heat between her legs with his fingertips and listening to her moan into his mouth.

When he stopped at the first door, Bailey shook her head but didn't stop kissing him. He took that to mean he was at the wrong room, so he moved a few more feet to the next and walked inside. He eased her down onto the bed and urged her onto her back. When he stood, he noticed the comforter and pillows were all a brilliant white, and the vivid colors of her dress stood out, making her look ethereal.

"Fuck, you're beautiful."

Her cheeks turned rosy as he ripped his T-shirt over his head. Her eyes moved over his bare torso. "Wow."

No doubt about it, he felt ten feet tall and bulletproof from the awe in her tone. He was grateful for his workout regimen, and while he wasn't beefed up like some of the hay-slinging cowboys he'd seen in town, he could hold his own.

Holt managed to toe off his boots, and he removed her sandals, but he left the rest of their clothes on. He wasn't eager for this to be over, and the clothes would add an obstacle that would force him to slow things down.

"I think you forgot a few pieces," Bailey said when he joined her, pressing his knee on the mattress between her thighs and moving over her.

"All in due time, little rabbit."

He kissed her, letting the tension build up again as she sighed and moaned. His muscles tightened when her soft, cool fingers trailed over his shoulders and down his back. He loved the way she touched him, the way—

"Oh, shit," he groaned as her nails scored down his back.

Holt punched his hips forward, pushing up on his arms as the thrilling sensation bolted through him.

"Do that again," he gritted through clenched teeth.

Her nails were gentler this time, but she scraped along his spine until he thought he would come out of his skin.

He wanted to tell her one more time, but Bailey had a plan of her own because she threw her leg over his hip and pushed him, forcing him to his side. He went without resistance, allowing her to straddle him. It put her in control, giving him a glimpse of the woman he hadn't seen much of.

"I asked nicely," Bailey said, dragging her nails lightly down his chest. "You didn't listen."

"No, ma'am." He chuckled. "I didn't."

Her fingertips dipped under the waistband of his jeans, and she quickly freed the button, inching back on his thighs so she could lower the zipper.

She dragged the tab down slowly, her gaze shifting to his face. "Nobody's ever made me feel like you do."

"Not even Rafe?"

He felt her brief pause, but Holt moved his hands up her thighs, sliding beneath the flowy skirt.

"We never even kissed," she said, her tone sturdier than he expected.

"But you wanted to?"

"Yes."

He sensed she was uncertain that was the answer he wanted, so he decided it was time they cleared a few things between them. "About Rafe—"

"I don't wanna talk about him right now." Bailey gripped the waistband of his jeans and tugged. "Maybe after."

"After what?" he teased.

Holt lifted his hips, helping her as she scooted down his legs, pulling his jeans and underwear off. He grinned when she took his socks off before joining him on the bed, straddling his thighs once more.

"After you make me come with this impressive piece of equipment," she said, teasing the head of his dick with her fingertip.

"I'm not sure if that's a boost to my ego or the beginning of a complex," he told her when she couldn't stop staring at his cock.

A smile formed as she curled her hand around him and gently squeezed.

Holt's hips lifted of their own volition, driving his cock into her fist. She pumped him a few times, bound and determined to drive him out of his fucking mind. He realized then that restraint didn't have a place in this room. If she wanted fast and dirty, he was more than willing to give it to her.

On his terms.

Sitting up, he slid one hand around her back, crushing her to him as he pressed his lips to her shoulder. He grabbed the thin strap of her sundress with his teeth and tugged, untying it. He trailed his lips across her chest and did the same with the other side. All the while, Bailey continued to stroke his cock between their bodies.

"Pull the dress down," he growled against her skin, closing his eyes because he wasn't sure he would survive seeing this woman naked.

She released his cock and tugged the stretchy fabric until her breasts were free. She wasn't wearing a bra, which meant there was nothing between his lips and her sweet fucking nipples. When he sucked one between his lips, Bailey clutched his head and pressed her chest forward. He sucked and laved, his body throbbing in tune with her sweet cries of pleasure.

"Holt ... yes... that feels..." She sighed, holding him to her as he suckled her breasts, alternating between them.

She rubbed her panty-clad pussy against his cock, and he could feel the heat of her. He wanted more. He wanted to feel every inch of her against every inch of him.

He released her long enough to pull the dress up over her head. He threw it to the floor, then got his first good look at her beautiful body. She was small-framed and perfectly proportioned. Not too skinny, either. He liked her womanly curves. No, he fucking loved them.

"Inside me. Please."

"I hope you don't like these," he said as he tore the delicate lace of her panties, ripping them from her body.

As soon as the last barrier between them was gone, Bailey gripped his cock and angled it between her legs.

Holt had barely enough sense to remember a condom. "Wait, wait, wait."

Bailey frowned down at him, and he could feel some of her heat cool instantly.

"Let me get a condom, little rabbit."

She nodded, and he sensed she was embarrassed that she'd forgotten that step. She shouldn't have because Holt had damn near forgotten, too, but protecting her was all that mattered to him.

Holt eased her off him so he could get to his wallet, which was in his jeans on the floor. He pulled out the condom he'd stashed earlier, ripped the foil off, and rolled it on, never looking away from her.

"You steal my fucking breath," he rasped as he joined her on the bed.

She welcomed him, so he moved over her, letting her think he would be in the driver's seat. But Holt had other plans for his sweet little rabbit. He happened to be quite fond of her when she was wild.

He pressed his cock along the seam of her pussy and rocked his hips, gliding through her slickness. She relaxed, and the moment she did, Holt rolled them so she was again on top.

She giggled with surprise, her hair cascading over her shoulders.

"I happen to like this view," he told her as he gripped her hips and positioned her over him. "Put me inside you."

Bailey's lips parted, her eyes glazed over, but she picked up right where they'd left off, angling his cock to the sweet heat of her one more time. Once the head nudged her entrance, he helped her to ease down on him, watching as her head tipped back on her shoulders as she took every inch.

"God, yes," Bailey moaned. "Holt … it's too good."

Good didn't even begin to describe it. She was so damn tight, her body clamping down on him as he pushed in as deep as he could. With his hands on her hips, he guided her back, exhaling as the friction caused his skin to tighten.

She rocked on him, her breasts swaying as she fucked him at her pace. Slow and steady and so goddamn perfect, Holt was positive he wasn't going to survive this. No way in hell.

Bailey tipped her head up, her eyes meeting his as she leaned forward. She planted her palms on his chest and took over, her hips lifting slowly, then dropping down.

"Fuck," he groaned. "Jesus, Bailey. Oh, yeah. Just like that. Fuck me."

He watched her as she became frantic, driving them both higher until they were at the summit, a razor-fine thread between perfection and ecstasy.

"Holt … I … oh, God. I … I'm coming!"

Her pussy locked down on him, her muscles gripping his cock so tight, it stole his breath and his sanity. She cried out his name one more time as she came. He didn't have a chance to admire her because his orgasm ripped through him, and they soared into ecstasy together.

Chapter Fourteen

Tuesday, August 16, 2022

RAFE WOKE UP ON TUESDAY EVENING FEELING like he'd been walking around in a dream since yesterday afternoon.

His life had taken a completely different turn with only a few words, and he knew the whirlwind was about to start.

He still couldn't believe Mack had sold him the bar for twenty bucks. It didn't seem real, but it obviously was because Mack had announced to everyone later in the evening, sealing the deal with a handshake and a promise to get all the documents they would need to make it legal. Rafe's first instinct had been to turn to Bailey so she could celebrate the news with him, but she wasn't there. Only Ivy. And it certainly wasn't the same.

When Rafe had left the bar at two, it had taken tremendous effort not to race over to the B and B and pound on the door so he could tell Bailey the news. He'd wanted her to celebrate with him. He'd wanted to watch her eyes glitter with excitement the way they always did.

God, he fucking missed her.

Although they hadn't yet signed any papers, Mack had laid out his plans to transfer ownership of the bar so Rafe could look over it. He informed him the paperwork was already in process, and once it was completed, they would sign on the dotted line. Until then, they would stick to business as usual, the schedule remaining the same until Rafe felt ready to take the reins fully.

Thankfully, Jeff had been there to clarify a few things, outlining that Mack was keeping the land, but he agreed to lease it to Rafe long-term for a price that boggled his mind. Rafe was responsible for the property taxes, but other than that, Mack was only charging him a dollar a month. The liquor license would remain with the property, and Rafe was responsible for renewing it when it was due in six months.

Rafe probably should've asked Jeff if they should be worried. Maybe Mack had a brain tumor because this all seemed too good to be true. Especially since Mack had a son, and if nothing else, Rafe expected Daniel to want first dibs on the place.

Not that it mattered anymore. Rafe knew Mack wouldn't do something like this without thinking it through. If he wasn't giving the place to his son, he knew there was a reason. So Rafe would wait patiently for the papers to be signed and notarized and for Mack to transfer all the utilities into his name. Jeff had gotten Mack to promise to help Rafe track profits and losses for the next few months until he got the hang of it. Mack would continue working regular shifts until Rafe hired someone who could help.

It was a lot to process. He'd already started making a list of all the things that owning a bar entailed. To be fair, it was a lot more than he'd expected. But as far as he was concerned, it would be worth it.

Sitting up, he dropped his feet to the floor at the same time his phone chimed. He glanced at the screen to see it was a text message from Rex.

I heard the news. Congrats, little brother. Jack and I will have to stop in for a beer to celebrate.

Rafe

⌣ Thanks, but don't stop by
tonight. I've got the night
off.

⌣ For the
record, owners
don't get time off.
Just ask Mack.

Rafe knew there was more truth to that than his brother meant, but he was okay with that, too. The only thing he wasn't okay with was where he stood with Bailey. With things falling into place, he knew he needed to fix that. Since he had the night off, he figured it would be the perfect time to seek her out. He owed her an apology, if nothing else. He only hoped she would accept it.

"WHAT ARE YOU DOIN' OUT HERE?" BAILEY asked in a hushed whisper when she found Holt in the swimming pool a little after ten on Tuesday night.

"Taking a break." He smiled up at her. "Why don't you join me?"

She peered around, hoping no one could hear them. "You know the pool closes at ten."

Holt's grin widened. "I know. Breaking the rules is part of the thrill."

"There are kids upstairs," she whispered as loud as she dared.

"Even if they were awake, their rooms don't face the back of the house."

He had a good point. "But other ones do."

"Are you worried they might see us? What are they gonna do? Tell the manager?"

Bailey couldn't help but smile.

"Plus, the possibility of getting caught is also part of the thrill."

She couldn't deny that the idea of it was appealing. Holt brought out the bad girl she never let loose, and Bailey was starting to really enjoy that side. It had resulted in some rather incredible orgasms recently.

He held out his hand to her. "Live a little. Come on. Join me."

Pretending to consider, Bailey stared at his hand. Even if she'd wanted to, she couldn't tell Holt no. The past few days had been a whirlwind. She'd been walking around on a cloud all day, thanks to Holt and the magical night they'd spent together. Passing up this opportunity because she worried someone might see them was something Good Girl Bailey would do. And she'd already learned that Good Girl Bailey got taken advantage of by men like Seth. Bad Girl Bailey got to set her own rules and not worry that she would get in over her head.

Joining Holt meant she would get a few minutes alone with him. Something she'd been wanting all day. One night hadn't been nearly enough, and Bailey was ready to explore the other dirty things she was capable of.

"Give me one minute," she told him. "I need to—"

"I already got you a towel."

Bailey scanned the darkened ground around the pool and found that there were, in fact, two towels stacked neatly near the end with the steps.

"I need to change into my bathing suit."

"No, you don't."

"Yes, I do."

"It's just you and me, Bailey."

"What if someone needs something?"

"Then I'm sure they'll text, but look." He gestured toward the house.

Bailey turned to look up at the second floor.

"All the lights are out except mine."

She counted the windows, and sure enough, there were no other lights except one in Holt's room.

"Now come on. Quit wasting time. Get in," he repeated, holding out his hand to her.

When he looked at her like that, as though she was the most important thing in his world, it was difficult for her to say no.

"Fine," she agreed. "But I *am* turning the pool lights off first."

There was no sense in taking unnecessary risks. At least with the pool lights off, even if someone did wander back here, they wouldn't be able to see that she was naked. And since she could clearly see that Holt was wearing swim shorts, it was only fair.

It took only a moment for her to flip the switch to turn off the lights and move the towels closer to the edge. You know, just in case. With her nerves rioting but her determination at an all-time high, she joined Holt at the shallow end of the pool. She stepped down onto the sun shelf, fully clothed. The water was only ankle-deep.

"You're still dressed."

"I thought maybe you'd like to do the honors."

Holt's eyebrows rose as he stood up. "Don't have to tell me twice."

She did her best not to think about someone peeking out their window while she stood there. If they did, they would only see silhouettes, which gave her some comfort. The moment Holt touched her, she stopped thinking altogether, focusing on Holt's hands slowly sliding up her legs, his thumbs teasing the inside of her thighs before grazing her mound.

"Take off your shirt," Holt urged as he unbuttoned her jean shorts.

"Shh. You need to whisper."

He chuckled softly, watching as Bailey tugged her T-shirt over her head and tossed it near the towels.

"And the bra," he whispered, tugging her shorts down her legs.

He allowed her to step out of them so they wouldn't get wet. Once she was standing tall again, she unhooked her bra and slid it down her arms.

And just like that, she felt entirely too exposed, which made her giggle.

"Now, the panties," he said as he moved back, dipping into the water as he watched her.

God, please don't let anyone be watching me.

Bailey slid her panties down her legs and tossed them with the rest of her clothes before walking down into the water to join him. With her nakedness shielded by the darkness, relief made her shoulders relax. So far, so good.

"You're naked," Holt said.

"And you're not."

As she approached, Holt's hands disappeared under the water. They came up with his shorts, making her giggle again.

"Better?"

She nodded, keeping her voice whisper soft. "I've never been skinny dipping."

"Never?"

"Nope. Have you?" she asked when he pulled her into his arms, allowing her to wrap her legs around his hips.

"Eh. Once or twice, maybe." He nuzzled her neck before bringing his mouth to hers.

Bailey relied on him to hold her up while she kissed him. His lips were soft, his tongue devilishly playful as he glided it over hers. The water seemed to cool, but she knew that was because her temperature was rising thanks to his rogue hands moving over her naked body.

His mouth traveled along her cheek, pausing near her ear. "You know what I've never done?"

"Hmm?"

"I've never feasted on a pussy poolside."

Heat the likes of which she'd never felt slammed into her like a lightning strike.

"But it's something I'd really like to try."

Holt moved toward the side of the pool, his hands shifting to her sides.

"We can't," she said, holding tightly to his neck so he couldn't lift her out of the water.

"No one can see us. It's dark out here."

"What if someone comes downstairs?"

"The lights are on, so if they look out here, they won't see anything."

She wanted to believe him, but only because she really, really, *really* wanted to have his mouth on her. He had teased her with his fingers, but she hadn't yet experienced the wonder of his mouth on her pussy. Something told her he would be as good at that as he was at everything else.

Holt pressed his mouth to her ear. "You know you want to feel my tongue on your clit."

His cock was hard, pressing against her belly. It would be much simpler to shift her hips, to take him inside her…

"My lips," he added.

Only they didn't have a condom. Bailey figured they should have the conversation about condoms at some point, but she didn't care to talk right now. She didn't have any diseases, so oral sex was definitely an option.

"You want me to suck that tiny nub until you come all over my mouth."

She groaned, her nipples tightening into painful points.

"Trust me, little rabbit. I've got you."

Her head fell back, and she gave in, releasing her arms so he could lift her out of the water. When her butt was perched on the edge, she scooted back enough to recline and put her ankles on the edge. She rested on her elbows to watch him when he stepped between her legs.

"Fuck, that's pretty," Holt said, teasing her with his fingertip while pressing kisses to the insides of her thighs.

Bailey felt entirely too exposed like this, but at the same time, she'd never felt more desired in her life.

RAFE STOOD AT THE FRONT DOOR OF the B and B, his hand poised to knock.

What the hell was he going to say to her if she answered the door? Was she even awake at this late hour? She would've been a few weeks ago when she worked at the bar, but her schedule was different now.

And what would he do if she invited him in? He couldn't go in that house. Ever. Nothing short of Bailey's life being in danger would get him past that threshold. Since Rafe was sure Holt was inside with her, he knew that wouldn't happen. No matter Rafe's feelings for Holt, he knew the man wouldn't let her get hurt.

As for whether he would break her heart or not … well, that was an entirely different story. Rafe had followed the news about the man for the past few years. He'd seen the numerous women that playboy thriller writer Holt Callahan had been linked to. Rafe even recalled an online interview where Holt proclaimed he would never settle down. Rafe had believed him.

Had something changed? Or did Holt have an ulterior motive for being here? Rumor was he was attempting to talk to the sheriff, but no one seemed to know what he wanted to discuss.

Admittedly, Rafe's feelings for Holt were biased. His experience with the man had shaped his thoughts and made him dislike him. Not because of what happened but because of what didn't. A part of Rafe had expected Holt to at least reach out to him afterward. Ask where he went, why he'd run off. But there were no phone calls and no texts. Nothing until Holt showed up in town just recently. If the man had given a shit, he would've come around a lot sooner.

Not that Rafe had expected Holt to chase after him, but it sure as shit would've been nice. Never in his life had anyone chased after him. He'd always been the one to insert himself into other people's lives. At first, he'd had no choice, and later because it was the only option in his quest for normalcy. Making friends allowed him to stop dwelling on the past and gave him an opportunity to move forward. Even when he came back here, he'd found himself in the middle of everyone else's life, pretending he fit in.

The only person who hadn't made him feel like an outcast or a burden or a box to check off had been Bailey.

And Rafe had gone and fucked that up.

Rather than knock, Rafe walked around the porch that circled the entire house. He figured maybe he could see in the windows. If he saw Bailey, then he would knock. Otherwise, he would simply come back during daylight hours.

He made it to the back of the house, alerted to the presence of people by the sounds coming from the swimming pool. The hedges that covered the pool equipment blocked anyone from seeing him, so Rafe kept walking. Maybe his brother was out here, and he could convince him to go in and get Bailey.

Rafe stopped when he realized that certainly wasn't his brother in the pool. He stepped to the right, peeking through a hole in the hedge. When he did, the security light on the furniture building came on, highlighting what they were doing.

Unlike the other morning when he'd come upon a similar scene, Bailey wasn't blocked from his view. This time he could see everything. Bailey was on her back on the pool decking while Holt stood in the water, his big hands gently pressing on her knees as his mouth feasted between her legs.

Every ounce of blood that wasn't pumping his heart took a detour, filling his cock and making it jerk against his zipper. At least now he knew his reaction the other day hadn't been an anomaly. No, Rafe found seeing them together intensely erotic.

And wasn't that just fucked up?

Worse, he was standing here watching like it was his right to do so. At the very least, Bailey should've been safe knowing he would never violate her privacy. Only Rafe couldn't move. Fuck, he couldn't even breathe. He wanted to strip off his clothes and join them.

Yes.

Join. Them.

Fucking hell.

"God, you're so sweet," Holt groaned, lapping at her pussy. "I want you to come on my face, little rabbit."

Little rabbit? *Since when does he get to give her a pet name?*

And now he was mentally talking to himself. Great.

Turn around.

Walk the fuck back the way you came.

Go. Now.

Rafe ignored the voice in his head, the one that came from a place of reason and common sense. He remained where he was, feeling lightheaded as he watched Holt push his fingers inside her, his tongue lashing against her clit.

"Holt!" Bailey grabbed his hair, holding him in place while she bucked her hips.

Rafe wanted that to be him. He wanted her gripping his hair while she tried to fuck his face. He wanted to make her come with his mouth.

And regardless of what he told himself, he wanted Holt to stand behind him while he did. He wanted to feel the man as he slowly pushed deep inside him, splitting him open before fucking him into oblivion.

The mental image took root, and Rafe gasped for air.

"Is someone there?" Bailey asked, sounding panicked. "Oh, my God! The light's on!"

"I've got you, little rabbit. If it's anyone, it's Rafe." Holt pressed her knees wider. "You like him watching, don't you?"

Like him watching? What the fuck?

"Yes," she whimpered as Holt's head dipped again. Bailey gripped his hair. "God, yes. Make me come."

She liked when he watched? Seriously?

Rafe was positive he would wake up any second because there was no way he'd heard that correctly. He was dreaming. Had to be.

"Make me come, Holt."

A moment later, Bailey cried out as her body trembled beneath the onslaught.

Rafe should've left when he had the chance, but he didn't. His feet were rooted in place as he watched Holt pull her into the water with him. She wrapped her arms around his neck, and their lips fused.

But it wasn't until Holt turned and Bailey lifted her head that he knew he'd been busted.

Only then did he leave.

"RAFE SHARPE! GET YOUR BUTT BACK HERE!" Bailey leaped out of Holt's arms and headed for the stairs, pushing against the resistance of the water, attempting to get out before Rafe could disappear completely.

Not that she knew what she would do if she did. She was naked, so she couldn't very well go running after him.

His truck engine sounded as she grabbed the towel to cover her nakedness. A second later, she heard it fade in the distance.

"I can't believe he did that again," she muttered, wrapping herself up tight and tucking the corner in to keep the towel in place. "It's a violation of privacy to watch someone while … while…"

"Bailey?"

She spun around to face Holt and snapped, "What?"

"Do you want to go after him?"

Guilt hit her like a two-ton hammer when she realized she'd bolted out of Holt's arms to go after Rafe.

"I … uh…" She brushed her wet hair back from her face.

"It's okay if you do." He came out of the water, all muscled and beautiful, looking like a god. Plus, he didn't seem to care that he was naked and anyone could see him.

Oh, God. She had yelled.

Her gaze shot up to the second floor, hoping she wouldn't see any additional lights on. She held her breath for a few seconds, waiting. Did that curtain just move? Was someone standing in the dark watching them? Had she woken them up? She exhaled heavily when no one appeared.

Holt's hand brushed her arm, and she spun around. "No," she said quickly. "I…" She backtracked. "Actually, yes," she said haughtily. "I do want to talk to him about this. He has no right to come over here and watch us."

Holt wrapped a towel around his hips and moved closer. "I don't know where he lives, but I'll drive you."

She waved a hand. "Over the bookstore. That's where his apartment is."

Suddenly, the adrenaline faded, and she didn't feel like talking to Rafe. She couldn't confront him about this until she'd had a chance to calm down. The last thing she wanted was to make assumptions about anything. Maybe he had a good reason for being here. Maybe it was an accident.

Twice? Sure it was.

"You know what?" She looked up at Holt. "I think I'm gonna go to bed."

"You sure?"

Bailey nodded.

"Okay. Want company?"

Although she felt guilty saying no, she did. "I think I need some time to think."

"Of course." He leaned down and kissed her.

Bailey kissed him back, leaning in and getting lost in his warmth again. She wished that Rafe would stop interfering because what she had with Holt was a good thing. A really good thing.

So why does it hurt so much that you can't have Rafe?

That was the question she intended to ponder. Alone.

"Sweet dreams, little rabbit."

"Good night," she said before grabbing her clothes and heading up the private stairs to her apartment.

Once inside, she tossed her clothes into the laundry hamper and grabbed her phone off the counter. She pulled up Rafe's number but rather than send a text, she called him.

"Why are you watching me?" she asked as soon as he answered.

"I'm not," he said, his tone clipped. "Not on purpose."

Her anger flared hot and bright. "Do you like seeing me with Holt? You like watching him make me come? Is that it?"

Rafe didn't answer, and Bailey felt childish and mean. Not to mention stupid. She knew the answer already. Rafe had never wanted her the way she wanted him. Throwing Holt in his face was the act of a bitter, desperate woman.

"I'm sorry. I shouldn't have said that." She took a deep breath.

"I came by to talk to you, Bailey."

He sounded sad, and it ripped at her heart. "You did?"

"Yeah. I miss you, that's all."

Her heart squeezed painfully tight in her chest. "I miss you, too, Rafe."

"Bailey…"

She held her breath, waiting for him to keep going. When he didn't, she realized that was Rafe's M.O. Pretending like he was going to give her a glimpse into his heart only to yank it away with non-answers or deafening silence. He wasn't going to open up to her. No matter how much she wished he would, Rafe wasn't going to use the sweet words that Holt used because that wasn't who he was.

With a heavy exhale, Bailey let the last shred of hope fade. "Good night, Rafe."

She didn't wait for a reply before disconnecting the call.

Rafe

Despite her best efforts, the tears began to fall, and she realized just how much she'd been holding out hope that Rafe would one day come around.

Chapter Fifteen

Wednesday, August 17, 2022

HOLT WAS SITTING IN THE BAKERY THE following day when Rafe appeared on the small porch in front of the bookstore.

Now that Holt knew the man lived in the apartment above it, it explained where he'd disappeared to that day. And it explained why Violet Anderson had been so protective of the man. He was her tenant, and she was protecting his privacy. Or maybe they were roommates. Could be either, but based on what Holt knew about Rafe, the man couldn't live with anyone. Hell, it was an act of God to get him to sleep in the same bed. Even though he'd managed that one time, Rafe had disappeared at some point, so Holt couldn't say whether Rafe had fallen asleep at all.

His thoughts drifted back to last night when Rafe had been standing on the porch watching him and Bailey. Holt had known he was there. Not at first, but he'd heard something and looked around, wanting to shield Bailey if necessary. The light over the metal building had come on, shining on a figure near the bushes. He hadn't been able to make out a face, but the cap had given Rafe away.

Rafe

Holt had expected Rafe to come storming back there, demanding Holt stay away from her. He knew the man wasn't thrilled that Holt was with her. He'd said as much. But Holt didn't think it had as much to do with Rafe trusting him not to hurt her as it was with Rafe being jealous. The burning question was whether Rafe was jealous of him or Bailey. Or both.

Good news was, there was a chance Holt was about to find out.

Rafe came toward the bakery, adjusting the cap on his head as he opened the door. He scanned the room, and Holt noticed the way Rafe's shoulders squared the moment he saw him.

"Good morning, Rafe," Ramona chirped. "What can I get you this morning?"

"Coffee."

"Comin' right up."

Holt watched as Rafe moved toward the register. He admired all the hard, sharp angles of the man's body, the smooth, rippling muscle. Rafe was tall and thin; every ounce of him comprised of tensile strength and admirable flexibility. That flexibility had worked in Holt's favor three years ago.

"I'll fuck you anywhere in this house, even on the balcony, but I'm not fucking you in this shower," Holt said, his mouth moving against Rafe's. "Not enough traction."

Rafe pulled back, and a wicked grin tugged at his mouth. Holt loved it when the man smiled, probably because it was such a rare occurrence.

Holt was the one grinning when Rafe turned and strolled out of the shower, soaking wet, his high, tight ass beckoning Holt to follow.

He had enough sense to turn off the water before strolling out of the bathroom after Rafe. He didn't bother with a towel, but he took a moment to grab a strip of condoms out of the drawer. He carried them into the bedroom, stroking his cock with his other hand.

Rafe was on the bed, his head propped on a pillow, his cock in his fist, eyes heated as they tracked Holt through the room. He moved to the far side of the bed, pulling a bottle of lubricant out of the top drawer.

"Ready for anything, I see," Rafe muttered.

"It's been me and my hand all summer long, cowboy. Don't go making assumptions."

192

That earned him a smile, but Holt made it his mission to eliminate it. He didn't want Rafe smiling; he wanted the man moaning his fucking name. He got his wish a few minutes later when he kissed him into submission, folded his long, lean body nearly in half, and impaled him, ensuring they were eye to eye the entire time.

"God Almighty," Holt groaned, gritting his teeth as he sank into Rafe's hot, tight hole.

Rafe grunted, gripping the headboard with both hands, holding on while he stared up at Holt. He knew he wasn't imagining the pure, unfettered trust etched on Rafe's exquisite features. It wasn't natural for him, he suspected, but at this moment, Rafe wasn't scared of him. And that ... that took the encounter to a whole new level.

The memory faded as Holt watched Rafe pay for his coffee. Before Rafe could make a hasty exit, Holt decided to make his move.

"You ready to have that conversation yet, or would you prefer to hide in the shadows a little longer?"

Rafe paused with his hand on the door. He peered back at him, his eyes narrowed, then shocked him with a clipped, "Yes."

"To which one?" Holt taunted.

If Holt thought Rafe was going to be civil and sit down with him, he learned that he was wrong when Rafe walked out the door, not answering the second question.

It took a moment for him to clear his table, but he followed Rafe outside. He found him leaning against the wall in front of the bookstore, sipping his coffee.

"Bailey called me last night," Rafe said as Holt approached.

That didn't surprise Holt. He knew they had to figure things out in their own way. And though Holt wished they would open up to him about it, he understood.

"When you hightailed it, I offered to take her to your apartment so the two of you could talk," Holt explained.

Rafe's eyes narrowed. "You haven't told her."

It wasn't a question. It was an accusation. One Holt took offense to.

"About what? Us?"

"There is—"

"No us. Yes, I know. You've told me as much." Holt leaned his shoulder against the post holding up the roof and feigned a casualness he certainly didn't feel. "And no, I haven't told her."

"Why?"

"Why would I? Does it matter anymore?"

Rafe pushed off the wall and stepped closer, body drawn up tight. "It matters because it's not a coincidence that you're here."

"You're right. It's not."

"But you're gonna let her think that it is."

Holt studied Rafe for a moment. "Why do you care?"

"I don't."

"The fuck you don't," he hissed, shedding the casualness as he stood tall.

"I don't," Rafe repeated. "Not about you. I care about her."

"And you don't think I do?" Holt stepped forward until they were nearly toe to toe. "This isn't a game for me. She's not a conquest. I care about her."

Rafe pulled back as though Holt had slapped him.

"Does that bother you? That I have feelings for her?"

Rafe didn't answer, but Holt could see it in his eyes. Something bothered him.

"I know how she feels about you, Rafe."

That glimmer of emotion vanished with Rafe's excuse. "We're friends. That's all."

"Bullshit." Holt wasn't buying that for a second. "She *loves* you."

"And what? You think you're tryin' to play matchmaker by…"

"By fucking her?"

Rafe grabbed his shirt and jerked. "Don't you dare disrespect her."

"Never," Holt bit out, leaning into Rafe rather than pulling away. "I happen to love her, too."

Rafe's eyes went wide. "What?"

"You heard me."

If Holt wasn't mistaken, that admission had hit Rafe like a gut punch.

Holt leaned in and lowered his voice. "But it doesn't change how either of us feels about you."

"Don't pretend you have feelings for me. If you did…"

"If I did, *what?* I would've come after you?" Holt had suspected that was Rafe's problem with him. It wasn't that he'd shown up after all this time. It was that he hadn't come sooner.

"Fuck you."

Holt kept his voice even, civil. "I want you, Rafe. I have since the day I met you. What we had … that doesn't happen every fucking day. But you're the one who walked away. Not me."

Rafe swallowed, his eyes bouncing over Holt's face.

"But I came after you. It took me a while because I needed to be right in the head before I did."

"You think you're right in the head now?"

Holt nodded. "I know I am."

"Is that why you're datin' her? Because you've got it all figured out?"

That was a damn good question. Holt didn't know how to explain Bailey because she was unexpected. And he wasn't lying when he said he loved her. He hadn't meant for it to happen, and he damn sure hadn't anticipated it, but it was true. He'd fallen in love with her in a matter of days. And now he had a decision to make. They all did.

"Are you gonna tell her about us?" Rafe asked.

"I thought there *was no us,*" he countered, mocking Rafe.

Rafe didn't respond, but Holt hadn't expected him to.

"I guess that depends."

"On?"

"Whether or not it matters anymore." Holt put his hand on Rafe's hip.

They stood there, staring at one another for several heartbeats. When Rafe didn't immediately shove him away, Holt knew that it did matter. He wasn't the only one who'd been emotionally altered that night. He couldn't pinpoint what had happened, but their time together had changed him. Meeting Rafe had changed him.

"Tell me it matters," Holt insisted, leaning in until they were practically breathing same air.

Rafe grunted, but he didn't pull away.

"Tell me."

"Fuck you," Rafe hissed right before he kissed Holt.

Rafe

The shock of his mouth had Holt tightening his hold on Rafe's hip. He held him there as his lips parted and their tongues thrashed. He groaned, and every fiber of his being came to life with memories of that night. Unfortunately, it was over as quickly as it started.

"No matter what I feel for you," Rafe said softly, "what I feel for her is ten times stronger."

"Ten's a big number," Holt said, breaking some of the tension.

"Yeah, well. You've met Bailey Weber."

Yes, he had. Which was why he fully understood.

"HEY, MOM," BAILEY GREETED, PUTTING HER PHONE on speaker so she could finish wiping down the tables and chairs in the dining room. "I can't talk long. I'm doing chores."

"I thought you said you were hiring someone for that."

"I'm interviewing people for the position," she corrected. "Rex would like to keep the hire local, and I agree, so I'm doing what I can until I find someone here or the perfect out-of-towner comes along. What's up?"

"So ... um ... I thought you said you were dating Holt. You know, the writer who's staying there."

Bailey grinned. "Yes, Mom. I know who Holt is." Relaying the details of her love life to her mom didn't thrill her, so she kept it simple. "And yes, we've gone on a few dates. Why?"

"Well, honey..." Her mother took a deep breath.

Bailey picked up the three-tiered tray she used for food in the mornings and carried it and the phone to the kitchen. It was clean, but she wanted to polish it now that she had a few minutes to do so. She set the phone on the counter and grabbed the silver polish and a rag.

"What, Mom? Don't tell me you're jealous. I mean, Holt is a catch and all." Bailey chuckled. "But he's—"

"Honey, I just saw Rafe and Holt outside Shelf Help."

Some of her amusement faded, but she responded without a hitch. "Yeah. And? They're friends."

"What kind of friends?"

Bailey put down the tray and picked up her phone. "Why do you ask it like that?"

"Well, because…"

"Because they were kissing!" Shelly shouted from somewhere in the background.

"What now?" Surely she'd misunderstood.

"It's true," her mother said, her tone dripping with sympathy. "They were outside talking, and it looked like it was getting heated. I thought for a minute Rafe was gonna throw a punch, and then…"

"Kablam! They were kissing!" Shelly shouted again.

Thank God Rex chose that moment to come in through the back door.

"Hey, Mom. Rex is here. I need to go. I'll call you back." She disconnected the call and tossed her phone on the counter before leaning back and gripping the edge, dragging deep breaths into her lungs, willing the tension in her chest to ease.

"You know you don't have to get off the phone when I come in," Rex said with a chuckle. "You live and work here, so…"

He trailed off, and Bailey was grateful. Holding a conversation right now was a lofty goal. One she doubted she could achieve. As it was, she was doing everything she could to keep herself together.

"Hey." Rex tapped her shoulder. "What's wrong?"

She took a deep breath and looked up at her boss. "Rafe was kissing Holt."

Rex took a step back and frowned. "What?"

Bailey nodded. "That was my mom. She saw them."

"She *saw* them?"

"With her own two eyes."

God, this was weird. Not at all the type of conversation she expected to have with her boss, but who better than Rafe's brother to talk to about it, right?

Rafe kissing Holt.

Holt kissing Rafe.

Her stomach twisted, and she thought for a moment she was going to be sick.

"Hey. You need to sit down." Rex took her arm and dragged her into the dining room before urging her into a chair. "I'm sure there's a perfectly good explanation for all of this."

Bailey's eyebrows flew up to her hairline as she regarded him with disbelief. "Seriously? There's just a simple explanation for why people *saw* Rafe and Holt kissing? I get it, Rex. I'm naive and all that but *come on now.*"

She didn't mean to sound hysterical, but she couldn't help it. The two men she happened to have feelings for were … kissing each other!

She figured that was one way to figure out the history they shared. The history they'd been hiding all this time.

An idiot! That's what she was. A freaking idiot!

"How did I not see it? How did—" She gulped air, trying to avoid a nervous breakdown, but seriously! "How do I fall in love with two men who are … are…"

"Bailey, I know this sounds cheesy, but you need to give them a chance to explain."

The hysteria kept bubbling up, pitching her voice higher. "Explain what? That I've been … like, their *beard* or something?" She gasped. "Oh, my God. That's what it is. I'm Holt's beard."

Rex barked a laugh. "I'm pretty sure it doesn't work that way."

She frowned. Her tone cooled as confusion set in. "Really? I thought that was what a beard was. Someone you used to conceal your sexual orientation."

"Well." Rex scrunched his nose and tilted his head from side to side. "In a sense, sure. But a gay man doesn't have … you know…"

"What?" Bailey squared her shoulders and gave him her full attention. "Have what, Rex? Tell it to me straight. I can handle it. A gay man doesn't have *what*?"

She might've pitched that last word a little too high.

It was obviously uncomfortable for him, but Bailey wanted to know. No, she *needed* to know. Had all of this been pretend? Had Holt used her to conceal the fact he was gay and he was with Rafe? Why her? Why would he lead her on like that? Was that why Rafe hadn't responded when she called him out for being a peeping Tom?

Oh, Jesus. She clutched her chest. She had accused him of watching her with Holt, but maybe it was the other way around. Perhaps he'd been watching Holt the whole time! Why hadn't she thought of that?

"How is this happening?" she groaned. "How can I be so stupid?"

"What's goin' on here?"

Bailey shifted in her chair and looked over to see Jack walking toward them.

Before Rex could speak, Bailey said, "Rex is explaining why I'm Holt's beard."

"No." Rex shook his head dramatically. "No, no. That is *not* what I'm explaining."

Jack frowned. "A beard? As in…?"

Bailey filled in for him. "You know, someone you pretend to be in a relationship with to conceal your sexual orientation."

Jack looked at Rex.

Rex shook his head. "She's not a beard."

"Who's the gay man in question?" Jack asked.

"Holt and Rafe," Bailey blurted. "Whoops. I think that's supposed to be a secret." She pointed at herself with both thumbs. "Beard. Coverer of secrets." She frowned. "Is that a word? Covererer … er?"

Ignoring her verbal vomit, Jack's eyebrows rose. "Holt? Like the author guy? And Rafe?" He looked at Rex. "Your…"

"Brother, yes." Rex sighed and looked at Bailey. "You need to talk to them."

"I'm a beard," she murmured, dropping her head into her hands. She wasn't sure whether she was about to burst into tears or laugh until she cried. How in the world could this happen to her?

"She's not a beard," she heard Rex tell Jack.

"I agree."

"Why?" She looked up. "Why's it so hard to believe? I'm good enough to be a beard. I mean, look, you didn't even know Rafe was gay, did you? It worked. I'm obviously good at it."

Oh, geez. And now she was promoting the idea? What was *wrong* with her?

"You're. Not. A. Beard," Rex said sternly, enunciating each word clearly.

Bailey threw her arms in the air, letting them fall in her lap. "We'll have to agree to disagree. I think I am."

"You're not," Jack chimed in.

She glanced between them. "Why not?"

"Well, for starters, gay men don't have sex with women."

"Pfft." Bailey felt her cheeks warm. "No one said anything about sex. What makes you think *that* happened?"

Rex cleared his throat, but Jack was the one who said, "You remember all those cameras we pointed out when you first started working here?"

Bailey felt every ounce of blood drain from her face as she stared at her bosses. "Oh. My. God."

"It's recorded for all time," Jack said. "You and Holt by the pool."

"We didn't watch," Rex clarified. "Het sex isn't our thing."

"Oh. My. God."

"Technically, they didn't actually *have* sex," Jack noted. "Just—"

Rex slapped his hand over Jack's mouth and shook his head. "No."

At that moment, the front door opened. Bailey tried to compose herself so she could greet their guest professionally, but then she heard Holt's voice.

"What's going on?"

"Uh…" Jack said.

"We were just leavin'," Rex added, shoving Jack toward the door. "Now, Jack."

"But." Jack looked back at her, his bottom lip protruding in a pout.

Bailey managed to get to her feet. She took a deep breath and squared her shoulders. Rex was right. She needed to talk to them about this. Surely it was a mistake. Her mother and Shelly must've seen two other men kissing outside Shelf Help. Not … not…

Holt approached, so handsome and charming and sexy. And so … gay.

"Are you okay?"

She said, "Yes," even as she shook her head.

Holt shifted, attempting to get her to look at him, but Bailey diverted her eyes each time he did. She couldn't look at him. If she did, there was a good chance those tears were going to burst free.

"Talk to me, little rabbit."

His use of the nickname he'd given her made her guts twist and her heart pinch. It also gave her the strength to confront him face to face. "Don't you mean, little *beard?*"

Holt's forehead creased, his eyebrows angling down. "What?"

She pulled every ounce of strength from her spirit, squared her shoulders, and tilted her chin, facing off with him directly. "My mom just called. You know, the woman who owns the bakery."

He smiled. Just a small one. "I know who your mother is, Bailey."

"The bakery that's perpendicular to Shelf Help?"

Holt appeared even more confused.

"The bakery with a direct line of sight to two men standin' in front of the bookstore. Kissing."

"Shit," Holt muttered and thrust his hand through his hair.

She had to give him credit. At least he didn't deny it.

"Why?" she asked, hating that her sinuses burned with the threat of tears. "Why would you make me have feelings for you if you're...you know? I mean, it explains why Rafe never... He didn't want to break my heart, so he..." Her eyes widened as it all clicked into place. "It makes perfect sense now. Oh, my God. That's why he never pursued me. Because he's gay."

"Rafe's not gay, Bailey."

She stopped and stared at Holt. "You understood the part where I said my mother saw you and Rafe kissin', right?"

His expression was somber. "He's not gay. I'm not gay."

"Then what? You're...?" She leaned forward, angling her chin and raising her eyebrow, waiting for him to fill in the blank. "I need you to tell me, Holt."

Her bravado failed her, and the first tear fell, adding to her shame and anguish.

Her voice was a harsh whisper when she said, "Tell me so I can understand what the fuck is goin' on."

If he answered, Bailey didn't hear him because the tears began to fall, and they didn't stop. He pulled her into his arms and held her against him, palming her head in an embrace that made her feel treasured and even more confused.

"How can I be in love with two men who love each other?" she sobbed, realizing he probably didn't understand a word she said because it came out in a jumbled mess.

Holt pulled back, pinching her chin and urging her to look up at him. She didn't want to, but she met his gaze.

His voice was pitched low, his tone serious. "Because those two men happen to be in love with you, too."

"*What?*" she croaked, positive she did not just hear what she thought she just heard.

"HEY. WHAT'S UP?" RAFE ANSWERED WHEN HIS brother called.

It was rare for Rex to call. Most of their conversations were via text, so he figured this was either important or urgent or both.

"You … um … might wanna come by and talk to Bailey."

"Is she okay?"

"Well…" His brother trailed off, but Rafe could hear him breathing.

"Rex, if you don't start talkin' right—"

"Her mother saw you kiss Holt, and now Bailey thinks she's your beard."

"My *what* now?" Rafe frowned. "I don't even know what that means."

"And I don't have time to explain it. I only know that Bailey's freakin' out because she thinks Holt used her because he's tryin' to hide his feelings for you. It's a mess."

It was Rafe's turn to be silent because he wasn't sure what to say. And he knew his brother was likely trying to figure out whether Rafe was in a secret romance with Holt Callahan. If he had to guess, that was exactly why Rex had called rather than texted.

Nosy fucker.

"It's not what you think," he told Rex, hoping that would appease him.

It didn't.

"And what do I think, Rafe? That I've watched my brother pine for the same woman for nearly three years now, and then suddenly this hot writer appears out of nowhere and suddenly claims to know you, and suddenly, you're gay!"

Jack's voice sounded. "You think the writer's hot?"

Never mind that Rex had used suddenly three times in the same sentence.

"I'm not gay," Rafe clarified.

"So you're straight?"

"I didn't say that either."

"You really think he's hot?" Jack repeated.

Rex ignored him. "And exactly how long has this been goin' on?"

Rafe barked a laugh because this conversation was absurd.

"Shit. I'm sorry," Rex said quickly. "It's none of my business. Your sexual orientation, anyway. I don't care. You know that."

He did know that.

"But Bailey is my business, and I don't like to see her cry."

"She's cryin'?" Rafe stood up, preparing to storm the farmhouse to check on her.

"Kinda. Maybe. I don't know. She's freaked out. And upset. Clearly. I think she's got feelings for…"

"Holt," Rafe noted. "It's all right. I already know."

"Do you?"

Rafe shrugged, knowing his brother couldn't see him.

He didn't know anything except that he needed to talk to Bailey. He needed to explain and tell her this wasn't Holt's fault. Rafe truly believed he would never do anything to hurt her. After all, Rafe was the one who kissed Holt, not the other way around. So technically, the man she'd been dating hadn't cheated on her. Well, besides the fact he kissed Rafe back, but—

"Talk to her, Rafe."

"I will."

"I mean it."

"I *will*."

"Okay."

Rafe disconnected the call and dropped back down into his recliner, trying to process what the fuck just happened.

Chapter Sixteen

HOLT WOULD ADMIT BAILEY HAD MADE HIM feel a lot of things. Things he'd never felt before. He figured that had something to do with the fact he'd been falling in love with her from the moment they met.

But the most potent thing she'd made him feel was fear.

Fear of losing her.

When he returned to the house to the sound of her raised voice, he'd come in expecting to find Bailey and Rex in some sort of heated argument over something simple and mundane, like why there were five biscuits in a small can and not four. Or whether there were more red loops in a box of *Fruit Loops*. He'd overheard Bailey having those exact conversations—one with Rex (biscuits) and the other with Jack (loops).

But they weren't having a crazy debate over food.

What he found wasn't an argument.

Nor was it in the least bit simple.

Now, as he sat on the living room couch near her, he tried to come up with a way to explain so she might understand and he wouldn't risk losing her forever.

"For a man who writes, you're not comin' up with many words," Bailey said softly.

She sounded sad. Beat down, almost.

The good news was the tears had dried up. She was now clutching a tissue in one hand and a roll of toilet paper (the first thing Holt had found of the tissue variety) in the other.

But she was right. He could fill pages with words when channeling the emotions of fictional characters, but when it came to speaking from the heart, he had absolutely no experience.

He rested his elbows on his knees and wrung his hands together, trying to come up with the words that would make everything all right.

Bailey spoke first. "Do you love him?"

Because he didn't want to lie to her, Holt nodded as he explained. "I haven't seen Rafe in nearly three years."

Bailey wagged a finger at him. "Is this the back burner story that I previously asked about?"

Feeling guilty for not telling her about it, Holt dropped his head and said, "Yeah."

"When was the last time you saw him? At the beach while you were workin' on your project?"

Holt lifted his head. "Yes. We spent a lot of time together for those couple of months, but nothing happened between us until … well, until the last day he was there."

"What happened?"

Holt forced himself to look at her. "I wish you'd ask him to tell you."

"Oh, I plan to." Bailey shifted so her knee was on the cushion, and she faced him directly. "But Rafe's not the one who led me on."

"I didn't lead you on, Bailey. I *am* in love with you."

"How does that work if you're gay?"

"Bisexual," he corrected. "Not gay. Not straight. I've always been attracted to *people*. It hasn't mattered whether they were one gender or another."

"Oh." Her lips pursed. "That does make more sense. But it doesn't explain what you expect out of all this. Did you think you could be with me *and* Rafe?"

Holt wanted to tell her he wasn't the one who had kissed Rafe, but it felt like a betrayal to blame the man when he wasn't there to defend himself. And he had kissed Rafe back, so that negated his innocence.

Bailey's eyebrows rose slowly. "Is that why you don't care that I have feelings for Rafe? Because that would benefit you?" She shook her head. "Oh, God. And that's why you thought it was okay that I've been fantasizin' about the two of you."

"What?" Holt sat up straight. "You fantasized about both of us?"

Based on her expression, she didn't realize that was something she hadn't shared with him yet.

"More like fantasies when I'm asleep," she muttered.

"Dreams?"

She chewed on her lower lip for a moment. "It doesn't matter. You were turned on when you thought he was watchin'."

"If I recall, you're the one who said *you* were turned on."

Bailey shrugged.

"But yes, I was turned on. More so by you than anything else, but the idea of it was ... I might have a penchant for exhibitionism, so thinking Rafe might be watching ... sure, it was hot."

Bailey's cheeks turned rosy, which seemed her default when the topic was sex-related.

"But I had no idea you fantasized about both of us." He inched closer. "At the same time?"

"Maybe." Her gaze dropped to her hands. "But that's not the point."

No, it wasn't. At least not right now. It would definitely be something they revisited later.

"Do me a favor, Bailey?"

"Hmm."

He tipped her chin up, needing her to meet his gaze. Her eyes were closed, but she finally opened them.

"I want you to talk to Rafe. Let him tell you his feelings on the matter. I honestly have no idea where we go from here, but I know one thing for certain, I don't want this to end. What you and I have ... it's real."

"Is it?"

"For me, it's as real as it gets."

"But I thought you were leavin'."

"When I came here, I didn't know what I was doing. Then I met you, and I knew I wasn't going anywhere. Now it's a matter of finding a place to live so I can put down roots. With you."

"And Rafe," she tacked on.

He opened his mouth, but he wasn't sure how to respond to that.

"Are you hopin' for that?" Bailey asked. "For the three of us…"

"Honestly, I don't know, but none of that matters until you talk to Rafe. You might not believe it, but he's in love with you. He told me himself. Told me that what he feels for you is ten times stronger than anything he feels for me."

"He said that?"

Holt didn't miss the wistfulness in her tone.

"He did. And the two of you need to get on equal ground before we can move forward."

"Okay."

Holt tilted her chin up as he leaned in and pressed his lips to hers. "No matter what, remember that what we have is real."

"I know."

"Do you?"

She nodded, her lips brushing over his. "Yeah. It's confusing, but it's real."

For the first time since he walked in, Holt took a deep breath.

He wouldn't deny his heart pinched just a little when Bailey walked out the front door a short while later. He had no idea what would happen between her and Rafe, but he hoped there'd be room for him in their lives when the dust settled. And he wasn't referring to being relegated to the sideline.

AFTER THE THIRD TEXT RAFE SENT TO Bailey went unanswered, he knew he would have to call her.

Problem with that was he didn't know what he was supposed to say. How did he explain to the woman he'd been pining for— as his brother had pointed out—that, yes, he had kissed a man?

Not just any man. One he'd once been intimate with before.

One who had come to Coyote Ridge for him.

One who was currently dating the woman Rafe was in love with?

How? How did you explain that?

Rafe

He had fucked this to hell and back.

Taking a deep breath, Rafe picked up his phone and tapped the screen. Before he could pull up Bailey's number, there was a knock on his door.

Perfect. A reason to procrastinate. Just what he needed.

The only person who ever came to his apartment was Violet, and that was generally when she needed his help with something in the bookstore. Something told him Violet didn't need his help, and she wasn't waiting on the other side of that door.

Which meant he had a fifty/fifty chance of guessing who was out there.

He glanced around to ensure the place was decent enough for a guest. There wasn't much he could mess up, and as long as no one went into his bedroom, they wouldn't know that he didn't bother to make his bed.

The knock sounded again.

"I'm comin'," he grumbled, unlocking the deadbolt.

He swung the door open, expecting to see Holt but found Bailey standing there instead.

Rafe swallowed hard and reminded himself to breathe.

"Can we talk?"

Was it possible? Yes. Could he at the moment? Probably not.

Figuring she didn't want to hear his excuses, Rafe nodded and stepped back from the door, allowing her to enter. She was only the fourth person to have ever been there. Violet being the first. Rex and Jack being the second and third.

"Not a carnival on a fall night, but it's nice," she said as she scanned the space.

"What?"

Bailey turned to look at him. "Nothing."

She looked good. She was wearing one of his favorite outfits, the white halter top that crisscrossed over her chest and tied behind her neck and across her lower back, leaving her tanned shoulders and back mostly bare, and a pair of frayed-edge jean shorts with the little jeweled flip-flops.

"I have one question to ask you."

Rafe stood before her, his chest constricting as he waited patiently.

"Are you gay?"

He didn't hesitate. "No."

Well, words were forming. That was a good sign.

"Are you sure?"

"That's two questions."

Her eyebrow twitched.

"Yes." He exhaled. "I'm sure."

"It's okay if you are," she stated. "I won't judge. I just—"

Rather than let her ramble, as she was prone to do, Rafe closed the gap between them, cupped her face in his hands, and sealed his mouth to hers.

Bailey gasped, her soft hands curling around his biceps as she parted her lips and allowed him entrance. He kissed her the way he'd wanted to kiss her for the past three years. He cradled the back of her head, tilted his, and deepened the kiss, lazily dragging his tongue against hers.

She tasted exactly as he'd imagined, like the orange gum she liked to chew. Only better. Sweeter.

He finally pulled back, forcing himself to release her.

"Is that proof enough for you?"

She touched her lips with her fingertips and nodded. A second later, her wonder faded, and she planted her hands on her hips. "If you're not gay, why didn't you want me?"

And *that* was the Bailey he knew and loved. Always ready to call a man to the carpet.

"I did, Bailey. I *do*."

"You have a funny way of showin' it." Her eyebrows pinched together. "Surely you knew how much I wanted you."

He noticed she used the past tense.

Before he could respond, she kept going. "When's the last time you saw Holt? I mean, before he came to Coyote Ridge?"

"Almost three years ago."

"At his condo on the beach?"

Rafe held her stare but didn't respond.

"Were you hopin' he would come here? After what happened between you back then?"

Realizing Holt had told her about their history, Rafe backed up a step and turned away. He brushed his hair back and gripped the back of his head, feeling the tension building in his shoulders. "Whatever he said, Bailey, it was only one side."

"He didn't *say* anything. He told me I had to get the story from you because it wasn't his place."

That surprised him. He figured Holt would find a way to use all of this against Rafe. Although he wasn't sure what his end game could be.

"That's why we're in this mess in the first place, Rafe. Because Holt didn't want to overstep. And since you're about as close-lipped as … as…" She threw her hand up. "As whatever's the most close-lipped thing. My point is no one's sharin' anything with anyone." Her hand returned to her hip. "So tell me your side of it. That's why I'm here. To understand."

He pivoted. "Understand what? How I fit in? I don't. I never did, Bailey. That's the way it works. Yeah. I was with Holt, and it was … surprising. But that ended when I came back here. And now you're with him."

Bailey huffed. "You are an asshole; you know that? How can you turn this on me? I tried … God, I tried *so hard* to get your attention, but you made it clear you wanted to be my friend, so I accepted that. Then I was with Seth. I thought I could get over you if I were with someone. It didn't work. And no, not only because I still had feelings for you. It just didn't work. And when I tried to tell you that, you threw it in my face. Said you wouldn't be my fallback guy. *As if* I would *ever* think of you like that."

Her words came fast and heated, and Rafe felt like the asshole she accused him of being.

"That's not what I meant," he said, feeling defeated. "You're right. I kept you in the friend zone, but not because I didn't want you. I do. That's never changed. But, Jesus, Bailey, I know you're not blind. What the hell do I have to offer you?"

"I don't need you to offer me anything," she bit out. "I wanted you to *want me*, Rafe."

"I do want you, dammit. I have for years."

She stared at him as though he'd just admitted to skinning cats.

"You deserve better than me, Bailey. You deserve a man like Holt. He's good for you. He can give you things I can't."

Her eyes glittered, and he realized she was on the verge of tears. "I thought we were friends."

"We are."

"Then how did you not notice that I've never needed *things*, Rafe? I get by just fine. I just wanted you to love me."

He stepped toward her. "I do love you, Bailey."

Her throat tightened as she swallowed.

Rafe moved closer and lowered his voice. "I only want to protect you. Even if it's from the likes of me."

A tear slipped down her cheek when she smacked him in the chest. "I don't need to be protected from you."

"You hear what they say about me. It's true. And those comments and accusations are gonna follow me forever."

She smacked him again. "I don't care."

"You should because you'd be the woman who loves a murderer."

She smacked him again, but this time he grabbed her arm and pulled her against him. He stared down into her beautiful face.

"Problem is," he whispered. "I want to do the right thing, but I'm not sure I can anymore."

"Why not?"

"Because I love you, Bailey. I didn't realize how much I'd miss you until I didn't see you every day. Not hearin' your voice, your laughter … it's killin' me."

"It's killin' me, too." She wiped a tear away. "But what about Holt?"

"What about him?"

"He kissed you. Obviously, you're the reason he came here. He says he stayed for me, but clearly, he's still got a thing for you."

Rafe shook his head, releasing his grip on her arms. "He didn't kiss me. *I* kissed *him*. He wouldn't do that to you, Bailey."

"But you would?" With her hand free, she smacked him again, her voice raising to a high-pitched squeal. "You kissed him knowin/ that he's with me?"

"I reacted," he admitted.

She smacked him again. This time he backed up.

"It's not an excuse, and it doesn't make it okay."

She pursued him, smacking his chest again. "But it means"— *smack*—"you've got"—*smack*—"feelin's for him."

Maybe. Probably. Feelings he hadn't acknowledged until last night when he saw the two of them together. Rafe had spent most of the day trying to unravel the confusion. To figure out how he could possibly want both of them. He'd never understood it, although he knew it worked for some people. Since returning to Coyote Ridge, he'd watched those relationships grow, and he'd never understood how anyone could love two people at the same time.

It was possible, but that didn't mean it would work.

"I don't know what it means," he said honestly. "But the last thing I want is to come between the two of you."

Bailey rolled her eyes. "You've been between us since the day he got here. I just didn't know the extent of it."

"What does that mean?"

Her lips twitched one way; her eyes moved the other. "I … umm…"

Rafe waited, knowing she would get around to it eventually. Probably when her face was as red as a sunburn, but still.

"I might've"—her voice lowered to nearly imperceptible levels—"fantasized about you and him."

"Fantasized?" Rafe couldn't hide his grin.

"And I might've told him about it."

"Really?"

Bailey swatted his chest. "You don't get to find this funny, Rafe Sharpe. Nothin' about this is funny."

"No, it's not." He grabbed her arms to stop the slapping and pulled her into him. "But it is kinda hot."

"You might not think that if you know what the fantasy entails."

Rafe's cock jerked against his zipper. He'd been hard since she walked through the door, but he was attempting to handle this the right way.

"Tell me."

"I can't."

"Yes, you can," he said as he stepped closer.

She stepped back and shook her head.

"I wanna know."

Her eyes met his. "And I want you to kiss me again."

Surprised by her directness, Rafe hesitated for a second too long.

Bailey's expression fell, and she tried to sidestep him. Before she could escape, he grabbed her around the waist and pulled her against him, her back to his front.

"Don't think that was me denyin' you," he whispered against her ear, inhaling her sweet lavender scent as he pressed a kiss to her jaw.

When his lips trailed to her neck, Bailey stopped resisting, leaning into him.

He dragged kisses over her shoulder, then back to her neck, his hands flattening over her belly.

She cupped his head and held him, tilting her head to give him freedom to explore the smooth expanse of her beautiful neck.

"Are you sure you want to do this, Bailey?"

She nodded.

"What about Holt?"

"He knows where I am," she whispered.

Rafe didn't know how he felt about that, but he couldn't bring himself to care. Having her in his arms, the only thing he cared about was sating this ache that had been building for three long, painful years.

BAILEY KNEW THE GUILT WOULD COME AT some point, but it was too hard to focus when Rafe was touching her.

She'd wanted this for so long. She'd fantasized about him, his kiss. Not even her most incredible fantasies had come close to being as explosive as what she felt when he kissed her the first time. She'd felt that kiss deep in her soul.

And now, as his breath fanned her neck, her skin felt too small to contain her. Every part of her was on high alert, aching and eager to feel him.

The gentle tug on the tie at her neck had her holding her breath. When it released, her halter top fell, freeing her breasts. She gasped as cool air chilled her skin seconds before Rafe's hands cupped her, warming her instantly.

"I've dreamt about this," he whispered in her ear.

He was leaning forward, staring over her shoulder as he fondled her breasts. Bailey kept her arm back, her fingers linked in his hair as he tormented her, plucking her nipples until they felt diamond-hard.

Reaching back with her free hand, she tugged on the other tie. It came free, and her top fell to the floor.

Rafe's groan made her skin prickle, giving her the courage to unbutton her shorts. She shimmied them down her legs, kicking them away along with her flip-flops. She stood there, her back against his chest, wearing only her panties and in desperate need of his body against hers.

His arms fell away, and Bailey suddenly felt a chill. He dragged his fingertips down her arm as he moved around her. She wasn't sure what was happening, why he'd stopped, but she started to feel self-conscious when he stepped back, his gaze moving over her from neck to ankle and back.

"You're even more beautiful than I imagined." His voice was deeper than usual, sending ribbons of desire curling in her belly.

When she started to move toward him, Rafe shook his head. "Stay right there. Let me look at you for a minute."

Her nipples tightened, and her pussy clenched as his gaze raked over her. What seemed a good idea a moment ago now made her feel slightly embarrassed. Here she was, throwing herself at him again, and Rafe was still fully dressed, staring at her.

Bailey was just about to chicken out when Rafe finally stepped forward, his gaze lifting to her face.

"You're so fuckin' beautiful, Bailey," he rasped darkly.

His words sounded so sincere, almost as though a sense of wonder had pushed them past his lips.

"Christ Almighty," he whispered when he stopped directly in front of her. "I've thought about you for so long." His eyes lowered to her bare breasts. "About all the dirty things I wanna do with you."

Her breath shuddered in and out of her lungs, her hands trembling as desire slammed into her.

She wanted to say something, anything, but the words wouldn't come as she waited for him to touch her. The next thing she knew, her back was against the wall, and Rafe was kneeling before her. Their height difference was never as apparent as it was now when he was on his knees, his eyes level with her breasts.

"Spread your legs."

When she did, he cupped her breasts firmly, his forearms pressed against her hips.

"Oh, God," she moaned, grabbing for his head when his lips covered her nipple. "Rafe…"

A deep rumble sounded from his chest, and Bailey held on for dear life as he devoured her, his lips and tongue rasping against her nipple, sending her skyrocketing toward the edge of that cliff. Just a little more, and she would be hurdled right over into the abyss.

"Rafe … I'm gonna …" Her pussy clenched, her clit throbbed, and when he sucked her fully into his mouth, she detonated.

The orgasm came out of nowhere, unexpected because he wasn't touching her anywhere else. Only his mouth on her breasts. But it was enough to make her body quake and tremble.

"Oh, fuck, you're so sweet," he moaned, lifting his head and finding her mouth with his. "You drive me fuckin' crazy, Bailey. So fuckin' crazy."

Yeah. She knew the feeling. It was a desperate ache, a hunger so powerful, it depleted the senses, made you forget everything except sating the urge.

When she fumbled with the buttons on his shirt, wanting to get him naked, Rafe stopped her, nipping her lower lip.

"Not yet, darlin'. I'm not done yet."

"I need you, Rafe. I need to feel you inside me."

A feral growl sounded from him as he put his hand behind her knee and lifted her right leg, angling it outward. When he tugged her panties aside, Bailey flattened her palms on the wall to keep herself steady, watching as he leaned in and pressed a kiss beneath her belly button. He shifted, sinking lower until she felt his warm breath on her clit. Her body clenched, her muscles locked, and she tried to hold still even as she shook from the inside out. She stared down at him as his head dipped, and his tongue teased her clit lightly, then more firmly. He worked her like that until her head spun and her pussy squeezed painfully hard, desperate to be filled.

He paused for a moment, releasing her leg so he could pull her panties off. Then he was there, lifting her leg, opening her to his mouth once more. It was all she could do to remain standing, her other leg weakening as he brought her closer and closer to another orgasm.

Heat blasted through her when he fused his lips to her clit, suckling the sensitive nub until she was jerking and twitching, dangerously close to coming again. And when he pushed two fingers inside her, Bailey exploded.

When she screamed his name, the only thing that mattered was the brilliant heat that flooded her veins and the ecstasy that consumed her.

Chapter Seventeen

RAFE COULD HARDLY BREATHE FOR WANTING BAILEY.

His cock throbbed as he stood, yanking the button on his jeans free, jerking the zipper down. He wasted no time lifting her off her feet, using the wall to balance her weight before he slammed inside her.

"Oh, God!" she screamed as her legs wrapped around his hips. "Fuck me, Rafe! Fuck me. Please … don't stop."

Rafe fucked her.

Hard.

Right there against the wall. He probably should've carried her to his bed, eased her down gently. He couldn't. This need for her had multiplied tenfold every month, year after year. At this point, the only thing he wanted was the tight clasp of her cunt on his cock. She was so wet, so fucking hot.

"Rafe … yes…" She grunted with every driving thrust, her fingernails digging into his shoulders as she held herself still, accepting him deep inside.

Somewhere in the back of his mind, he knew he had forgotten something, but he couldn't bring himself to care.

"More," she hissed. "Harder, Rafe. Fuck me harder."

Those words coming out of sweet Bailey's mouth were like a drug. They heightened his senses, made him feel invincible. He slammed into her again and again, his cock tunneling deep, slick with her juices.

"Bailey … fuck, you feel good." Rafe held her gaze as he tried to gain some of his composure. He failed miserably, his hips pistoning forward, back. Over and over as his fingers dug into the flesh of her hips, holding her still so he could take his pleasure, giving as much in return.

She moaned and groaned, a husky sound that spurred him on. The way she chanted his name made his heart slam against his chest.

He rammed into her so hard that the picture on the wall rattled. He didn't care. Neither did she.

"I'm gonna come again," she said with a sharp breath as he impaled her. "Make me come, Rafe."

They were both out of control. The lust so powerful it bordered on pain.

He growled, urging her to come so he could do the same. While he wanted this to last all fucking day, there was no way to make that happen. He was more animal than man, and the only thing that mattered was bringing them both to orgasm.

When Bailey's pussy gripped him, Rafe groaned, trying to hold back a little longer because it felt so damn good. Her pussy milked him until he couldn't hold back, couldn't contain the pleasure that ripped through him.

Rafe thrust his hand in her hair, pulling her mouth to his as he filled her, coming hard and fast in a roar muffled by her sweet lips.

As they fought for air, Rafe managed to move, to get his legs sturdy beneath him as he carried her into his bedroom. A few steps and he had her on the bed, her soft, warm body under him, exactly where he wanted her to be.

"You okay?" he asked, lifting his head to peer into her eyes.

He was still inside her, his cock hard as stone even though he'd come once already.

"Better than okay," she answered on a shaky breath.

"Good. 'Cause I'm not done yet."

Her smile blinded him. "No?"

Rafe shook his head.

"You don't need a break?"

She was teasing him, and it warmed him from the inside out. No woman had ever teased him before.

"Not even close." He sucked air into his lungs as he shifted his weight, pushing his hips forward, burying himself as deep as he could.

Bailey reached up, pulled his head down until their mouths were centimeters apart. "Good. Let's do that again."

Rafe nodded, then kissed her hard and rough. He wanted to be gentle, but he couldn't. He would have to make sure to cuddle with her later. Right now, he had to fuck her, had to take her because he felt he would go insane if he didn't.

When Bailey began rocking her hips, trying to get him to move, Rafe pulled out, flipped her over. She squealed, then giggled as he jerked her hips back and thrust into her again.

"Ohhhh *fuck*, yesssss!" she hissed, her back bowing, her chest pressing against the mattress while her perfect ass stayed right where he wanted it.

Rafe drove forward, retreated, his hand sliding down the sweet curve of her spine toward her neck. He reversed, his fingers trailing back to those cute little dimples in her lower back, then between the crack of her ass. He massaged her ass, pulling her cheeks apart with his thumbs, watching as his cock slid into her cunt. Her asshole clenched tight when he pushed in deep, so he teased the little rosebud with his index finger. He wanted to fuck her there, to claim her in every way possible.

Not that he would. Not yet, anyway.

But that didn't mean he couldn't tease her.

"Rafe…oh … that feels…" Bailey rocked back against him when he added more pressure, the tip of his finger slipping inside.

"Tell me," he insisted, driving his cock into her welcoming pussy as he teased her asshole.

"It's … different."

"Hurt?"

"No."

"Want me to stop?'

"No."

This woman was going to be the death of him.

Rafe reached beneath her, slicking his thumb with her juices before teasing her again. This time he pressed his thumb into her ass, holding it there while he pumped his hips, fucking her hard and deep.

Bailey began meeting every thrust, rocking back against him, her pussy taking his cock, her asshole fucking his thumb. Just the sight of it made his breath falter for a moment. Rafe wasn't going to last any longer than he had the first time.

"Fuck me," he urged. "Fuck my cock, Bailey."

While she slammed back against him, Rafe held himself as still as possible. The sweet warmth of her pussy made his cock swell.

He remained like that as she took her pleasure from him, her moans growing louder until she cried out his name again. When her pussy tightened, squeezing him like a velvet vise, Rafe pulled his thumb from her ass, gripped her hips with both hands and drilled into her repeatedly until his cock exploded, his seed shooting deep inside her.

It was only then that he realized what he'd forgotten.

"SHIT," RAFE HISSED, LAUNCHING HIMSELF OFF THE bed.

Bailey stared after him, confused.

"I'm sorry, Bailey."

Oh, Jesus. No.

No, no, no. He did *not* get to do this. He did *not* get to have regrets after something as incredible as that.

Intending to give him a piece of her mind, Bailey started after him when he disappeared into the bathroom. It wasn't until she stood up and felt the warmth trickle down her thigh that she realized they hadn't used a condom.

She glanced at the bathroom door, down at herself.

It probably wasn't the sanest reaction to a situation like this, but Bailey grinned as she marched to the bathroom to get a towel.

"Rafe?"

"Be out in a minute."

"I'm comin' in," she warned before opening the door.

He was still naked, standing at the sink, his hands pressed down on the porcelain sides, his head hanging low.

She was about to blast him when she saw his back, the scars that marred his sleek golden skin. There was a large triangular-shaped one on his right shoulder blade and several small round ones scattered down his left side, a few more up near his neck.

Figuring now wasn't the time to ask where he got them, she stuck to her original plan to rip him a new one about his unwelcome apology.

"If you're in here because you regret what happened, I'm gonna kick your ass," she said, opening the small cabinet above the toilet in search of a washcloth.

He lifted his head and met her gaze in the mirror.

She smiled. "And if you're in here because you realized we didn't use a condom, you can stop freakin' out. I'm on birth control. And if you're worried about me, I always used condoms with Seth. Before him, I'd been tested at one of my routine appointments." She paused, then opted to add, "And Holt and I use condoms."

His eyebrows had hitched up an inch or so as though he was shocked by her revelation.

"Your turn."

Rafe took a deep breath, his chest rising, then falling slowly. "I haven't been with anyone in three years."

Bailey's jaw dropped open. "Seriously?"

A smile tugged at his beautiful mouth. "Seriously."

If that had been a question on a pop quiz, Bailey would've gotten the wrong answer. All these years, she'd thought he'd merely been good at being discreet.

"Does that have something to do—"

Rafe interrupted with, "Let me just put this out there. If you insist on standin' here naked, I *am* gonna fuck you again."

Bailey peered down at herself. She'd honestly forgotten she didn't have on clothes. Weird thing to forget at a time like this, but whatever.

"Noted," she said, taking her washcloth into the living room.

She hurried to clean herself up, then gathered her clothes and pulled them on while Rafe was still in the bathroom. When he didn't emerge immediately, she perched on the edge of the recliner and waited. She was beginning to wonder if he would remain in there all night when he finally emerged, his hair wet from obviously taking a shower.

"I have to get back to the B and B," she told him as she stood.

He came over to her and pulled her into his arms. "This isn't a one-time thing."

Bailey would admit she'd needed to hear that. She needed some sort of validation from Rafe that what they'd done had meant something to him.

"Technically, we did it twice," she informed him.

His smile reached all the way to his eyes, and she tried to recall if it ever had before.

"I know you've got some stuff to figure out, but what I said earlier was true."

Bailey pulled back. "What do you mean, I've got some stuff to figure out?"

"With Holt?"

"What about him?"

Rafe looked confused. "I figured you'd end things now that…"

"Now that what?" Bailey felt her ire rise. "Now that we've fucked."

The word tasted funny in her mouth, but that was what they'd done. They'd surrendered to the potent attraction and *fucked*.

Rafe shook his head. "I guess I'm confused, then. I don't know what it is you want from me."

Bailey stared at him, realizing she didn't know what she wanted either. She'd come over here to talk and ended up having sex with Rafe. Now she had to go back and talk to Holt, to tell him what happened. Where would they go from here? Any of them?

She honestly hadn't considered what the next steps were.

"I need to go," she blurted and started for the door.

"I'll take you."

"No. Thanks, but no."

"Bailey!" Rafe called after her as she rushed out of his apartment. She followed the narrow hall to the end of the building and hurried down the stairs.

She felt like an idiot. Not because she'd had sex with Rafe but because she'd had sex with Rafe knowing she wasn't willing to give Holt up. And maybe she'd done it partially because she figured Holt expected it. But now what? Were they gonna fuck and decide the fate of this … this … strange triangular threesome?

Exhaling heavily, she hurried across the street and through the park. She emerged on the other side, wondering if she smelled like sex. What if Holt decided he wanted nothing to do with her now? She wouldn't blame him because this could be construed as cheating, right?

Figuring the best thing would be to avoid potentially running into him, she raced around the side of the house and up the private stairs to her apartment. She didn't even reach the hallway when someone knocked on the front door.

Bailey came to an abrupt halt and stared at it. She knew it was Holt. He'd probably watched her as she came up the drive. It would've taken him the same amount of time to get up here as it did her.

Crap.

Another knock.

She took a deep breath and decided to be a grown-up about this. This wasn't her doing. They were the ones kissing in the middle of town, throwing her perfect world into chaos.

When she opened the door, she looked up into Holt's beautiful blue eyes, and a second later, she burst into tears.

BAILEY HAD BEEN AVOIDING HIM.

And though Holt accepted that something had likely happened between her and Rafe, he hadn't expected her to cry in his arms, but that was what she was doing now as he picked her up and closed the front door.

He carried her into the living room. "Talk to me, little rabbit."

Her sobs grew louder as she clutched his T-shirt in her fist.

"I'm sorry," she blubbered. "It just happened. I'm not sorry that it happened, but I'm sorry I did it to you. You don't deserve that."

Figuring there was only one way to end her rambling, Holt cupped her face and forced her to look at him. He applied gentle pressure to her cheeks to get her attention. Bailey's eyes opened, and she stared at him.

It was then he saw it. She was heartbroken.

The question was, why?

"Tell me what happened." He relaxed his grip and leaned back with her in his lap, her feet on the other cushion. He pulled her against him and wrapped his arm around her back to hold her. "But do it slowly."

Bailey rested her head on his chest. "I fucked Rafe."

Well, there was no way to hide the fact his cock thickened since it was pressed against her ass. Holt ignored it but wasn't sure how long that would be possible.

"Did you at least get to talk to him?"

"He told me he loved me. Then like the pathetic moron I am, I fell into his arms and—"

"You're not pathetic," he said gruffly. "And you're damn sure not a moron. You're human, Bailey. And you've been in love with him for years."

She sighed, her body relaxing against him. "Rafe thinks he has nothin' to offer anyone. That's why he kept me in the friend zone." She hiccuped. "Not because he's secretly gay. I'm not a beard after all."

He couldn't stop the smile. This woman.

Holt had already suspected that Rafe thought he was unworthy based on his conversations with him years ago. The man had lived a traumatic life and didn't understand the concept of unconditional love. Somewhere along the way, he'd convinced himself he had to be able to give more than he received to be worth something. And since he was convinced he had nothing to offer, he would forever be alone.

"I told him it's never been about *things*; I just wanted him to want me."

"And clearly he does."

Bailey nodded, her cheek rubbing his chest. "And I love him."

"I know you do."

She pulled back, her fingertip tapping his chin. He peered down at her.

"But I also love you."

It was the first time she'd said as much.

"Rafe thought I would end things with you because of what happened."

Holt figured that wasn't an illogical assumption. "And? Are you?"

Her arms moved around him, and she squeezed. "No."

"So you're ending things with Rafe?"

Her grip on him loosened when she pulled back. Gone was the sad, sobbing woman. In her place, one who thought men were stupid. "Why do both of you assume that's how this ends? It's like you've both forgotten that you were kissin' in the middle of downtown."

Bailey eased off his lap, and he reluctantly let her go.

She started to pace. A few steps that way, a few back. When she stopped, she planted her hands on her hips and glared at him. "I think you need to figure this out for yourselves."

"I'd say we do have some things to talk about. At the very least."

Her arms dropped to her sides, and her shoulders slumped. "Are you gonna ... you know ... whatever the two of you do together?"

"Fuck?" he supplied.

"Sure. Let's go with that." She brushed her hair back from her face. "Because it would only be fair. I cheated on you. You cheat on me."

Holt stood quickly, grabbing her and pulling her into him. He tilted her head back and stared down into her surprised face.

"First of all, you didn't cheat on me. I knew when I suggested you go over there that something might happen. I would've put up a fight if I was worried about it."

"So this is you bein' okay with me sleepin' with other guys?"

"Hell no." He leaned in closer and lowered his voice. "This is me being okay with you trying to figure things out with Rafe. Don't think for a second that I'll be okay with you fucking anyone else. It might not look like it, but I'm a possessive man, baby."

"Ditto," she chirped. "Woman, I mean. Not ... you know what I mean. I'm just not sure I'll be as okay with you and Rafe ... doin' stuff."

God, she was fucking adorable.

"Stuff?"

"Yeah. You know, sex stuff."

Holt chuckled.

"Don't laugh at me."

"Trust me, little rabbit. I'm not." He released his tight hold on her and pulled her in so he could hug her close. "I'm not saying anything'll happen but tell me what concerns you about me talking to Rafe privately."

"I just... Y'all have history, and I don't want y'all doin' stuff that might make you forget about me."

Now, *that* wasn't what he expected her to say at all.

He slid his hands down her back and cupped her ass. "What if you *are* there?"

Bailey's hands slipped under his shirt. "Are we doin' hypotheticals here? Like fantasies?"

"Sure. Let's call it that."

"Well, if I happened to be there, then I could just ... you know, keep an eye on you both. Then maybe I wouldn't feel left out."

"Are you saying you'd like to watch?"

She shrugged one shoulder.

Holt smiled and realized he wasn't the only one who'd given this serious consideration. Bailey might not know it yet, but she was directing the play to her advantage. And from his vantage point, Holt could only see it as a win-win-win.

But would Rafe see it that way? Or would he find a way to throw a wrench into the works before they even had a chance to see if this was something all three of them needed?

Chapter Eighteen

BAILEY WASN'T SURE WHAT PROMPTED HER TO tell Holt she wanted to watch.

Well, she kinda knew. It had more than a little to do with the fact both men in her life thought she was the one who would have to make the hard choice between the two of them. Why? Why did they immediately think she would choose *either* of them? Just thinking about it was infuriating. They were the ones who started all of this. All. Of. It.

Except for her intensely erotic dreams. She was certain they couldn't be blamed for that. Neither had even been aware she'd fantasized about having two sets of hands on her, two mouths, two impressive cocks…

Okay, she was getting carried away. That or someone had turned the air conditioner off because suddenly she was sweating.

However, they'd infuriated her enough with their assumptions that Bailey was determined to stick to her guns. If she couldn't have both of them, she wanted neither.

Not that she was willing to tell them that. No. Determination was one thing. Stupidity was another. She was in love with both of them, and an ultimatum like that could very well have her crying herself to sleep every night.

So, for now, she was going to play this cool. She would set the scene, and they'd see where things went from there. Who knows? Perhaps everything that happened had been building up to this.

Rafe

Although she knew it was a long shot, Bailey texted Rafe and asked him to come to her apartment. When his response came in, her heart sank.

> You know I can't go in that house. It's not that I don't want to. I can't.

> Technically, my apartment is connected to the house, but it was originally the attic. I'm hoping you don't have bad memories of the attic.

She waited patiently for the three dots to signal he was responding. When seven minutes passed, she texted him again.

> You don't have to go through the house to get up here. You can come in through the back stairs. I assure you it doesn't look anything like an attic.

Again, she waited.

"He's not comin'," she told Holt, who was sitting on the couch.

After their conversation earlier, Holt had given her a few minutes to gather herself. She'd taken a shower, pulled on clean clothes, then texted and asked him to come for dinner. That was after she texted Rex and told him she would need the night off to handle a few things but would still be in the house if something came up. He'd quickly responded, asking if she was okay and letting her know he would cover anything that might arise, but since their full house of guests seemed only to be needy first thing in the morning, Rex figured there'd be no issues with covering for her.

Clearly, he hadn't realized she was attempting to sway his brother to come over and venture through a house that gave him nightmares. If he had, the overprotective big brother might change his mind.

Rex was a great boss, and it bothered Bailey that she was dragging him into her drama, but it couldn't be helped at this point. This was her life, and at the moment, it was warped and twisted, so she felt the need to give it the attention it deserved. During her shower, she tried to imagine waking up tomorrow and not having Holt *or* Rafe around. The mere thought of it had been enough to set off the waterworks. It was true, she was in love with both of them, and if someone insisted she choose one over the other, there was no way around it, she would have to give up both.

What a horrible, *horrible* choice that would be.

Bailey continued to stare at her phone like that might make Rafe respond faster. She was still doing so when Holt came over to her.

"Tell you what. Why don't you call the diner and place an order? I'm sure you know what Rafe likes, and you can get me the chicken fried chicken. I'll swing by Rafe's apartment, drag his ass out of there, pick up the food, and be back before you know it."

She studied him. She wasn't an idiot. She knew it wouldn't be that simple, but in all fairness, he did deserve a chance to talk to Rafe without her hovering. It wasn't that she was worried that they'd have sex. If they did, they did. What worried her the most was that they would no longer want her. And yes, that made her selfish, but she couldn't help it. The heart wanted what it wanted. In this case, hers wanted to be the center of their world. She didn't care if they were together, but she didn't want to be left out.

And all this time, she'd wondered how in the world Kylie Walker could've ended up married to two men who happened to be in love with each other. It wasn't nearly as convoluted as she'd once thought.

Bailey took a deep breath. "Okay." She tucked her phone in her pocket and looked up at him. "But don't forget about me, please."

It sounded needy and clingy, but she didn't care. Bailey had never fought for what she wanted before, but this was far too important for her to be complacent. She didn't want to sit on the sidelines and wait for them to decide. She wanted to be an equal partner.

"If he happens to show up, just text me."

Bailey was sure he would see Rafe before that happened. Their paths would have to cross for them to trade places, but she nodded anyway.

"Order the food. I'll pay for it when I pick it up."

She nodded again.

Holt tapped her chin. "I love you, Bailey. That won't change in the next few minutes."

She forced a smile, hoping that was true.

IT HADN'T OCCURRED TO HOLT THAT RAFE hadn't come into the B and B once since he arrived nearly three weeks ago. Based on the brochure, the place was owned by both Sharpe brothers but managed by Rex and his husband, Jack. And Bailey, but she was a new hire, so the brochure was a bit out of date.

He didn't need to be a genius to know that Rafe's absence was related to the traumatic events that had taken place in the house. Not only the deaths of his mother and father but also the abuse Rafe had suffered. Not that Rafe had gone into great detail when he'd told Holt the story back when they'd first started hanging out, but he'd told him enough. And research had filled in a lot more of the blanks for Holt. He'd even seen pictures in archived articles of what the house had looked like previously, both inside and out. He had to admit Rex had done an impressive job converting it into an inviting space. If Holt hadn't known it was the same house, he would've been hard-pressed to tie them together.

Could a man really avoid something like that forever? Would it benefit Rafe to come inside and see that it didn't hold the ghosts of his past?

Holt wasn't a shrink, so he honestly didn't know. But he was a man who wanted to make the woman he loved happy, which was why he'd offered to find Rafe and drag him back if he had to.

Not that he would, but he wasn't above putting a guilt trip on the man. After all, Bailey was worth it, and he had no doubt that Rafe realized that.

Since Holt had seen Rafe come down the stairs at the end of the building, he figured that was the way to get to the apartment above. He learned he was right when he came to the second door on the second floor. The first had a sign that read: REAL ESTATE OFFICE. USE FRONT DOOR. The second door had the numerical address with the letter B.

He knocked on the door and took a step back, leaning against the iron railing that lined the top floor walkway. A moment later, the door opened. Rafe appeared briefly, then disappeared back into the apartment. Holt took that as an invitation to come in, so he did. Closing the door behind him, he scanned the space. It was nicer than he imagined it to be. For some reason, he'd pictured an overflow storage area with a cot in the middle where Rafe laid his head at night. But it was an actual apartment, complete with gray wood-plank flooring, light gray walls, and a few pictures that he was positive Rafe hadn't put up. Probably Rex since they were very similar to the decor at the B and B.

As for the furniture, it left a lot to be desired. Rafe obviously didn't have people over often because there weren't many options in seating, only a recliner in what served as the living room. The kitchen didn't appear large enough to cook a meal in, but it had a rolling island that doubled the prep area. There were two other doors in the space, one that looked like a bathroom, the other, he figured, led to the bedroom.

"Bailey's waiting for us," Holt told him. "She's calling in an order at the diner. I told her I'd drag you back by the hair if I have to."

He could almost see the beginning of a smile on Rafe's face. "I'd like to see you try."

"Never underestimate a man simply because he spends his days with fictional characters."

This time Rafe smiled but didn't move to the door. Good thing Holt hadn't expected this to be simple.

"I thought for sure the next time I saw you I'd have your fist in my face," Rafe said, leaning against the small island.

"Don't count it out just yet," Holt said, checking out the view of the park through the wood-framed windows.

"She told you?"

Holt peered back over his shoulder. "She didn't have to. I knew where she was going." He shrugged his shoulder. "I knew what would happen."

"You claim to love her, but you let her come here knowin' I would fuck her."

"First of all, I didn't *let* her do anything. Bailey's not mine to command. The two of you needed to work this out."

"And I *fucked* her," Rafe said, obviously intent on pissing Holt off.

Holt didn't dignify it with a response.

"And you don't want to punch me in the face?"

"Of course I do. But not for that." Holt turned around to face Rafe. "I'd like to because she's over there waiting for you, twisted up in knots because you gave her an ultimatum, and she doesn't want to choose."

"An ultimatum? Is that what she said?"

"No," Holt clarified. "I deduced it based on how upset she was."

"It wasn't an ultimatum. It was an assumption."

"That she'd pick you over me?"

"I've known her longer."

"What you mean to say is that you've *loved* her longer."

Rafe's eyebrow twitched—as though to say, *of course*.

Well, Holt had news for him.

"As far as her heart's concerned, I loved her first. From the moment I saw her, I've been there, Rafe. I didn't push her away and pretend not to have feelings for her."

"I never claimed to be perfect," Rafe snapped. "I don't deserve her."

Holt shook his head. "If I thought that was merely you feeling sorry for yourself, I *would* punch you in the face. Goddammit. If I had to guess, you ask for absolutely nothing and expect even less. Can't you just accept that there are people who love you?"

"You mean Bailey?"

"Not only her, Rafe. Your brother loves you. I figure your brother-in-law also loves you."

Rafe's eyes narrowed.

"And me," Holt snarled. "You need me to say it, I'll say it. I love you. Does that make you feel any fucking better because it does nothing for me? I know you don't feel the same, goddammit. But it's out there now. I. Fucking. Love. You."

"That's not even possible," Rafe countered, standing tall and crossing his arms over his chest. "One night? You don't love someone after one fuckin' night."

"*One night?*" Holt barked a laugh. "You think I fell in love with you the night I fucked you? Jesus, you're dense."

"Fuck you."

"It was all the days and nights that led up to that, Rafe." Holt stepped forward. "We had an entire summer together. Maybe we didn't fuck like rabbits all that time, but sex doesn't equate to love. I didn't fall in love with you because I enjoyed fucking you."

Holt could tell he'd surprised Rafe with that statement. He moved closer, not stopping until they were toe to toe.

"But I did enjoy fucking you," he whispered. "And you can pretend all day long, but I know you enjoyed it, too."

Rafe's gaze shifted away from his face, but Holt wasn't letting him ignore him this time.

He gripped Rafe's jaw, not surprised when Rafe attempted to jerk away. But Holt held firm, keeping him there.

"It was incredible. I haven't been with a man since then," he admitted.

Rafe's eyes snapped to his face.

"It's true," Holt said softly. "I've relived that night again and again in my head, but I've never tried to recreate it. I knew it would be pointless. It's you I want, Rafe. You and Bailey ... if I can have both of you, my life'll be complete."

"Both of us?" Rafe's incredulity practically dripped from the words.

Holt nodded.

Rafe jerked back. "Are you fuckin' serious?"

Damn right, he was. And he wasn't ashamed to admit it.

"As a goddamn heart attack."

RAFE COULDN'T BELIEVE WHAT HE WAS HEARING.

Holt loved him. One night together, and the man loved him? Was he insane?

There wasn't a damn thing about him to love. Seriously.

"What the hell do you think I have to offer you?" Rafe bit out. "You *or* Bailey?"

Never mind that Holt implied that the three of them should be together. How would that work? If Rafe couldn't provide for one, how the hell was he supposed to provide for two?

"What is it you think we need you to offer us?" Holt asked, his tone bordering on condescending.

"Stability, for starters."

"Yeah? Have you met Bailey Weber? I can guarantee she would fight either of us tooth and nail to prove her independence. She doesn't need you to provide stability for her. And me? Shit. I'm doing well enough to support all three of us for a long damn time, Rafe. But it's not about that."

"Then what's it about?" Rafe backed up again, needing to put some space between them. He couldn't think when Holt's intoxicating scent was drowning out everything else.

"It's about caring for someone. Being there when they need you. Having their back during the hard times."

Rafe had never had anyone like that in his life. Except for Rex, that was. But Rafe had proven he wasn't worth it because he hadn't been able to protect Rex when it counted. When people depended on him, he ultimately failed them. Even if they didn't realize it.

"You're your worst critic, Rafe." Holt moved toward him again, refusing to let Rafe put the distance he needed between them.

"I can't change that," Rafe admitted. "It's who I am."

"That night ... when you came to my condo ... you put all that shit away for a little while."

Rafe stared at Holt, remembering that night like it was yesterday. The sandwich. The blowjob. The shower. The fucking. Rafe shook his head, trying to dislodge the memories. Holt had shown him a side of himself he'd never known existed. And while the fucking had been intense, it had also been soul-searing. The bed had been the beginning, and by the time dawn broke, Rafe had given himself to Holt in damn near every room of that condo.

"You gave yourself to me, Rafe. Nothing bad happened. You can't keep expecting the worst in everything. What's the point of living if you can't enjoy it."

"I enjoy it just fine." He did. He went to work. He had a few friends. People depended on him to help when he could. He enjoyed life just fucking fine.

"You go through the motions, but you don't enjoy it. Spend one night with Bailey and see how different you feel. I can tell you from experience that there's nothing like waking up to her in the morning."

Rafe swallowed hard. The thought of never having the chance to experience that for himself hurt more than he wanted to admit. At the same time, he'd robbed himself of having that opportunity with Holt by running away that night and never looking back. How could he possibly want both? More importantly, why would he deserve both of them?

"She's over there right now waiting for us to come back."

"I can't go in that house."

"You mean you won't. You can. Physically, you're capable. I assure you I won't let anything bad happen."

Rafe stared back at him, clinging to that promise in a way that scared him. Rex had made that promise once, and look what happened? They'd both endured hell, and neither of them had been able to do a damn thing to stop it.

"One night, Rafe." Holt held up a hand before Rafe could argue. "One *hour*. Give it one hour. Or hell, we'll take it minute by minute. Just give her this. You owe her that much."

"And what do I owe you?" Rafe asked because that was what it came down to, right? He had to pay his penance for walking away from Holt.

"Nothing. You owe me nothing. That won't change how I feel about you. That's why they call it unconditional love. It's not based on what you can provide."

Rafe was seriously considering it. One minute at a time. Surely he could do that. He wanted to see Bailey. After she left this afternoon, all he could think about was her. To spend just a few more minutes with her would ease some of the chaos.

"Fine. But I'm not makin' any promises. If I want to leave, I'm leavin'."

"Understood."

Rafe took a deep breath and headed for the door. Before he could reach it, Holt's hand curled around his wrist, jerking him back. The next thing Rafe knew, he was up against the wall, Holt's big body pinning him there. Their mouths crashed together. It was all Rafe could do to hold on, pressing his fingertips into Holt's flesh. He kept himself together by sheer will. Try as he might, Rafe had never been able to forget that night or the change that had taken place within him after he'd been with Holt. He hadn't been the same since, and he knew if he walked away from this man again, he would forever be altered once again.

"Tell me it's still there," Holt whispered against his lips. "Tell me you feel it, too."

"Yeah." Rafe reached between them and ground his palm against Holt's erection.

Holt grabbed his wrist and stilled his hand. "I wasn't talking about that."

Rafe's exhale carried with it his fear. "I know."

"Tell me," Holt said. "I need to know it's more than that."

Rafe hated to admit it because it made him look weak, but he couldn't deny this man. He'd never been able to, and though he didn't understand it, he couldn't fight it.

"I feel it," he whispered. "I don't want to, but I do."

He sensed Holt getting emotional. Rafe didn't want the upheaval to ruin his night, so he gripped Holt's wrist, pulling his hand away.

Holding Holt's stare, he resumed rubbing Holt's cock.

"Ahh, fuck." Holt planted his hands on the wall beside Rafe's head and looked down, watching as Rafe rubbed him through his jeans. "I've thought about this so many times."

Rafe had too. More than he could count. That night had been incredible. He hadn't gotten nearly enough of this man, but he'd run fast and far because he thought he had no choice. He chose self-preservation over happiness because that was his default setting.

But that night, Rafe had held back. He hadn't given Holt everything because he'd been scared. The man's dominance had brought back bad memories. It had taken months for Rafe to be able to let those fantasies play out fully, and once they did, they'd been on repeat.

"Keep it up, and you'll have to finish me off," Holt warned.

"Maybe that's what I want."

Holt met his stare. "Is it?"

"Yeah."

From the gleam in Holt's eyes, he was on board with the idea, but when Rafe reached for the button on Holt's jeans, Holt stopped him.

"Not yet."

"Why?"

"Bailey." Holt groaned. "She wants to be with us."

Rafe's hands fell to his sides, shock and disbelief gripping him by the throat. "Y'all've discussed this? Do you know how *fucked up* that is?"

Holt took a step back, his expression hard. "It's not fucked up. And no, we haven't discussed it at length."

"What did she say then?"

"That she doesn't want to be left out."

Rafe shook his head and moved away. "I don't know if I'm up for that."

This didn't make sense to him. Maybe it didn't necessarily feel wrong, but it didn't give him a warm fuzzy feeling either. Watching them when they weren't aware was one thing. Joining in … sure, it was a great fucking fantasy, but it seemed like a whole other beast.

Rafe thrust his hand in his hair, gearing up to tell Holt he was out, but his words died on his tongue when Holt pressed up behind him, his arm banding around Rafe's chest.

"Don't move for a minute."

Rafe took a deep breath and remained where he was.

Holt's hands slipped beneath his shirt, sliding over his stomach, higher. "Imagine her on her knees right now."

Rafe looked down as though he might see Bailey kneeling before him.

"She's touching you. I'm touching you. Both of us. Tell me you haven't thought about that."

Rafe couldn't because he had. In fact, he'd jacked off to that very fantasy the night he'd watched them in the pool together. Rafe had imagined himself eating Bailey's pussy while Holt fucked him.

Holt kissed his neck, and Rafe tilted his head.

"I've thought about it," he admitted. "More than once."

"Then let's go to her apartment, have dinner, and see where the night leads us."

Rafe sighed, leaning against Holt, although he didn't want to.

"There're only two ways this ends," Rafe mused.

"How's that?"

"We do this, and we need more. It works out. Or we do this, and it's awkward, and we end up unable to look each other in the eye. What then? There are no other options. It works, or it doesn't. The middle ground disappears completely as soon as we're together."

Holt's arm tightened, his breath rasping against Rafe's neck when he said, "You don't have faith it'll work."

No, he didn't. Because never in his life had he wanted anything as much as he wanted Bailey or Holt. And the two of them together? That was his version of nirvana. How could this possibly work out when he didn't deserve either of them, much less both?

"Minute by minute," Holt repeated.

Clearly, Holt needed proof that Rafe could fuck this up. Who was he to deny the man that? Maybe then he would get it.

"Okay," he said reluctantly. "One night."

Holt released him when Rafe turned to face him.

"But Bailey's in charge. What she wants…"

Holt nodded. "Understood."

"And I'm drivin' myself."

Another nod.

Since Rafe had no more demands, he headed for the door. And this time, Holt didn't stop him.

Chapter Nineteen

By the time Holt and Rafe appeared at her back door, Bailey was seconds away from giving up.

She was also on her third glass of wine, which meant she was feeling no pain, and forgiveness came quickly and easily.

"Come in," she said, motioning for them to join her.

Holt crossed the threshold carrying two large plastic bags filled with Styrofoam containers. Rafe wasn't quite so enthusiastic. He remained outside the door, his gaze skimming what he could see of the inside.

"It's an apartment," she said. "Two bedrooms, one bath. A kitchen and living room. Rex had the ceiling redone to accommodate. I can't imagine it looks anything like before."

Rafe's gaze slipped to her face.

Bailey held his stare, willing him to know that she would take care of him no matter what. The last thing in the world she would ever want to do was hurt him, and if she thought for a second he couldn't handle being inside, she would've willingly gone to his apartment. And yes, maybe she was selfish in wanting him here, but Bailey didn't know how they could possibly have a chance at a future if he couldn't come inside the place she lived, much less where she worked.

"Please," she whispered, holding out her hand.

Rafe took a deep breath and twined his fingers with hers as he stepped into the space. While she closed the door, he continued scoping the place out. When he didn't move, Bailey released his hand so she could help Holt with the food.

"Would you like a beer?" she offered. "Or there's wine."

"Beer's good," Rafe answered.

"I'll get 'em," Holt said, maneuvering behind her so he could reach the refrigerator.

Bailey realized tonight was going to be awkward. She'd expected it to be, considering. But she was bound and determined to do this because she couldn't see another option. For some inexplicable reason, their worlds had collided. All three of them. And to find happiness, she wanted them to figure out how this could work.

Not that she was holding her breath or anything. How did something like this even work? She'd often wondered how the throuples in this town had come to be. She'd imagined that their intimacy had come about organically. Like, one minute, the three of them were talking, the next, they were kissing. Sure, she'd oversimplified it, probably. Now that she was in the thick of it, she couldn't fathom how this would start without someone intervening.

Someone was going to have to make the first move.

"Would it help if she got naked?" Holt asked.

Bailey nearly spit out her wine. "Me?" She chuckled and looked at Rafe. "I mean, if it'll help…"

Rafe's eyes heated as they moved over her.

"It might help me," Holt said, a hint of hopefulness in his tone.

"I'm not gettin' naked," Bailey told them. She wasn't. Making the first move, especially one so bold and brazen, might come easy for some, but not her. She was just getting to know Bad Girl Bailey. She definitely wasn't pushing it.

"What if *I* get naked?" Holt offered, picking up his plate and beginning to eat from where he stood in the kitchen.

"That's a much better idea," Bailey agreed, glancing at Rafe. "It would be even better if you got naked, too. I mean, there's no harm in takin' in a show with dinner, right?"

Rafe rolled his eyes, but she sensed he was relaxing a little. However, he wasn't getting naked.

Not that she was serious. Mostly. Of course, she wouldn't look away if either of them happened to strip down to skin.

Realizing her thoughts were running fast toward the gutter, Bailey reined them in.

"Since no one's gettin' naked, why don't we talk?" she suggested, carrying her plate into the living room. The kitchen table was small, so she figured they could spread out more here. Plus, it would force Rafe to move away from the back door.

"What would you like to talk about, little rabbit?" Holt asked when he joined her, sitting on one end of the couch while she sat in the small rocking chair.

"Why do you call her that?"

Rafe's abrupt question startled her, but she looked at Holt for the answer.

"Growing up, we had rabbits in our backyard. Not pets," Holt explained as though it was completely natural. "They would come and go, stealing the birdseed that fell on the ground. We had a dog. He would sit out on the back porch and watch them as they snuck up closer to the house." His grin grew wide. "They were these little daredevils, taunting the dog until he'd give chase. They'd run and hide when he went after them, but they always came back for more."

Bailey stared at him in shock, a smile on her face. Honestly, she'd never considered there was a story behind the nickname. She figured it was something akin to *honey* or *sweetheart*. Just something someone said.

"You're the little daredevil taunting the big dog," Holt said with a wink.

Bad Girl Bailey really liked that comparison.

Bailey looked at Rafe, wondering if that explanation was sufficient. When he didn't say anything, she steered the conversation once more. "You were gone for a while. Did you two get a chance to talk?"

"A little." Holt took a bite, chewed.

"What did you talk about?" She looked at Rafe, hoping he would contribute or, at the very least, come into the living room.

He did neither.

"Simple stuff," Holt supplied around a mouthful.

When he didn't say anything more, Bailey took a bite. Rafe hadn't made a move to get his food, and she suspected he was debating on making a quick exit. Whatever he was doing, he wasn't making an effort, which meant all of this had been for nothing.

A few more minutes passed, and Bailey hopped to her feet. With all eyes on her, she marched into the kitchen. She set her plate on the counter, somehow resisting the urge to throw it. This wasn't what she'd wanted. She wasn't interested in awkward silence. She didn't have to endure it when she was with them separately, and she didn't think they had a problem when she wasn't around, so why couldn't they do this? The only answer she could come up with was that it wasn't meant to work like this.

And that hurt more than she was willing to admit.

"I can't do this," she said, grabbing the bottle of wine and her glass. "If you two can figure out how to make this work, I'll be in my room."

With that, she turned and stomped across the room, down the hallway, and into her bedroom. She slammed the door behind her for good measure.

"AREN'T YOU GONNA GO AFTER HER?" HOLT asked Rafe.

Rafe glared at him. "Me? I'm not the one who came up with this stupid idea."

"You really think it's stupid?"

"I think it's backfirin' in your face. You can't force somethin' that's not there."

Oh, it was there, all right. Not all of this tension was due to Rafe being somewhere he didn't want to be, and Bailey being torn between two men. An underlying passion connected the three of them, and Holt had no doubt that if they'd give it a chance, it would work. *How* he knew that, he couldn't say, but he'd always trusted his gut.

Holt got to his feet. He obviously wouldn't be eating until they cleared the air. And he knew one surefire way to ease the tension.

He returned to the kitchen to set his plate on the counter by Bailey's, then took a swig of his beer. He set the bottle down and walked over to Rafe.

The man's eyes tracked him, watching Holt like he was a black bear looking for an easy meal.

"What are you doin'?" Rafe asked when Holt took his hand.

"We're not goin' far."

Holt felt Rafe's reluctance to follow.

"Trust me, Rafe. If nothing else, know that we're not here to hurt you."

Skepticism glittered in Rafe's brown eyes, but he managed to take three more steps so that he was standing at the threshold between the breakfast nook and the living room. The space was open to the kitchen, but support beams created separators between the two spaces, and this post was all Holt needed.

With dramatic movements, Holt turned Rafe so that his back was against the wide beam wrapped in smooth, glossy cedar. Rafe's expression was a mix of curiosity and confusion, but he wasn't running for the door, so Holt considered that a good thing.

He caressed the hard line of Rafe's jaw with his thumb and forefinger. "I'm gonna kiss you. And you're gonna kiss me back."

"Bailey's—"

Holt cut him off by pressing his mouth to Rafe's. He hadn't forgotten about Bailey. He knew where she was, and he figured she would eventually emerge when she was curious about what they were doing. And when she did, they would have their answers on whether this would work. And while he wasn't projecting his uncertainty, Holt silently prayed that this would not backfire in his face as Rafe said.

"Kiss me," Holt murmured against Rafe's mouth. "Like you did that night."

A soft hum came from Rafe's throat, his shoulders relaxing, his lips more pliant.

Holt didn't relent until he felt the urgency building in Rafe. It didn't take long before it mirrored his own, that desperate need awakening now that they were together. It had been so long. Too long. By far, the one night he'd had with Rafe had been the most intense of his life. He wanted to experience that again. Only he wanted Bailey to join them because, with both of them, a night of passion would blow his previous best night to smithereens.

Holt flicked a button on Rafe's shirt open. "You good?"

Rafe nodded, leaning into Holt.

Holt took his time, relishing the sweep of Rafe's tongue against his own. It started slow, but it didn't take long before their hunger took over. The brief teasing session at Rafe's apartment had left Holt on edge, but he wasn't doing this for himself. He was offering a distraction. One he knew Rafe couldn't resist.

Once Rafe's shirt was open, he planted his palms on his sides and felt those rock-hard muscles tense beneath his touch. The man's body was nothing but finely chiseled muscle and sinew. Holt dragged his thumbs along the line that bisected Rafe's abs, moving upward slowly, feeling every groove of his perfectly sculpted torso. He kept going until he was palming Rafe's chest, the soft, dark hair tickled his palms as the muscles flexed.

Holt leaned into Rafe, letting him bear his weight while their mouths ate at one another. He teased Rafe's nipples, gently tugging before sliding his hands down, curling them over Rafe's hips, and dipping his thumbs and fingers into the waistband of his jeans. Their grunts and groans grew louder as the temperature in the room soared from the heat churning between them.

"You remember that night?" Holt prompted, sliding his lips along Rafe's jaw. "We were on the back deck when I kissed you for the first time."

Rafe moaned.

"Were you expecting it?"

"No," Rafe said softly. "But I was hopin'."

"I couldn't resist." Holt nipped his earlobe. "I'd wanted to touch you the first night I met you, but I knew you weren't ready for it then, so I waited."

Rafe tilted his head when Holt licked his neck. Holt took the offer, sucking the warm skin until Rafe shivered.

Rafe

Testing the waters, Holt reached for the button on Rafe's jeans and was surprised when Rafe didn't attempt to stop him, instead turning his head so their lips met again.

"I've waited a long damn time to get my mouth on you again," Holt mumbled against his lips as he opened Rafe's jeans. "Push them down."

Rafe shifted his feet, steadying himself as he pushed his jeans down his hips.

"If this isn't what you want, tell me now. Otherwise, I'm gonna suck your dick until you're begging me to let you come."

Rafe's breath expelled from his lungs, and his hips thrust forward.

"Tell me," Holt insisted. He wouldn't do this unless he knew Rafe was willing.

"I want it," Rafe rasped. "God, just fuckin' touch me."

Holt curled his fingers around Rafe's thick shaft and stroked him once, twice. He teased the head, rubbing the precum that had formed there.

"Fuck." Rafe's head fell against the wall as his chest expanded with every gulp of air he took.

"I'm gonna put my mouth on you," he warned. "If Bailey comes out of her room, she's gonna see you fucking my face."

Rafe trembled.

Holt didn't wait for verbal approval. He'd already warned him; if Rafe didn't want this to happen, he could stop him anytime. He kissed Rafe's lips one last time before trailing his mouth down his chest, his stomach, going to his knees as he descended.

Rafe was watching him, completely in the moment. That was an aphrodisiac in itself. To know that Rafe was there with him, not trying to shy away from his touch, but accepting that what they'd once had was still burning hot between them.

Holt kissed the head of Rafe's cock, loving the way it twitched in his fist. When Rafe's eyes met his, Holt opened his mouth wide and took him inside.

"Oh, shit." Rafe swallowed hard.

Holt sucked him. Slowly at first, relearning every ridge and vein of Rafe's cock. When he took Rafe deep, the man groaned low in his throat.

Rafe grunted, gripping Holt's head with both hands, holding on while Holt bobbed up and down, letting the broad head hit the back of his throat each time. During their one night together, Rafe had been very vocal, but he was holding back now. Holt had a feeling that would change with time. The sounds he made grew louder the longer Holt worked him with his hand and mouth, bringing him closer and closer to release.

The squeak of a door opening had Rafe's hands tightening in Holt's hair. He waited for him to shove him away.

"Let me do this," he urged. "Let her watch."

Rafe met his gaze, and for a moment, Holt saw what looked like fear. Holt understood it because he felt the same. The fear of losing Bailey because of this.

"Give it a chance," Holt said, licking Rafe's cock like an ice cream cone.

Rafe hissed, the fear fading as Holt resumed his efforts, licking and sucking with eager abandon but ensuring Rafe knew he was completely in charge.

Footsteps sounded briefly, but then they stopped.

Holt's back was to the hallway Bailey had disappeared down, so he had to rely on Rafe's reaction to know when Bailey appeared.

Her soft gasp was a good sign.

"I want you to come," Holt told Rafe, keeping him in the moment. "I want you to come down my throat while she watches."

And though he was telling Rafe what he wanted, Holt gave him a moment to decide.

RAFE WAS TORN BETWEEN MIND-NUMBING PLEASURE and heart-stopping fear.

Surprisingly, it had nothing to do with *where* he was. For the moment, he couldn't think about the house, and he wasn't haunted by the memories of that long ago time. Both pleasure and fear came from seeing Bailey appear while Holt had his mouth on his dick.

He couldn't explain it, but her presence heightened the pleasure ten-fold, but he couldn't keep from worrying that this would ruin any chance he could have with her. Then Holt's words rang in his head.

If I had to guess, you ask for absolutely nothing and expect even less. Can't you just accept that there are people who love you?

Rafe hadn't wanted to admit it, but there was so much truth in that statement. He didn't ask for anything, and he expected absolutely nothing. From anyone. So, could this work? Could he have both Holt and Bailey? The only two people he'd ever loved? Had all his sacrifices made room for this?

There was only one way to find out.

Something inside him clicked, and he took the chance. He decided to go for it because this was already an all-or-nothing situation. He would have them both, or he would have neither. He couldn't see any other way.

"Suck me," Rafe barked, dropping his head back, acquiescing because it felt like the right thing to do. To surrender and take a chance.

His cock was enveloped by the wicked heat of Holt's mouth once more, and the only thing Rafe could do was hold on.

"Come here," Rafe rasped, staring at Bailey.

She hesitated but only briefly before padding barefoot across the floor. As she neared, her gaze shifted to his cock, watching as it tunneled in and out of Holt's mouth.

Once she was close enough, Rafe reached for her hand, pulling her into him. The warmth of her skin lit him up, and the way her hand caressed his chest had his cock twitching in Holt's mouth.

"Aw, hell," he groaned. The sensations were intense, and he was grateful for the wall at his back. Otherwise, he would've been a puddle on the floor.

"How does it feel?"

He didn't expect her question, but he responded as though it was normal to answer her while getting a blowjob from someone else.

"Perfect. You. Him." He pumped his hips, trying to fuck Holt's mouth while he tightened his grip on Holt's hair. "So fuckin' perfect."

He could feel Bailey's hand trembling against his chest, and he noticed she was breathing heavily as she watched Holt suck him off. Her eyes were glazed, her plump lips parted slightly. She wasn't repulsed by what she saw; she was so turned on she was trembling.

Holt groaned, and the vibrations traveled up Rafe's shaft, causing his balls to tighten as his release barreled down on him. He couldn't hold back. He wanted to because the hot, wet drag of Holt's tongue on his shaft felt so fucking good, but he couldn't. He needed to come. More than that, he needed to come down Holt's throat while Bailey watched.

"Fuck ... I'm close..." He pumped his hips, holding Holt's head in place as he chased the inevitable release. And when the electricity fired in his spine, Rafe tightened his hold on Bailey's hand and let himself go.

Holt drank him down, not missing a drop as Rafe gasped for air, letting the ecstasy move through his entire being. His ears rang for a moment as the orgasm faded.

Rafe panted, using the beam for support, watching as Holt stood up and grabbed Bailey. He pulled her against him and crushed his mouth over hers. She whimpered, her arm coming around him while her other hand remained firmly on Rafe's chest.

"Can you taste him?" Holt asked Bailey.

Rafe's cock jerked, still semi-hard despite the orgasm.

"Yes," she moaned, her hand falling from Rafe's chest, but she grabbed his shirt to keep from releasing him as Holt assaulted her mouth.

"Your turn, little rabbit."

When Holt lifted her off her feet, carrying her to the couch, she didn't release Rafe's shirt, so he was forced to follow, jerking his jeans up as he went.

"Take it off, Bailey," Holt demanded. "Take it all off because I want you bare when I fuck your pussy with my tongue."

Rafe suddenly remembered how vocal Holt had been the night they were together. Barking orders and commands like he had a right to do so. When Rafe hadn't been tossing out his own, he had surrendered to every single one. Obviously, the man was doing something right.

Between the three of them, they undressed Bailey within seconds. Before she could recline on the couch, Rafe pulled her onto his lap so she was straddling him, her breasts crushed to his chest. He kissed her hard, loving that she immediately kissed him back.

"Did you like that?" she asked, nipping his lower lip. "His mouth on you?"

"Did *you*?" he countered.

"So much ... it was so hot." She arched her back as Holt licked his way down her spine. She repositioned, shifting her hips toward Holt, urging him to continue.

Rafe slipped his hand between her legs, teasing her slick folds with his finger, loving how she gasped when he touched her the right way.

He felt movement against his knees, then a tickle on his knuckles. He realized Holt was sitting on the floor, leaning back so that his face was between Bailey's legs, the crown of his head pressed against Rafe's balls.

Rafe helped Holt out, separating Bailey's pussy lips with his fingers, feeling the slick slide of Holt's tongue as he teased her.

"Oh, yes," Bailey cried, her head falling back.

Rafe helped her move back so that she was straddling Holt's face as he ate her pussy. Rafe was jealous. He wanted to taste her again. This morning he hadn't gotten nearly enough of her. But this was good, too. He understood why she'd said it was so hot to see Holt's mouth on him because watching the erotic encounter added a level of ecstasy.

Rafe focused on her tits, tugging on her pretty pink nipples while she rocked her hips, riding Holt's face.

"How does it feel?" Rafe asked, throwing her question back at her.

"So good. His tongue... More, Rafe. I need more."

Rafe pinched her nipples harder. Bailey cried out, thrusting her chest toward him.

She groaned. "I'm gonna come. Holt ... Rafe ... oooohhhh ... yeeessssss!"

Rafe held her while she trembled, waiting for her to come down from the orgasm. When she did, she fell against him, her mouth sealing over his. She kissed him gently, almost reverently.

"I didn't know it would be like this," she whispered.

He brushed her hair back from her face. "Like what?"

"Exquisite."

"I'm not done with either of you yet," Holt said as he stood.

"Who said we were done with you?" Bailey asked, peering back at him over her shoulder.

Holt's eyebrow lifted in question. "What is it you plan to do with me?"

Bailey looked at Rafe as though seeking an answer, so he offered one.

Rafe held Holt's stare. "What I wished I'd done all those years ago."

Holt's smile was slow and wicked. "Yeah?"

"What did you wish for all those years ago?" Bailey asked, glancing between them.

Holt answered for him. "He should've fucked me."

Bailey moaned.

"I think she likes that idea."

"Oh, she does," Bailey agreed. "She definitely does."

"Problem is her bed's not big enough for all three of us," Holt noted.

"I can fix that." Bailey hopped up and hurried across the room, her bare ass jiggling as she scurried toward the hall. When she returned, she was concealed by the fluffy white comforter she was dragging along with her. It took her a couple of tries, but she spread it out on the living room floor before kneeling on it.

Rafe knew that no matter what happened, he would enjoy this for as long as it lasted.

Chapter Twenty

Although Holt wanted nothing more than for Rafe to fuck him, he was mindful of the situation. More importantly, he recalled Bailey's concern that she would be left out, and he wanted to prove that she was the one they wanted to focus on. She was the glue that would hold them together if they chose to pursue this beyond tonight.

"Before we get to that," he told her, joining her on the blanket. "I think you need some attention."

"One orgasm wasn't enough for you?" she teased, staring at him as he pulled his shirt over his head.

"Little rabbit, I want you to come a dozen times. And then a dozen more."

Holt released the button on his jeans, then got to his feet. He glanced at Rafe, nodding his chin, urging him to do the same.

"Do you have lube?" Holt asked Bailey.

"Umm…" She shook her head.

He grinned. "No worries."

Since she was an avid baker, he figured she had something in the pantry that would work as a lubricant. Plus, it would allow Rafe to spend a few minutes with her. Which he was obviously hoping for since Holt barely made it to the kitchen when he heard Bailey sigh. He peered back to see Rafe kneeling over her, kissing his way down her chest.

Holt paused in his pursuit of all-natural lube to watch them. As he'd expected, it was intensely erotic. He had never been able to explain his potent attraction to Rafe. It had come on instantly from the moment they met, and even after their summer ended, Holt had never stopped thinking about him. Before Rafe, Holt had been with a few men, but his preference had always leaned toward women. Rafe was the exception. For the years since, Holt hadn't been with another man because he hadn't met one who could hold a candle to Rafe.

And Bailey … well, Holt figured that was far easier to explain. She was one of a kind, so it only made sense that he'd been ensnared from their first encounter. No other woman compared to her. She was beautiful, both inside and out.

And together, they were … breathtaking.

Bailey moaned softly, her back arching as Rafe shouldered his way between her thighs. He licked her slowly, leisurely, as though feasting on her was the only thing he'd ever wanted to do. Holt certainly understood the appeal.

Turning back to the pantry, Holt moved a few things around until he found a bottle of liquid organic coconut oil.

That would do.

Holt retrieved the condom from his wallet, then left the wallet on the counter before returning to the couple in the living room. He set the coconut oil aside, along with the condom, and decided to join them. But not before he stripped off his jeans. As he did, Bailey's gaze shifted to him. Her heated gaze did wonders for his ego, but her touch set him aflame. When he went to his knees, she reached for his cock, stroking slowly while gasping as Rafe continued to eat her pussy.

"I want you in my mouth," she said, meeting his stare as though he might deny her request.

Inching around, he knelt near her head, his cock hovering hard and heavy above her. He leaned forward, holding himself up with one arm and angling his dick toward her mouth. Her lips parted. A soft swipe of her tongue followed. Then she was licking him like she'd found her new favorite treat. But when she took him into her mouth, her teeth lightly scraping, a fiery chill ran down his spine. For the first time in his life, he feared he might detonate before he was ready.

"Slow," he urged. "When I come, I intend to come in your sweet little ass."

She moaned, and the vibrations traveled up his shaft.

"That excites you." He chuckled when she moaned again.

Twisting his upper body, Holt sucked her nipple between his lips while she sucked him. He loved that she fumbled when he sucked harder, her chest thrusting upward in offering.

"I think they need more attention," he said, dislodging his cock from her mouth so he could focus on her tits.

Holt stretched out alongside her, sliding his hand under her thigh to open her legs wider, allowing him to watch as Rafe tongued her slowly.

"He's drivin' me crazy," she moaned. "He's teasin' me."

"Looks like he's savoring you."

Rafe grunted.

"What do you need?" Holt asked Bailey. "You want his fingers?"

Bailey moaned.

"Or do you want his cock?"

She hummed and nodded.

"Tell him."

"Rafe … oh, God … please…"

"All you have to do is ask, little rabbit. We'll give you whatever you need."

"I want you both," she whispered. "I want you both at the same time."

Rafe lifted to his knees, his mouth sliding up her torso until he reached her mouth. Holt watched as they kissed, a heated exchange that told him the foreplay had reached its limits, and it was time for the three of them to consummate this relationship.

But if Holt thought this would be a slow expedition, he learned he was wrong when Rafe pushed Bailey's knees back and rammed his cock deep inside her. He wasn't wearing a condom, and Bailey didn't question the action, so Holt didn't either. Evidently, they'd already had this conversation which he took to mean there'd been considerable progress between them.

Holt took that as a good sign.

As soon as Rafe thrust inside her, a sense of overwhelming urgency brought her nerve endings to life.

She didn't want slow and gentle. She wanted fast and hard. She wanted to lose herself in this moment with these men. She'd never wanted anything as badly as she wanted both of them, and having them at the same time, filling her, fucking her ... it was all she could do to breathe as he urged Rafe onto his back so she could take the reins.

"Damn, you look good like that," Holt murmured, watching as she sat astride Rafe, rolling her hips as she fucked him.

She watched as Rafe turned his head and Holt leaned in, their lips melding together. The way they touched ... this wasn't merely about sex, although she would bet money Rafe would claim that was the case. He seemed present and willing, but Bailey sensed he was still holding back. Before the night was over, she hoped his hesitance had faded because she'd lost every ounce of uncertainty the moment she saw Holt on his knees with Rafe's cock in his mouth.

Never in her life would she have imagined two men could look so hot together.

As the memory assaulted her, Bailey whimpered, planting her palms on Rafe's chest so she could move faster, take him deeper.

"I think our little rabbit needs more," Holt said, breaking the kiss.

"Yes," she bit out. "Fuck me. Both of you."

Rafe's eyebrows lifted, and he turned his full attention to her, gripping her hips and holding her still so he could fuck her. He drove his hips up, impaling her deeper than she thought possible. Sparks burst along her skin, leaving tingles in their wake.

The next few minutes were a rush as she fought to hold on while they brought her extreme pleasure with their hands and mouths. But the moment she felt the firm press of Holt's fingers against her back hole, she thought she would come out of her skin. She'd never imagined she would want to be fucked there, but after Rafe had teased her that morning, she couldn't stop thinking about it. She'd never experienced it with the few men she'd been with, but now that she'd had a little taste of it, she wanted to binge.

Leaning forward, she rested her chest on Rafe's, her lips moving with his as she rocked her hips against those intruding fingers, trying to take them deeper. She expected it to hurt, but there was only slight discomfort when Holt inserted two fingers.

"Please," she groaned. "Fuck me, Holt. Fuck me now."

She heard his raspy chuckle, felt his thighs when he shifted closer, pressing against her. She held her breath and waited, expelling it when he pushed the head of his cock against her anus.

"That's it. Bear down. Let me in."

Bailey pushed back against the intrusion, taking him in her ass. Holt slipped inside slowly, fighting her body's natural resistance until he was lodged so deep, she thought she would break in two.

"Slow," he urged, gripping her hips when she attempted to pull forward so she could take him again.

She conceded, allowing him to guide her, his cock retreating slowly before sliding in again. Rafe cupped her face, forcing her to look at him. She met his gaze, holding steady as Holt sank inside her inch by glorious inch.

They filled her to the point of pain, but she rode it out until it morphed into pleasure.

Holt stilled inside her. "Bailey?"

"Hmm?"

"You okay?"

"Better than okay," she admitted, still holding Rafe's stare. "I'll be better if you both fuck me now."

The smile that pulled at Rafe's mouth was the most beautiful thing she'd ever seen.

And then they were fucking her. Alternating at first, pushing in deep and slow, retreating while the other slid inside. Her nerve endings sang as pleasure coursed through her, making her skin tight and her nipples tighter. Every glorious sensation came together, culminating in the deepest parts of her, then expanded slowly, growing more intense by the second.

"Make me come!" Bailey pressed her face into Rafe's shoulder as they plowed into her, harder, deeper, faster. "Oh, God, yes!"

She cried out, gritting her teeth as wave after wave of ecstasy crashed through every part of her, moving from her center to her fingertips and her scalp. The intensity blinded her until she felt them still and heard their soft grunts and groans as they came, filling her at the same time.

"That was amazing," she gasped.

She remembered nothing after that except the smile on her face as she succumbed to physical exhaustion.

When Holt got up, Rafe remained where he was, his arms banded around Bailey, holding her while her breaths deepened.

She had passed out cold, relaxing against him.

Holt returned with a washcloth, tending to Bailey while Rafe listened to the soft rasp of her breaths. He didn't want to leave, but the panic was churning. He'd thought for a minute he'd dodged the bullet, but now that the evening had crescendoed, he was left with only his thoughts. And as usual, they were taking him down a very dark path, one he didn't want anyone to have to venture with him.

"Let's take her to bed," Holt said, moving to her side and lifting her into his arms.

Bailey curled into Holt, her arms sliding around his neck as she held onto him.

"Give me a minute," Rafe told him, staring at the ceiling.

Holt grunted, then left the room with Bailey.

A minute passed, and Rafe felt the twisting intensify in his gut. When it spread to his chest, he knew there was nothing he could do. Staying wouldn't prove anything other than he was a pathetic excuse for a man because, try as he might, he couldn't fight the demons that still haunted him. Not even his love and desire for the two people he wanted more than his next breath was powerful enough to keep him there. He knew if he closed his eyes, if he let sleep claim him, the demons would appear in his dreams. They would have him in their clutches. There would be no escaping them.

Rafe

As quietly as he could, Rafe got to his feet. He pulled on his jeans and his shirt, grabbing his boots before rushing out the back door.

Like a thief in the night, he fled, only he didn't take anything with him.

Instead, he left his heart back there with Bailey and Holt.

Chapter Twenty-one

BAILEY WOKE AGAINST A HARD, WARM BODY. Something in her brain told her not to move, so she came awake slowly. She let the light filter into her foggy mind, the sounds register—the air conditioner, someone breathing deeply.

Holt.

She was snuggled up against him, the comforter covering her, his heartbeat steady beneath her ear.

It only took a moment to realize that, at some point, someone had moved her to her bed.

"Morning," Holt whispered, his beard stubble brushing against her temple.

Bailey reluctantly pushed herself up onto her elbow, smiled. As soon as she did, all her synapses started firing, and she realized there was far more sunlight filtering in than should be if it were six o'clock.

"Oh, shit!" She launched herself out of bed. "What time is it? I need to start breakfast. Shit, shit, shit."

She raced to the living room to find her phone. She needed to check to see if there had been any text alerts. They had a houseful of guests, plus one set leaving and another arriving, though she couldn't remember when. Regardless, it wouldn't look well if everyone arrived for breakfast only to find there wasn't anything to eat. Not a great precedent to set for a bed and *breakfast*.

She found her phone on the kitchen counter next to the plates of food that they hadn't finished last night.

"Oh, thank God," she mumbled when she saw no alerts and no text messages from Rex.

The sound of footsteps sounded behind her, then disappeared at the same time the bathroom door closed.

It was seven forty-five—nearly two hours after her normal start time—which meant there could very well be an angry mob downstairs waiting to be fed. And if Rex was here…

Deciding she should be the one to apologize before Rex had a chance to question her, she pulled up his contact information and sent him a quick text. Simple, to the point.

> I overslept. I'm so sorry. I'll be down to start breakfast in a few minutes.

His reply was almost immediate.

> Hmm. That's strange. There were bagels, muffins, and scones when I came by earlier. You didn't make those?

She was about to respond that she hadn't but figured it might be better to know who had beforehand. And since she could only think of one person who could pull off a spread like that so early in the morning, Bailey called her mother.

"Did you bring muffins this mornin'?"

"Good morning to you, too, honey."

"Sorry, Mom. I overslept. I'm a little grouchy."

Ramona chuckled. "Yes. Holt called me a few hours ago. He said you had a long night and asked me to help out."

Wow. Just … wow.

"He's a good man, Bailey."

Good wasn't the word for what Holt was, but she didn't want to get all gushy with her mom on the phone.

"He is," she agreed. "Well, I need to head down and check on the guests. Thanks for doin' that, by the way. You're the greatest Mom in the whole wide world."

Ramona laughed again. "And don't you forget it."

After disconnecting the call, Bailey took a deep breath, squared her shoulders, and decided a shower was in order. She was already late, which meant she would have to make up for the time, but she wanted to be clean before she got messy again.

Holt was coming from the hallway when she turned to go down it.

"Oh. Shit," she squealed. How she'd forgotten he was there, she had no idea.

"Everything all right?" He peered down at her, his palm rasping his scruffy jaw.

"Yeah. You called my mom this mornin'."

"I did."

"You saved me from gettin' fired."

He smiled. "I doubt Rex would fire you for being late one time."

"You're probably right. But that doesn't mean I can be complacent. They pay me to take care of things, and makin' breakfast is still something on my task list."

"I wanted you to sleep in. I could tell you needed it. You can tackle breakfast tomorrow," he said, pulling her into him.

She tilted her head back and looked at him. "I could make you somethin' now."

"It's tough to think about breakfast when you're standing there naked."

As she pressed against his warm body, she realized he was right. She was definitely naked.

And then all thoughts of breakfast fled because she was embarrassed that she'd raced out of the bedroom buck naked when—

Bailey stopped and turned toward the living room. "Where's Rafe?"

Holt's expression lost its luster. "I don't know. He left sometime during the night."

"Did he go to bed with us?"

"No."

Was that his way of telling them he wasn't interested in seeing this through? Had he regretted what happened?

"Bailey?"

She snapped her gaze to Holt's face and realized she was frowning.

"It's not for you to worry about right now. I'll talk to Rafe in a little while."

"Okay." She nodded as though enforcing the notion that it was okay. "I don't have time to think about it right now. I need to shower."

Holt stepped back out of the way. "I'll be outta your hair in a minute."

She grabbed his wrist before he could walk away. "No. I don't want you to go."

His eyebrows rose slowly.

"You know what I mean. I don't want you to think you have to leave. We can go downstairs, and I'll make you coffee."

"I like that idea. But I'll need to put some pants on first."

Which meant he needed to get by her because their clothes from last night were strode across the living room.

"I'm gonna shower," she told him as she watched him walk away, admiring the smooth flex of his back muscles. Her gaze drifted lower to his absolutely delicious ass. It really was a shame that he had to get dressed.

Knowing she had to focus on what was important, Bailey put Holt out of her mind. As best she could anyway. After rummaging through her dresser, she pulled out clothes and hurried to the bathroom. She used the bathroom first, then flipped on the shower so it would heat, and set to work checking off the items on her hygiene list. While she dragged the toothbrush over her teeth, she stared at herself in the mirror and fought the urge to cringe. She looked like a woman who'd been well-fucked by two incredibly hot men last night.

One of those men stayed.

The other ran.

What was she supposed to think about that? Should she be hurt even though it didn't surprise her? Or should she be worried about Rafe? He had come into the house he swore he would never come in. Was he okay?

"No time to worry about it," she reminded herself.

Once steam started billowing out from behind the glass, she got in, letting the spray beat down on her while her body tingled at the memory of what they'd done. She'd had sex with two men at one time. Never in her life had she even fantasized that she would do that. It had been incredible. They'd made her feel sexy and desired, not to mention safe and cared for.

Would they ever have that chance again? Or was his disappearing act meant to be the line that they would no longer be able to cross?

Her optimistic heart told her that, provided Rafe hadn't gone off and let his thoughts take over, there might be a chance. But Bailey knew Rafe; if she had to guess, he was at his apartment belittling himself for getting caught up in it. But he'd been a willing participant.

God, the things he'd done with his tongue. Not only when he'd had his head between her legs but also when he'd kissed her. His mouth had sealed to hers when Holt slid inside her, and there had been something distinctly possessive about that kiss. For a moment, Bailey had worried Rafe was going to put a stop to it.

He hadn't.

No, he'd fucked her like he had wanted to possess her. And he had. They both had. Now what were they supposed to do? Did she assume that the three of them would continue seeing each other like that?

What surprised her was that she was no longer worried about what Rafe and Holt would do when she wasn't around. In fact, she kind of hoped they would find a way to get closer. Just the two of them. They had some serious chemistry, but they also had history. They needed to clear the air before there was a chance for anything to work.

She only hoped they didn't ask to take things slow. She was tired of slow. She wanted to spend her nights doing what they'd done last night. And she wanted them to want that, too.

Bailey was washing her hair, head tipped back, eyes closed, when she thought she heard the door opening. She held her breath, trying to hear any noises over the water pounding on her head.

"Holt? Is that you?"

She chuckled softly. That was a stupid question. Who else would it be? It wasn't like he would leave when she'd asked him to stay, right?

"I'm hurryin'," she told him, her words echoing off the tile. "I promise I'll be out in a jiffy."

Bailey spun around, grabbed her conditioner, and squirted it into her hand. She was coating her hair, water beating down on her chest, when she felt the air stir behind her.

"I hope you don't mind company."

His warm hands slid over her slick hips, moving upward as his chest pressed to her back. No, she didn't mind company.

"Not at all."

Every cell in her body zinged to life, heat swamping her from head to toe. If he kept this up, she would get fired because as long as he was distracting her with the gentle caress of his hands, she wasn't going to make it downstairs.

"Bailey."

She smiled to herself. "Holt."

She let her hands drop but didn't turn around to face him. When his warm hands slid over her shoulders, she sighed. As they inched down her chest, his rigid cock pressing against her butt, she moaned. He hugged her, his long arms wrapping across her breasts.

"This can't be a mistake, Bailey," he whispered, his lips brushing her ear.

He kissed her neck, and she held her breath, silently willing his hands to wander.

"I don't want this to be temporary," he added.

"I don't either." And she didn't. She wanted forever.

They remained like that, her breathing rapid as her pulse raced. His stubble tickled her neck, and her skin prickled with awareness when his hands began to move over her lightly. Ever so lightly, teasing her skin.

"Definitely not temporary," she said with a soft moan as she leaned into him, her chest pushing forward, pressing her breasts into his palms while she let her head rest on his chest. "I'm not done with you yet."

"I should probably make love to you after what we did last night." His voice was a deep, dark rumble against her senses. "But I don't have that sort of restraint."

Make love? Restraint?

"I'm not a gentle lover, Bailey. I'm not sure I know how to be. But I could learn. It'll take some time, though."

"Good thing we have all the time in the world." She gasped when he plucked her nipples.

"So, you do want me to make love to you?"

What was he talking about?

Then it hit her.

She chuckled softly, tilted her head to the side, and allowed his lips to tease her neck. "It was a figure of speech. I don't need gentle. I need…" She lost her train of thought when Holt's teeth scraped her ear lobe. "Oh, God. I just need you."

"That's good because fucking you is the only thing I can think about."

Her insides coiled tightly, her breath expelling from her lungs in a whoosh when he nipped her ear. Fire sizzled through her bloodstream, her pussy throbbed, and a torrential downpour of need slammed into her.

Holt continued to knead one breast with his big hand while his other slid down her stomach, his fingers inching downward until he was parting her pussy lips, grazing her clit, making her inhale sharply.

"Ah, sweet little rabbit … I'm warning you now. Patience isn't my best quality."

Bailey shook her head adamantly. "Don't want patient. Need fast … dirty… Oh, God!" She cried out when he pushed his finger inside her, filling her so perfectly. "Holt… More."

She leaned into him fully, spreading her legs wider, giving him room to maneuver as he finger-fucked her. She was lightheaded, sucked into a cataclysm of heat and light and the most delicious friction she'd ever imagined.

Holt's mouth slid to her neck. He sucked on her skin as he added another finger, pushing in deep, driving her closer and closer to the edge with the glorious thrust and retreat of his fingers.

Unable to resist, Bailey shifted in his arms. Thankfully, his fingers didn't slip from where they were, but Holt's mouth settled over hers, his tongue insistent, demanding as he kissed her roughly, his fingers still fucking her thoroughly.

Her body morphed into one giant ball of sensation, coiling tighter, burning hotter until there was no way to contain the electrical current that started in her core and shot outward.

Bailey broke her mouth from Holt's as she screamed in ecstasy, her orgasm stealing her breath and obliterating her mind.

When she put her hand on Holt's face, staring into his eyes, she saw him smile, and her heart skipped a beat.

"I think it's time for you to go to work," he whispered, his hand sliding over her hair in a sweet, comforting gesture.

"Yeah? You give me the orgasm of a lifetime, then send me on my way?"

Holt leaned in and kissed her. "Tonight, when you come home, I promise, there'll be more where that came from."

"Home?" She smiled. "Hmm. I like the sound of that."

"Me, too."

Holt kissed her quickly, then traded places so he could be underneath the spray. As she got out, Bailey stared at him, her mind and body still floating from another incredible orgasm.

RAFE WAS PULLED FROM A DEEP SLEEP by someone pounding on his door.

"Goddammit," he growled, forcing himself up when it was clear they weren't going to stop.

The banging grew louder when he emerged from his bedroom. The clock on the wall said it was only nine, which meant he was supposed to be asleep since he worked nights. So whoever the fuck was trying to knock the damn thing down with their fist needed a lesson in civility.

He didn't bother looking out the security hole, flipping the lock and jerking the door open. "What do you—"

Holt stood there with an expression that said he wasn't happy, which was a polite way of describing the murderous glare that had his eyebrows angled into a furious V and his nostrils flaring.

Rafe gripped the edge of the door, prepared to close it. "I'm sleepin'. Come back later."

Holt obviously didn't care because he planted two palms on the door and shoved, knocking Rafe back a step before he stormed into his apartment.

"Good mornin' to you, too," Rafe muttered, slamming the door. "Don't you know I work nights, so I sl—"

"If I ever wondered why you've been single all these years, now I fucking know."

"What the hell are you talkin' about?"

"You left her." Holt shook his head. "You fucked her, then left without so much as a goodbye."

"What the fuck did you want me to do? Damn. She was asleep. You were with her," he said, not in the mood to be chastised like a child. "And I told you, I can't be in that fuckin' house. It was all I could do to…" He waved a hand.

"To what? Get your cock sucked and then fuck her? Bareback?"

Rafe laughed, but it lacked mirth. "Is *that* what you're so pissed about? Because I fucked her bare?"

Holt continued to glare. "I figure it's something you have a conversation about first."

Shrugging his shoulders, Rafe rolled his eyes. "And you think the only conversation that takes place is when you're in the room? Fuck you. We *did* have a conversation. When she came over here yesterday mornin', we fucked. I forgot the condom. She said she was on birth control and that she's clean."

Holt stared at him, his mouth set in a thin line.

"What?"

"Are you done being a dick?"

Rafe snapped. "Fuck you, Holt. Fuck you and the goddamn horse you rode in on. I've done every fuckin' thing you've wanted me to do since the day you got here. I even fucked the woman I loved while you tag-teamed her. That ain't enough for you?"

Holt shoved him. "If you ever talk about her like she's a conquest, I'll—"

"You'll what?" Rafe sneered. "You'll come over here and expect me to fuck you, too? That's what I'm good for, right? An incredible night? Is there a book on how to draw the murderer in and get him to play house with you? Lemme guess. You found the chapter that said, *let's give him a blowjob!*"

Holt's expression was one of shocked horror.

Yeah, Rafe knew how he sounded. He was a complete asshole. No one was disputing that, but goddamn.

Rafe ran his hand through his hair and groaned. The muscles in his neck and shoulders were knotted, and he feared he was dangerously close to hitting Holt in the fucking face.

"How dare you come to my apartment and tell me I screwed shit up." Rafe spun and pointed at Holt. "You're the one who screwed this all up. You came rollin' into town lookin' to wrangle up a couple of people for your little orgy. Oh, hey!" He waved his arms. "Look, there's Bailey Weber. She'll go good with a side of Rafe Sharpe."

"What the hell is your problem?"

Rafe honestly didn't know.

No, that was a big fucking lie. He knew, and it was his own guilt that was turning him into a dickhead. He hadn't wanted to leave last night. He'd tried to convince himself to go back, but the more he thought about it, the more panic set in until the walls were closing in on him, and he couldn't breathe.

But it was easier to pretend it had been his choice than to let Holt know about that weakness. He didn't want the man's pity.

"Are you telling me what happened last night was a mistake?"

Rafe heard genuine concern in Holt's tone and decided to dial down his fury a notch.

"It should be," Rafe admitted.

"Why?"

Rafe took a deep breath, preparing for a tirade, but the moment he saw Holt's downtrodden expression, it lost its luster.

He opted for the truth. "Because I had a fuckin' panic attack, all right?"

Holt took a step toward him.

Rafe held up a hand. "Stop. Don't you dare feel sorry for me. And don't you dare tell me that time heals all wounds because that's a fuckin' lie. If it did, I would've been able to go in that house at least one of the thousands of times my brother invited me over the past three years. But I can't because when I do, all I see is—"

"What, Rafe? What do you see?"

"It doesn't matter."

"It does." Holt moved toward him. "It fucking matters."

Rafe shook his head.

"I read about what happened," Holt said, his tone lacking any of the fury it held a moment ago. "What she did to Rex that night. Is that what you see?"

Rafe knew he should simply agree. Tell him that he was traumatized by that horrific scene. It would likely be a sufficient explanation and not untrue.

"If only that were the worst of it," he muttered, unable to look Holt in the eye.

"Your brother said it only happened one time," Holt continued. "That's what he told the police. Was that not true?"

Rafe shrugged. "Probably."

"Look at me."

He didn't want to, but he forced himself to lift his gaze.

"Rex wasn't the only one she hurt, was he?"

He held Holt's stare and shook his head. He didn't mean to respond, but for some goddamn reason, this man made him feel safe.

"Talk to me. Please," Holt whispered.

At the very least, he figured Holt needed to know why Rafe was too fucked up to let this go too far.

FOR THE FIRST TIME SINCE HE MET Rafe all those years ago, Holt saw real torment on the man's face.

All this time, he'd thought Rafe was rebellious because people accused him of being a cold-blooded murderer. He'd figured the thick skin was a direct result of those accusations, and Rafe's stand-offish behavior had been born from that.

269

Rafe

Based on what Rafe alluded to a moment ago, Holt feared there was much more to the story. A darkness that Rafe had kept to himself all these years. Something that went deeper than the physical abuse they'd suffered at the hands of their father.

"Tell me what happened, Rafe," Holt urged. "Tell me what happened after your mother died."

"After she was murdered, you mean," Rafe snapped. "Because she didn't die from fallin' down the stairs."

Holt swallowed, hoping Rafe would continue if he didn't interrupt.

"That bastard said she'd been drinkin', and she fell down the stairs," Rafe hissed. "Mama didn't drink. Not like he said she did. He killed her."

"You saw it happen?"

Rafe shook his head. "No. If I had, I would've killed him that night. Rex and I were sleepin', but they were always fightin'. Nothin' we did was good enough for him. Not Mama. Not me or Rafe. I don't think Billy Don loved anyone but himself."

"Did you see your mother's body?" Holt had seen a dead body or two and knew firsthand that it wasn't the same as seeing one on television. He'd signed on to work with the Biloxi PD when he was researching his second novel and thought that a stint with the homicide division might give him insight into the mind of a killer. He'd tried to look at it from a clinical standpoint, but he hadn't been able to do it. After seeing one dead body after another, he realized it wasn't something he could do. He had a new admiration for the men and women who fought to get justice for the dead after that, and he decided to leave the difficult tasks to them.

"Yeah."

"It's understandable that seeing her like that would make it hard to go back in that house."

Rafe's eyes lifted, meeting his. "You think that's what it is?" Rafe snorted. "If only."

Holt decided not to push him, but he wasn't walking away, either. He wanted Rafe to open up, but only if he were willing. Holt couldn't drag the horror out of him, and honestly, he didn't know if he wanted to. But he did want to help Rafe. Somehow. Someway.

"He'd been fuckin' her before Mama died," Rafe finally said. "Jolene Snyder. Town meth-head. Only twenty-two. More than half Billy Don's age. He had no fuckin' business with her."

Holt held his tongue, praying Rafe would keep going.

"The first time she came to the house was the day of the funeral. She stayed there while we went and laid Mama to rest. When we returned, Billy Don sent us to our rooms, tellin' us not to come out until he said." Rafe paced across the floor. "I didn't care. I didn't want to be around him anyway. But then *she* came to my room. Introduced herself."

Holt noticed Rafe's tone had gone cold, as though he was reciting the events he'd read about.

"She hugged me and told me she'd take care of me. I remember thinkin' she smelled rotten. I didn't want her anywhere near me, but I knew if I said somethin', Billy Don would make me because that was what he did. He got off on that shit. Forcin' us to do things we didn't wanna do. He thought it was funny."

Holt's heart thumped hard in his chest.

"Turned out Jolene liked me." Rafe cringed. "She told me as much that night when she came to my room again. I woke up to find her sittin' on my bed with her fuckin' hand up my shorts. I wasn't even twelve yet. Not for another month, but that didn't bother her. The nasty bitch."

Holt felt the blood drain from his face. Was he saying…?

"For months, that bitch came to my room at night. Sometimes durin' the day if Rex wasn't home."

Oh, Jesus.

"Did Billy Don know?"

"Yeah." Rafe's throat worked on a hard swallow. "He liked to watch."

Holt forced himself not to react, but his stomach clenched, and his chest filled with a rage so potent, it was a damn good thing that bastard was dead.

"Have you ever talked to anyone about this, Rafe?"

"You mean a psychiatrist?" He shrugged.

Honestly, that wasn't the response Holt had anticipated. He'd expected Rafe to claim that it wouldn't help. Now Holt had to wonder.

"You might consider it."

Rafe nodded. "I'm sure it disgusts you to know all that about me. That I was some nasty bitch's play toy."

"*What?* Of course not. What she did to you … that wasn't your fault." How could he possibly think that it was?

"I know that," he snapped. "But I let her because she told me she'd move on to Rex if I didn't. I didn't want her touchin' my brother. I didn't want him to have to go through that. I knew he didn't like girls."

Holt recalled the court transcript. It read like a horror novel, complete with a detailed depiction of the woman determined to exorcise the gay out of Rex. That was the reason she'd been in his room that night. So even though Rafe had endured to protect his brother, it hadn't mattered.

"I'm not disgusted," Holt repeated.

Rafe's expression turned arctic. "Then would it disgust you to learn that I'm the one who gave Jolene the drugs that she overdosed on? I made sure she had more than she could handle. Essentially, I killed her, too."

Rafe was staring at him, expecting a response, so Holt gave him the truth. He approached slowly, sensing Rafe's defense mechanisms falling into place as he neared.

Holt leaned forward and pressed his forehead to Rafe's, not touching him any other way. "I think you're a survivor. I think you've suffered far more than anyone should. And no, it doesn't disgust me to learn any of this. It makes me love you more."

"If I'd told someone, I could've protected Rex," Rafe whispered, his voice ravaged with pain.

Holt stood tall and looked Rafe in the eye. "I read in an article from back then that Rex fought to get the sheriff to investigate your mother's death. He claimed your father did it, but the authorities didn't believe him. There's a good chance you coming forward would've had the same result, Rafe. There's no way to predict what could've happened. Not with any certainty. You need to forgive yourself."

"I don't know how."

"You let me and Bailey love you. That's a start."

Rafe swallowed, and Holt anticipated a rebuttal coming, but Holt's cell phone rang before Rafe could get the words out.

He saw it was Bailey, so he answered, still holding Rafe's gaze.

"Hey. We were—"

"This is Rex. There's been an accident." He was quick to add, "Nothing life-threatening, but I think you should get back here."

"What happened?"

"Bailey cut her hand pretty bad. I think she's gonna need stitches."

"I'll be right there."

"What's wrong?" Rafe asked when Holt ended the call.

"Bailey's hurt. She cut her hand. Rex thinks she needs to go to the hospital."

"Let me get dressed."

Three minutes later, they were pulling into the B and B parking lot. A minute after that, Holt was kneeling on the couch in front of Bailey.

"How bad is it?"

She held out her hand, and he gently unwrapped the towel to see that she'd sliced an impressive gash into the side of her middle finger.

"Well, at least it's still attached." Holt stood. "Let's get you to the emergency room."

Bailey stood, but the instant she saw Rafe standing in the living room doorway, she went still. It didn't take a doctor to understand why. Rafe was white as a sheet, as though he'd just encountered a ghost from his past.

"Breathe," Holt insisted, moving to Rafe. "Breathe, now. Slow."

Rafe looked at Bailey. "I'm—I'm sorry."

A second later, Rafe was racing out the door.

"Son of a bitch," Rex growled.

"You need to go after him," Holt told Rex. "We were talking." He swallowed. "I think I might've coaxed open some ancient wounds. He needs you right now."

Rex nodded. "I'll take care of him. You get her to the hospital."

Holt put his arm around Bailey and helped her out to his truck.

"Is he gonna be okay?" she asked when he strapped her seat belt across her.

The woman never ceased to amaze him. Of course she would be on her way to the hospital with a physical injury and worried about someone else.

"Yeah. But coming face to face with your demons after you've avoided them most of your life … it's not easy."

He got in, started the SUV, and backed out of the driveway.

"I find it hard to believe that walking into that house could be that traumatic. I don't get it. It's so different."

"Not in Rafe's mind, it's not. But I don't think it was walking in that did it. We were talking about the past when Rex called."

Bailey's big hazel eyes were on him. "About what specifically?"

He hated that he couldn't share with her, but it wasn't his place.

"Oh, I get it. Rafe opens up to you, but I'm still shut out."

"That's not what happened."

She crossed her arms over her chest, cradling her hand. "Whatever."

"Bailey…"

"No. Just take me to the hospital. I don't wanna talk about it."

After such an incredible night, this certainly wasn't how Holt had seen the day going. Too bad there wasn't a reset button.

Chapter Twenty-Two

"RAFE?"

Rex followed the wraparound porch to the back of the house where he'd seen his brother run to. When he saw him sitting on the rickety gardening stool that used to belong to their mother, Rex paused. The last time he remembered seeing his brother on that stool, Rafe had probably been eight or nine, and he'd been helping their mother plant the tulips she was constantly replacing. Rafe had been happy back then. Carefree and wild. A far cry from the man Rex knew today.

To say he'd been surprised when Rafe came storming through the house looking for Bailey would've been an understatement. Yeah, Rex had been shocked, but he'd always figured there would one day be a powerful enough motivator to break through some of his brother's fears. It appeared Bailey Weber was that motivator.

But his brother's reaction when he realized where he was hadn't been one of someone who'd merely been rebellious and ornery about the place. Rex hadn't realized until then that the horrors Rafe had faced were much darker than he'd suspected.

"Wanna talk about it?" Rex asked as he moved closer.

"What's there to talk about? I'm fucked up." His words were muffled because he was bent at the waist, breathing rapidly.

"No more fucked up than the rest of us."

Rafe lifted his head. He was pale, and his breaths were still shallow and fast. "I hate this shit."

"What? The panic attacks?"

Rafe frowned. "What do you know about panic attacks?"

Rex hooked his thumb on his pocket and leaned against the porch railing. "I know I've had them. Not so much anymore, but they still sneak up on me now and then."

"Why?"

Rex shrugged. "No idea. I've never figured out the pattern."

"Me, neither."

"I think it's safe to say there's no pattern," Rex decided. "And here I was thinkin' I'd done a damn good job makin' this place over. I didn't think there was a hint of the past in there anymore."

"There's not," Rafe said. "Not that I saw, anyway."

Well, that was a ray of light on an otherwise cloudy day. Rex truly wanted to believe his brother could one day come back, and that meant eliminating the triggers. Evidently, he'd missed something.

"Somethin' triggered you."

Rafe slowly pushed to his feet, standing straight. He took a deep breath and exhaled slowly. "I was talkin' to Holt about … *things* when you called."

"Things? Like what happened after Mama died?"

"Yeah."

"I'm glad you've got someone to talk to. Did it help?"

Rafe shrugged. "Maybe."

Rex tucked his hands in his pockets and shifted his feet. "I know you might not wanna hear this, but you could go see Piper. I've gone to see her a few times. It helps."

Piper Briggs was one of their many cousins on their mother's side. She also happened to have a psychiatric practice here in Coyote Ridge. And while Rex wouldn't go bragging through town that he was under the care of a shrink, he figured it didn't hurt to open up to his brother about it.

Rafe stared at him like he had tentacles growing from his upper lip.

"What? I have. She—"

"I'm sorry, Rex."

The torment in his brother's tone had Rex standing tall and dropping his hands to his sides. "For what?"

"For not sayin' somethin' back then. For not tellin' someone what she was doin'. If I had, she wouldn't have…" Rafe trailed off, nodding toward the house.

Rex didn't need him to finish the sentence. He knew who Rafe was referring to.

"You have no reason to apologize," Rex told his brother, his voice cracking. "I'm the one who should apologize to you."

Rafe's upper lip curled. "For what?"

"For not speakin' up when I could have." Rex swallowed past the lump in his throat. "I suspected she'd been inappropriate, but I kept hopin' I was wrong. If I'd told someone… If I'd confronted her… None of this woulda happened."

Rex had already informed Dr. Briggs that he had suspected their father's girlfriend had molested his little brother. He had nightmares about it, sometimes waking up screaming with his hands tightly gripping the blankets in his efforts to suffocate the crazy bitch. Only Jolene was only in his dreams. She was dead like their father, no longer a threat to either of them.

"Holt said you told the sheriff Mama's death wasn't an accident."

Rex couldn't say he was surprised by the subject change, so he went with it. "I tried. Sheriff Monroe wouldn't listen. But he was Billy Don's friend. He was loyal."

Right up until Rex's story came out in court. At that point, Carl Monroe couldn't stand in the man's corner anymore. Not even to defend a dead man. Not too long after that, Carl Monroe learned that he'd lost the respect of the community when he wasn't re-elected. Unfortunately, Rafe hadn't been around for long to see that their new sheriff was someone they could depend on to stand up for what was right.

"I don't think either of us should be apologizin'," Rex told him. "What Billy Don and Jolene did to us … that's on them. But they're the ones who must pay for what they did. Not us. We have to move forward, Rafe. We have to live our lives."

"That's what Holt keeps tryin' to tell me."

"So you and Holt. That's a thing?"

Rafe shrugged. His brother had shrugged a lot as a kid too. Always when he didn't want to admit to something, but he wasn't going to deny it either.

"And Bailey?"

"That's a thing," Rafe confirmed.

"Wow. That's … two of 'em. I'm impressed, little brother."

Rafe gave him the middle finger, but he smiled. It faded as quickly as it came on.

"I don't know how to go in that house and not remember."

"It's not easy. I know from experience." Rex looked at the house. "But I can tell you what worked for me."

"I'm probably gonna regret askin'…" Rafe muttered.

Rex grinned. "I started by tacklin' every room. I went through and forced myself to remember the good things. And after I did that, I made new memories in there. Memories that are strong enough to drown out the others. Pretty soon, you'll find that the ghosts are only there when you summon them."

Rex knew it sounded simpler than it had been, but he'd done it. He had forged through because he refused to let Billy Don and Jolene control his life anymore. Of course, it had taken the love of a good man to help him get to where he was today. Since it looked like Rafe had a chance at love times two, Rex figured it might just work for him, too.

"In case you're wonderin', there's no one in there right now. The only guest still checked in is Holt. At least until tomorrow."

Rafe grunted as he peered at the back door.

Leaving Rafe with that knowledge, Rex headed toward his house, hoping his little brother would take that first step now that he had the incentive to do so. He'd seen it in Rafe's eyes. Holt and Bailey were the motivation he needed to finally break free from the past. The only thing Rex could do was be there when and if Rafe needed him. This time he vowed he wouldn't let his brother down.

AFTER REX LEFT HIM, RAFE SAT ON the back porch and stared out at the pool and the acres of land beyond, waiting for Bailey and Holt to get back. He'd received text updates from Holt since they got to the hospital, relaying what the doctor said. Thankfully, it sounded like the cut wasn't too bad, but it did require a few stitches.

While he appreciated Holt letting him know, Rafe couldn't help wondering what exactly he brought to the relationship. His efforts paled in comparison to Holt's and Bailey's. Holt seemed to have everything figured out, and he had no demons haunting him. And Bailey ... well, she was Bailey. Her bright, sunny smile was all a man needed to know that his world had been turned upside down.

But what did Rafe bring? What did he have to offer?

And, no, he wasn't talking about material things. Bailey had set him straight on that, and Holt had reinforced it. Rafe wouldn't make the mistake of thinking they needed him to be the breadwinner, but he was confident they needed him to contribute in some way.

Perhaps he was a little less focused on the financial aspect since he would be more stable with a bar of his own, but it would take some time and a lot of hard work to get it where he hoped it would be one day. But he was dedicated and determined to make it work.

Was that what he had to offer? He wouldn't half-ass anything he set his mind to. They could rely on him for that. If he redirected his attention to a relationship, could he make it grow? His gaze shifted to the flowerbed near the edge of the porch. Rex had planted tulips in a variety of colors. Unlike their mother, Rex didn't seem to have to put much effort into keeping them alive. But that was one thing about their mother that Rafe had admired. She never gave up. Even when she probably didn't have a reason to keep trying.

Yes. He could channel his mother's determination. She'd put her heart and soul into creating a happy family. Rafe had loved her more than anything, even when he hated her for suffering at the hands of his bastard of a father. Adele Jameson never quit.

It was something, Rafe figured. Especially since, up to this point, the only thing he'd contributed to this relationship was a couple of orgasms, and while that was always a plus, he knew that wasn't the only thing he could be good for.

He needed to prove to Bailey and Holt that he wasn't a broken fuck up. Or at least that he wasn't *only* a broken fuck up. He loved them, and it was his job to find a way to prove that they could rely on him while they all had their clothes on.

Rafe

Rafe glanced back at the house. Was Rex right? Did it start by tackling the house first? If, by going inside and facing what haunted him, could he begin to move forward? Maybe if no one was around, he could tackle that fear and show that he was making an effort. That would be a start, right?

Getting to his feet, he brushed his hands on his jeans and stared at the back screen door. It only took him seven minutes to make it past the threshold and into the kitchen.

He took deep, slow breaths, willing his heart to remain steady as he studied the place. He noted the differences, reminding himself that the place was basically new. Rex had replaced far more than he'd repaired, so in theory, the ghosts of his past had been tossed out with the old.

Rafe noticed the large knife on the kitchen counter. He walked over, picked it up, and saw Bailey's blood on the blade. Before he knew it, he was washing the knife, removing any evidence that it had ever taken place. When it was as good as new, Rafe returned it to the butcher block holder.

If only it were that easy to erase the evidence of his fucked up childhood. Unfortunately for Rafe, it was forever etched in his mind. And while he couldn't see the old wallpaper he'd stared at when Billy Don had forced him to sit beside Jolene and endure her gross touch, the memories remained.

His heart rate sped up, and his breaths became labored, but Rafe pushed himself to continue.

He made it to the dining room, noticing it was completely different. Forget the wallpaper; not even the walls were the same here. Rex had opened the space so that there was a full line of sight from the front door almost to the back. A single wall offered a small amount of privacy, sealing off the kitchen from where the guests would have their breakfast.

Gone were the dingy flooring and the shadowy corners. The windows had been replaced, some with larger panes to bring in more light.

Rafe walked over to the reservation desk, noticing the book on top and the lockbox mounted on the wall. He hadn't noticed it when he'd come in through the front door a short while ago because he'd been too worried about Bailey. It was definitely different. He could almost picture Bailey standing here greeting guests as they arrived. He knew how much she'd wanted this job, and he could only imagine she was good at it.

He passed the stairs, his gaze snagged by the newel post. It had been replaced entirely. The new one was square when the original had been curved. If he had to guess, it wasn't loose anymore, either. He touched it to see.

A smile formed, and suddenly, he felt as though he was in someone else's house, not the childhood house of horrors he'd grown up in.

Rafe ventured toward the front and checked out what had once been the parlor. It had been converted into what appeared to be an office, but it wasn't full of papers or shit like that, which meant it was a place for guests.

The living room came next, and unlike a short time ago when he'd stood in the doorway, Rafe saw the entire room for what it was today, not what it had been back then. Most of the windows were new, no longer painted shut as had been the case when he was a kid. The fixtures had all been updated, the walls and trim painted. Rex had done a damn good job.

For a solid hour, Rafe walked through the entire house, even checking out a couple of the guest rooms. He hadn't wanted to, but he'd looked in the rooms that occupied the space where his and Rex's old bedrooms once were. Nothing was the same, and knowing his brother, Rex had likely removed everything down to the studs and replaced it. Had it been intentional that he'd redesigned the space, moving the walls so that the original rooms weren't there anymore?

It was a relief. Try as he might, he couldn't even imagine where Rex's old bed had been or even the closet in relation to it.

And to think, he'd been haunted by this place for so long.

Rafe

As he was going down the stairs, the front door opened. He paused as though he'd been caught doing something he shouldn't. Bailey walked in first, her eyes slamming into him as she stopped in the doorway. Holt nearly plowed her over but stopped just in time, his gaze following hers.

"Rafe?"

He forced a smile and continued down the stairs. Surprisingly, he felt as though a weight had been lifted off his shoulders. The only frustration was that he'd waited this long to do it. He'd wasted three years back in Coyote Ridge trying to outrun those fucking demons.

"What are you doin' here?" Bailey asked.

"Exorcising my demons, apparently."

Holt urged Bailey inside so he could close the door behind him.

"Are you all right?" Rafe asked, nodding toward Bailey's bandaged hand.

"Yeah." She rolled her eyes. "It was a stupid accident, but I'm fine. A couple of stitches."

"Four," Holt corrected.

Bailey rolled her eyes again, and more weight seemed to fall from Rafe's shoulders. For the first time since he was twelve, Rafe felt ... *hope*. Yeah. He was pretty sure that was what it was. He had hope for them now.

"I have to work tonight," Rafe said, glancing between them. "But I was thinkin' maybe the three of us could have breakfast tomorrow mornin'."

Bailey nodded. "We've got guests comin' in at some point tomorrow, but I'm sure we can figure somethin' out."

Rafe stepped closer. He tilted her chin up and pressed a kiss to her lips.

"I'm sorry," he whispered.

"For what?"

He met her wide eyes. "For a lot of things. But I promise, I'm gonna do things differently from now on."

"Meaning?" Holt prompted.

Rafe smiled, sidestepped Bailey, and kissed Holt on the lips before moving to the door. "You'll have to wait and see."

As he walked across the park to his apartment, Rafe was already making mental notes of all the ways he could prove he had something to contribute to this relationship. And he knew exactly what he needed to do first.

"Did that just happen?"

Holt kept his eyes on Rafe's form as it got smaller the farther away he got. "I think it did."

"You think he's really okay?"

Closing the door, Holt took Bailey's arm and escorted her into the living room. "I think something changed."

Holt could still feel the lingering sensation of Rafe's lips on his. He'd kissed him like he'd done it a million times before walking out the door. It was … dare he say, normal?

"I don't need to sit down," Bailey said as Holt helped her onto the couch. "I cut my finger. I didn't break my leg."

"You can rest while there's no one else here."

"No. What I can do is clean the guest rooms so that when someone *is* here, I'm not rushing around to take care of things."

Figuring she had a point, Holt nodded. "I'll help. What can I do?"

"You could start by findin' me someone who wants to work here," she grumbled. "I've interviewed three people, and no one wants to do the work. And the one woman who was willin' said she couldn't work for me."

"Why?"

"She said I was too young to take orders from."

"I certainly don't mind taking orders from you," he said, hoping to make her smile.

It worked. She relaxed, and a grin teased the corners of her mouth.

"I think I might have an idea," he said.

"If you tell me you're gonna clean toilets, I—"

Holt put his finger to her lips and shook his head. "I have no desire to clean toilets."

"Yeah, no one else does, either."

Grinning, he leaned in and kissed her. "Let me run an errand, and I'll be back shortly. You rest until then."

"Fine."

Holt knew she had no intention of sitting still, but he left her there and headed over to Moonshiners. Since Rafe said he worked tonight, Holt figured Mack was manning the bar until then.

When he walked in, he found Mack sitting at one of the tables in the corner, staring at the room as though seeing it for the first time. Holt cleared his throat to get Mack's attention as he approached, not wanting to startle him since he appeared lost in a daydream.

Mack's gaze shifted, his eyes clearing. "I didn't take you for an afternoon drinker."

Holt smiled and motioned toward the empty chair. "Mind if I sit?"

Mack sat back and crossed his arms over his chest, nodding curtly. "You here to talk about me sellin' the bar to Rafe? 'Cause that's a done deal. All that's left is to sign the papers."

Frowning, Holt attempted to catch up. "I … uh…No. I didn't even know that was happening."

Mack looked surprised. Holt knew the feeling. He wondered why Rafe hadn't said anything.

"Then what brings you by?"

Shoving the other topic aside for a later date, Holt nodded toward the bar. "I was here the other night. I was talking to Chester. I didn't get his last name."

"King," Mack supplied.

"Okay. Anyway. I was talking to him, and he mentioned his niece had dropped out of her college classes and was moving back home."

Mack nodded. "Chester raised both Maya and her brother, Cassius. Why?"

"I was just curious if she'd want to work at the B and B. Rex and Bailey are looking to hire someone who can clean. It's not the most glamorous job in the world, but Chester said something about her needing to find something that interests her. I'm not saying that cleaning up after people is her ultimate goal, but she'd get to see firsthand what it's like to run a B and B."

Mack pinched his lips together and nodded. "I think you're onto something."

"You think you could pass that along to Chester?" Holt asked. "And if she's not interested, that's cool, too. Like I said, not everyone's cup of tea."

"I'll give him a call."

"Great." Holt pushed his chair back. "If she's interested, just have her call Bailey."

"Will do."

Holt stood and pushed the chair in. "I didn't realize you were parting with this place."

That distant look returned as he glanced around the space. "I'm not goin' far. Rafe said he'd keep me on part-time. I think it'll be good for both of us. That kid's got a lot of ideas, and the only way to make it work is to give him the opportunity to run with it."

"Knowing Rafe, he'll outperform all your expectations."

Mack laughed. "Funny how the rest of us see that in him, but he doesn't see it in himself."

That was for damn sure.

Chapter Twenty-Three

Sunday, August 21, 2022

"Do you know what this is all about?" Bailey asked Holt when they pulled into the parking lot of Moonshiners.

It was Sunday, so the bar closed early, and the parking lot was empty except for Rafe's truck.

"He didn't say. Just that he wanted to talk to us, and he wanted it to be tonight."

Bailey had been busy the past few days with the B and B. They'd had guests coming and going, most of them short stays, which required more work since she was constantly stripping the room and cleaning it for new guests. Yesterday, she'd had a surprising phone call from Maya, Chester King's niece. She'd heard there was a job and wanted to know if it was still available.

Her initial reaction to the idea was skepticism. Bailey knew Maya and her brother, Cassius. Both were what the town liked to consider wild and out of control. They had been, for sure, growing up. But Maya had started college last fall, so Bailey hoped she'd gotten some of the wild out.

Turned out, she hadn't really, but she seemed eager to do something other than sit around and listen to her uncle bitch about her getting a job. As far as incentive to work went, Bailey wasn't sure that qualified, but since she hadn't had any other candidates willing to try, Bailey had hired her on the spot. Only time would tell whether the nineteen-year-old would work out, but as usual, Bailey was optimistic.

They had to knock on the door because it was locked, but a moment later, Rafe appeared, allowing them inside and locking the door behind them.

"Thanks for comin'," he said, gesturing toward a table set up with glasses of water. In the center was a manilla folder.

"What's goin' on?" Bailey asked as she looked around. "Is Mack here?"

"Just me."

She managed to take a seat when Holt pulled out her chair for her. Bailey kept her eyes on Rafe. He seemed nervous but not fidgety. They hadn't talked much since she came home from the hospital to find him coming down the stairs. Rafe had come to the B and B the following morning for breakfast as he'd proposed, but other than that, he'd been MIA. Except for a few text messages to check in.

Bailey was still harboring some animosity since, from what she could tell, Rafe had opened up to Holt about his past. It hurt that neither of them thought it was important to share with her, but she was doing her best to be patient. Like them, it wasn't her strong suit.

"What's this?" Holt asked, tapping the manilla folder.

"Open it," Rafe said, pacing in front of them.

Holt pushed it closer to her, so Bailey picked it up and opened it. There was only one sheet of paper inside. A bill of sale.

She skimmed it, a smile forming as she realized what it was. Her eyes were glassy with tears of joy when she looked up at Rafe.

"Mack sold you the bar."

He nodded, and she was almost positive his eyes were shiny too.

"That's wonderful!" She launched herself up from the chair and right into his arms. "Congratulations! It's crazy, but I'm happy for you." She pulled back. "Why didn't you tell me?"

"We just signed the papers yesterday," he said quickly. "I wanted to wait until we could have a few minutes to talk."

She stepped back, reluctant to hear what this conversation entailed. Knowing Rafe, he was going to say he would now be focused on the bar full-time and wouldn't have any to spare for them. If he did that, she would have to smack him. They'd made some progress this past week. Not a lot, but it was still progress. No way was she going to let him backtrack on her now.

"What brought it about?" Holt asked. "Mack selling the bar?"

Bailey returned to her seat, wanting to hear the story.

"To be honest, I'm still not sure. He called me in last Monday and told me. We'd never talked about him sellin', but he said it was time."

"Was it weird?" Bailey had worked for Mack for quite a while. She could only imagine how that conversation went.

"I thought he was firin' me," Rafe admitted, a smile pulling at his lips.

Bailey laughed. Now, that she could see Mack doing. Most people didn't see his mischievous side, but it had come out more since he married Jeff. She figured happiness brought out the best parts of people.

"Did you take out a loan?" Holt inquired.

Rafe shook his head. "I own it free and clear. He sold it to me for twenty bucks. The exact amount I left for a tip a few weeks ago."

Bailey could feel her chest expanding with warmth. She was so happy for Rafe, but she was equally as concerned for herself.

"Are you gonna convert it into the roadhouse like you wanted?"

"A roadhouse?" Holt nodded. "I can see it."

Rafe nodded. "That's the plan. I'm not in a rush. I'll do most of the work myself, and I'm hopin' Rex'll help. He's good at shit like that."

"He definitely is," she agreed.

"And I was hopin' the two of you might wanna pitch in. Even if it's only to hang out while I work."

She was near tears, so overwhelmed with relief she could hardly hold them in. Since her voice wouldn't work, she nodded in agreement.

"That is if you're plannin' to stick around," Rafe said, directing his comment at Holt.

"Depends."

Bailey looked at him. "On?"

"On us. What we're doing. The three of us."

Was that a question? Did he expect her to answer? Confused, she looked at Rafe.

"If we're doin' this, we're doin' it right," he said, sounding more assertive than she'd ever heard him. "We're not gonna drag it out any longer. We commit or we don't."

"And by commit, you mean…?"

Holt had asked the question, but Bailey was hanging by a thread, waiting for the answer.

"I've wasted too damn much time already," Rafe explained, glancing between them. "I'm ready to start livin' my life. And I'd like to do that with the two of you."

A sob choked her.

Rafe looked at her. "I was thinkin' we could move into the B and B for a while. Unless you're opposed to that."

She shook her head. "I'm not opposed."

Rafe glanced at Holt. "I'm sure we'll outgrow it since you'll need a space for writin' and whatnot."

Holt grinned. "I might've talked to Rex about renting one of the rooms for a while. As a writing space."

How had she not known that? "You did?"

"Not officially." Holt smiled sheepishly. "More like I put a bug in his ear."

"Or we could keep my apartment above the bookstore," Rafe suggested. "You could convert it into a writin' spot."

Holt's eyes widened. "Now *that's* not a bad idea."

It really wasn't.

Bailey's head was spinning. A few minutes ago, she'd been worried Rafe was about to kick them to the curb. And now they were talking about moving in together. A future.

"But before we jump into the deep end," Rafe said, drawing her attention. "I need to tell you a few things."

"Like?"

"My past, for starters. I think you deserve to know—" He cleared his throat. "You need to know what happened to me. It might change how you see me."

Bailey shook her head. "No."

Rafe's eyebrows arched upward. "No? You don't wanna know?"

"I do. But not like this. What happened to you, Rafe … whatever it was, it shaped who you are. And I love you. Just like this." She gestured toward him. "Flaws and all. That won't change. I know it was bad. I can tell. And I want to listen when you're ready to tell me. But only then."

Rafe glanced at Holt, then back to her.

"I don't want you to tell me because you think I need a warnin'. I don't. Nothin' you could say will change how I feel about you."

He came toward her, his eyes glassy once again. When he went to his knees before her, Bailey gasped. Rafe rested his head on her thighs and whispered, "I'm sorry I wasted so much time."

This man. Even when she was happy, he had a way of breaking her heart. She loved him so much it hurt.

"Just gave me more time to fall in love with you," she said, running her fingers through his hair.

"Just think, if you hadn't wasted all that time, I couldn't've come along and upended your whole world," Holt said with a grin.

Rafe lifted his head. He was smiling. "You are good at that, though. Upendin' my life."

Holt winked at Bailey. "Based on the outcome, I don't think that's a bad thing."

For the first time, it was possible they were all finally in agreement.

Chapter Twenty-Four

ON MONDAY EVENING, HOLT FOUND BAILEY IN the kitchen preparing everything for tomorrow's breakfast. She didn't seem to care that he was currently the only guest in residence. According to her, breakfast was a morning staple, and as long as there were people around, she was going to make it.

He couldn't really argue with that. Especially since he knew Rex and Jack looked forward to her breakfast.

"While you finish here, mind if I go up to your apartment? Rafe's picking up dinner."

"Is he back yet?"

"He will be in a minute."

Bailey glanced at the clock as she dug in her pocket. "I need about fifteen more minutes." She shook her head, passing him the key. "Make it twenty. I forgot about the load of laundry in the dryer."

He took the key and kissed her. "We'll keep it warm, and we won't start without you."

As he walked out of the kitchen, Holt smiled to himself.

If he had his way, they would be starting without her. Not dinner. No, that could wait until she arrived. Holt had other things on his mind, thanks to the conversation he'd had with Rafe earlier. How they'd gotten on the topic, he didn't know, but when Rafe started describing the look on Bailey's face when she first came in to find Holt sucking Rafe's cock, Holt's brain had frozen on the mental image.

Rafe

Now *he* wanted to see her face when she walked in. It was only fair, right?

When he got to Bailey's apartment, he unlocked the back door for when Rafe arrived, checked to ensure Bailey had a bottle of wine in the refrigerator, then began pulling out plates and silverware. A few minutes later, Rafe walked in carrying the white plastic bags from the diner.

"Is Bailey here?" he asked as he set them on the small rolling stand that served as the island.

"She's finishing up downstairs. Why?"

"I'm starvin'."

Holt grinned. "I can think of something to tide you over."

Rafe's eyebrows lifted slowly, his gaze tracking him. "What did you have in mind?"

The rasp in his voice said he already had some idea, but Holt didn't mind spelling it out for him.

He moved over to the same column Rafe had stood against the other night. Pressing his back against it, Holt pointed to the floor in front of him.

Rafe's throat worked on a swallow, but he didn't hesitate, coming closer. Rather than let him get right to work, Holt grabbed his shirt and pulled him closer, fusing their lips. It hadn't been quite a week since their first and only encounter in this room, but it felt like an eternity. Now that they were beginning to mesh as a throuple—a word he'd never heard until Bailey said it—Holt hoped they could make time for more of it.

"Mmm," Holt moaned when Rafe unbuttoned his jeans, slipping his hand in and fisting Holt's cock.

"She's gonna come in and see us," Rafe said, easing down to his knees.

"I know."

"That's what you want."

It wasn't a question, but Holt said, "Fuck, yes, I do. I want to see the heat in her eyes."

"She likes to watch," Rafe noted, tugging Holt's jeans down his thighs before stroking him firmly.

"I like that she does." Sliding his fingers in Rafe's hair, he pulled his head forward, urging him to put his mouth on him.

A sigh escaped, and his knees weakened when Rafe's hot, wet mouth enveloped him. No preliminary lick, no light tease. Rafe simply took him to the root.

"Oh, fuck that feels good." Holt released his grip on Rafe's hair, allowing him to control the motion, but he kept his hand resting on his head simply so he could touch him.

Thankfully, Bailey was as timely as always. She walked in only moments later, her eyes wide as she faltered at the door.

Holt watched her face, storing to memory every nuance of her expression as she moved closer. Yeah, that was definitely heat in her gaze. The way she moistened her lips, as though eager to participate, had Holt's cock thickening inside Rafe's mouth.

Bailey met Holt's gaze. "Findin' creative ways to pass the time while you wait?"

"He was hungry."

Rafe chuckled, sending vibrations along Holt's dick.

"I'm hungry, too," Bailey said, her eyebrows raised as though seeking a suggestion.

"Two options," he said, his words raspy as the pleasure intensified. "We can pause this for later and have dinner."

"Or...?" She prompted.

Rafe lifted his head. "Or you can get down here and join me."

Bailey's eyes flashed hot. She wasted no time getting to her knees. Rafe shifted so that she was in front of him. With his hand on Holt's cock, Rafe guided it into Bailey's mouth. Holt stared at them. He'd never seen anything as erotic as the two of them on their knees. Bailey's sweet beauty and Rafe's devilish good looks made for an enticing aphrodisiac. Hell, he could probably come without their mouths. They were that hot.

Holt grunted and groaned as his release built. They traded places, and he fought to hold on a little longer. When Bailey's mouth was on him again, Holt slid his hand into her hair.

"I wanna come in your mouth, little rabbit," he hissed.

She whimpered, her eyes pleading as she bobbed up and down on his length.

"Fuck, baby. It's too good."

Rafe's hand curled around the back of Holt's calf while he watched Bailey suck him deeper.

Holt couldn't hold on any longer.

"All the way," he ground out, resisting the urge to pull her onto his cock.

Turned out he didn't have to because Bailey took the lead, enveloping him nearly to the root. As soon as the head of his cock bumped the back of her throat, he came, her name tumbling from his lips.

ALL THROUGH DINNER, BAILEY SQUIRMED IN HER chair.

She couldn't help it.

Walking in to find Rafe on his knees with Holt's cock in his mouth had been so freaking hot. Ever since the night she'd walked in to find them in a reverse position, she'd thought about it. Fantasized about watching the two of them together. She had no idea why it was hot to watch, but it was.

She was sure Holt had insisted they eat dinner simply to mess with her. He had to know she was hanging by a thread. If the sparkle in his eyes and the twitch of his mouth were any indication, he was enjoying her discomfort.

Thankfully, no one wanted dessert.

"I'll do the dishes," Rafe offered when they were finished.

Bailey stared at him in disbelief.

"What?" He smirked. "I know how to wash dishes."

She knew he did because she'd worked with him at Moonshiners long enough. But it wasn't the cleaning she was surprised by. It was how easily he was moving around the apartment. Whatever happened the other day when he'd exorcised his demons had changed him. Bailey was grateful. Not because she would have to worry about him slipping out in the middle of the night, although that was a plus. No, Bailey was grateful because some of the dark clouds had disappeared from Rafe's eyes. She was sure he wasn't completely healed, but he had taken the first steps.

"While he does that, I'm in the mood for dessert," Holt said.

Before Bailey could tell him he was SOL because she wasn't waiting any longer, Holt picked her up and tossed her over his shoulder. Only then did she realize dessert was a euphemism for exactly what she hoped for.

He carried her into her bedroom and tossed her onto the bed. She bounced and giggled while he quickly stripped her of her shorts and T-shirt. He followed suit, discarding his clothes before settling between her thighs.

"Ohhh," she moaned when he dragged his tongue from her entrance to her clit.

The man had a wicked tongue.

Time stood still while she succumbed to the exquisite pleasure of his mouth. He didn't rush, seeming to savor. She realized it was a stall tactic when Rafe appeared in the doorway. His eyes burned hot as soon as he saw them.

Bailey patted the bed, urging him to join them. After ridding himself of his clothes, Rafe stretched out by her side, his cock in his fist. As soon as Holt saw it, he deviated from his task, sucking Rafe into his mouth.

More heat flooded her veins.

They were so beautiful together.

Holt didn't leave her waiting, though. He caressed her clit with his thumb while he sucked Rafe, then stroked Rafe while he licked her. It went on for a few minutes before Bailey couldn't take it any longer. She needed more, and since she wanted to watch them, she knew exactly what to do.

"Where're you going, little rabbit?" Holt asked when she scooted to the far side of the bed. She leaned over, opening her nightstand drawer to retrieve her vibrator.

When she held it up, she was almost positive she saw the disappointment in their eyes.

"You'd rather use a toy than…?"

Bailey smiled. "I wanna watch."

"Watch what?"

She knew Rafe asked the question to get her to say it. Her face heated, but she pushed past the embarrassment and said, "I wanna watch you fuck Holt."

"Jesus," Holt rasped softly. "She's gonna be the death of me."

Rafe chuckled even as he moved so quickly neither of them had time to anticipate the move. Rafe straddled the back of Holt's thighs, pinning him to the bed.

Bailey gasped when Rafe pressed his cock between Holt's ass cheeks, sliding between them.

Okay, so clearly, she had underestimated their ability to turn her on. There was a good chance she didn't even need the vibrator. She might come from watching this.

"Lube," Rafe said, holding out his hand to Bailey.

She gave him a questioning look.

"It's in the drawer," Holt said, his words muffled because this face was pressed into the mattress.

Sure enough, she found a small bottle of water-based lubricant in the drawer, still sealed in plastic. She ripped it away, then passed it to Rafe.

"Do I need a condom?" Rafe asked, his question directed at Holt.

Bailey held her breath. She'd already had this conversation with Rafe, though it had been reactive rather than proactive.

Holt turned his head. "I'm clean, and I trust you. Both of you."

Rafe looked at her.

"I'm on birth control, and I take it religiously. I don't have any diseases."

"I haven't been with anyone but Bailey in three years."

Holt twisted, and Bailey noticed his shock. It was similar to her response when Rafe originally told her.

"Seriously? No one?"

"No one," Rafe confirmed.

"No condom," Holt said gruffly. "Just fuck me already."

Bailey leaned back, propping herself on pillows so she could watch the action.

"I better see you using that toy," Holt said, his eyes on her as Rafe shifted behind him.

She turned the vibrator to its lowest setting, bent her knee, and pressed the silicone tip against her clit. Holt and Rafe both watched, which made it all the more thrilling.

After a minute, Rafe leaned forward and kissed Holt's shoulder. "She wants to watch."

Holt grunted.

"Turn over," Rafe commanded.

Rafe lifted up, giving Holt room to turn over onto his back. Without hesitation, Rafe pushed Holt's leg back, his knee close to his chest. Holt put his hands behind his knees and held himself open while Rafe angled his cock at his hole.

Bailey held her breath as Rafe sank inside him slowly. Oh, so slowly.

She tossed the vibrator aside, too entranced by them to focus. Shifting to her knees by Holt's head, she watched as Rafe began fucking him while they stared at one another. Hot didn't begin to describe what this was. This wasn't a mere joining of bodies; it was an exchange of ... everything. She could see it on their faces, in the way they touched each other as Rafe pushed in and retreated.

It was apparent this had been a long time coming, and she would've felt like a voyeur intruding on their moment if Holt didn't take her hand, placing it under his thigh.

"Open him wider," Rafe instructed.

Bailey pulled Holt's leg back and wide, staring at where their bodies were joined. Holt's cock was hard as steel between them, but neither of them touched it. She wanted to but didn't want to disrupt what they were doing.

Suddenly Rafe paused.

"Turn over."

Bailey released Holt's knee and was about to get off the bed, but Rafe stopped her, grabbing her hand.

"You lay down."

Confused but so turned on she physically ached, Bailey lay on the bed. A moment later, she realized Rafe's intention because Holt moved over her.

She reached between them, guiding his cock to her entrance, and whimpered with sweet relief as he pushed inside.

"Oh, fuck, yes," Holt groaned. "You're so tight. Oh shit." He hissed. "Without a condom...I might not survive this."

She giggled. "You will. I'll make sure you do."

Bailey felt Rafe's leg brush against her feet as he moved into position behind Holt. She watched Holt's face, the way his eyes closed and his lips parted. His hips shifted forward, his cock sliding deeper inside her. Rafe was fucking Holt while Holt was fucking her.

"How does it feel?" Rafe asked Holt. "To have us both at the same time?"

"Heaven," he groaned. "Fuck."

"That's what I intend to do," Rafe said.

A moment later, Rafe began fucking Holt.

Hard.

Deep.

Fast.

With every thrust, Holt fucked her deeper. When Rafe rammed in, Holt hit the perfect spot inside her. Bailey saw stars. Her scalp tingled as pleasure coursed through her veins.

"Fuck, yes," Holt hissed, his eyes opening as he stared down at her. "Come for us, Bailey. Come all over my cock."

She was so close, her pussy clenching and releasing as she tried to hold on a little longer. Her insides coiled as a sparkler of sensation detonated in her core. She couldn't stop it. The orgasm made her cry out, arching her back as Holt slammed in so deep she swore she would feel him for eternity.

"You're so fuckin' beautiful," Holt bellowed. "Fuck, Rafe. I can't … oh, fuck … I'm coming."

Rafe's deep, booming roar followed as the bed shook one final time.

"That was…" Bailey couldn't find the word.

"Amazing?" Holt supplied.

"Mind-numbing?" Rafe added.

"Perfect," she decided. "That was perfect."

They fell to their sides beside her on the bed, the warmth of their bodies prolonging the sweet sensations still moving through her.

"I know one way it could've been better," Rafe said after a moment.

Rafe and Holt lifted their heads and looked at each other over her.

"She needs a bigger bed," they said in unison.

Bailey giggled, then it morphed into a full laugh as she snuggled into them and accepted that she'd finally found her happily ever after.

RAFE WAITED UNTIL BAILEY AND HOLT FELL asleep before he slipped out of bed. He went to the bathroom to clean up. Since a shower was just as fast, he went that route, soaping up and rinsing off, hoping he hadn't woken them in the process.

When he finished, he went to the kitchen for a bottle of water.

As he went through the motions, moving around Bailey's apartment—what would soon be shared by all three of them—he kept waiting for the panic to hit. He stared out the window at the front of the house, noticing that downtown Coyote Ridge was only now beginning to close. There was a light on in the bookstore, which meant Violet was closing out her receipts for the day. The barber shop sign had stopped spinning, Mr. Harris gone for the evening.

Interesting how it looked the same from here as it did from his apartment. A week ago, he would've said it was completely different. Then again, he felt completely different now. He wanted to claim that walking through the house had exorcised his past, but he knew that wasn't the case. Those demons likely lurked and would return when he least expected it, but he felt strong enough to face them now. And one trek through the house hadn't given him that strength.

His brother had by reminding Rafe that he was still the same brother he'd looked after when they were younger.

Bailey had by opening her heart to him and letting him see that he would never be alone as long as she was with him.

And Holt had. Perhaps Holt had given him the most strength because he'd shown Rafe that he was more than he'd ever given himself credit for. Holt had let him open up, and he'd never once looked at him with pity or shame. That had given Rafe the strength he needed to live a life worth living.

And now he was.

It didn't hurt that he'd gone by Piper's office yesterday and chatted with her for a few minutes. It only took that long for him to feel comfortable enough to ask her if he could come back again. Only time would tell whether it would help, but Rafe was willing to try.

Whatever it took to be worthy of Bailey and Holt.

He moved to the couch and took a seat, his gaze shifting around the room. Again, he waited for the panic to come, but it wasn't there. His stomach didn't twist, and his chest didn't tighten. He wasn't itching to run out the door.

This was where he wanted to be.

Rafe

The sound of footsteps had him staring at the end of the room, waiting for someone to emerge from the hallway. He expected Holt, geared up to give Rafe a scolding for attempting to flee.

Bailey was the one who appeared. She was naked and so beautiful it made his chest ache to look at her. He loved her so damn much.

"You okay?"

Rafe held out his hand, urging her closer. She came to him without pause, placing her hand in his. He pulled down so she was straddling his hips.

"I'm better now," he admitted.

She placed her hand over his heart. "Are you havin' a panic attack?"

"No."

"Would you tell me if you were?"

"Yes." As soon as the word was out, he realized it was the truth.

"I'm glad." Her hands slid up to cup his jaw. "But I want you to know I'm here if and when you do. Even if it's only to sit quietly by your side so you know you're not alone. I'm here."

Rafe cupped the back of her head, pulling her mouth to his. He kissed her slow and deep.

"I love you," he whispered. "I always have."

"I love you, too." She leaned into him, her elbows on his shoulders, her fingers playing with his hair.

They were both naked, and her touch was affecting him. Just as he always knew it would. He managed to ignore the throbbing of his cock between them, but Bailey didn't fare quite so well.

"Make love to me," she whispered, shifting her hips, angling so his cock moved between her legs.

He heard a sound, noticed Holt was standing near the hallway, his shoulder leaning on the wall.

"How about you make love to me," he said softly, angling his cock to the sweet juncture between her thighs.

"I can do that."

And she did.

Right there, in the house Rafe had been terrified of for so long, Bailey made love to him while Holt stood across the room, quiet and content to watch. The second of many memories they would make in this house and together. The first was one Rafe would never forget for as long as he lived. The three of them joined as one.

But this ... this was good, too.

No, amend that.

This was better than good.

It was perfect.

Epilogue

Thursday, September 1, 2022

TRAVIS WALKER STEPPED INTO THE DINER, HIS eyes adjusting to the dim interior as he scanned the dining area, looking for the sheriff. The call he'd received forty-five minutes ago assured him he would find him here.

Sheriff Jeff Endsley was the one who called to give him a heads-up about the topic Holt Callahan was interested in, a topic he had no business discussing with anyone. Although Travis would've preferred to put Holt off a while longer, he knew Jeff wasn't thrilled with the idea. He'd already done it once at Travis's request, but he wasn't willing to wait any longer.

At that point, Travis had skimmed the email Gage had sent him on the man Jeff was meeting with before pawning the rest of his shit on his brothers and leaving Alluring Indulgence Resort, coming straight here.

And there they were.

Sheriff Endsley was sitting at a table in the back, Holt Callahan directly across from him. From his place near the front door, Travis could only see a partial profile, but the photo he'd found on the internet was definitely of the famous thriller writer who'd recently graced Coyote Ridge with his presence.

Travis had heard rumblings about the stranger who'd wandered into town a month ago and holed up at the B and B. He figured since he hadn't been formally introduced, now would be a damn good time. Preferably a hello and goodbye in the same conversation. He wasn't sure how long Holt intended to stay, but if Travis had his way, the man would be on his way out in the next few minutes.

As Rachel approached to escort him to a table, Travis waved her off. "I'm meetin' with the sheriff."

She nodded. "Can I get you something to drink?"

"No. Thanks, though."

She smiled and returned to the kitchen. Only a couple of customers were lingering, but they were scattered throughout the restaurant, which he figured was why Jeff had chosen this place for the conversation. He appreciated that they could talk privately, but Travis didn't require privacy. He didn't require a damn thing because he had no intention of discussing his wife with a stranger. He didn't give a fuck who the guy was.

Travis approached the table slowly. Holt's back was to him, so Jeff saw him first.

"Hey, Travis," Jeff said, slowly getting to his feet. "Let me introduce you to Holt Callahan."

Showing he had proper manners, Holt got to his feet and held out his hand. Travis could tell when a man was sizing him up, and Holt's laid-back demeanor was merely a facade. He clearly realized Travis wasn't here to shoot the shit.

"Have a seat, Mr. Callahan," Travis stated after shaking his hand. He turned to Jeff. "Thanks for the call. I'll catch up with you later."

"It was great to meet you," Jeff told Holt, his expression rife with apology.

"I always knew I'd one day ask the wrong question," Holt said when Travis took a seat. "I can only assume you're here to tell me to back off."

"You read people well."

The corner of Holt's mouth tipped up. "Maybe it'd help if I explained why I'm here."

Travis didn't need to hear his bullshit excuses. "I know why you're here. You came to Coyote Ridge because you intend for it to be the backdrop of your next book."

His smile wasn't hesitant or half-ass this time. "Actually, no. Well, yes *and* no."

Travis leaned back and put his arm on the back of the seat. "Enlighten me then, Callahan."

"I didn't choose Coyote Ridge randomly on a map."

"You chose it because you know someone," Travis filled in. "Rafe Sharpe. He's my cousin, in case you didn't know that."

"I know many things I probably shouldn't know about Rafe."

"And why, dare I ask, are you stalkin' him?"

"And here I thought the grapevine was more thorough in small towns. There's no stalkin' involved." His expression turned serious. "I'm in love with Rafe."

Admittedly, Travis hadn't heard that part. The moment he'd learned of Holt Callahan's presence in Coyote Ridge, he'd had him investigated. Gage had uncovered quite a bit of detail, including the man's lucrative career as a thriller writer. Travis had assumed he'd chosen to come here because he knew Rafe. And why not use that friendship, and this town, for his own personal gain?

Clearly, Travis hadn't dug deep enough.

"Surprised you, I know," Holt said. "That's not something I tend to share with strangers."

"Or something you share when you're datin' Bailey Weber," Travis noted. "Keep in mind; this is a small town. Someone notices every single thing you do. And that someone tells someone else."

"Then tell me, why do you seem to be a week behind in the news? I heard the rumor mill was reliable around these parts. Apparently, that's not accurate."

Holt Callahan was too damn cocky for his own good.

"Doesn't mean you're not stalkin' him," Travis retorted.

"Does when we're livin' together." His expression remained cool. "I moved in with Bailey and Rafe a few days ago."

Well, shit. Travis would have to admit he'd gone off half-cocked on this one. Then again, he didn't give a shit about Holt Callahan's personal life or his romantic interests.

Travis jerked his chin. "That brings me to my next problem."

"I hadn't realized the first was a problem. Least of all for you."

Travis didn't want to admit it, but he was starting to like this guy.

Leaning forward, Travis put his elbow on the table. "Why are you here askin' questions about my wife?"

Some of Holt's cockiness faded. "Unfortunately, that's not as simple to explain as how I got here."

"I'm a smart guy. Lay it out for me, Callahan. I bet I can keep up."

HOLT HAD KNOWN THE SHERIFF WAS STALLING when he'd first sat down. After a quick introduction and hearing Jeff's confirmation of what Mack had told him about Holt being one of his favorite authors, Holt attempted to get to the point. Jeff had redirected the conversation every step of the way.

Now he knew why.

As he sat across from Travis Walker, he had to admit the stories he'd read about the man hadn't done him justice. Many referred to him as a businessman with a steely determination and a laid-back demeanor. The steely determination was obviously on point, but Holt had yet to see anything that resembled laid-back since the man appeared.

"You're right when you said I intend for Coyote Ridge to be the backdrop for my next book. A lot about this town appeals to the writer in me. And it's the perfect setting for my protagonist." Holt turned his coffee mug, then met Travis's eyes again. "I like the idea of a mystery unraveling in a small town that rarely sees any crime. Finding a place like that is rare. At least for me. So, when I learned about the small town Rafe grew up in, I did my research."

"My wife's death was national news," Travis said through clenched teeth. "I don't see why you're diggin' for more information. If you think you're gonna use this tragedy to line your pockets, you're—"

"No," Holt said firmly. "I have no intention of doing any such thing. My book has no resemblance to anything that happened to Kylie. And if you don't believe me, I'll gladly let you read the first draft before I send it to my editor."

"That's a given."

Holt smiled. "Don't mistake my offer for fear. I'm not doin' it because I'm threatened by you."

Travis's gaze shifted over his face. Holt figured not many people stood up to this man, but that was too damn bad. Holt was not going to be bullied by anyone. He understood Travis's reason for coming here. He even understood the confrontation. What he didn't understand were the assumptions Travis made without any facts.

"I didn't intend to investigate Kylie's death when I first came across it. As I said, it has no bearing on my book. However…"

Travis's eyebrows rose. "What?"

Holt huffed. "It was when I was reading about Kylie that I came across a few things that didn't add up to me. And no, I'm not a detective. However, my life's work involves creating a mystery. My goal's to make it difficult to unravel, keeping in mind that everything can be unraveled. It may take time, but you can pull on the thread and see how every response to the previous action led to another and then another. A chain reaction, if you will."

"If this is your convoluted way of sayin' my wife's death was the result of someone's reaction, you're right. Juliet Prince hated me. And that bitch killed my wife because of it."

Holt had done his homework on Juliet Prince as well. As far as he could tell, the woman who had run Kylie down with a car was a byproduct of something else. If he was right, she was merely a side character who happened along at the exact right time so that everything looked like it was her fault. Not that she was innocent by any means. She was the one behind the wheel of the car that struck Kylie. They had eyewitness accounts.

"I'm not disputing that, and this is gonna sound bad, but I think Juliet Prince was a red herring."

Travis's face hardened. "She killed my wife. She ran her down in the goddamn street. I don't know how you can think we were led to *believe* she was the bad guy. It's a proven goddamn fact. She killed—"

Holt shook his head. "That's not what I mean."

"Then what the fuck *do* you mean?" Travis growled.

Holt glanced around, noticing Travis's heated words had drawn the waitress's attention.

"I'm not debating that it happened. It did. I know that. Everyone in this town remembers that day like it was yesterday."

Travis growled again.

Holt lowered his voice. "If I tell you this, do you think you can refrain from punching me in the face?"

Travis's blue-gray eyes narrowed to slits. "No. I can't. But you're gonna fuckin' tell me anyway."

Despite his hostile temper, Holt admired the man. At least he was honest.

"I think there's more to this story. I think..." Holt steeled himself for a punch he prayed didn't come. "I think what happened to Kylie resulted from something that happened eighteen years ago."

Travis glowered. "Eighteen years ago? I didn't know Juliet Prince then."

Holt met Travis's stare. "Which is why I don't think any of this has to do with you *or* Juliet Prince."

"Then who the fuck does it have to do with?"

"Meredith Prescott."

Travis's frown deepened.

"Kylie's mother," Holt clarified.

"I know who the fuck she is," Travis snapped. "That makes no fuckin' sense at all. She left when Kylie was in college, and no one's seen her since. She abandoned her family."

"I don't think that was the case," Holt told him, keeping his tone even. "I think one of two things happened. Meredith Prescott went into hiding, or she's dead."

Travis looked bewildered and pissed, which didn't bode well for Holt. "Why the fuck would you think that?"

"Because she disappeared shortly after the FBI tried to strong-arm her into testifying."

Travis's chin jerked. It wasn't dramatic, but Holt could tell that wasn't something he'd been aware of.

"Testify for what?"

"She witnessed a mob hit."

Travis sat up, preparing to get to his feet, his expression morphing into disbelief. "A mob hit. That's what you're goin' with? I think you're confusin' fact with fiction, Callahan."

"Am I?" He peered up at Travis as he stood. "Then I suggest you do some digging because it wasn't difficult to find."

Travis glared down at him. "What wasn't?"

Holt held his gaze. "The details of the sole witness who saw Maximillian Adorite kill a man. Her testimony's a big deal. It has the power to bring down the Southern Boy Mafia once and for all."

Travis barked a laugh. "Now I know you're full of shit."

Holt remained where he was even after the bells over the door jingled, signaling Travis Walker's exit.

If he had looked back, he would've seen Travis with his phone in his hand, dialing the number for his cousin, Brantley.

ACKNOWLEDGMENTS

I'll admit it took me some time to write Rafe's book. I knew from the moment he met Bailey that he would fall in love with her and vice versa. That was about all I knew when I started writing it a couple of years ago. I would write a little more and a little more, but it never resonated with me, so I kept setting it on the back burner to return to later. This time when I started, a few things had been clarified for me, so I felt more confident about where they were going. As for Holt Callahan ... he was a complete surprise. A welcome one but totally unexpected. I guess he had the same impact on Rafe and Bailey. I really hope you enjoyed their journey together, and I can say you'll be seeing more of them in the future since Moonshiners happens to be the town's favorite (and only) watering hole.

As is always the case, I have to thank my husband because he tolerates me. Most importantly, he finds my excitement amusing when I tell him about whatever story I'm working on. He might not get it, but he loves me enough to pretend.

I have to thank Chancy Powley, who is always there to cheer me on and to ask the difficult questions when she reads the book. She always gives me something to ponder when I'm looking back at her notes.

And Jenna Underwood, you are the one who ties it all together and finds the little things that the rest of us have missed.

Nicole Nation 2.0, for the constant support and love. You've been there for me from almost the beginning. This group of ladies has kept me going for so long I'm not sure I'd know what to do without them.

And, of course, YOU, the reader. Your emails, messages, posts, comments, tweets… they mean more to me than you can imagine. I thrive on hearing from you, knowing that my characters and my stories have touched you in some way keeps me going. I've been known to shed a tear or two when reading an email because you simply bring so much joy to my life with your support. I thank you for that.

About Nicole Edwards

New York Times and *USA Today* bestselling author Nicole Edwards lives in the suburbs of Austin, Texas, with her husband, their three fur babies, and the youngest of their three children, who has threatened never to leave home. When Nicole is not writing about sexy alpha males and sassy, independent women, she can often be found with a book in hand or attempting to keep the dogs happy. You can find her hanging out on social media and interacting with her readers - even when she's supposed to be writing.

Connect with Nicole

I hope you're as eager to get the information as I am to give it. Any of these things is worth signing up for, or feel free to sign up for all. I do my best to keep each one unique and interesting.

NIC NEWS: If you haven't signed up for my newsletter and want notifications regarding preorders, new releases, giveaways, sales, etc., then you'll want to sign up. I promise not to spam your email, just get you the most important updates.

RAMBLINGS OF A WRITER BLOG: My blog is used for writer ramblings, which I am known to do from time to time.

NICOLE NATION: Visit my website to get exclusive content you won't find anywhere else, including sneak peeks, A Day in the Life character stories, exclusive giveaways, cards from Nicole, or join Nicole's review team.

NICOLE NATION ON FACEBOOK: Join my reader group to interact with other readers, ask me questions, play fun weekly games, celebrate during release week, and enter exclusive giveaways!

INSTAGRAM: Basically, Instagram is where I post pictures of my dogs, so if you want to see epic cuteness, you should follow me.

NAUGHTY & NICE SHOP: Not only does the shop have signed books, but there's fun merchandise, too—plenty of naughty and nice options to go around. Find the shop on my website.

YOU CAN ALSO FOLLOW NICOLE ON

Website:	www.NicoleEdwards.me
Facebook:	/Author.Nicole.Edwards
Instagram:	/NicoleEdwardsAuthor
TikTok:	/@nicoleedwardsauthor
BookBub:	/NicoleEdwardsAuthor
Goodreads:	/nicole_edwards

BY NICOLE EDWARDS

THE WALKERS

ALLURING INDULGENCE
Kaleb
Zane
Travis
Holidays with The Walker Brothers
Ethan
Braydon
Sawyer
Brendon

THE WALKERS OF COYOTE RIDGE
Curtis
Jared (a crossover novel)
Hard to Hold
Hard to Handle
Beau
Rex
A Coyote Ridge Christmas
Mack
Kaden & Keegan
Alibi (a crossover novel)
Trey
Rafe

BRANTLEY WALKER: OFF THE BOOKS
All In
Without A Trace
Hide & Seek
Deadly Coincidence
Alibi (a crossover novel)
Secrets
Confessions
Bounty

AUSTIN ARROWS
Rush
Kaufman

CLUB DESTINY
Conviction
Temptation
Addicted
Seduction
Infatuation
Captivated
Devotion
Perception
Entrusted
Adored
Distraction
Forevermore

DEAD HEAT RANCH
Boots Optional
Betting on Grace
Overnight Love
Jared (a crossover novel)

DEVIL'S BEND
Chasing Dreams
Vanishing Dreams

MISPLACED HALOS
Protected in Darkness
Salvation in Darkness
Bound in Darkness

OFFICE INTRIGUE
Office Intrigue
Intrigued Out of The Office
Their Rebellious Submissive
Their Famous Dominant
Their Ruthless Sadist
Their Naughty Student
Their Fairy Princess
Owned

www.ingramcontent.com/pod-product-compliance
Lightning Source LLC
Chambersburg PA
CBHW060402260626
47160CB00006B/2400